The Disappearance of Emily Marr

Louise Candlish

SPHERE

First published in Great Britain as a paperback original in 2013 by Sphere

MORAY COUNCIL
LIBRARIES &
INFO.SERVICES

20 36 80 73	
Askews & Holts	
F	

ISBN 978-0-7515-4356-8

Typeset in Sabon by M Rules
Printed and bound in Great Britain by
Clays Ltd, St Ives plc

Papers used by Sphere are from well-managed forests
and other responsible sources.

MIX
Paper from
responsible sources
FSC® C104740

Sphere
An imprint of
Little, Brown Book Group
100 Victoria Embankment
London EC4Y 0DY

An Hachette UK Company
www.hachette.co.uk

www.littlebrown.co.uk

For Lynda Alison Candlish
(1944–2012)

Acknowledgements

Thank you to Emma Beswetherick and Dan Mallory of Little, Brown for the early championing of this idea, and to Rebecca Saunders for guiding the novel to fruition and for being so patient and clever with it. Thank you also to David Shelley, Lucy Icke, Cath Burke, Hannah Green, Kirsteen Astor, Carleen Peters, Felice Howden and Emma Stonex. Thank you to Vicki Harris for her excellent copy edit and to Emma Graves for the cover design.

Thank you to Claire Conrad, Rebecca Folland, Kirsty Gordon and Jessie Botterill at Janklow & Nesbit, London.

Thank you to Natalie Downing for information about dementia and to Michael Orr for advice about psychiatric disorders – any mistakes are, of course, mine. Also to the helpful staff at Southwark Coroner's Court, Tennis Street, London EC1. The description of the medication Quetiapine is based on one given at www.netdoctor.co.uk.

Thank you to Jojo Moyes, Rosamund Lupton and Dorothy Koomson: it's not always easy for busy authors to read books and give quotes and they have been generous enough to find the time to consider mine.

Thank you to Jacqueline Miller and the McCarrys senior and junior for their respective parts in making life easier for me during the writing of this book. Thank you also to my supportive family and friends, especially Nips and Greta.

Lastly, a grateful acknowledgement of the novel *Die verlorene Ehre der Katharina Blum* (The Lost Honour of Katharina Blum) by Heinrich Böll, which has been a great source of inspiration to me.

'Although every attempt is made to avoid any upset to people's private lives, sometimes, in the interest of justice, it is unavoidable.'

A Guide to Coroners and Inquests,
Ministry of Justice

'I did not recognise myself, either in the media's depiction of me or in the altered woman in the mirror before me. I felt as if I was dissolving, disappearing. It was as if Emily Marr no longer existed.'

Emily Marr

Prologue

Sussex, July 2011

She had never in her life seen terror like it. It was stark and primitive, the elemental response of a person who knew he was about to die.

A young person, too.

When the car came off the road, Lisa Hawes was sitting in stationary traffic on the southbound dual carriageway opposite. The standstill was what made it possible for her to witness the accident with the level of certainty that the police, and later the coroner, would require of her. She was in the outside lane, a couple of feet from the central reservation: a front-row seat.

Having not taken this route for weeks, she had forgotten about the roadworks taking place throughout the summer, necessitating a reduced speed limit and the merging of two lanes into one. Last time, there had not been a blockage like this, only a few minutes of impatient crawling, but perhaps there'd been an accident or there was some other unlucky factor at play. Her brother had once tried to explain to her the 'wave' dynamics that caused traffic to bottleneck and clot in this way, but she had not listened properly.

'Just one idiot slowing right down and you're all screwed,' she remembered him saying.

Well, if the driver of the oncoming Saab was an idiot then he was a dangerous one: far from slowing down, he was accelerating recklessly, the car drifting between lanes and towards the central reservation, on direct course for the car in front of Lisa's own – so close, so fast, that she recoiled, right forearm to her face. She could make no sense of the motion at the wheel or the fact that there appeared to be three heads in the front, not two. In any case, her attention was seized by just one of them, the boy or young man in the passenger seat, by *that* face. The simian grimace, the ghastly stupefaction in the eyes, the rigidity of throat and mouth as the jaw strained in a scream: the sight of him riveted her, froze her heart.

Then he was gone. An instant before certain impact with the barrier, the vehicle jerked to its left, overcorrecting, changing direction with a thrilling, skidding clumsiness you'd associate with a dodgem car or a go-kart. There was the briefest glimpse through the driver's window of a bowed head, blond hair tipped forwards. A woman. Lisa's brain processed then what the three heads had signified: someone in the back must have reached between the front seats to grab the steering wheel, his face drawing level with theirs. This third person was in control of the vehicle, not the woman in the driver's seat.

But for no longer. Feeling visceral dread before any relief at being spared from harm herself, she watched first in her wing mirror and then through her rear side window as the car shot across the outside lane, off the carriageway and down the embankment. The decline was steep enough for her to lose sight of it but nonetheless there could be only one outcome: the car would plunge directly into a dense screen of trees that would be hardly more absorbent than a brick wall. The roar of impact was not as loud as it would have been had her own car not been filled with the oblivious talk and brash laughter of a radio show selected half an hour earlier to keep her awake. (The irony! It would be three nights before she could sleep again.) Silencing it, she turned off the engine and reached to

2

open the door. There was a claustrophobic moment when her heart pulsed too loudly, her blood too full for her skin, and then she climbed out.

She stood with difficulty, knees soft. There was nothing to see where she judged the Saab to have gone off the road, only the tops of the trees. She expected, if not pieces of the wreckage itself, then certainly smoke, billowing like in the movies as if from a bonfire, but there was none. And there was no residual noise, either, at least not any that could be heard above the drone of oncoming cars, continuing northbound at speed. It seemed incredible that the drivers now approaching would have no idea what had just happened, no instinct that they were passing through an aftershock. They might hear of the accident later but they would never know that pure luck had saved them from having been in this tragedy themselves.

For these were her first thoughts that morning at the scene, her natural assumptions as she stood by her own car, not yet ready to act: that the Saab must have hit something in the road further back, if not another vehicle, then perhaps an animal or an object swept into its path by the wind. The driver had been too stunned or panicked to react and the passenger had intervened. He had not been successful.

Replanting legs that now trembled badly and using her hands to steady herself, she tried to decide if it was safe to step over the barrier and cross to the other side. The traffic was not heavy, it was not like the work-day sprint to London, but it was fast, and coming in both lanes. You would need to do it in one dash.

The sound of car doors opening and closing in the queue of traffic behind her brought an injection of courage, as well as a sense of deliverance: others had seen what she had seen, some may even have had a view of the crash itself. Others were stepping from their vehicles and preparing to cross to the scene and search the wreckage for survivors.

Others were putting phones to their ears and calling for help.

3

Chapter 1

Tabby

France, May 2012

'You need to leave,' the voice ordered. 'You can't stay here.'

Tabby pretended to sleep, stirring her body under the sheet as if dreaming too deeply to be pulled awake at first call. The fact that she was not able to place the identity of her commander did not trouble her enough to raise her heart rate.

After all, sometimes when she woke up she didn't remember which *country* she was in, much less whose company.

Talking of which ... She half opened her eyes and allowed her vision, if not yet her memory, to focus. She was in a big wooden double bed with soft sheets (Lord knew, it had come to the point where neither the bed nor the sheets were to be taken for granted) and the room was white and blue. Smooth white walls, rough blue beams, white bedlinen, blue rug, white dresser, blue vase: someone had been very strict about this, evidently. There were two windows set deep in walls of pale stone, the shutters closed. Shutters, here was her clue: she was still in France, of course! She had been in the country for a month or so now, mostly sleeping in budget fleapits in Lyon and then Paris, and could bring to mind no particular plan to evacuate.

Where would she go, anyhow? Back to England? Never – at least not yet. Not until her money ran out.

The flare of unease this thought set off was extinguished by the sight of a male figure moving across her eyeline. He was much older than she, twice as old, perhaps – at twenty-five, she did not distinguish much between forty and sixty – and his appearance was defined by the topmost few inches of him. The hair was thick, about half of it silver, and elegantly swept from a tanned brow corrugated in such a way as to suggest a lifetime of intellectual vexation. Or perhaps simply the immediate difficulty of her.

'Come on, you must wake up now!'

He spoke English but sounded French (I'm firing on all cylinders now, she thought) and the tone was not at all unpleasant. Meeting his eye, she saw that his expression was purposeful, devoid of personal doubt in a way she could only envy. 'You need to go,' he repeated. 'My family will be here today.'

'Oh,' she said, and as if hearing the instruction for the first time she wriggled upright.

What was his name? Either they'd only met yesterday or she really was suffering from amnesia this time, but she couldn't have amnesia because she'd remembered France and anyway her mind held the same weight of knowledge it always did first thing in the morning: knowledge that her father was gone, her mother a lost cause, her friendships mostly lapsed; knowledge that the person she had most loved – and still did – had told her he didn't want her anywhere near him. He didn't even want to know which country she was in, only that it should not be the same one as he.

And now, this man did not want her either. It was as if she were some sort of pest, a liability, and sooner or later everyone she met understood that about her.

Don't cry, she told herself. They've got it wrong. You're fine.

'The taxi will take you over the bridge. The airport is close by, or do you prefer the train again? The station is in the centre of the town, for Paris or wherever you want to go.'

What bridge? The centre of which town, if not Paris, where she was now certain she had woken up yesterday? *Wherever you want to go*: he made it sound like a romantic adventure, simply the next one after this, for theirs had been a romantic adventure, or a sexual one, certainly. Her mind began to sift recollections of the trip they'd taken to get to this blue bedroom: a dusk train from Paris, the journey involving a succession of drinks; the cool interior of a station building with soaring space overhead; a waiting taxi.

She had an image then of this man handing her backpack to the taxi driver. That was a detail worth celebrating because she had her whole world in that backpack, or what was left of it, and she wasn't ready to relinquish it yet.

He was at the windows now, pulling the panes inwards, pushing the shutters outwards. He did it slowly and with deliberation, as if in ritual. Perhaps he hoped that when he turned around again she would have vanished, his problem solved. She heard the hushed murmur of the sea a fraction of a second before she saw it, and when she did she had to narrow her eyes, for it was more like a plane of light than a body of water. Chill air rushed to her skin, reminding her that the month was May.

'Where are we?' she asked.

'We are in a village called Les Portes. I told you this.' He turned, regarded her form beneath the sheet with an ambiguous expression, and she saw she'd been wrong: he had not decided yet whether she had become a nuisance or remained a temptation.

'Ah.' Les Portes. *Le village à la pointe nord* ... the village at the northern tip. She remembered that phrase from yesterday, and now came images of the backpack coming out of the boot of the taxi, an empty street with white walls, cash changing hands. Cash. The uneasy feeling of a moment ago returned,

7

sickening her stomach, and she could no longer stave off the most crucial of all memories: she had no money. Not just none in her possession or in her bank account, but *no access to any*. As of yesterday the cash dispensers of Europe dispensed to her no more, her overdraft limit having been exceeded and her account suspended. If her phone had not run out of credit, she would undoubtedly have received a message from the bank's call centre notifying her of the ruinous impasse. Her train ticket had been bought for her yesterday by this unnamed patron, as had the drinks. She'd come here with him because she'd reached the point at which anywhere would do, and on any terms. That wasn't to say that she hadn't been attracted to him when they'd spied each other in the bar near the Gare Montparnasse, before he'd picked up the bill and relieved her of the need to present a bank card guaranteed to be declined, because she had. He had an air of affluence and protection, the kind that women responded to generically, even those with homes to go to. She would have been happy to stay longer than one night if invited.

Instead, he was throwing her out. The only power she had at her disposal was what had brought her here in the first place and she reached out a bare arm and opened the bed covers in invitation. He moved towards her, sitting close to her on the bed, touching her thighs.

'Your hands are cold. Come in and warm up.'

He sighed. '*Then* you must go.'

'Don't keep saying it, please,' she said. 'I get the message.'

This was a guest room, she thought as she drew his body against her own; not the room he shared with his wife. Someone – his wife, probably, or perhaps an interior designer – someone had once stood in the doorway and looked at the empty space and thought, Blue and white, that's what I want. Like a house by the sea is supposed to look. In the bathroom there were probably white towels embroidered with fish motifs

8

or perhaps anchors; a length of weathered rope for a handrail; a framed old photo of the village from the days when people covered themselves from head to toe for a visit to the beach, travelling *en vacances* by steam train; an oar with hooks to hang your clothes on.

But she was getting carried away now.

'Before you get rid of me,' she murmured, 'do you even know my name?'

'Of course I know your name. It is Tabitha.'

'That's right.' Occasionally, since parting ways with Paul, she had used a different name, not because of any fear of entanglement or to conceal any crime, but because you could do things like that when everything was impermanent, when you were itinerant. You could use any name you liked because no one cared what your real name was; you could do it if only to see if it would change the story you told afterwards, or the actions you next decided to take.

But she'd used her real name with this man; not even Tabby, but her full name, one that she associated with teachers and step-parents and border patrol officials. She must have wanted to impress him. The thought made her arch her torso more urgently, not so much in desire as in gratitude.

The taxi driver spoke no English and she didn't care to reveal her passable French just yet and expose herself to conversation. He knew he was delivering her 'over the bridge', but she would wait until the last possible minute before deciding which mode of transport she would pretend to be taking while knowing full well she could not afford to take it. And she could not face the humiliation of admitting that she was not sure where she was.

It was a beautiful place, wherever it was, remote and low-lying, the land flattened as if by the light itself, which was yellow and colossal, the vast sky wobbling with it. She squinted into the blue as she sought road signs with place names.

The first, Les Portes-en-Ré, had the diagonal red line through the words that meant they were leaving the village behind. Soon, a pattern had developed: Ars-en-Ré, Loix-en-Ré, Saint-Martin-de-Ré. They were in Ré, or *on* Ré, because one minute the water appeared in one direction and the next a seawall rose into view in another: a peninsula or an island, then. The bridge must connect it with the mainland.

Ré. Her brain had returned to full working order and she knew she had never heard of the place when her man – Grégoire, it had come to her just as they said goodbye – had proposed the trip, for he had been going to spend the weekend in his holiday home, arriving a day earlier than his family in order to meet with an artisan about his leaking roof. And why should she have heard of it? It was not on the checklist of the budget traveller, but clearly the location of expensive properties owned by people like him, Parisians, rich, established ones for whom weekend tranquillity was a birthright.

Presumably it was only in weaker moments that an interloper was picked up at the station and offered a bed for the night.

At last, after a smooth stretch between dark wood and flat field, the ribbon of sea visible once more on the left, she saw the bridge. It was a mile or so away, a long, curving black spine that made her think of the tail of a dinosaur, and in the distance, on the far shore, there were industrial buildings, cranes and huge ships. The parting village, by contrast, was delightfully small-scale, the water of its bay still and shining and massed with seagulls. The taxi passed a smart hotel weatherboarded in grey, a pier with sculptures on it, an expensive-looking *boulangerie* with terrace furniture in ice-cream pastels ... Forget weekend tranquillity, Tabby thought, this was a place you might choose to live permanently if you had the luxury of choice.

'Stop,' she told the driver, and he did so without argument.

She had been given fifty euros by Grégoire for the taxi, the driver wanted twenty for the aborted trip, so she was up thirty on yesterday. Beyond this she had only her last loose change, the coins she might fish from the folds of her luggage.

She retraced her route to the hotel they'd passed and found in the lobby a map of France by which she was at last able to locate herself: Rivedoux-Plage on the Ile de Ré, off the coast of La Rochelle. It was about halfway down the Atlantic coast, south-west of Paris, north-west of Bordeaux. Calais was several hours away and Saint-Malo, which she knew had ferry services to England, was half as near. She refused to think of the distances to either in terms of hitchhiking.

At the reception desk, she asked how much the cheapest room was for a night.

'One hundred and twenty euros.' They had entered high season at Easter, the girl pointed out, which pushed the price up. Tabby only faintly recalled Easter, for one of the strange things about travelling was that you had no relationship with bank holidays or long weekends or annual festivals. You drifted through the calendar as you drifted across the map.

In any case, the tariff might as well have been one thousand and twenty euros as far as she was concerned.

She changed her approach: did they happen to have any job vacancies at the hotel?

'What sort of work can you do?'

'Any sort. Bar work. Cleaning. I could be a chambermaid?'

The receptionist shook her head. 'But there are many more hotels and restaurants in La Flotte and Saint-Martin. You should try there.'

She gave Tabby a tourist map and a bus schedule. The next bus for the proposed villages, which were back the way she'd come, was not due for an hour and so she began to walk along the main road, soon detouring along cycle paths through the pine woods she'd earlier passed in the taxi. She felt strangely fearless, charmed, like a character from a fairy tale, safe from the wolf's eyes thanks to some invisible protector. No one knows I'm here, she thought, enjoying the sensation of secrecy and solitude. I am completely alone. Free to start again.

As a waitress or a chambermaid, if she was lucky.

She reached La Flotte. It was a larger place than Rivedoux, with a pretty port, cobbled quayside and windswept promenade. No doubt life here was busy by its own standards, but it ran at a fraction of the pace she'd been used to in Paris and the other cities that had come before. There were, however, dozens of bars, cafés and hotels and she tried every one she came to, only to find that none needed an English worker with broken French.

Flagging, she continued to Saint-Martin, the capital village, but by now her legs and spirits ached too much for her to resume her search straight away. Besides, the port here was intimidating in its smartness, its bistros and art galleries reminding her of the chi-chi neighbourhoods of Paris that had had no place for the likes of her – and with rows of pristine yachts and speedboats to reinforce the divide. She sat on a bench on the waterfront and watched the people, out-of-season tourists, some in furs and designer sunglasses, with pre-schoolers wearing coats more costly than any she'd ever owned. Thirty euros was not going to buy a hotel room here, either, and only a miracle would produce any sort of hostel. She was going to have to make alternative arrangements.

'Alternative arrangements': how coy that sounded! She'd never done it before, slept rough. Two Australian guys she had met in Paris had said they'd done it all the time on a Greek trip the previous summer, and they made it sound like camping without a tent. You stayed up as late as you could bear, they said, then kipped in some secret nook for a few hours until sunrise, which was all very well in August and with old fishing boats strewn conveniently at the foot of sheltering cliffs, but did it work on the Atlantic in the first week of May, too? Would she be at risk of hypothermia or, in a place like this, police arrest?

Instinct told her to head from the exposed and populated edges of the island to its empty interior: what about the woods she'd passed through, might there be a little hut or barn she could slip into there? The thought was half-hearted, however. The hours remaining till dusk might be shrinking fast but she still clung to the belief that something would save her before they disappeared completely. Something.

Thirty euros. She wasn't a vagrant yet.

Hungry, she struck off from the waterside and into the pedestrianised heart of the town in search of a *boulangerie* or supermarket. She bought a small stick of bread and settled halfway up a street of souvenir shops to eat it straight from the paper sleeve, her backpack at her feet. It was not high season, no, but there were numbers of shoppers. She watched one group come out of the nearby linen shop, tried to imagine how it must feel to be on holiday here and not near-destitute, up on your luck and not down, with the money – and the desire – to buy table runners and bathmats, cushion covers and oven gloves. For the twentieth time, she wondered what she had in her pack that she might sell.

'Oh, for God's sake, come on!'

Her attention was caught by the sound of English being spoken – and in clear annoyance. Just a few feet away, down a narrow passageway to Tabby's left, a woman was standing at a green door, stabbing with her index finger at the security pad on the wall, saying letters and numbers aloud in what was evidently an attempt to remember the correct entry code. She cursed when she got it wrong a second time, gaining access only at her third attempt ('*B* one one nine oh three N, *thank* you …'), and the sound of her native, unaccented tongue released in Tabby the same peculiar flare of emotion that came with catching your favourite song in an unexpected place: here, at last, was hope! She could knock on the door and ask this woman for help, ask to borrow some money, one Englishwoman to another. But that was absurd. Why would anyone, compatriot or otherwise, lend a stranger money?

No, she needed to find a public phone, ring her bank in the UK and beg for a last extension to her overdraft, enough to get her home and into someone's spare room (anyone's but her mother's and stepfather's), enough to feed herself while she looked for a job, any job that paid because beggars could not be choosers and she was a beggar. She had to admit that here, in the cobbled and picturesque streets of Saint-Martin-de-Ré, she had come to the end of the line.

She finished her bread and wondered how much a bottle of water would cost in this town. It would be more prudent to get tap water for free. She needed the toilet, too, would set about finding a public one or a café that would let her use its facilities without requiring her to buy a drink.

Down the alleyway, the woman had reappeared at her door, now carrying a backpack of the size you took on to planes to avoid checking in luggage. She pulled the door shut and hurried to the corner, head down, giving Tabby no more than a glimpse of drab-yellow anorak and the bleached ends of a head of cropped mouse-brown hair. She turned uphill in the direction of the church, leaving town, Tabby supposed idly. Imagine leaving a great place like this by choice, to go back to Britain! But she was forgetting that this was what normal people did. They came to the end of their holiday and had a home to return to, one they looked forward to seeing again, however restful the trip. Or, if they lived here, then they had jobs to hold down and places to be. They would come and go.

Leaving town ... Places to be ... Come and go.

To her credit, there was a civilised interval before the bad idea struck. When it did it caused as much revulsion as it did excitement, followed by the sensation of having been relieved of command of herself, of acting outside her own jurisdiction. And then, indecently quickly, it took hold of her completely.

B11903N.

She stepped into the alleyway towards the green door and without risking a glance to either side of her she keyed into the pad the same sequence of letters and numbers she'd heard said a few minutes earlier. There was an affirmative click, and when she pushed at the door it gave way. She slipped quickly through the gap with her eyes down, pushed the door silently behind her, then stood facing it for several seconds, waiting and listening. The weightless sensation had gone and now her lungs squeezed, painful and arrhythmic, like bellows operated by a lunatic, jolting an explanation from her. What are you doing? What on *earth* are you doing?

She turned and looked ahead of her. A short passageway drew her into a small, dark ground-floor room with two shuttered windows and a glass door, which appeared to open on to a sliver of outside space too narrow for any furniture and shaded from the sun by a tall brick wall. There was a galley kitchen along the far wall, the units in a state of near-dilapidation, the worktop disorderly but clean enough. The sight of a single mug on the draining board reignited her thirst and she went straight to the tap and drank, returning the mug to its spot and looking about from her new vantage point. There were two small sofas by the fireplace, both ancient and fraying, an oval dining table with cheap cane chairs and various other junk-shop pieces: lamps, books, all the furnishings of a modest home. In the right-hand corner of the room there were stairs: so it was a house, a small, cavernous one, hidden from the street, open to the light only at the back.

Right, she thought, think. The place did not appear to be any kind of holiday unit and even if it was the woman had left possessions about the place and so could not have checked out. Best-case scenario: she lived in England and used the house only occasionally (why else could she have needed three attempts to get the code right?); she had left for the airport (hence the carry-on bag) and was returning home, perhaps not coming back again until summer. Tabby could stay here for weeks, come and go using the code, not catch anyone's eye, not answer any questions. It wouldn't matter if the electricity supply had been turned off, she needed only water which she already knew she had.

She tested the lights: working.

Worst-case scenario: the woman would be back in five minutes, having gone to the gym or to the shop to pick up dinner. There could be any number of explanations why a person might choose to leave her house at five o'clock in the afternoon with a medium-sized bag, and relatively few involved fleeing the country. Whoever she was, she was here alone, for the items about the place came singly: one bike propped against the wall, one pair of wellington boots by the door, one jacket and one fleece on the coat hooks; that lone mug on the draining board.

Tabby took the stairs, moving on soft feet like the prowler she was, careful not to scuff walls with her pack. There were two bedrooms, and from the door of the larger one she noted the handful of items on the chest of drawers – a leather-bound notebook, a small bottle of perfume (an upmarket English brand, bluebell, less than half left), a laptop of a size and manufacturer that made it, even to her uneducated eye, out of date. Tucked into the corner of a wood-framed mirror was a postcard of a painting, a swirl of red and pink, one of very few personal touches in the room. But she had no wish to touch and snoop: she was too tired and, besides, she had *some* principles. That made her smile, and the sensation of smiling in a situation like this – finding it funny! – brought on a deep sense of unreality.

If she couldn't trust her own responses, could she trust that this was actually happening and not playing inside her mind as she snoozed in the sun somewhere?

Her need for the loo was real enough and she used the one next to the bathroom, willing the sound of the flush to fade quickly, in case the woman came back. She thought, I should get out of this place, forget I was ever here. No one will ever know I was.

But fatigue was taking her in the opposite direction, up a run of three stairs and towards the door of a second bedroom at the rear. It was less spacious than the first, no larger than the cabin of a boat, and was furnished with only a small double bed under the window, a chest of drawers and a stool. It looked as if no one had stepped into the room for months. She pulled the door to behind her, not quite closing it, and sat on the bed.

Her second guest room of the day, her second stranger's bed. Though neatly made, the covers and pillowcase had the damp coldness of fabric not touched or turned for a long time.

She laid herself on top of them and closed her eyes. Even in this context, her last waking thought was of him, Paul.

Dreamlessness ended with physical touch: she was being shaken. There was a rough clutch on her left shoulder and hot breath on her face, and she could feel the anger in both.

'Who are you? What are you doing in my house?' The words were in English at first, frantic and involuntary, and then repeated in French.

Tabby opened her eyes properly. It was the woman she'd seen in the street, of course, her wan English skin flushed, dark eyes ablaze with fear. The light in the house had dimmed: it was evening now.

She struggled upright. In her sleep she had pulled the covers around her and they were tangled at the ankles and knees, shackling her. 'I'm sorry,' she began, voice gruff with sleep, 'I'm so sorry. I just needed somewhere to rest. I didn't think you were coming back ...' But she gave up almost at once. There was nothing she could say that would alter the fact of her trespass, the clear illegality of it. She needed to escape – and quickly.

'Hang on, you're *English*?' If anything, the discovery appeared to intensify the woman's distress, deepen her skin to a feverish red. Her grip tightened. 'Who are you, tell me? How did you find me?'

Tabby did not understand. 'I was so incredibly tired, I didn't know what to do, and when I heard the entry code—'

'What do you mean, you heard the code? You were watching me, then?'

Tabby disregarded the suspicion that they were talking at cross purposes: after all, they hardly had a common one. 'No, I mean I saw you key in the code, and you said it out loud as well. I haven't got any money and I needed somewhere to sleep, so I let myself in—'

The woman interrupted once more: 'Are you *completely* mad? You can't just overhear codes and *let yourself in*! This is a private home, not some sort of doss house!'

'I know, it was wrong. I'm really sorry.' How inadequate the words sounded: insultingly so, as if she were not respectful enough to try harder.

'This is unbelievable, it's breaking and entering. I'm going to phone the police.'

'Don't do that, please. I was going to leave as soon as I woke up, I promise. I wasn't going to steal anything, honestly.'

'"Honestly"?'

Tabby sensed a paralysis in the other woman that gave her her first hope, perhaps even a momentary advantage: if she made a dash for it she might outrun her discoverer. Her legs now free from the bedding, she began to slip from the woman's grasp, heading through the open door and towards the stairs, but she was quickly pursued, footsteps menacing on the wooden stairs behind her. Emerging into the main room, Tabby stumbled and felt a twist in her left knee, at the same time remembering her backpack, still upstairs, at the foot of the bed. She knew she couldn't leave it behind and turned in surrender.

Trying her knee, the pain caused her to crumple to the floor and before she could compose herself she'd succumbed to whimpering into her hands. 'Please, just let me go. I promise you'll never see me again . . .'

'Oh, for God's sake, look at you!' the woman cried, her voice hardly more controlled than Tabby's own. Indeed, she could not continue for a moment or two, breathing hard as she calmed herself. 'Why don't you get up from the floor and sit on the sofa. I'll make you a drink. You obviously need a few minutes to get yourself together.'

'It's too late for that,' Tabby sobbed. 'I might as well just throw myself off the bridge and be done with it.'

The woman stared at her, at a loss. 'I'll make some tea,' she said finally. Only when she turned her back did Tabby rise to her feet and limp to the sofa.

The kettle seemed to take a long time to boil, long enough for Tabby's tears to subside, leaving her too desperate to feel any embarrassment. She became aware of the other woman's scrutiny and then of its removal as the water was poured, the fridge door being opened and closed. Neither spoke, but it was not hard to guess the other's thoughts. She'd had the fright of her life – to find a stranger, an adult female, in your home! It was a miracle she had not turned and fled the moment she saw her, returning only with a pair of police officers. (Tabby had seen the police booth next to the car park in the port, no more than two minutes away.) What would *she* have done in such a situation? But the notion of being the home owner, the occupier, was so heartbreakingly foreign she could not answer the question. She thought, inevitably, of Paul, not in accusation of his having caused her to fall so low, but in hope of him coming to raise her again. Rescue her.

She had never felt more pathetic in her life.

'Right, here we go. How's the leg?'

Tabby looked up in confusion, for the woman's tone had

altered completely. It was gentle and soothing; *kind*. Not only that, but as she approached the sitting area, bearing a tray with tea things, Tabby saw that her whole demeanour had changed: her shoulders were lowered and her facial muscles relaxed. Though she couldn't say why, Tabby understood that this could not be the product of a natural draining of fear and adrenalin, but had to be something more deliberate. It was as if, in the time it had taken the kettle to boil, the woman had reinterpreted her own part in this unscheduled drama and committed herself to a different, less likely role.

'I think it'll be OK,' Tabby said. 'It's just my knee, I've twisted it slightly.'

The woman placed the tray on the coffee table and handed her one of the mugs. 'Drink this and let's get to the bottom of what just happened here.' She settled herself on the sofa opposite Tabby, her movements loose and easy. There was a trace of humour in her eyes, a reversal of mood confirmed by her next question: 'So what's your name? I assume it's not Goldilocks?'

Tabby paused. If she gave her real name, she could still be reported at any time, and perhaps this was the thinking behind this change of approach. There might even be a sedative in the tea! With nothing to guide her but her gut instinct, she made the decision that this was no trick, no trap, but a chance.

Raising the mug to her lips, she smelled the warm, woody aroma of the tea and said, 'No, it's Tabitha. Tabby.'

'Well, Tabby,' the woman said. 'I'm Emmie.'

Chapter 2

Emily

London, December 2010

It was 12 December 2010 when I met Arthur Woodhall, and I honestly believe that until that date I had not been properly activated. I had not yet become myself. I was thirty years old and, extraordinary as it may sound now, given all that's happened since, I'd made little impression on the world. True, people often said I had an attractive face, but I'd come to learn that it never quite seemed to fit. People said I had a big heart, but I'd reached the conclusion that it might never be able to tolerate its own capacity.

I suppose what I mean is I'd never been happy before.

It was a Saturday and the occasion was the Christmas party of our neighbours, the Laings of number 197, a bash they were giving for the Friends' Association of Walnut Grove. Such events, I was told that night, were held in rotation by certain members, mostly those owning the bigger houses on the street, houses worthy of opening up and showing off. Though Matt and I were not Friends, we were invited because the bedroom of our new rental flat at 199 adjoined a portion of the sitting room of 197 and it was thought the music might disturb us. The Laings did not want to risk being remembered as the ones who hosted the year someone called the police about the noise.

'They don't expect us to actually turn up,' Matt said. It was he who had answered the door when Sarah Laing called round and he had described her to me as 'posh and bossy'. 'They're just covering themselves in case it all kicks off. Let's go to the pub instead.'

'Oh, no,' I said. 'Come on, let's see how the other half live. Think of the free booze.'

Finances being painful and Matt an uncomplicated sort, this was all the enticement he needed. I bullied him into the shower while I dried my hair and did my make-up in the Fifties style I liked: dark brows, curled eyelashes and liquid liner, soft and dewy pink lips. Then I costumed myself in a dark red silk dress I'd found in the vintage shop near work. The style was off-the-shoulder and the skin of my chest and shoulders glowed white in the bedroom mirror – I felt like a strawberry dipped in cream.

'That's a bit revealing,' Matt said, with neither approval nor disapproval – with little sense of relevance to him whatever, in fact. After five years of steadily decreasing sexual attraction between us, we were flatmates, not lovers, our recent signing of a new lease together an act of apathy, like failing to switch from an underperforming bank or a negligent GP. Better the devil you know. We were friends who shared a bedroom because we could not afford one each. And we *were* friends, I want to be clear on that. We may have stopped sleeping together, but we had not stopped liking each other.

As we walked down our front path and up the Laings', I felt ashamed of the contrast on behalf of our landlord. While our garden was a horror of neglect – dirty bins with the flat numbers daubed on them in yellow paint, the dead remains of lavender in borders rife with weeds – theirs was artfully stocked and professionally maintained, dustbins out of sight in a timber pen painted some heritage shade of green and at the door two potted firs encrusted with fairy lights. More Christmas lights blinked at the first-floor window, where beyond the ceiling-skimming tree the party was taking place, and the contained boom of conversation behind the glass quickened my blood a little. I know now that while Matt genuinely doubted the value of the entertainment on offer that night, I had different motives. Though I liked to believe I opposed all that the Friends stood for, I secretly craved membership of their elite society. To possess one of these narrow black Georgian houses with their rows of high sash windows, to own a piece of a street scouted frequently by the makers of period drama, to have a marriage, a social life – a Christmas party! – like that of Marcus and Sarah Laing: what a declaration it made to the world that you were *someone*.

After an unnerving delay, the door was answered by a short, muscularly built man I guessed must be Marcus. Though losing his hair, he was youthful for his age, which I judged to be about fifty, and bounced on the balls of his feet with enthusiasm. 'How nice, some young blood at last!' he cried, speaking over the rush of party sounds in the tones of a pantomime actor. His wife, materialising on the crowded stairs behind him, was younger by five years or so and not quite tall enough to carry off the flowing, full-length dress she wore – I feared a tripping as she approached. But she arrived smoothly enough, a cold smile cast in my direction. She greeted only Matt, seizing him from my side as if agreed in advance, and the two of them vanished into the throng without a backward glance. I was left feeling as if my bag had just been snatched from my hands.

'Right, alcohol,' Marcus shouted into my ear, 'give me one second,' and he promptly disappeared into one of the ground-floor rooms. I worried he'd never come back, was just contemplating turning on my heel and fleeing home when he was by my side once more, pressing a glass of champagne on me and proposing to lead me upstairs for introductions. Already I could think of nothing to say; for the first time in weeks, I craved a cigarette.

In the sitting room, the furniture had been moved to the edges of the room to make way for the central mob of Walnut Grovers, the space above their heads dominated by an enormous chandelier that hung white and motionless, like a fountain frozen at the point of eruption. I could not see Matt. Surveying the crush, Marcus turned to me with a mock-helpless expression, before spotting a group of middle-aged men near the window at the back and launching me towards them.

'A treat for the menfolk!' he announced, to my embarrassment. 'Meet our new neighbour Emma!'

'Emily,' I corrected him, blushing under my make-up.

'Emily, forgive me. Sarah must have misheard.'

He stayed to supervise the introductions, standing very close to me and making me excruciatingly conscious of my cleavage (what had I been thinking, choosing this dress? It was so *burlesque*). There were three other men in the little cluster, each of whom emitted the body heat of one who'd been drinking for some time.

'What do you all do?' I asked, shyness making my voice too bright.

Marcus was a City solicitor, Arthur a consultant at the nearby hospital, Ed a journalist, and the last, whose name proved one too many to remember, a voiceover actor whose voice I did not recognise. I'd been told by the rental agent about the vibrant mix on the street, which was close enough to the hospital to attract senior staff, costly enough to interest City lawyers and bankers, and romantic enough to draw the artistic type. (As a web developer for a bike retailer and a glorified shop assistant, Matt and I scarcely qualified for the final category.)

All the men were in their forties or fifties, which validated Marcus's opening claims of my relative youth. Though I'd seen a handful of teenagers on the stairs and noticed one or two small children in the doorway now and then, presumably visiting from a more diverting zone elsewhere, I could find no one else here in their twenties or thirties. The music was from the decade of my birth.

'Are *you* a Friend?' the voiceover actor asked me, a little doubtfully.

I swallowed. 'Well, we haven't joined the association or anything, no, but we live next door. We just moved in a few weeks ago. Flat B.' There were still times when I clung to the plural of Matt and me, and this was one of those times.

'Flat B,' the guy repeated, as if sharing a joke with the group, 'we'll have to remember that.'

His neighbour, Ed, sniggered. 'What, next time you lose your keys and need a bed for the night, try Flat B?'

'I can't think what you mean,' I said, smiling. 'Besides, it would be a tight squeeze: there's my boyfriend as well.'

'There are some on this street who'd say that made it even better,' Ed said, chortling. The instantly risqué turn to the conversation could only be explained by the speed with which they were all guzzling the Laings' champagne. It was high-quality stuff, creamy and soft as it effervesced on my palate. I couldn't remember the last time I'd tasted something so expensive.

'Careful Nina doesn't get wind of that sort of talk,' Marcus said. 'That's Ed's wife,' he added, for my benefit. 'She's not someone you'd want to cross.'

I didn't want to cross anyone, but the conversation was moving much too fast to allow me to protest.

'Nina writes for the *Press*,' the voiceover artist explained. 'She's claimed more scalps than the Comanches.'

I did not often read the *Press*, a national tabloid, and had not heard of the Comanches, but it didn't matter because ignorance was expected of me, I saw. I'd already been judged lacking in the sphere that counted the most: connections (or perhaps money). I was only decorative, the quintessential dumb blonde; perhaps by dressing in the style of a bygone era, I attracted bygone attitudes. 'What do you mean, scalps?'

'You know, all the people she's hung out to dry over the years. Ministers, actors, pop stars. Oh, that TV presenter with the red hair – she's in the Priory now, right, Ed?' He crowed at my blank expression. 'The TV presenter, I mean, not Nina. Sarah's friendly with her, isn't she, Marcus?'

'Not as friendly as she'd like,' Marcus said, and given his wife's cool reception of me I couldn't help thrilling to this small disloyalty. Raising an eyebrow at Ed, who remained modestly silent on his wife's behalf, Marcus sought the opinion of the only one of the men yet to contribute. 'But Arthur'll tell you, won't you, mate? His wife Sylvie's a founder member of the feared Grove coven.'

But Arthur remained aloof from the banter, absorbed in his thoughts; it wasn't clear that he'd been following the conversation at all. Unlike the others, he did not press physically, or *im*press particularly. He was no taller than me in my heels, with a boyish slightness to his build and a pronounced weariness in both posture and expression. Whereas the others ogled my neckline in exactly the manner I deserved, his gaze moved only reluctantly across me, as if over a display in a shop he'd been forced to enter when he'd expressly stated a preference to wait outside.

'I'd love to be able to write,' I told Ed. 'That's my ambition. But if I did, I don't think anyone would want to read it.'

'That's not a million miles away from how I feel myself,' he replied. 'Let's swap jobs, eh?'

'What *do* you do?' Marcus asked me. 'I don't think I know.'

'I work in the pottery café on Linley Avenue. We do children's birthday parties, half-term classes, that sort of thing.'

But Earth, Paint & Fire was below their radar, evidently. Ed's was the only face to clear and he was not quite fast enough to conceal his contempt: 'Is that that place where kids paint spots on an egg cup and the parent gets charged twenty quid for the privilege?'

'God, is that what it is? I've always thought someone who actually enjoys working with small children must be a bit *touched*,' the voiceover artist said.

'Oh.' Even without their comments, mine had already sounded an insignificant way to earn a living next to their grand careers, and I thought it best to accept my inferiority with a good grace. 'It's not for ever,' I said, smiling. I imagined myself in a year's time – same party, different house – but with a raised status. I'd be a trainee reporter or a novelist with a work in progress. I'd be one of them.

Marcus left us after that, and as Ed and the voiceover artist returned to the subject of Nina's latest victim, I waited for the opportunity to make eye contact with Arthur. I felt an urgent need to redeem myself, to see something finer reflected in his eyes than the top half of my own breasts. 'So which number are you?' I asked him, when at last our glances intersected.

He paused, as if judging the meaning of my question from an extensive list of options. 'Eleven. Right at the other end of the street.' It was the first time he'd spoken since giving his name in greeting and I loved his voice instantly: it was low-pitched and earnest, a voice designed for discretion.

'Have you lived on the Grove long?' (This was how you referred to it, I had learned, as if there could be no other.)

'Since before the children were born, twenty years, something like that. They're much too old for your egg cups, I'm afraid.' So he *had* been listening.

'That's OK. I'm not here to drum up business. I get no share of the profits, more's the pity.' 'More's the pity' was not the sort of expression I used often, but, as I say, there was something about Arthur that made me want to try harder. I was pleased when he gave a little smirk in response.

'Is your wife here too?' I asked.

'Somewhere, yes.'

With the famous Nina, presumably, co-founders of the Comanches or whatever the clique was that the men found so amusing. Everyone here knew each other, by definition, of course: if you put a finger in the air you'd be able to touch the threads of the entanglements, the cat's-cradle of private connections and presumed knowledge. There was a smugness in the room's energy, a self-satisfaction bordering on glee. No one was casting about for a better bet in that way you often find at parties, all were utterly fixed on the person or people they were with. I felt sure that if my little group disbanded I'd be left alone, ignored until I left. Indeed, Ed and the voiceover artist were already drifting from Arthur and me. Did he hope to follow? I had the unsettling impulse to reach for his hand.

'I don't know a soul here,' I told him. 'I feel like a gate-crasher.'

'Well, if you've just moved into the area,' he said. Now we were out of earshot of the others he had lowered his reserve somewhat, eyeing me if not in appreciation then with encouragement.

'I haven't even met anyone in my own building yet – I've not been home much since we moved in, still got half the boxes to open. My dad's very ill, you see, and I visit him after work whenever I can, then when I get back I just feel so tired the last thing I want to think about is unpacking, let alone decorating.' Though I always tried to be friendly with new people, it was not like me to pour forth to a stranger in this confessional way, and I couldn't understand what was making me do it; the champagne, I decided at the time – by then I'd dispatched my second glass and accepted a third. Later I understood that it was Arthur's bedside manner, a mild-mannered charm common to many hospital consultants. Designed to calm and reassure, it acted on me as a reverser of inhibition.

28

'What's wrong with your father?' he asked. His eyes met mine with deeper interest and I saw the colour of the irises properly: acorn brown flecked with amber, like tortoiseshell.

'He's got Alzheimer's. It's pretty advanced. They don't expect him to make it to the end of next year.'

He raised his brows a fraction. 'They've said that to you?'

'Not in so many words, but reading between the lines, you know.'

'He's in a care home, I assume?'

'He was until recently, yes, but now he's been transferred to the hospital unit. He's not eating enough, he keeps getting infections.' Feeling distress rise in my gullet, I took a gulp from my glass to wash it back down. 'But I hope he'll go back to the nursing home. It was nicer there.'

'How old is he?'

'Sixty-two.'

'That's pretty young.'

'Some of the people I've met there are a lot younger. It's such a sad place.' I felt suddenly very low, both for the poor patients in Dad's unit and for my situation as a whole. I had nothing, I thought with sadness, no one. Looking down at the strawberry dress, the garment seemed to me to symbolise the mistaken nature of my position; it was not the statement of arrival I'd hoped for but the announcement of a permanent error of judgement. Compared with the tailored black dresses of the other women here, the expensive, heavy fabrics designed to skim and conceal, not cling and expose, it was out of place. I'd done it again: come somewhere I didn't belong. And, as was becoming customary, I might as well have come alone. When I'd said I felt like a gatecrasher, what I'd really meant was I felt lonely.

'Are you all right?' Arthur asked, and there was gallantry to his mien, a paternal tenderness unbearable for the associations it stirred.

'I think I'd better go and find Matt,' I said, though I didn't move. 'I haven't seen him since we got here.'

'Well, if I can advise in any way, you only need ask.'

I looked at him, not understanding.

'I mean about your father,' he said.

'Oh. Is that your field of medicine, then? Dementia?'

'Field of medicine' sounded wrong, too formal and outdated, but he didn't seem to mind. 'No, no, I'm an eye specialist.' Since he did not expand, I preferred not to disappoint him with clichéd first questions ('Don't you get squeamish touching eye-balls?' being the most common, I later discovered). 'I just meant generally,' he said. 'Degenerative illness is very tough on close family. You might have questions you can't get straight answers to at the hospital. They'll be understaffed. I know what it's like.'

My morale lifted irresistibly in response to this unexpected offer. 'Thank you. That's very kind.'

'Not at all. That's what all of this is for ...' He gestured to the mêlée, which struck me now as a distant carnival from which the two of us had fled: 'neighbours helping each other out.'

'Really? Even the ones renting crummy one-bedders half the size of this room? Non-"Friends"?'

'Yes. Everybody counts,' said Arthur Woodhall, and his face had a soulfulness in it that moved me. In spite of his credentials, his eminence – and I had no idea then just how eminent he was – he felt out of place too, I could tell, and partly perhaps by virtue of that last opinion, which was unlikely to be shared by many others in the room. I wished then that I hadn't said I was going to find Matt. As I turned, though I was the one moving away, it felt like it does when you watch a train leave the station, understanding only after it's gone from sight that it was the one you should have taken.

Chapter 3

Tabby

Right from the start, Emmie was an enigma to her. Tabby could not make her out at all. But that was beside the point: what Emmie made of her was what mattered, and that she should make anything that did not involve the bringing of criminal charges was a cause for celebration. And yet, to take her in, to sit her down and try to understand the circumstances that had led her to this desperate intrusion: that was tantamount to a miracle.

Then again, this was a day in which nothing had been predictable, least of all her own actions. The best Tabby could hope for was to survive till morning.

She talked for two hours or more that first evening, long enough for the windows to turn black and reflective and for the house to grow silent but for her own voice or, in occasional prompt or query, Emmie's. She told all about her travels with Paul, how they'd begun seven months ago with a flight to Bangkok, just the two of them against the world – or *for* the world – and how by the time of their arrival in India three months later they had disassembled into something she neither understood nor desired: a travelling couple who couldn't bear to be in the same country together, much less the same room.

'There was no one thing,' she said to Emmie. 'Every day a

few more threads broke.' But in trying to explain to a stranger how each new place Paul had set eyes on, each new person he'd met, had cast a brighter light by which her own inadequacies might be exposed, she encountered only the same bewilderment that had made the actual break-up so impossible to process. If she'd understood how to stop it, she would have. How could Emmie know what it felt like to live every moment as the one before the axe fell? She wouldn't wish her to know!

And when it did fall, there'd been no relief in it, only the splitting pain she'd anticipated. 'Don't you get it? We're history,' he'd said, changing the tense of them just like that. Why, she had asked, of course. Why? And when he struggled to express himself she saw that it wasn't that he couldn't find the words, but rather that he had hoped to spare her the truth of them.

'You're too . . .'

'Too what?'

'You're too *much*,' he said, finally.

Now, she repeated to Emmie, 'It was no one thing.'

Emmie nodded, with her eyes as much as her head. She had listened to Tabby's account with an air of gracious impassivity, almost as if she were a therapist who had had the session scheduled all along. It was only when Tabby told her how Paul had abandoned her, literally walked away from her in a street in Varanasi, leaving her without map or guidebook or (for all he knew) money, that the other woman broke her composure and interrupted.

'That's disgusting,' she cried, indignant. 'Anything could have happened to you, left on your own like that. You could have been robbed or raped!'

Tabby gave her a grateful smile. Given the circumstances, she had not expected to gain sympathy so easily. 'Well, there were lots of other travellers about and in the end I just picked up my stuff from the hostel and found out where the train station was. I still had some money, I wasn't destitute.'

Not like now.

'Even so, you must have been devastated. We all know how it feels to be totally shut out by someone.' Emmie glared with a sudden scorching intensity, and there was a new significance to her body language, a bracing of the torso, as if challenging Tabby to demand how she had come by this awful knowledge. Indeed, Tabby felt her natural curiosity surface, but the fierceness of Emmie's face discouraged her from pursuing it.

'It's terrible,' she agreed. 'He was like a different person. He just did not resemble the man I knew.' *Thought* I knew. 'But people change when they travel, don't they? I was warned about that, but I thought we were ... we were ... *together*.' Will I *ever* heal? she asked herself. The drifting that had followed Paul's desertion, the way in which she had turned her escape from real life into some sort of penance for having left it, it all stemmed from the day of the break-up. And today had been her most desperate to date; was she then not only failing to heal but actually starting to self-destruct?

She gazed at her unlikely confidante with fresh despair, willing her to supply the answers. Instead, Emmie had another question, one she put with some eagerness:

'Was he married?'

'Paul?' It was a peculiar idea, Tabby thought, since married men were not known to set out on year-long backpacking odysseys with their lovers, though it was true she had met a few divorcees along the way. 'No. The last thing he wants is to get married.'

'To *you*, you mean.'

Tabby was taken aback by the bitterness of this remark. Coming so soon after the one about being shut out, it pointed to Emmie having suffered a recent relationship catastrophe of her own, perhaps a broken marriage. Again, she dared not ask, could not risk giving offence and reminding the other woman that rather than wasting time with this torturous heart-to-heart she should be turning her out into the street and setting about changing her locks.

'So what brought you to Ré?' Emmie asked.

'Nothing in particular.' Tabby decided not to tell her about her one-night stand with Grégoire, not least because of that bitter indignation about married men. *She* knew she was a good person, but when you added casual adultery to criminal breaking and entering the evidence rather pointed against it. 'I got a cheap one-way ticket from Paris. I thought I might find work here. It's a big holiday destination, right?'

'Yes, when the summer season starts. But that's not till late June. It's very expensive here. I've probably got the cheapest rental on the island. This place isn't in good enough shape to let to tourists.' Emmie looked about her as if dismissive of a hovel, though to Tabby the house was a paradise of comforts. 'It seems an odd place to choose if you're down to your last cents,' she added. Her expression – apparently somewhat changeable – once again brimmed with suspicion.

'I suppose I didn't want to go home and so I took the next available offer,' Tabby said, truthfully.

'Why don't you want to go home?'

'I'm not close to my family, not since my dad died. My mum is . . . well, I'm not really welcome there. I don't get on with my stepfather.'

'Why not? You don't think she should have had a new relationship so soon after your father's death?'

Tabby took a moment to process the leap in the other woman's logic. 'No, not that. They split up years before he died, they both had new partners.' Much as she wished to cooperate, on the subject of her parents' post-divorce relationships there were no words, not yet, not when she had succeeded for so long in burying the memories. Besides, there was enough dirt flying about without the need to unearth more.

'No brothers or sisters?'

'My father had two stepdaughters, but I never really got close to them and we didn't keep in touch after he died.' How wretched this all sounded: as if she had failed every one of her relationships. If her earlier actions had not been repellent enough, then she was not selling herself any better with this summary of her family history.

'How long have you been away?' Emmie said.

'Seven months.'

'That long?'

'Yes, since October.' Once more, she was ready to make the same enquiry in return, but the rigid set of Emmie's jaw reminded her that this was not an exchange between equals. *She* was the one being asked to explain herself here, Emmie the one whose trust was to be won. 'I don't know about you but I'm totally out of touch with home,' she added blithely, keen to avoid long pauses that might allow Emmie to reconsider her position. 'Anything could have happened and I wouldn't have a clue.'

At this, there was another sharpening of interest in Emmie's eyes. 'You mean you haven't spoken to anyone in England this whole time you've been away?' She was incredulous. 'You haven't followed current affairs at all?'

Tabby thought of the weeks and months that had slipped by without her having given a thought to the wider world. 'Well, you know, for the first few months, when I was still with Paul, I was just on the beach or travelling on buses from one place to the next. I liked not knowing what was happening anywhere else.' It was true that at first there had been a sense of deliberately casting herself away, a natural embracing of a freedom she'd never tasted before, but later, less commendably, she'd been too fixated on her own heartbreak to consider the outside world; self-pity had been a continent all of its own, anything beyond it hopelessly out of reach. 'I haven't really thought about the news at home.'

Embarrassed though she was by the admission, it seemed to hearten Emmie. 'Then that means . . .' There was the lift of optimism in her words, though she did not finish, only averted her eyes and smiled to herself.

'Means what?' Tabby said, encouraged.

'Nothing. Forget it.' Emmie drew herself up and collected the empty mugs, her demeanour relaxed once more. 'It's good that you don't know anything. It's not relevant.'

Baffling as this was, Tabby was more interested in the fact that Emmie was heading to the kitchen and refilling the kettle, preparing for a second round of tea. Her stay of execution was prolonged.

Then, bringing in Tabby a sensation close to deliverance, Emmie called out, 'You must be hungry – would you like something to eat?'

When it grew very late, Emmie said Tabby might as well stay the night. For Tabby, the irony of this invitation was immense, inescapable, but she strove to contain her gasps lest Emmie came suddenly to her senses and remembered she was dealing with a person semi-vicious enough to consider squatting acceptable. The thought of a night in some doorway down by the port, with its still, dark water, the cold Atlantic beyond, was not appealing.

'You know where the spare bedroom is,' was the only clue Emmie gave that she recalled the earlier part of the evening at all. She added that she had to go to work in the morning and Tabby should take her time getting up, have a bath and rest her sprained knee.

'Thank you, that would be fantastic, Emmie.' Talk about my lucky day, Tabby thought. She didn't deserve this generosity, she wasn't at all sure why she was receiving it – her story of rejection had struck a chord with Emmie, evidently – but she was damned if she was going to turn it down.

From the moment she closed the bedroom door behind her,

she entered a state of being that was nothing less than bliss. To go to bed in a room all her own, knowing she could wake up in her own time and get up without harassment. To not worry about having her pack tampered with (though, frankly, there was nothing left in it to steal), or her person, for that matter. How extraordinary life was, that the things you took for granted in childhood should at the age of twenty-five have become so novel they felt like blessed gifts: the clean bed, the full stomach, the quiet night.

And, in the morning, church bells, blue skies, a long, undisturbed bath. The taps ran painfully slowly, but she didn't care because the water was hot; the tub was a huge old rolltop, long enough for her to lie totally submerged, her skin itching with the forgotten luxury of it, her injured knee rapidly losing the last of its soreness. Above her head the paint on the ceiling peeled, the roof tiles visible through the skylight were ancient and eroded, but sun poured in, bringing charm to the irregular angles of the room. Whatever Emmie said, the house was superior in a hundred ways to the hostel in Paris she'd slept in a few nights ago, the dormitory conditions she'd grown used to, the communal bathrooms, the shared odours.

As for Grégoire's house, already it was as though she had conjured it in a dream. She looked down at her body under the water, at its tonal changes, arms and legs still stained dark by the southern sun, the middle part paler, more vulnerable, and tried to imagine herself as she had been the previous morning, in his hands. She felt detached from the memory already, as eager as ever to rewind her mind to the one before, the only one. Paul.

She wondered, as she did every day, where he was now, and if he was back in England yet, and who he had been with since they parted, and whether he ever regretted ending their relationship, and if he had returned to the spot where he'd dismissed her from his life (she'd waited a full hour for that very reason), and . . . on and on the wondering went, suffocating her with pain. She had trained herself to stop after a certain number of what-ifs, just as she had trained herself not to check his activity on the social networking sites he used to update family and friends on his travels, an abstinence that had been easier since she'd been unable to spare the euros for the use of a computer. She had long run out of credit for her mobile phone. At first it had felt frightening to be cut off, but soon it felt only natural, even preferable.

She recalled noticing a laptop in Emmie's room, but it was out of the question that she should use it without permission. The paradox of this struck her with less shame than it perhaps should have, for already it seemed inconceivable to her that she should yesterday have committed the crime of breaking into a stranger's house with the intention of occupying it for as long as she could get away with. She couldn't have done anything like that, could she?

No, it was impossible.

Emmie returned to the house at lunchtime. Tabby was waiting to thank her, her backpack by the door, the mug she'd used for her morning tea washed up and returned to the cupboard (there were spares, it turned out). Charitable and forgiving though Emmie had been, she knew she must now set about finding somewhere to stay and a job to pay for it. The best way of combining the two was hotel work, and her immediate plan was to obtain a list from the tourist office and work her way down it. Was it cheeky to ask Emmie if she could leave her backpack here while she did this? It would look better not to be seen to be lugging her ragged possessions like a refugee. After her bath and the use of a hairdryer and iron, she looked more like a normal person, the sort who might get a job on merit as opposed to pity.

She had notions of delivering Emmie a thank-you gift when she was back on her feet.

'Everything all right?' Emmie asked her. Having expected a

more sombre mood, an impatience to see her trespasser on her way, Tabby was surprised by how light-hearted she was, even pleased to see her again. In daylight she could see how attractive Emmie was, too, or at least would be if she wanted: she had strong, symmetrical bones, her eyes wide-set and large, her teeth straight and white. She would have suited her hair longer than the careless, slightly lopsided style she wore. Not that I'm one to talk, Tabby thought; before the bath, I must have looked like a fisherman.

'I've been thinking,' Emmie said, eyes and voice bright. 'I know how it feels to have everyone turn against you, so if you really have no other options, you can stay here until you sort yourself out. Be my lodger for a while.'

Tabby gaped, her heart racing at the prospect of lightning striking a second time. 'Really?'

'Yes.'

'That's incredibly kind of you, but the problem is—'

'Money, obviously.' Emmie shrugged. 'If you really can't get any from home, then you can owe me the rent. Just pay it when you've got it. Fifty euros a week or something like that will do. I'm not charged very much myself.'

Though this was extremely generous – a week in this delightful place for little more than a night or two in a squalid hostel – it did not change the fact that fifty euros was more than Tabby possessed. Even half that and she would not be able to eat for long.

'I could give you twenty to begin with and the rest as soon as I get work? I was just about to go down to the port and ask around for bar shifts.'

'I might be able to get you something with the woman I work for,' Emmie said. 'I think she's still looking. You only need basic French and she'd probably pay cash. You don't have to fill in forms or anything. She doesn't even know my name – surname, I mean,' she added when Tabby looked puzzled.

'What sort of work do you do?' Emmie was well spoken and gave every impression of being well-educated, qualities Tabby associated with white-collar, professional roles. She herself had limited office skills. Before travelling, she had suffered from an inability to settle in a job, her last, as an administrative assistant for a property management company, having taxed her organisational skills in spite of its entry-level demands. She couldn't imagine producing documents in French and she did not want her ineptitude to reflect badly on Emmie.

'Cleaning,' Emmie said, as if reminding her of information she'd already given. 'You could do that, couldn't you? Most of the houses here are second homes or holiday units rented out weekly, so there's going to be more work now we're coming up to summer. It's crazy over July and August, apparently, getting houses ready for their owners and doing all the changeover days for the lets. But it's decent work, takes your mind off other things.'

'Cleaning, right.' Tabby was careful to conceal her surprise. 'Have you been doing it for long?'

'Since I came here, about a month ago.'

Very recently then, which explained the paucity of personal belongings in the house. And an odd time of year to have come, if, as she said, work was to be had mostly in high season. Presented with Emmie's open and generous mood, Tabby was sufficiently encouraged to venture a further question or two. 'What did you do before, in England?'

In an instant, Emmie's expression neutralised. 'Not this.'

'You just wanted to live in France?'

'Not particularly, no.'

'So it didn't work out back home?'

'No, it didn't.' There was a pause as Emmie took her time choosing her words, eyeing Tabby narrowly before averting her eyes altogether. 'You're not the only one with traumas to forget, you know.'

Tabby very much wanted to ask her what those traumas were, what 'things' Emmie needed her mind taking off, why she had had cause last night to say, 'It's good that you don't know.' Know what? But Emmie's replies had been evasive enough for her to hold her tongue. With an offer like this on the table she could not afford to speak out of turn, not when there might by the end of the day be no other alternatives bar stealing or hitch-hiking.

Emmie sighed. 'So do you want to stay or not?'

'I'd love to,' Tabby said.

Chapter 4

Emily

Before I continue, I should like to say that I am writing this for myself, not for anyone else, and certainly not for the public record. Of course, there are people who I'd like to think *ought* to read it – my side of the story and as honest an account as I can make it – but I don't plan to give them the opportunity. They wouldn't accept it, in any case, not while events are so recent, the pain so raw. On the contrary: they'd like to see me properly punished, an Anne Boleyn or a Ruth Ellis, both of whom have been invoked in media articles about me – or at least about the Emily Marr they've decided I am.

IS THIS BRITAIN'S MOST HATED WOMAN? one newspaper asked, and it wasn't even Nina Meeks who wrote *that*.

Why put pen to paper at all, then? Why torture myself by reliving the horror moment by moment? It's not for reasons of pride or posterity, that's for sure. I probably won't ever re-read this, nor even print out a copy and make a material memento of it. When I told Ed Meeks at the Laings' party that it was my ambition to be a writer, I could not have imagined in my darkest nightmares subject matter like this. But perhaps nothing less could have impelled me to do it.

No, the reason is simple: I want to rid myself of it. If I shed the words, empty them from my head, then hopefully I'll be able to refill the space with new words, new stories. A new life.

Hopefully. I have to hope, you see. I have nothing else left.

The second time I met Arthur it was in an unlikely context: the pottery café where I worked. The fathers of teenage boys were not the demographic most typically represented in Earth, Paint & Fire, or males generally: decorating milk jugs and eating cupcakes was incontestably a mother-daughter indulgence. But there he was one Saturday in January, right at the end of the afternoon, approaching me in the studio behind the shop as I cleaned up after the chocolate-fountain finale to a fifth-birthday party. The acoustics were painful back there and the squeal of young girls' voices remained in my ears, that particular pitch of excitement I'd learned to recognise as a tipping point: on one side noisy joy, on the other the kind of delirium that led to children being carried out over their parents' shoulders like so many broken dolls.

So when he spoke, the words made restful, consoling sounds. I wanted to touch them, hold my wrists in their cool flow and feel my pulse settle.

'Hello again. I don't know if you remember but we met at Marcus and Sarah's party? Arthur Woodhall.'

'Of course I remember. How are you?' I was self-conscious in my apron, with its paint spatters and chocolate smears (it was possible I even had chocolate on my face), and my general disarray. My hair, which at the party had spilled down my back in an extravagant show of blondness, was today pulled into a workmanlike ponytail. My work leggings and overall were stained and my pumps scuffed. By contrast, his weekend dress of jeans and blazer scarcely concealed a natural neatness, the polish of wealth. 'You're not collecting someone from the party, are you? I think they've all gone home now.'

He glanced at the remaining devastation. 'Is that what this was? A party? Looks more like the remains of a pitched battle.'

I laughed. 'They're virtually the same thing. And you have no idea how good it feels to speak to someone who isn't about to burst into tears.'

'Well, try me on another day and it could be a different story,' he said.

We looked at each other, smiling. I felt the disarming sensation of certain knowledge that I would agree to anything he cared to suggest.

'So how can I help you?' I asked.

'I've been sent to pick up some sort of plate.' He said this as if speaking of an obscure artefact, not an everyday household item. 'My wife was here with her niece a couple of weeks ago and they painted one. She says it should be ready by now.'

'Do you have the receipt with you?'

'Sorry, no.'

'Well, if it was a couple of weeks ago it will have been in one of the last batches we fired, last Monday, or possibly the one before. All the finished items are on display in the café; let's have a look.' I led him to the enormous dresser opposite the counter, which held the many hundreds of items awaiting collection. There were battalions of glazed figurines, cats and dogs and ducks and turtles, fleets of gravy boats and milk jugs and teapots. Some were a dashed-off mess, destined to be tucked out of public sight, others painstakingly composed and deserving of pride of place. Collectively, every conceivable blend of colour had been used, squirted from the banks of plastic bottles we replenished daily. Sometimes I wondered what would happen if the dresser were to come crashing down; it was like trying to picture Armageddon.

I turned back to face him, my attitude of indulgence the same one I used with any hapless male who'd come at his spouse's bidding – OK, perhaps a shade more flirtatious. 'What are we looking for exactly? Any idea of size?'

'Big, I think. It's a birthday gift for Sylvie's sister and

44

apparently it has the date of her birthday on it. That should be a clue.'

But when presented with three dinner plates and one platter bearing commemorative dates in the next two weeks, Arthur confessed he couldn't remember his sister-in-law's date of birth after all.

'Do you know what colours they used?'

He didn't know that either. 'My preparation for this mission has been woeful, I'm afraid,' he said, looking entirely unafraid, and I found the phrasing exciting – no other customers spoke to me in this formal, bold way. It was not unusual, however, for them to be so vague about the item for collection. Mothers would spend hundreds of pounds on a pottery party for their children and then barely pay attention to its taking place, standing in the café talking to the other adults. Sometimes, after casual Saturday visits, they would not bother to return to collect the fired article even though they'd already paid for it. It was an expensive way to amuse a child for an hour.

'You might need to come back another time,' I said, sensing that my tone had changed to something more overtly inviting than it should have been. 'I can't let you take one in case we get it wrong, and the other customer is bound to come in the moment you walk out the door.'

'No, that's fine. We can't do that.' The echoed plural seemed to establish a conspiracy between us, but before I could register my pleasure in this he had already upgraded it by asking if I had finished for the day and, if so, did I want to stroll back to the Grove together? I was astonished by my body's reaction to this suggestion: blood rushed faster and air grew lighter, as if I'd been summoned to a paradise island with a movie star, his private jet standing by on the street outside.

'Sure,' I said, struggling to sound cheerful rather than elated. 'That would be lovely.'

It was the standard Saturday situation of my shift having

overrun, with neither extra pay nor Brownie points to be gained (I'd long ago realised there was no chance of promotion when the manager was also the owner of the franchise and her holiday cover her sister-in-law), and so I decided to leave without finishing cleaning up and without asking Charlotte's permission.

'I have to go on time today,' I called to her. 'I'm due somewhere else.' She was at the till, just starting to cash up, and frowned without glancing up. 'It's almost done back there, just the floor still needs sweeping – could Aislene do it?' Aislene, the Saturday girl, was paid by the hour and could not be expected to work overtime for free, I thought.

Arthur a step ahead, I followed him out of the door, rebellious, the worm that had turned, Cinderella cutting loose.

'Shall we go through the park?' he suggested. 'Or is it too dark now?'

'No, let's, if it's still open.' I would not have dreamed of taking the park route on my own at this time of year, for not only was it unlit, but it was also less direct than the road option. Both, this evening, were advantages: we would not be seen and, if we dawdled, it would take half an hour to reach the Grove. I wondered if this had occurred to him, too.

'I'm glad I saw you,' he said, as we waited for the lights to change at the crossing. 'I wanted to ask how your father's doing.'

Feeling my smile sag, I willed the muscles to lift it again. I didn't want him to see me as the despairing kind, I didn't want to *be* the despairing kind. 'Not very well, to tell you the truth. On my last two visits, he hasn't been conscious. It's getting hard to believe that it's worth my going – from his point of view, I mean. Even if he's awake he doesn't always recognise me, or he'll need to see a photo of me when I was younger and even then he can't make the link.'

'No new memories. That's part of the disorder, isn't it? Apart from childhood or earlier adulthood, everything is as if for the first time?'

'That's right. There's no point arguing or trying to persuade him to remember. Usually I just agree with whatever he thinks and if he seems anxious about it I try to distract him with something different.'

'That sounds kindest,' Arthur said.

The park gates were still open. Out of the street light, our deserted path flanked by silent, black conifers, I felt the same urge to confide that I'd felt at the party. 'The thing is, sometimes I really feel like he *wants* to be able to understand it all again. Everything he used to know. To be who he used to be. But I know that's just me projecting my own feelings. It's an irreversible disease and he's long past that stage.' I sighed, partly to pre-empt the choking-up of my speech. 'There's a student nurse there who he's more attached to than me. Even though all of their interaction must be like the first time, he feels a connection with her. Not that I mind – I'm glad he does, you know, with anyone.'

'Still, that must be very upsetting for you.' Arthur's voice was full of sweet condolence, and of the personal kind, as if we knew each other well, as if my pain were his pain. It was impossible not to compare that with Matt's enquiries, which were dutiful but offhand, all too expectant of the bleakest of responses.

'No, it's OK. Honestly. It's been years now and I've accepted what it is. Now I'm preparing myself for what's next.'

I was not as brave as I sounded. It was probably truer to say that I was preparing myself for *having* to prepare myself for what was next.

'Your mother's not in the picture?' Arthur asked.

'No, she died when I was nine. That's why we're so close, Dad and me. Why it's all so hard.'

In the dim light I caught the blink of surprise, the pluck of compassion at his mouth. 'You've been unlucky, Emily.'

'Maybe. But luckier than some people.' For instance, hearing him speak my name for the first time made me feel magnificently lucky. I wondered what he would say if I told him that. I wondered what he would do if I slipped my arm through his, pleading fear of the dark, perhaps, or pleading nothing at all.

'It's good that you think that way,' he said. 'It's very easy to feel persecuted by health problems. I see it all the time. People always want to know why it's happened to them, as if it's some sort of punishment or personal injustice.'

'It hasn't happened to *me*,' I pointed out. 'It's far worse for him. And he doesn't think in terms of punishment or justice. Maybe that's the one good thing about it.'

'Do you not have brothers and sisters to share the responsibility?'

'I have a brother. He lives out in Newbury, but he visits once a week. To be honest, when he does I take the night off.' This was an unfortunate consequence of Dad's hospitalisation: Phil and I were the only ones who could give each other a break and so rarely saw each other.

'Still, it's a tough situation. You're handling it very well, I would say. And working full-time in the café, you've got a lot on your plate. Excuse the pun.'

'Oh, it's manageable. It's not as if I've got children as well,' I added, my glance having fallen on the outlines of the swings and climbing frames in the distance, too dark now for there to be any families still out playing. 'I have plenty of spare time compared to a lot of people.'

'But you'd like children one day?' The way he said it made the unspoken 'obviously' perfectly audible to me. And he looked candidly at me, keen to learn the answer. Then, when I failed to reply, he remembered himself. 'Forgive me. I suppose I'm used to reading between the lines. It's none of my business.' But he held my gaze well beyond the natural threshold, the prolonging of it forcing us to slow our step. At last he looked away and lengthened his stride once more. 'It's getting cold,' he said.

I scurried to catch him up. 'I would like kids, yes,' I said in a rush, as if fearful of having missed my chance. 'Of course I would. But my boyfriend . . .'

'He's the one you were at the party with? Matt?'

'Yes. He doesn't want to start a family. Not that I would want to with him, anyway, so it's not a problem. He doesn't want *me*. I don't want *him*.'

This was a bold declaration by anyone's standards, but Arthur responded smoothly, as if he heard this sort of thing routinely. 'I see. It's like that.'

'It's like that,' I agreed, calming myself. 'And he wouldn't be at all bothered to hear me say it. I call him my boyfriend, but we're really just friends these days, flatmates. We had to find somewhere to live in a hurry and there wasn't time to sort out an alternative. We should have just called it a day.' The stupidity of signing a new lease with Matt had never been clearer to me, the *wastefulness* of it. We both deserved better than love by expediency. 'You're very good at getting people to tell you their secrets, aren't you?' I said, for this was the second time I'd found myself treating a casual conversation with this man as a confession. I was struck by the absence of embarrassment on either of our parts. 'But in a very tactful way, I mean. No offence.'

'It's my job, I suppose,' Arthur said. 'You learn to discover the information you need to know.'

I tried not to ponder whether my relationship status was information he 'needed' to know; he himself was married, after all. 'Of course, you're a surgeon at St Barnabas', you must deal with every type of person and get told all sorts of secrets.'

'I certainly do. I don't always want to know them, however.'

I smiled. 'Do you use euphemisms, like Dad's doctors do? I bet you've never actually used the word "death" with your patients, have you?'

For the first time in my company, he laughed, a spontaneous chuckle of delight that made me giggle too. 'Well, since I'm mostly correcting squints, the subject doesn't tend to come up.'

I pulled a face at my mistake. 'I suppose someone might encounter complications with the anaesthetic?'

'That's true, but the anaesthetist will have outlined the risks of that with the patient. I just concentrate on solving the vision problems.'

It was all too easy to imagine him at work: he'd be utterly unflustered, focused to the point of severity. He'd probably known from an early age what he would become and trained at the top medical schools – unlike someone like me, who had not been to university and was as easily distracted from jobs as she had been in falling into them. I was not climbing any ladder, only stepping on to the nearest unoccupied rung of the next one along, determined not to notice how close to the ground I remained. (Maybe mine was a vision problem, too.) Pulling myself back from such thoughts, I blurted, 'I've never had an anaesthetic. I can't imagine what it's like.'

'That's something to be pleased about, believe me. You've obviously never needed surgery.'

'No. Have you?'

He smirked, raising his eyebrows only fractionally. 'Maybe I ought to know you a bit better before I reveal that sort of detail.'

It was one of the most bizarre conversations I'd ever had with anyone. Confiding in him about my father, telling him my relationship was a sham, asking if he'd had surgery! With anyone else I would have considered that I'd made a fool of myself, but with him I felt as if I'd been only direct and agreeable. It seemed a thing of wonder that two people could lead

such different lives, one so accomplished, the other so unre-
markable, and yet still have so much to say to each other, still
feel a powerful connection. It was a connection I did not yet like
to name, though I must have known what it was, of course, and
it had nothing to do with sharing a postcode.

We reached the park gate and he held it open for me. The
park would be locked at any minute, we were probably the last
to leave. Back under street light we quickened our step, soon at
my end of the Grove, at the gateless path of 199. The windows
of my flat were dark: Matt was out. I lingered with Arthur,
nearly suggested he come up for a drink, almost but not quite
willing to ignore the mental picture of my kitchen, the sink
stacked with last night's dinner dishes, Matt's cycling gear
strewn about, the laughable lack of anything to drink but cheap
lager. 'I'd love to invite you in for a cup of tea,' I said, 'but the
place is in such a state, I'm embarrassed for you to see it.'

Arthur's smile, mild but rueful, implied that such an invitation would not have been turned down. 'If you'd ever laid eyes
on my elder son's bedroom, you'd know I've seen a lot worse.'

I pictured his home at the opposite, smarter end of the street,
the family waiting, a wife eager to inspect her pottery. With the
exception of the son's pit, the house would be immaculate,
along the lines of the Laings', full of chic, expensive furnishings,
walls of inherited art, a piano in the library perhaps. They'd be
going out that evening to some grand dinner party or charity
do, or perhaps to the ballet or opera. They'd be Friends, of
course. And yet, it seemed to me already that all of that might
in fact be immaterial to him, that he held within him nobler
concerns.

'Well, another time,' he said, smiling.

'Definitely.'

We stood looking at each other in the dark, only a couple of
feet apart and close enough for me to see that the skin around
his eyes was fragile and bruised, as if rubbing with fingertips

had worn it thin. Neither of us turned to leave and I had exactly the same feeling I'd had at our first meeting, reluctance in the form of a physical tugging – not heartstrings, not yet, but bits of my gut, maybe; something bodily and fundamental.

'You look different,' he said at last, his tone thoughtful.

I realised he meant different from the night of the party. 'What, as in worse? Run ragged?' I laughed. 'I would agree with that.'

'No, that's not what I meant at all. I like both ways.'

'Thank you.' I didn't know what else to say.

Now he left me, casting a quick glance up at the Laings' house as he went. Though in reality the two families were probably friends, I liked to imagine that Arthur was praying he would not catch one of them coming or going, just as I did whenever I walked past.

It was his wife, Sylvie Woodhall, who came to collect the plate the following Saturday. As I squatted a short distance from the cash desk, unpacking a delivery of ready-to-paint jewellery boxes, I could hear her announcing her name and describing the piece to Aislene. 'I did send my husband in last weekend, but he's obviously not to be trusted with such a task.' And then she cried out, 'That's it there, on the bottom shelf, that big yellow one! I don't see how he could possibly have missed it.'

'Must need his eyes testing,' a female voice replied, followed by a single sharp bark of laughter that set Sylvie off, and without being told I knew this wisecracker must be the scalp-hunting journalist Nina.

I adjusted my position behind the raised lid of my cardboard box so I could study the two of them more discreetly. Both women were in their late forties or early fifties and very well dressed: expensive-looking woollen coats and wedge-heeled suede boots, cashmere scarves in understated shades twined casually about the neck and shoulders, handbags about a hundred times

52

more costly than any in my possession. Arthur's wife had a shower of natural-looking blond curls, angular features and a pink English complexion, Nina dark bobbed hair and the kind of polished-pearl skin that spoke of high-end facials. As they queued together at the till, the huge plate now held in Sylvie's arms like the Wimbledon trophy, they chatted openly about personal matters, quite heedless of who might be in earshot. Admittedly, this was not unusual behaviour for customers and I'd long ago learned to zone out of the myriad soap operas going on around me; this time, though, I found myself listening closely. Finishing with the jewellery boxes, I started on a package of piggy-banks that were supposed to have waited till later, dallying over the job and hoping Charlotte would not come on to the shop floor from the office upstairs to notice my breach of protocol.

'Anyway, if you ask me, you're doing brilliantly,' the Nina woman said in the strong, carrying tone of a public announcement. She exuded a sense of command you rarely encountered in real life, as if she could quite unselfconsciously bring the room to silence and start an impromptu rally for the cause of her choice. 'It's almost two years now, isn't it? That's pretty good for him.'

'As far as I know, yes. Pathetic, really, to be congratulating him on it.'

'I think you should be congratulating *yourself* for getting safely to the other side, not beating yourself up because you're not Pollyanna.'

'I just can't help it, though. Every so often the resentment just bursts through.' Sylvie's voice was higher in pitch than her friend's, making her sound a little wheedling. 'Not just about *that*, but about the balance of power in general. You know, like we've said before, Neen, all the domestic inequalities, the stuff it wouldn't occur to him to know about. It's all so far beneath him it might as well be taking place underground.'

Sighing, Nina removed her gloves – leather, a beautiful smoky blue – as if settling in for a prolonged debate. 'And it only seems to get worse as they get older, doesn't it? You wouldn't believe the self-importance of Ed these days, you'd think he was the Foreign Secretary, not someone who just tries to get a question in at press briefings. He's far too pivotal to the future of our democracy to book a restaurant or stay in for the plumber. At least Arthur has a secretary to do his dirty work. For most of us, we've been saddled with the job without having ever applied for the bloody thing. Maybe they're cleverer than we think, eh?'

'Maybe.' Sylvie Woodhall stood further from me than Nina and her voice did not carry as clearly, but I could still piece together most of what she said. 'The problem I have is there *is* an imbalance, a real one. I'm not like you, my job can't begin to compare with his, not on any level.' She sighed. 'But it's not like that's news to anyone so I don't know why I bore myself by going on about it.'

I wondered what it was that Sylvie did. I suspected amateur interior design or some unprofitable enterprise involving semi-precious stones; she'd be her own boss, certainly, no kneeling on shop floors among the piggy-banks for her. As for Arthur, I had of course Googled him since our last meeting and knew now that he was celebrated and revered, one of the top specialists in the world in an area of eye medicine called strabismus, his reputation having been established many years ago when he had treated a member of the Royal Family who had suffered problems with his vision following a stroke. My fifteen minutes on Matt's laptop had also told me that he worked in a private practice in Harley Street as well as at St Barnabas', and had in fact two secretaries, not one, to make his restaurant reservations and calls to the plumber. There were strings of letters after his name, a name he lent, along with several days' surgical time a year, to a charitable enterprise in a

West African country. He appeared occasionally in the society pages.

'Well, I don't see why it *shouldn't* compare,' Nina said, 'just because he's a famous surgeon. I mean it's not like it's anything heroic, is it? Like A&E or heart transplants for babies. It's just squints. Double vision. Come on, most of us can cure that by cutting down our wine intake a couple of nights a week.'

'Yes, well, *I* did, I suppose, didn't I?' They both hooted at this private allusion, Arthur's wife's laugh a low, bitter sound that lasted longer than Nina's barking staccato. Though Sylvie's humour was self-deprecating, I could tell she greatly enjoyed this opportunity for irreverence towards her husband. I supposed it didn't come her way very often, not if my own rapt response to him was anything to go by, and that Nina gave her the confidence to rebel. I sneaked a longer look at Nina. Though nervous of her in a primal way, I could easily appreciate her appeal: she was bold and strong and funny. It was she who drove the mood of the conversation, championing her friend with a gusto none of mine did me (nor I them). How had Sylvie, a pale, complaining creature, won her as a friend – or Arthur as a husband, for that matter? Had she once been different? I longed to know the full story of it. And so did other people, for I could tell that I was not the only one eavesdropping: several customers had let their own conversations lapse in order to listen in. Even for this place, Sylvie and Nina were being indiscreet, something I put down to pure arrogance. At parties or when among their own kind, they were probably more vigilant, but somewhere like this, where it was mainly mothers with younger children, or people who'd travelled from other, lesser postcodes, or staff who were by definition below consideration (so far below as to be underground, I thought wryly), there was no need for caution. Everybody counts, Arthur had said to me, but for women like these two that was not true. No one else mattered, except for those in their own lofty sphere.

That wasn't to say that once in a while someone or something outside it would not catch their eye, as I did now when I shifted my position on the floor and rolled back my tensed-up shoulders to ease the beginnings of an ache, sliding the half-full box closer to the storage unit.

'I know you, don't I?' Nina called out, regarding me with interest. As Sylvie reached the front of the queue and handed over the plate for wrapping, she took a step towards me, evidently enjoying this test of her memory. 'Where would it be from ...?'

'You might have seen me here before?' I suggested timidly. Under her direct beam, my skin reacted, stinging with sudden high colour.

'That's not it, I never come here. Weren't you at Marcus and Sarah's party at Christmas?'

'I was,' I said, swallowing. 'I live next door to them. But I don't think we met, did we?'

She looked amused by the idea that I might not be sure, might be able to consider her in any way forgettable. 'What's your name?'

'Emily Marr.'

'Emily Marr,' she repeated, not exactly with distaste but with a certain precision, as if sensing it would benefit her to remember it. 'Nina Meeks,' she offered in return, and her name caused a noticeable catch in the atmosphere. If anyone had been in any doubt as to who this droll, charismatic woman was, they knew now.

'I'm at the other end of the Grove from Sarah,' she told me. 'I won't say which number out loud, though. You never know where your enemies might be hiding.'

I thought it interesting that she should withhold her address when she'd been so happy to air her private thoughts about her husband – and Sylvie's.

'And this is another neighbour, Sylvie Woodhall. Have you met before?'

As Sylvie turned at the sound of her name, I rose, unwilling to remain on my knees, subservient and reduced. 'No, we haven't. It's nice to meet you. I think I might have met your husband,' I added, but regretted it at once because it was clear from her glower that, whatever her similarities with Nina, she did not possess the other's self-assurance. The idea that I knew her husband (and had stood to announce the fact) was not received as the casual claim I'd intended it to be. She was an anxious, suspicious spouse, evidently, and I knew better than to show I'd recognised this by blurting some unnecessary detail.

The exchange ended as Aislene handed Sylvie her wrapped package. 'There we go. I hope your sister likes the design. It's come out really well, hasn't it?'

Sylvie just nodded, evidently too preoccupied to respond to the pleasantry, while Nina turned dismissively from me, from this port of call and back to her friend. 'Right, Sylv, I think we deserve some lunch, don't you?'

As they left I heard her say, 'You hope what?' There came more of that distinctive, lupine laughter. 'Oh, *don't* be ridiculous, darling. No chance, he wouldn't dare, not after last time.'

My shelves restocked, I began collapsing the cardboard boxes, wondering what fear of Sylvie's Nina had pre-empted, wondering when 'last time' had been and whether it was anything to do with the achievement of 'almost two years' that she had earlier been urging her friend to celebrate.

Wondering why my face burned so hot.

Chapter 5

Tabby

Emmie's employer was an Englishwoman called Moira, the proprietor of an agency that managed seasonal lets and supplied cleaners and maintenance staff to the owners of second homes on the island. She lived with her French husband and children on the mainland, travelling to her office in La Flotte across the same bridge with which Tabby was determined to avoid being reacquainted. She was in her fifties and had a pleasant face, blurred but not ruined by the decades, and a quiet, measured manner that Tabby guessed must once have been brisk and eager.

'Tell me a bit about yourself,' she said.

This was not a question that could ever silence Tabby; the trouble was selecting from the ready outpouring those details that might actually be relevant. 'I'm twenty-five and I'm in France for the summer, maybe longer if things work out. I have *huge* amounts of energy.' It was true that since taking residence at Emmie's she had avoided getting under her benefactress's feet by taking long walks along the coast and through the vineyards, exploring her temporary home with the wonder of a newcomer to Eden. 'Emmie sent me,' she added. 'She said I had the right experience.'

At Emmie's advice, she had turned up at Moira's office without an appointment at twelve-thirty. During the lunchtime hours of noon till two, when the French did not do business, the British had time to fill. She had been admitted at once.

Moira listened to her plea, complete with claims of experience that were not quite true but that Tabby was reasonably confident could be lived up to, and seemed content to accept them as reference enough. Even at first glance Tabby could tell she was one of those middle-aged women who had retained a soft spot for the young, even a fond memory of it, as opposed to the envy or begrudging of it that you were sometimes faced with in women past their best (her mother sprang to mind, though Tabby was expert in the rapid extinguishing of any thought of *her*). Perhaps it was this that made it so easy to imagine how love had once led Moira to this foreign place – she'd met her husband on holiday, Tabby decided; it had begun as a seasonal romance – and how, twenty or thirty years later, as she worked from a small first-floor office above an *immobilier*, an estate agent, in La Flotte, the exhilarations of love had had to be consigned to history, her marriage now moribund.

But she was being ridiculous. There was nothing in Moira's face to suggest disappointment or resignation. She needed to conquer this compulsion to project her own miseries on to everyone she met. She needed to stop the self-indulgent fantasies and focus on raising herself from penury.

'I'm *very* keen to work,' she declared, not sure if she had already said this. 'No job is too low.'

'Well, I can always use a hard worker,' Moira said, 'and your timing is good.' This was not a comment Tabby had heard much lately. 'I have several clients who are letting their homes from the end of this month right through to late September and there'll be regular changeover work on the weekends.'

'What does that entail?' Tabby asked in earnest tones.

'Basically, you clean up after one lot and get it brand-spanking-new for the next. A quick inventory check in case anything's missing or broken. We usually do check-out at eleven in the morning and check-in at three, so you've got four hours to turn it around. But sometimes it's just a couple of hours. It's very hard work, especially in the summer months when it gets very hot here. Do you think you can handle it? Are you fit?'

'Very. I just walked here from Saint-Martin and yesterday I walked twenty kilometres to Loix and back.'

'That's quite a hike. Do you not have your own bike or car?'

'Not yet. I'll use the bus.' The idea of owning a car was about as likely as being crowned the Queen of Sheba. 'Would I need my own cleaning materials?' This could be a deal breaker; she couldn't afford to buy products, and even if she had the cheek to ask to borrow some from Emmie, her new friend would surely need them for herself.

'No, it's all stored in the individual houses. If you need to get something urgently, you buy it and I'll reimburse you when you submit a receipt.'

Tabby prayed that wouldn't happen before she was paid. Having given Emmie twenty, she was down to her last few euros now.

A thought occurred. 'I wouldn't be taking work from Emmie, would I? She would still get first refusal?'

Moira eyed her with interest. 'I'm impressed by your loyalty, though, as I say, there should be enough jobs to go around.' She paused. 'How do you know her? You came to the island together, did you?'

'No, we just met a few days ago, actually. I'm staying in her spare room in Saint-Martin. I came along just as she was thinking of getting a lodger. I've been very lucky.'

'Yes.' Moira drew her lips between her teeth and bit down. Tabby wondered what she was trying not to say. 'Emmie's not everyone's cup of tea,' she offered finally, 'she keeps herself to herself. But if you're as diligent as she is, I'll be very happy.'

'I will be.'

'For your first job, I'll come along and show you the ropes. There's a bit of juggling at first but you'll soon get the hang of it. What's your phone number?'

'My phone isn't working at the moment,' Tabby admitted, 'and I don't think we've got a landline.' Nor was there an internet connection in the house, Emmie had told her, and sooner or later she was going to need to find a way to get online. 'Should I call in every so often instead?'

'Yes, or I can get you on Emmie's mobile, presumably? I've been texting her her client details a day or two before each job. It'll be easier in a few weeks when you get regular slots and keep a set of keys yourself.'

'I'm sure that would be fine,' Tabby said.

As she pedalled back to Saint-Martin on the bicycle she'd borrowed from Emmie, she marvelled once more at her extraordinary reversal of fortune. As if those inauspicious beginnings had never occurred, Emmie had in the space of forty-eight hours assumed the role of landlady, colleague, even mentor. That a sensible private citizen should take in a penniless drifter, offer her a home and expect rent only in arrears; that she should find her work and share her only means of transport: it was almost too good to be true – and at exactly the point at which Tabby had thought things too awful to believe.

What was it that had made Emmie choose to trust her? For that was what it was, a deliberate choice, that almost magical moment when she had turned to Tabby with the mugs of tea, her face alight with the decision that she was going to give her the benefit of the doubt. She was going to give her a break. Tabby was not at all certain that she herself would have been so generous had their positions been reversed. Well, she would learn from Emmie, she vowed. Just because kindness had become a rare commodity, it didn't mean it should be treated with suspicion.

Besides, she had a good feeling about the island generally. Not yet swollen with the throngs she knew to expect in high season, it was a tranquil place, a haven from the Atlantic, which at full tide lashed savagely at the sea walls. When the tide was out, the shores heaped with glossy black seaweed and scarred with oyster beds, it felt more as if the place was forgotten, abandoned even by the ocean, a mood that suited her circumstances perfectly.

Her walks over the last two days had revealed a join-the-dots trail of small, low villages with old cobbled streets and handsome stone churches; she'd seen an antique bandstand, a medieval market, row after row of shuttered fishermen's cottages. By chance, Saint-Martin appeared to be the jewel in the crown, the warren of streets contained within grand, star-shaped fortifications built centuries ago by some famous military engineer called Vauban. She'd studied a booklet from the tourist information office, feeling a certain pleasure in not being a tourist. She had switched sides, she was to be a cleaner *for* tourists. She would clean, she would save her earnings and live frugally, she would make some sort of plan, build herself a future.

What had Emmie said about forgetting traumas? Well, this would be the perfect place to forget her own – or to try to, at any rate.

She'd insisted on having them laid bare, her faults – or rather the single consuming fault of her being Tabby Dewhurst. 'Too much in what way?' she asked him, and she had to squint into the brightness, close her ears to the street. Varanasi: it was an epic, intense backdrop, though she was not sure anywhere would have suited humiliation of this sort.

'Too needy,' Paul said. 'Too clingy. Too serious. You want me to be everyone.'

She was indignant, already desperate. 'No, I don't. Who? Who do I want you to be?'

'Friend, counsellor, family.' He took a breath then, deciding whether or not to continue. But you had nothing to lose when you'd already decided to rid yourself of everything and so he *did* go on: 'I'm sorry your father died, but I can't be him as well as everything else. I'm sorry you don't speak to your mother, but I can't be her, either. The friends who've let you down or you say don't listen to you, I can't be all of them. Especially not here. I'm not some kind of travelling therapist. I'm not any kind of therapist!'

She listened, aghast. It was true that he had been far more than a partner to her in the four years of their relationship; he'd been a saviour, a crutch. She couldn't have survived her father's death without him; she couldn't have come to terms with estrangement from her mother; she couldn't have filled all the holes.

'But that's what boyfriends are supposed to be,' she said, 'and girlfriends. They give each other whatever is needed.'

'Not all the time,' he said, 'and not to the point where they want to stand in the street and scream.'

He wanted to scream.

Tabby began to tremble. 'I'm no different from how I've always been, Paul.' But straight away she saw she'd hanged herself with that, she'd made his argument for him. The unbearable neediness of her was cumulative.

And there was worse to come, before he walked away, before he left her swinging.

'I've tried to tell you before,' he said, 'but you never get the message.'

That choked her badly, made the single syllable hard to mouth: 'When?'

'Like before we left England, for one.' His hands gestured with frustration. 'That would have been ...'

He did not finish the sentence, but she heard it anyhow: it would have been better, cleaner; he'd wanted to travel alone. Or he had wanted to go *in order* to bring an end to them, it had been the only way he could see to loosen her suffocating hold. The man she loved had been prepared to leave the country to shake her from him and not only had she not recognised this but she had insisted on going with him! She'd had no idea she was sharing a mission to escape herself.

'You *never* said you wanted to break up,' she protested. 'Why didn't you spell it out? I can't read your mind.'

This time his expression answered for him: pity and fear. Pity that she had no one else, fear that when she fell apart he'd be too far away to do anything about it. The pity remained, but the fear had been overcome.

'This trip was what I needed,' she said, with a conviction she could not feel. 'I'm over all of that now. I'm over the past.'

'So am I,' he said.

Later she would understand that he had been the only one speaking the truth in that conversation. But this was not the sort of realisation you made on the spot, in the moment, when despairing eyes and helpless hands distracted you, when inflating lungs and deflating hearts competed with words and won.

As it went, Moira found work for her just two days later. Another of her cleaners, a local girl called Sophy who lived in the southern village of Sainte-Marie, had fallen sick and there were four remaining weekly clients to be covered: could Tabby step in? The thrilling – and unfamiliar – sense that she had found herself in the right place at the right time deepened.

As promised, Moira instructed her at the first appointment. It was straightforward enough work, pretty much what she had done unpaid while living with Paul, what most women did but faster, and she worked ceaselessly to impress her new employer, the muscles in her arms hot and aching by the end of the three-hour shift.

'Very good,' Moira said on inspection, and paid her cash. Folding the notes in her hand caused a surge of tears to her eyes: she felt relief and gratitude and something close to a renewal of faith.

Now trusted to work alone, she set about her tasks with exactly the same vigour as the trial session, mopping tiles and vacuuming rugs and scrubbing toilets as if her life depended on it – because it did. In those first houses in La Flotte and Saint-Martin, empty of occupants during her working hours, she hardly took a break at all, much less thought to indulge her natural preference to lie on the most comfortable bed in the house and fantasise that she was the owner.

She had been in very few private homes in the last seven months and there was much to satisfy her curiosity. The houses were French-owned, either weekend homes or occupied full-time, and she enjoyed seeing the unfamiliar furniture styles and bathroom fittings, even the French cleaning products. Hers was an imagination easily sparked, and the smallest personal clue – a family photograph, a sports trophy, an old Larousse with an inscription on the flyleaf – was enough to set her off, picturing these people in their daily lives, devising lifestyles for them, inventing little histories that couldn't possibly be true but that made the hours sprint by.

By the third house she was already slipping open the bedside drawers and bathroom cabinets, casually auditing the items her clients kept private, the books and trinkets and contraceptives, in one case a padlocked teenager's journal. She was scanning the tops of wardrobes and poking into the backs of deep shelves with the thoroughness of a participant in a treasure hunt, but there was nothing to find of course, at least nothing exotic, only an out-of-date soup mix or a pair of scratched swimming goggles. The faint suspicion that her interest might be in some way perverse was easily eclipsed by the conviction that she was dedicating herself to the service of cleanliness and order.

The fourth place was a holiday unit that was let all year round and bereft of all personal clues – a sniffer dog would be in and out in two minutes – and this, she knew, was typical of what she could expect of all her jobs when the summer season began. A locked cabinet held what must be the only private items, otherwise it was a case of removable sofa covers, stacks of IKEA basics in the kitchen dresser, cupboards absent of any surprises. She'd been advised by Moira to throw away opened kitchen products in the holiday lets, and Emmie had said it was permitted for the cleaners to take them instead for themselves if they wanted, but the shelves in this one were empty, waiting to be filled by the next set of arrivals. Only in the last ten minutes did she find an abandoned item, a three-pack of apple juices – the branding was Sainsbury's, she supposed a British family must have stayed here last – but since the pack was intact she followed the rules and replaced it on the scrubbed cupboard shelf.

Five minutes later, preparing to leave, she found herself in a peculiarly nervous state of mind: it seemed that the unre-markable discovery had disturbed an emotion, a memory of her father she had kept tightly folded these last years, as she had so many concerning him from the period following his divorce from her mother. A triple pack of apple juices, little green boxes with straws, the kind you gave to kids in their packed lunch: something *this* innocuous was reviving a vignette that encapsulated much of her feelings during her teenage years, feelings of isolation and failure, intense ones. Locking up and beginning the walk back to Saint-Martin, she pictured her-self as a sixteen-year-old, the day she'd arrived at her father's house having argued with her mother about her stepfather Steve.

'Tabitha. We weren't expecting to see you today.' Her father's wife Susie had answered the door, her welcome just a grade warmer than if it had been the gas man come to read the meter in the middle of dinner. She wavered visibly between asking Tabby to come back at a more convenient time and just letting her in and telling her to make it snappy. Her eyes dipped to the bulging canvas bag her stepdaughter carried, but she made no comment.

'Come on in. Mike's in the garden with the girls.' She never said 'your father', always 'Mike'. It wasn't a conscious strategy, Tabby noticed – and in fact it had an inclusive quality, a suggestion that she was one of the adults now – but it was consistent, she never slipped.

In fact her father was just coming indoors himself. He must have been playing some particularly energetic game because he was breathing heavily and looked hot in the face. He was overweight these days, well fed by his new wife. Close behind him, Susie's two girls appeared from the kitchen, tearing the plastic off a pack of juices and needing their stepfather's help to extract the cartons. They called him Dad now, no Mike for them. He took the third one for himself and was just putting the straw to his lips when he noticed her.

'Hello, love! When did you get here?'

'Just this second.' She wanted to hug her father, but did not. Shows of affection felt awkward now and were easier avoided. 'Hi, girls, have you had a nice game? What were you playing?'

'Football,' her father replied on behalf of the two small girls, who were sucking their drinks in that dramatic way small kids did, as if on the brink of acute dehydration.

'Would you like one of these?' he asked her.

'I think we've run out,' Susie said.

'That's OK,' Tabby said. 'I'm not thirsty. Maybe later.' She could see Susie did not relish that 'later'. It wasn't that she didn't like Tabby or begrudged her basic refreshment, no one thought that; it was just that she planned her family's weekend with some precision and did not welcome spontaneity.

67

'Everything all right?' her father asked her.

'Yes – I mean, no, not really.' Tabby faltered, flooded by a sudden sensation of disorientation. The sight of her father as a resident in a house where she was merely a guest, even the way the light bounced off him here: it was like meeting his doppel-ganger or travelling to the future and seeing how he would become after she no longer needed him. And yet she did need him still, that was why she was here. Perhaps the problem was that she had spent so little time in this house there was nothing familiar about it or its contents; when picturing this scene *en route*, she'd misremembered the colour of the sofa, the size of the garden, even the height of his second wife, whose house this had been during her first marriage. Would it be different if Tabby's mother had moved out of the family home and Susie and the girls in? Or would that only have made it heartbreaking in a different way?

'I wondered if I could stay with you for a little while,' she said, careful to include Susie in her appeal.

'Stay?' Susie repeated. 'You mean sleep here?'

Knowing that the lack of a spare room had been cited fre-quently as a reason for her not to stay the night, Tabby added pre-emptively, 'I don't mind sleeping on the sofa. Or in a tent in the garden if you like.'

'A *tent*? Don't be soft, of course you can stay,' her father said, just as she'd hoped. (His agreeability had been part of what had allowed Susie to install him as her own with such ease.)

'Can I have a word, Mike?' Susie said, inevitably. She dis-patched the two girls to the TV at the far end of the room, presumably to keep them out of range should the discussion get heated. But Susie did not allow heat, Tabby should have remembered that. She was what Tabby's mother called passive-aggressive. The conference took place in pained murmurs in the kitchen and before too long Susie could be heard stalking up the stairs, then moving items about in one of the bedrooms. Layla, the elder daughter, followed her up, asking what was happening, as her father returned to deliver the verdict.

'It's no problem,' he told Tabby, though his flush suggested otherwise. 'The girls can bunk up together. You can have Layla's room.'

On cue, Layla could be heard protesting at the top of the stairs. 'It's only for a night or two,' Susie was saying. 'Like when your gran comes to stay.'

'Why can't she have Jessica's room? Why does it have to be *mine*?'

'Are you sure?' Tabby said to her father. Desperate though she was, she half regretted this invasion.

'Of course. It's not for long, is it? So what's happened this time then?'

She'd planned to tell her father the real reason for her decampment, had rehearsed the words, the true ones, imagining herself saying them in one breathless go, perhaps not quite meeting her father's eye as she did: 'Steve's been pestering me. He says he's got a picture of me in my underwear and he's put it on some internet site for other men to rate. He said he's had messages saying how they understand his torment with jailbait like me in the house. I can't tell Mum, he said he'd deny it and say *I* was coming on to *him*, and he's right, I know she'd take his side . . .'

It was this last fear that distressed her most, more than the claim itself, which may or may not have been true. How could he have taken a picture of her in her underwear? She could not see any opportunity, though the suggestion itself was horrible enough. No, the suspicion that her mother *would* accept his word over hers: that was the frightening part. She had ended her marriage for Steve; mightn't she be willing to risk her relationship with her daughter, too?

All of this Tabby had planned to tell her father, to ask him what he thought she should do next and hear him say that whatever it was he'd do it with her or for her, that she would never have to suffer this kind of harassment again, but being here, in a house with two small children within earshot, she felt that she would contaminate the air they breathed, make herself even more undesirable to Susie than she already was.

'We fell out,' she said at last.

'What about?'

'Nothing in particular.'

And that was that. She had not told her mother and now here she was not telling her father either. Perhaps she'd known all along she wouldn't. Perhaps she wanted to test him, to see if he would take her in for no other reason than that she asked him to.

Which he had. It would have to be enough that he nodded in protective concern, even though he probably thought the episode was something and nothing and that it was his place to err on the side of something until such a time as Tabby declared its nothingness and returned home. Until she was eighteen, home was always going to be where her mother was. Everyone knew that offspring remained with their mother after a divorce, even those old enough to have a considered preference and whose considered preference was for their father. Instead, 'Mike' went on living in a stranger's house, with another man's children, and just as he got Layla and Jessica to care for, Steve, who had no children of his own, got Tabby.

She stayed a week or so before returning, following pressure from both sides. Her only strategy was hope, hope that Steve would never again speak to her as he had done, hope that he'd not speak to her at all when they were alone but just go back to contenting himself with staring at her legs or her breasts or her lips, never raising his eyes to hers, just going on staring until she got up and left the room.

She fixed a bolt to her bedroom door. Only later did she find she'd barred the wrong door.

*

'What's your surname?' she asked Emmie one evening towards the end of their first week together. She'd glanced idly at the mail that had come through their letterbox the last few mornings, but there was nothing for Emmie, all envelopes addressed to a M. and Mme Robert, presumably the owners of the property.

Emmie looked up from her book, a defensive cast to her face.

'I just remember you saying Moira didn't know it,' Tabby said. 'And I realised when I was talking to her that I didn't know either.'

Since the first evening, when she'd shared her life story in a hysteria of soul-bearing so unchecked she could now scarcely remember what she had revealed and what she had kept to herself, she had not had a conversation with Emmie of anything approaching the same intimacy. Lack of opportunity was a factor, of course. Not only had both of them been busy working, but Tabby had continued with her walks too, completing circuits of the town ramparts and of the cycle paths to neighbouring villages. It surprised her how quickly she'd come to feel as if she'd been walking these routes for months, down the coastal paths where oyster shells crunched underfoot, inland through open country, past neat rows of vines and walled estates. Perhaps it was because her thoughts remained the same: thoughts of Paul that had to be suppressed, thoughts that she still needed him in exactly the ways that had driven him from her. What was becoming depressingly evident was that her love for him was enduring, and apparently in no way connected to whether *he* loved *her*; it was like an addiction or an eating disorder: she would never again live without it, but could only manage its dormancy. She was as defined by his absence as she'd been by his presence. And there were moments when it hardly seemed to matter which.

Returning from those expeditions to their shuttered house in its hidden lane, not wide enough for two to walk abreast, she'd trained herself into the habit of early nights, which prevented her both from spending money and from intruding on Emmie's private time. Whenever in the same room with Emmie, she was careful to match the other woman's mood, which, rather to her surprise, was more often than not silent and preoccupied. Twice, Emmie had spent the whole evening in her bedroom at her laptop.

But Tabby was naturally gregarious, some might say garrulous, and her self-imposed discretion could not last for ever. There was that inquisitive streak, too, the one that had already led her to investigate the more private corners of Moira's clients' properties, and she awaited Emmie's answer now with real interest.

'It's Mason,' Emmie replied at last, with an exaggerated sense of surrender.

'Emmie Mason,' Tabby repeated, to get a feel for the name. 'It sounds like an old movie star or something.'

'Well, that's what it is,' Emmie said.

'Of course.'

This added one more item to the modest list of facts she knew about Emmie. Emmie had been in Saint-Martin for five weeks or so, staying at first in a guesthouse in the newer quarter of the village before finding this place inside the old walls thanks to an advertisement on the noticeboard in one of the supermarkets. The rent was low because the place was in urgent need of upgrading; nothing in the house worked properly, Emmie said (this, Tabby had found for herself, was true, or at least in so far as nothing electrical in the house worked at the same time as anything else). Though she appeared to have settled here for the foreseeable future, she had no plans to open a French bank account and had utility bills included in her rent, dealing only in cash and living 'on the black', as the French called it, an arrangement Tabby was keen to emulate. Her French was excellent, certainly strong enough for her to have found shop work, but she was happy enough to clean. Tabby had not asked her her age, but judged it to be early thirties. Nor had she yet voiced her theory that Emmie was suffering from – and had been driven into solitude by – the same critical illness as her own: heartbreak.

'Why do you want to know, anyway?' Emmie said, eyes restless.

Why do you want to know why I want to know? Tabby thought to herself, for it had hardly been an invasive question. What's your *name*? It wasn't like asking someone her blood group or preferred hair-removal method or tally of sexual partners. 'No reason, I'm just interested. You know my name is Dewhurst, right?'

'Right,' said Emmie, as if humouring in Tabby an unnecessary and embarrassing compulsion to confess her fetishes. The contrast between this and that initial display of interest and compassion was marked, and in different circumstances might have hurt Tabby's feelings.

Instead she gave Emmie a look of warm amusement. Whatever her own inclinations, she had no intention of finding fault with her new landlady. She opted for a joke: 'You're like someone on a witness-protection programme, Emmie. You know, make no eye contact, leave no paper trail. Are the mob after you or something?'

Emmie smiled, relenting a little. 'I'd hardly have invited you to move in if I was completely anti-social.'

'Maybe you thought you needed a bodyguard?' Tabby said mischievously. 'To protect you from whoever it is that's after you?'

Emmie took this in better humour than Tabby might have expected, given the unpromising start to the exchange. 'Yes, next time I find a stranger asleep in the spare room I'll be sure to call for your support.'

They both laughed then, and Tabby revived the hope that the

two of them were on their way to becoming great friends, discovering that crucial shared sense of fun in one another. What did it matter that Emmie was naturally rather more private? As she'd pointed out, she'd shared her home, hadn't she? You didn't get much more open-hearted than that. This reluctance to divulge personal information came from living alone for weeks on end, possibly months. Unlikely though their teaming-up was, it would do Emmie good to have Tabby's company. She'd soon have her sharing war stories as single women usually did.

'That's exactly what *I* thought,' Emmie said just then, though Tabby had made none of these comments out loud.

'Thought what?'

But Emmie just returned her questioning look with one of her own, making Tabby wonder if she had spoken up after all and been too absent-minded to notice. Either that or Emmie was one of those people whose thoughts flowed so loud and clear in her own ears that she mistook them for having been part of general conversation.

Again, the sort of thing you might do if you'd lived on your own for too long.

And so Tabby did the decent thing and pretended not to notice. 'Shall we open the shutters?' she suggested. 'It's not dark yet.' It was brighter longer here than in Paris and, even with the high wall beyond their windows, there was a well of natural light that she longed to expose.

'I like them shut,' Emmie said.

Chapter 6

Emily

I won't spend time on my family background. I can't work on this story indefinitely, but will soon need to find work and earn money again, and in any case, there isn't any need for a full autobiography. I want this to be about Arthur and me, that's all, and in all honesty I don't believe my childhood is relevant. It goes without saying that I don't agree with the media's speculation about what kind of tragic, motherless upbringing made a man-eating sociopath of me – any more than I agree that I'm a man-eating sociopath in the first place. Nor am I interested in claiming some psychological condition that made me a victim-in-waiting. I fell in love: that was what happened. It was of itself, a one of a kind.

I suppose it *is* fair to say that as the year opened I was beset by strange new emotions. Knowing that I might lose my father during the months ahead was giving me previously unknown urges to seize the day, to make life count while I was young and healthy enough to appreciate the difference. Of course, I see now that I had my head up at exactly the time when I should have been keeping it down.

But I don't regret it. Even now, I don't regret it.

*

As Nina Meeks would tell it, I brazenly seduced Arthur. I was less a neighbour than a Venus flytrap positioned on the other side of his garden fence, carnivorous and hungry, every hair on the surface of me alert to his approach. But it wasn't like that at all. The night it happened, he couldn't have been further from my mind.

I'd been to visit Dad after work. Visits were never more surreal than on a Saturday evening, when that contrast between the outside world, which throbbed with the heartless energy of young lives being led, and the inside one, a muted, ageing, heartbroken realm, was at its most pronounced. Saturday night was also when I was at my most tired, too tired sometimes to raise the bonhomie required to make the visit enjoyable for Dad.

The hospital was just outside London, in Hertfordshire, well over an hour by tube and train from my neighbourhood south of the river, and the dementia unit was a sobering place to visit at the best of times, as I suppose would be any medical facility where security was strictly monitored. With some patients liable to wander out of bounds, it was necessary to ring and wait for a member of staff to admit you through several sets of locked doors. Sometimes, if they were short-staffed, you waited ten minutes simply to gain entry.

Something had happened on this visit that had unsettled me, though I tried not to let it. Making my way to Dad's ward, I smiled at an approaching nurse and her elderly charge in a wheelchair, who I recognised as Ronnie, a one-time neighbour of Dad's at the nursing home. Though his dementia was not so advanced, his physical health was fading fast and he had the frail skin-and-bones frame I was accustomed to seeing here.

'Hello, Ronnie,' I said, though I knew not to expect him to recognise me. Even so, I was not prepared for what he did do as we came close to passing: reached up towards me with startling abruptness and ran outstretched fingers over my breasts, finishing with a quite painful squeeze. As I cried out, the carer gently removed his hands.

'*Sorry* about that,' she said, in a jolly tone that would curdle any crisis. 'They lose their inhibitions. Impulses we know not to act on, they act on them.'

I'd been told about this – 'disinhibition', they called it – many times and in all sorts of contexts, often to do with personal habits we all indulged in alone but which patients gave rein to publicly. Damage to the frontal lobe meant Ronnie, my father and every other patient here, to a greater or lesser extent, were no longer the socialised, civilised creatures they had once been. All the work Ronnie's parents and teachers must have put in when he was a child, the tens of thousands of reproaches and corrections, had now unravelled and returned him to square one.

'It's absolutely fine,' I said. 'Please don't worry about it.' And I smiled at Ronnie as if I were not thinking what anyone in my position would think: does the person *I'm* visiting do things like that, too?

At the nurses' station I was told that there was a surprise for me. For the first time in two weeks Dad was out of bed and seated in the lounge. He'd been tucked under a blanket, like an injured fox cub someone had found in the woods and put in a warm corner to build up his strength. Even though he'd been bedridden with infections for some time now, I still felt the same slicing wound of disbelief every time I saw him. It was the physical depletion as much as the mental deterioration: once, he'd been muscular and forceful and undefeated, had raised two children on his own. Now, he was feeble and could not raise himself. I stooped to kiss him on the cheek before settling next to him and giving my name as I always did. He seemed to know who I was or at least not to think I was a stranger.

'You don't need the IV any more?' I made a point of asking

him and not the nurse, for I'd developed an aversion to conversations across patients' heads in which the subject was presumed deaf or unconscious.

'He's been eating a lot better, haven't you, Vince?' she said, because someone had to answer.

'That's brilliant,' I said. 'Well done!'

Dad looked momentarily pleased, but soon anxiety seized his face. 'I was looking for Lesley,' he said. 'I couldn't find her. I looked everywhere.' Lesley was my mother. I knew, of course, that I should not tell him she was dead, it would be a bombshell as devastating as the twenty-year-old original and he was in no condition to handle the grief of new widowerhood. The same went for his own parents, both long passed away but often sought by his dislocated mind.

'Do you remember when we had that day out in London and sat on the steps in Trafalgar Square?' I said, plucking an occasion from infanthood. Occasionally he connected with those, though most of his reliable memory was of his own childhood. 'And the pigeons kept landing on Phil's sandwich and he freaked out, and Mum laughed and laughed. He couldn't stop screaming and she couldn't stop laughing.'

'Phil never liked birds.' Dad was chuckling too, and, mercifully, allowed the subject to turn to the dinner he'd just half eaten, the flavours of yoghurt drink he most liked and disliked. 'I'm glad you're here as well,' he said. 'I don't like visiting on my own.'

'I know what you mean,' I agreed, and I held his hands in mine to reassure him that we were both visitors, that the visit was finished and we were just taking a little break before going home. I did this every time now, even though I was not supposed to tell him outright lies; I had done it ever since the time I'd insisted he understand that he was the patient and I the visitor and he had become very distressed.

Occasionally I added little false details to cheer him up, such

78

as that I would drive him home in my new top-of-the-range convertible and show him my house, a beautiful old place on the famous Walnut Grove. Perhaps the embellishments were as much for myself as for him.

Sometimes he demanded to know who it was we'd been visiting and I would make up a name on the spot, but today he did not.

No, I was not thinking of Arthur when I came home. I was thinking, in fact, of Matt; I was thinking that I would phone him and find out which drinking hole he and his friends had climbed into, join them in it. Somewhere along the line I'd stopped thinking of them as 'our' friends and recognised them as his, recognised too their common aim: to prolong their twenties into their thirties and devote themselves to the dance of dodging next steps (while denying that such a dance existed). Those who succumbed to marriage or parenthood were either mocked or marginalised by the group, while those who remained knew to keep any nobler ambitions to themselves. It was absurd.

But tonight I didn't care about any of that. Tonight I needed to be among the old crowd, to sit in a group of consciously self-centred adults and be absorbed into the Saturday-night smoulder of the living world, to remind myself that the hospital unit was a capsule I could enter and leave at will. If I could have, I would have bent time back to the start of Matt and me, to when the wandering hands on my body were his and not those of a dementia sufferer.

As I'd expected, the flat was empty and had been left by him in the usual disarray. Less explicable were the signs in the bedroom of hasty packing; on closer inspection I found that his backpack was gone. There was nothing sinister about this, for we had long since reached the point where we no longer included each other in weekend plans – I worked every Saturday

79

and went to the hospital either the same evening or the following afternoon, while Matt had every weekend free – but it was a first to find him gone and to have no idea where.

I dialled his mobile. 'Are you away for the night or something?'

'I'm in Scotland.' Raucous sound effects placed him in the very bar of my dreams.

'Scotland? What for?'

'Biking with the sales team. I told you the other day, Em.'

I vaguely recalled talk of mountain bikes and trail grades, but I was fairly sure I hadn't been apprised of any forthcoming dates. 'Oh, OK. I must have forgotten. When are you back? Tomorrow?'

'Not till Monday.'

Something – a thwarting of that need for physical contact, a final acknowledgement that the clock could not be turned back and this man would always be in a different country from me, even when in the next room – made me say what I should have said months ago. 'Can we talk when you get home? About us.'

'What about us?' His tone became slippery, that of a man being unjustly hounded by an ex-girlfriend. Which I was, I understood; ex in all but name.

'Everything.' But I spoke gently. I did not want to insult him. 'I don't want to go on like this and I don't think you do, either.'

I heard him sigh. There would be no struggle, no wires crossed or cut. 'Fine. Monday night. But I've got to go now.'

The conversation did nothing to quell my urgent need for a drink. There was no alcohol in the flat and so I left at once for the off-licence on the high street, already rehearsing in my head the conversation Matt and I would have on Monday evening: candid and personal or cautious and indirect? In their own ways, each would bring sorrow, if only for old times' sake.

Walking past the pub on the corner of the Grove and the high street, I saw Arthur Woodhall sitting with two or three others at a table in the window, his face square to the glass, and I waved to him, slackening my pace a little in the expectation of a return gesture. When it didn't come, I hurried on, telling myself that the glare on his side of the window meant he'd not caught my face, only general movement.

But in the wine shop I became aware of someone arriving in the doorway soon after me and I knew before looking that it was him: he had seen me, followed me.

'Oh,' I said. I felt an immediate orchestra of effects inside my body and knew I had no hope of silencing them. 'Didn't I just see you in the pub?'

He looked briefly about him in mild surprise, as if not quite clear where it was he had found himself. 'I told them I left my wallet at home.'

This was not an answer to the question I'd actually asked, but since I was peering at him as if at an apparition, I thought it possible he was doing something similar aurally. 'But you didn't,' I said, simply.

He scratched at the centre of his forehead and left a pink mark. Our eyes locked, bringing a stutter to my pulse at the sight of his expression: fascination, vague fear, as if I were an exotic creature he'd accidentally cornered. 'I'm with some neighbours,' he said. 'I wondered, would you like to join us?'

I hesitated. 'That's very kind of you, but wouldn't they find it odd if you came back with me instead of your wallet?' I'd noted his use of the singular – '*I'm* with some neighbours' – and needed to hear the crucial clarification. 'Anyway, what would your wife say if you suddenly reappeared with another woman? She might not like it.'

'Sylvie's in Sussex this weekend with the boys.'

'Sussex?'

'We've got a place there.'

Of course they did. The Woodhalls' life would be one of second homes and pieds-à-terre, Michelin-starred suppers and weekends in deluxe hotels. And yet here he was in a grungy off-licence, apparently transfixed by . . . me.

'I'm on my own as well. Matt's gone on a biking trip to Scotland.'

'Right.'

As he stepped aside to let a chain of new customers enter, my mind turned over a dozen possible outcomes to the question I burned to ask. The worst of these was that I'd be rejected outright and later be confronted by Sylvie or one of her friends (I refused to allow the face of Nina Meeks to come into focus), laughed at or snubbed in the street, whispered about. But this was London, even streets with residents' associations like the Grove afforded a certain measure of anonymity to those who stepped out of line. People were too busy with their families and careers to conduct witch-hunts. No, the worst that could happen was still worlds away from what I'd seen earlier in the evening.

Goodness knew how long it took me to think all of this but Arthur just waited in silence while I did, an actor whose colleague is having difficulty with her lines but who has no helpful improvisation of his own to hand.

'After the pub, come and have a drink at my place if you like,' I said at last, and in not making a question of it, it seemed to have less criminal intent.

He did not speak. Nothing of him moved, not even his eyes, but I knew the answer was yes.

'Do you remember where I live?'

'One-nine-nine, Flat B.'

'That's right.'

It was a tense, skeletal exchange of desires. When he turned and left it seemed to me that the meeting might not in fact have taken place, but was a desperate fantasy brought on by the events of the day, the hospital visit and the flight of Matt; the fiction of a woman too tired to conjure dialogue any sharper. I half expected the man behind the till to ask me what I thought I was doing talking to myself.

Nonetheless I chose a much nicer wine than I normally would, bought two bottles instead of one, and hurried back to the flat, my earlier exhaustion evaporated. Tidying up would have to wait while I addressed my personal hygiene. I showered and scrubbed off the smells of hospital and tube and rubbed rose oil into my skin, dressed in jeans and a silk blouse, heels in place of the trainers I'd been wearing. I dried my damp hair and twisted it from my face, put on lipstick and eyeliner. I was neither the exaggerated confection I'd been at the Laings' party nor the colourless drone I must have appeared just now in the off-licence. Then I cleared up the one decent space in the flat, the living room with the tall Georgian window, and lit orange-blossom candles to sweeten the air.

It was ten o'clock by then. I didn't know what time the pub closed or how much longer he'd want to spend there. As I waited, the suspicion returned that I'd misconstrued our encounter, suspending me breathlessly between fear and hunger. Half of me prayed it *was* a delusion, that I *had* invented it; the other half wanted to commit suicide if it did not turn out to be true, if he did not come. My head swam with the recognition that somehow, with neither warning nor logical justification, Arthur Woodhall had become the person I most needed to see in the world. No one else would do.

He arrived at close to eleven. As he came through the door he exhibited none of the commotion I was experiencing; only when I caught sight of myself in the mirror by the door did I realise mine was not outwardly evident either. I *looked* utterly com-posed. I was clean and shiny-eyed and wholesome, like someone who'd just showered after a run. I didn't look anything like an adulterer beautified for seduction.

'Hello again.' I stepped aside to let him in, not sure how to proceed. I'd imagined him kissing me at once, a bold, greedy kiss in place of spoken greeting, but that now seemed both an absurd assumption and an adolescent cliché. In the living room I gestured to the sofa – our only seating – and went to the kitchen to fetch the wine. Returning, I sat next to him, turning primly inwards as if I were the guest and he – easy and expectant, left arm hugging the back of the sofa, right foot resting against the coffee table – the host.

'Sorry about the flat,' I said. 'It must be the only dive left on the whole street.'

'I like it. It reminds me of one of the places I lived years ago when I was training.' Hearing himself, Arthur apologised. 'Maybe I should rephrase that.'

'Oh, don't worry, I completely agree. It *is* like student digs. Not that I ever went to university, but even if I had it would be long enough ago by now that I should have worked my way up to something more salubrious.'

'"By now"? How old are you, Emily?'

'Thirty. How old are you?'

'Forty-eight.'

Eighteen years. It was about what I had guessed.

'An old man to you, huh?' Arthur smiled.

'No.' I thought briefly of Ronnie in the unit, of the heedless infant his condition had made of him; I thought of my father, shrunken and ancient.

'Have you had a rough day?' he said, narrowing those flecked eyes a fraction, and I thought he must be some sort of mind reader. But then I realised he was commenting on the speed with which I was draining my wine.

'Yes, as it happens. Terrible. But I feel much better now.' Now you're here. I put down my glass and turned to face him properly, waiting, hoping. All at once I was terrified. The prospect of rejection was a thousand times more powerful here than it had been in the wine shop. Now it felt as if it would be the end of my world if this went wrong, that I'd have to leave the area, and in a hurry, overnight. Matt would have to report me as a missing person. So stricken was I by this thought that when Arthur began to move towards me I remained perfectly motionless, which caused him to hesitate, and we hovered uncertainly in the space in front of one another.

'Have I misunderstood this?' he asked, anxious not to offend me but evidently not at all self-conscious.

'No, no, you haven't. Of course you haven't.' But still I couldn't move, mesmerised by the closeness of him, this man who was both a stranger and someone I seemed already to know as well as I did myself.

'Good. I didn't think so.' His face came closer and warm skin touched mine, mouth first, hands soon after. His kisses were hard and precise, almost formal, his fingers gentle and vague, entirely *in*formal, and the two in conjunction sent me leaping over any last barrier of inhibition. Soon we were having sex on the sofa, clutching and straining and groaning, and it was the most alive I had ever been, my responses outside the limits of normal sensations; as I said, it was like being activated, set in motion for the first time. Afterwards, I was almost limp-limbed with the new knowledge of it, the giddying sense that everything had been made better, all the faults of my life corrected, the future blessed.

Which I *know* sounds ridiculous, an overreaction by anyone's standards.

'I feel like I'm under the influence of some mind-bending drug,' I told him as we lay flattened against one another. I adored the stinging heat of his skin, the sharpness of his collarbone against my cheek, the beat of his pulse. 'Did you spike my wine with something from the hospital pharmacy?'

'I'm not sure I needed to,' he said. 'And endorphins *are* very similar to opiates.' He stroked my damp hair for a time, growing more serious. 'Just for the record, I don't want you to feel bad about this: *I* pursued *you*.'

'You did follow me down the street and into an off-licence,' I agreed.

'And I came to your work.'

'For the plate? I thought your wife sent you?'

'I offered to go. I came another time as well, after the plate business, but you were on your lunch break.'

'Oh? I didn't get any message.' I thought of Charlotte – or perhaps it had been Aislene – with rose-tinted fondness, knowing she couldn't have been aware of the magnitude of her oversight.

'I didn't leave one,' Arthur said. 'I hoped I might see you in the street some time – which I did.'

'You were happy just to leave it to chance like this?' The thought that it might so easily not have happened was appalling to me.

'It just seemed inconceivable that it wouldn't,' Arthur said.

I absorbed all of this. He had a very easy way of switching his tone between wry and serious that made it hard to judge which to respond to. 'Well,' I said, 'I wouldn't exactly call that hot pursuit. Are you disappointed you didn't have to work harder to get me?'

He smiled, the near corner of his mouth curving with feminine prettiness. 'I'm not remotely disappointed. Quite the opposite.'

I pressed myself closer still, arms around his neck, fingers in his hair. As our body heat faded a little, I shivered, pulled a throw over us. The scratchiness of its fibres seemed to advertise the cheapness of me. 'Do you have to go home? Will your wife phone from Sussex?'

'No, we spoke earlier. She won't call again, she knows I'm out tonight.' He paused. 'Besides, she's working very hard at not giving in to her suspicions.'

'Suspicions about me?' I was alarmed enough by this to disentangle myself from him and sit upright.

'No, not you. Any woman. All women. I haven't exactly been a saint over the years.'

There was not a trace of arrogance in this admission, more a general air of melancholy regret. (I would learn that Arthur was not one of those people who claimed to regret nothing. That was a philosophy he and I shared, and one that went against prevailing fashion: you were allowed to have regrets about your life, it was conceited *not* to have them.) His remark made sense of those snippets I'd overheard between Sylvie and Nina in the café – 'It's almost two years now, isn't it? That's pretty good for him' – and could hardly have come as a surprise in any case, for however special I felt that evening I had presumably been attracted by the same sexual charisma other women had, including Sylvie herself. Weren't we all responding to the fabled godliness of surgeons? Offering ourselves on a plate one after the other – a perk of the job, perhaps, as it must be for any other high-ranking male, from captain of industry to household-name actor.

'In that case, maybe she shouldn't be working on not giving in to her suspicions,' I said. 'Maybe she should be acting on them?'

Amused by this – 'Whose side are you on, Emily Marr?' – he pulled me back to him and began moving his hands over my skin again. I could feel a sense of wonderment in his fingers that matched my own response exactly. It was as if possession of each other demanded proof in the form of constant physical contact, neither of us a shade less intense, less avid, than the other.

'Your side,' I told him. 'I'm on your side. But you know that already, don't you?'

He kissed me over and over, and then drew back again, regarding me with unambiguous delight, as if I'd been lost and recovered, a little miracle. No one had looked at me like that since ... since childhood. 'You are very beautiful, Emily, even more than I thought. You could have been a model.'

I pulled a face. 'No chance. I'm too short, anyway.'

'Really? I think of you as tall.'

I reached a hand for one of my shoes, discarded on the floor by the sofa. 'Heels. Very high heels.'

He took it from me and examined it. 'I like the very high heels.'

I held up my bra next. 'Also, too curvy. I'm fat by fashion standards.'

'I like the fat-by-fashion-standards as well.' He groaned. 'I like everything about you, as you can probably tell. I can't stop touching you, Emily . . .'

We made love again – there was more of that wild euphoria I'd never felt before – and we drank and dozed and murmured ourselves awake, resuming our besotted talk. I wish I could remember every line, because it was the most entrancing conversation of my life, but most has faded now. This, I won't forget: 'You have something special about you, Emily. Something I've never seen before.' And he was intent on defining it there and then. 'You're too innocent for your age, *that*'s what it is.' Even now I don't know if he meant my age in years or the time we lived in.

My head was filled with his compliments that night, with his star-maker's favour, his connoisseur's desire. But the next morning – he had left as I slept, when it was still dark – I warned myself not to expect anything more. It had been exactly the night of joyful spontaneity I had craved, a deficiency replenished, a self-contained piece of madness that I should treat as a catalyst for pulling my life into better shape. When Matt came home the following day I would tell him that when the first six months were up on our lease and the break clause active we would be parting ways. I would draw up a financial plan for myself and follow it, even if it meant starvation. I would begin looking for a retail management position, something better-paid than my current job that would allow me to keep the flat on my own or else rent a smaller place.

No, Arthur Woodhall was an important man who had decided he wanted me for the night, and by his own admission, he'd had many such adventures. And he was, after all, married. That could be ignored, if not excused, for one night, but certainly not indefinitely. I was not that sort of girl. It was going to have to be enough to be the woman he pursued down the street one Saturday night in winter, the girl he thought too innocent for her age.

Of course, I didn't know then that Arthur would not be willing to rationalise or subdue his instincts as I was mine; that he was not thinking in terms of self-contained pleasure or short-term conquests. I did not know that he would return that evening and we would continue headlong, never once closing an encounter without the promise of a next.

I did not know then that I was different from the others, different from his wife too, and it was a difference that would come to define me.

Chapter 7

Tabby

Having enjoyed the easy pace of the village in low season, Tabby was dismayed, if not surprised, when the place transformed itself in June into a seaside destination on which the whole world apparently demanded a foothold. Vehicles queued for the car park that had until then been a wasteland at the edge of the village, tour groups clogged the ramparts, cyclists passed in wobbling shoals, and tourists stood ten-deep at the ice-cream shop on the quayside. Suddenly there were oyster cabanas and waffle stands, donkey rides and vintage carousels. All the shops pulled racks of their wares into the streets, so that when you stood at the top of rue de Sully or rue Jean Jaurès you looked down on an open-air market of island apparel: silver sandals and turquoise sarongs, waxed jackets and sailor tops, scarves and pashminas, long pieces of soft cotton knotted in the middle, the two ends billowing in the breeze.

Tabby had not bought a new item of clothing for months and could not imagine being in a position to spend eighty euros on a beach kaftan or forty on a sunhat. Such sums were beyond the reach of someone starting again from scratch. The weekly budget structure she had devised for herself was simple: before all else, she had to earn fifty euros to give Emmie towards the rent, and then enough for food and bus travel; any surplus was saved towards her goal of the several hundred euros needed to travel back to England – preferably London – where she'd be able to find better-paid employment and tackle her overdraft. It was unthinkable to splurge thirty euros on one of the pale-hued North African *foutas* that were on sale everywhere. Still, she had to admit it was lovely, when passing, to touch the fabrics, to let the softness of washed linen fall over her hand and wrist.

Emmie appeared oblivious to the sudden influx of tourists, her sphere of influence contained in that tucked-away house, forays for work or food rarely yielding more than the most general observations. 'I hope there won't be too many English people,' was all she said when Tabby reported her latest eavesdropping from the breakfast queue at the *boulangerie* (one euro a day for the still-warm baguette that she and Emmie took it in turns to buy).

'I hear quite a few now,' Tabby told her. 'It must be the half-term holidays, maybe?'

'I thought it was mainly French who came here,' Emmie said, frowning.

At first Tabby had hoped there might be potential among the holidaying Brits for the kind of temporary friendships she'd enjoyed on her travels, but she quickly saw that these were not the type to be interested in her: affluent families with an air of self-satisfaction, parents calling out to one another as they rode their bikes across the cobbles, telling each other how *glorious* the place was as they took a terrace table by the water and ordered their children feasts of *moules et frites*. Sometimes whole families would dress in the striped mariner tops available in every shop in every size, and in the vintage tennis shoes that came in sun-bleached greys and pinks.

'I've come across the type,' Emmie said when Tabby described them. 'I used to think that's what I wanted for myself.'

Surprised by this exceptional offering of personal information, Tabby was slow to draw her questions. 'What, you mean a husband and family? Money? Nice holidays?'

'I don't know what it was, really. Just ... belonging.' She spoke in the wondering tone Tabby knew preceded a withdrawal into her own thoughts, and Tabby used the silence to enjoy a brief reverie of Paul, of the two of them riding about the island together and calling out to each other in that enviably self-confident way, debating where to stop for a plate of oysters (not a food she had ever tried, admittedly). She was confident that Emmie was doing the same, the only difference between their fantasies the face of their respective former lovers.

'Maybe you belong *here*,' she told Emmie kindly.

'Maybe,' Emmie said.

The season for weekly lets now began in earnest and the two women had their first experience of changeover day. Though generally a Saturday, this was also scheduled in certain properties for Sundays or Fridays, which meant more work for both of them, more cash for Tabby's savings fund. From now on she would associate weekends with the clatter of luggage on cobbles, a sound effect that began early in the morning and continued till late.

The work was strenuous and varied little. Moira had issued a schedule for the day to ensure that everything was completed in the correct order. Before all other tasks, beds had to be stripped and linen and towels put in the washer-dryer, which meant the beds could be made with the fresh linen at the end of the session. In between, the rest of the house had to be restored to the spotless, sweet-smelling standards required by the incoming holidaymakers, many of whom had paid thousands of euros for a single week's rental. At first Tabby ran into unpaid overtime to get everything done, on one occasion still mopping the kitchen floor of her Saturday house on the rue du Rempart when the new arrivals' taxi pulled up outside, but her efficiency soon improved enough to allow breaks. These she spent sitting in the garden or courtyard, admiring the ultramarine glow of the sky, absorbing the damp aroma of the sea in the air. Regarding the houses with a different eye, she would imagine how it felt to come to Ré as a holidaymaker, expectant only of pleasure. Did anyone ever consider who had lain on the mattresses the night before, drunk coffee from the mugs, wiped feet on the doormat, thumbed the folder of restaurant recommendations? Sometimes she thought she caught a scent, an energy, left in the house from the departed; it was her job to extinguish it, but she liked it, that heat of other lives lived.

Of course, some clients only needed their house preparing for themselves. They did not offer it to paying strangers, it was a second home, *une maison secondaire*. The mere notion of this staggered Tabby: houses that were fully furnished and stocked, right down to dustpan and brush and aerosols of stain remover, tennis racquets and *pétanque* sets. So many people with a reserve set of equipment for life, when she did not yet have the original one.

She did not permit herself to think about the flat she'd rented with Paul in the years before their trip; that could only lead to the shameful admission that she would swap France, the salty Atlantic air, this second chance she'd been so serendipitously awarded, swap it all in a heartbeat to return to that small flat in Guildford she'd shared with him. Back when he still loved her.

For the larger properties, Moira needed two girls, and it was not long before Tabby was asked to join Emmie on a job. She was pleased by the mid-week bonus: not only was it unexpected extra earnings, but there'd also be some company – cleaning involved a solitary confinement she did not always relish. The disadvantage was that, with only one bike between them, Tabby would have to get the bus, which was busy now with tourists village-hopping or travelling to and from La Rochelle. She had started to wonder if it might be an idea to keep her eye out for an old bike being sold off by one of the hire outlets, and it surprised her that she was thinking in such terms, that she might intend staying on the island long enough for the investment to be worthwhile.

But, examining the address details Moira had texted her, Emmie said, 'This place is much too far to cycle, we'll both have to get the bus. It's right up near Trousse-Chemise.'

'Where's that?'

'Miles away, past Les Portes. I'll check the timetable.'

Tabby was happy to let her take charge.

Walking together to the bus stop, she called out greetings to the shop and restaurant staff she recognised. She enjoyed the exchange of civilities that was customary here. Emmie, however, walked on without saying a word, waiting for Tabby at the corner with her eyes cast to the ground. She'd lived here two months now and yet gave little impression of wanting to be anything but an outsider in the village.

'Do you think you'll get any visitors here this summer?' Tabby asked her as they reached the bus stop.

'Visitors? The place is packed with tourists.'

'No,' said Tabby, suspecting Emmie had deliberately misunderstood. 'I mean will *you* get visitors? Family and friends from England?' Then it occurred to her that if visitors came she could lose her bed and so she shifted the emphasis. 'Where do your parents live back home?'

Emmie looked towards her but not quite at her before replying, 'Nowhere. They're both dead.'

Tabby was taken aback. 'Oh, Emmie, I'm so sorry. I had no idea we have that in common. I mean my father, of course.' She wanted to take Emmie's arm or even give her a hug, but Emmie was not the tactile sort and she thought better of it. 'Is that the trauma you mentioned before, your parents passing away? Did it happen recently?'

'I don't want to talk about it,' Emmie said.

'Of course. I understand.'

They waited in silence. As personal details went this was an important one for Emmie to have omitted to mention; it was also one on which Tabby was qualified to advise, were Emmie ever to decide she wanted to confide in her. Her father had died following a stroke three years earlier and she had cried herself to sleep for months afterwards, struggling for over a year with insomnia and anxiety. Gradually she had learned to detach herself from the sense of loss, to hold at bay the memory of hearing the news from her mother that Tuesday afternoon and being engulfed almost instantly by a darkness she grew so used to that she'd been astonished when it finally lifted, unveiling once more the sensory world she had forgotten was there.

She rarely thought now of the faces at the funeral, the ones that had once haunted her: her stepsisters Layla and Jessica, devastation so raw on their young faces she feared it might permanently disfigure their still-forming features; and Susie's, too, a more mutinous grief, the type that was quick to transform into blame. At first, Tabby had felt relief that she had not seen her father in the days before his death and so could not be held responsible for the stroke in some way, but this was quickly replaced with a terrible regret that she had not been there. Either way, Susie didn't want to share him in death any more than she had wanted to in life. Tabby felt the same. After the funeral she had made no attempt to see Susie or the girls again.

Her mother and Steve had been there, of course. She'd avoided his eye, though it had been difficult, her glance attracted to her former tormentor like a ghoul's at the scene of a road accident. How grateful she'd been to be leaving with Paul, to be no longer under her mother's jurisdiction or Steve's sordid surveillance.

She was jolted by the memory of confiding all of this to Emmie in their very first conversation, of telling her, 'He didn't suffer. It wasn't one of those situations where he hung on in agony for years, not being able to do anything for himself. Everyone said it was better the way it was, quite merciful, really.' She had not heard the word 'merciful' much before in her life and it had never come up since, except, just possibly, that very night, the night Emmie took her in. 'Any one of us could be struck down at any moment. I know it's a cliché, but it's true.'

Of course, now, in light of Emmie's own revelation, Tabby cursed herself for these loose-tongued remarks: *Any one of us could be struck down* – poor Emmie must have been thinking then of her own losses. And what if one or both of Emmie's parents *had* 'hung on in agony'? How could Tabby have been so thoughtless? And yet, how much easier it would be to be sensitive and tactful if Emmie would only open up a little, reduce the potential for upset in every one of Tabby's attempts at conversation.

All of this she considered as the bus arrived and they took their turns to board. Emmie chose a seat across the aisle from her and turned her face to the window, perhaps to spare herself any more of Tabby's blundering small-talk. Tabby closed her eyes and relaxed. It took an age to reach the other end of the island, the warm air and constant stops and starts eventually sending her to sleep, so that Emmie had to poke her awake at their destination. The house was a ten-minute walk from the bus stop, on a remote road towards the beach, and the gates they passed concealed properties far larger than the fishermen's cottages and seaside bungalows she had worked in to date. She realised they had ahead of them a hard afternoon's labour, wished she could simply sneak off in the direction of the beach and snooze the afternoon away in the dunes.

96

Their client's house was a broad, two-storey building, the grounds dotted with cypresses and fruit trees. There was a glamorous stone terrace and a narrow blue pool, a lawn that stretched towards the beach. It was a beautiful place, with sea views on two sides, no neighbours within earshot, a sense of being at the end of the world. The shutters were the same shade of blue as the sky.

Emmie took care of entering the required security codes and, once inside, deactivating the alarm. 'Look at this place, it's already clean!' She pivoted in the spacious hallway, assessing the scale of the job. 'It'll be spotless by the time we finish,' she added with indecent cheer, ending any hopes Tabby may have had that they might slacken their usual standards. Tabby surveyed the expanse of antique terracotta tiling with new weariness, a sudden vision in her mind of the thousands of other floors on the island gathering dust and waiting for her to arrive to mop them. Temperatures would soon rise, and not all of the houses – if any – would have air-conditioning. If she couldn't face her job today, how on earth was she going to endure it in high season?

Because you have no choice, she told herself sternly. Remember, you could have been in a homeless shelter by now. Or worse.

'Right, better get on with it,' Emmie said, and, after locating the storage cupboard, instructed Tabby to take the kitchen and entrance hall while she handled the vast open-plan sitting room at the rear. 'We'll need to sweep the terrace as well. If they've got a high-pressure jet wash, we'll use that.'

She began sweeping her allotted zone with focused intensity. This, according to protocol, would be followed by vacuuming and mopping, though in recent days Tabby had begun to omit the vacuuming stage when on her own. And it had never occurred to her to clean stone terraces or tidy courtyards, not unless the tasks were on Moira's list.

She set to work too. It was a testament to how well she had settled into her new life that she had virtually forgotten its inception and therefore only recognised where she was when, after an hour in the kitchen, she paused for a glass of water and looked at the family photographs on the dresser while she drank it.

Then she fetched a second glass for Emmie, who had finished downstairs and was starting on the first of three bathrooms on the upper floor.

'I've been here before,' she told her.

'Have you? That explains why it's in such good nick.' Emmie was scrubbing at the skirting boards with demonic energy, as if she'd found them thickly coated in syrup. 'The owners probably haven't set foot in the place since then. Had the oven been used? Moira says some people don't ever cook, even when they're here for weeks. They must pay her a retainer, I guess, get the place cleaned even when no one's been here. It's all right for some.'

'No, not on a job for Moira,' Tabby said, ignoring the last comments, though not before noting that Emmie was only ever talkative on impersonal, inconsequential matters. 'I don't mean that.'

'When, then?' Emmie asked the question with an air of sufferance rather than interest.

'When I first came here ... I haven't told you about what happened before I turned up at your house.'

Emmie looked for a moment quite startled, but her face cleared as soon as Tabby added, 'I was with a man, the owner of this place. That's how I came to be on the island.' She hardly needed add that it had been an illicit extramarital liaison, for the evidence of family life was all around them, the portraits that had caused the penny to drop in the first place, the bikes and surfboards and tennis racquets, the rows of teenagers' sports shoes.

'You had an affair with him?' Emmie said, dispiritedly, and Tabby could not tell if it saddened her to hear the confession or simply to be having to hear anything more of Tabby's history at all.

'Not an affair, just one night. He picked me up in a bar in Paris. Or I picked him up, I don't remember. Do you hate me?'

'Why would I hate you?'

'Well ... some people might disapprove. Most people would. He's married. He's got, oh, I don't know how many kids.'

'Two. I saw the pictures. Both boys.'

'*I* disapprove of me,' Tabby told her.

But Emmie shook her head. 'Why did you leave the city with a complete stranger? Let him bring you somewhere so remote? He could have murdered you.'

'I don't suppose there's been a murder here for centuries,' Tabby said mildly.

'Yes, but it could have been the murder capital of France for all you knew.'

'I wasn't thinking about murder,' Tabby said, frustrated by this line of enquiry. Emmie *never* gave the predictable response, or the desired one. One moment she'd correctly detect a faint implication you hardly knew you'd made, the next she'd take you at your word when you couldn't possibly have meant it. 'I'd had a few drinks. And I had that good vibe about him, you know, like I already knew him well and could trust him?'

Emmie didn't reply, but Tabby thought she could see in her face that she did know.

'Anyway, he threw me out the next day. He had a meeting with a builder, and his family were arriving in the afternoon.'

'So what were you expecting?' That ambivalent sorrow reappeared in Emmie's eyes.

'Nothing, I suppose. I just remember it felt a bit sordid afterwards. Like I'd done it for money.'

'He paid you?'

'No! Well, he paid for the train and taxis. My expenses.'

'Well, one night isn't anything to fuss about, is it?' Emmie made a dismissive face, as if the subject were closed, causing Tabby to jump in with an emotion that took her by surprise.

'The thing is, Emmie, he was the first man since Paul. It felt like, are they *always* going to end with me being sent packing? It makes me feel, you know, like I get close to a man, he gets close to me, and then he takes it back again. He changes his mind about me.' She heard the lurch of despair in her own voice, frightened herself by how quickly she could abandon optimism and descend into inarticulate self-pity. 'Nobody wants me,' she was about to add, but pulled herself together. 'Oh, forget it, I'm just feeling sorry for myself.'

But all at once Emmie was on her feet, not only interested but gazing at her with true compassion, the intense, livid kind Tabby had not seen in her since the night they met. 'No, I know exactly how you feel, Tabby. When he says there's nothing to be gained any more. Nothing to be gained from *love*. I think it's horrible to be denied, whether the other person is married or not.'

'Denied': it was a sweet, old-fashioned way of putting it, Tabby thought, but she hadn't really been denied by Grégoire, only by Paul; she would have left this house of her own accord, if not that morning, then eventually. He'd been old enough to be her father. And she'd never said anything about *loving* him, had she? But she didn't want to hurt Emmie's feelings by pointing this out.

'Emmie, can I ask you something?'

'You can ask,' Emmie said.

'Were you "denied", too? Dumped, like me? Is *that* why you came here? Are we in the same boat?'

Emmie looked at her, the familiar shade of self-protection drawing over her face. 'No, our boats are not the same at all, Tabby. I wish they were.'

Tabby burned inside and out with the need to know more.

And it was more than plain curiosity: she longed to be able to reciprocate the kindness she had received from Emmie. As she understood it (and whether or not Paul had credited her with the knowledge), support worked both ways. 'But what *is* your situation? You've never told me. I might be able to help, you know. Even just talking about it might be useful?' When Emmie did not reply, she continued recklessly, 'Do you remember when you discovered me that day in the house?'

'How could I forget.'

'You said, "How did you find me?"'

Emmie's face tightened. 'I don't think so.'

'No, you did, I'm sure you did. Why did you think I was looking for you, Emmie?'

'I have no memory of that,' Emmie said, 'but presumably because it wouldn't occur to me that you could be in my house for any other reason.'

It was a typical evasion and one that should have silenced Tabby, but, fired now to temperatures she could not control, she persisted. 'Not like my situation: OK, so is it the opposite, then? You're hiding from someone who *does* want you? You thought I might know him?' She imagined now an obsessed lover, a hunter for Emmie's heart, and registered momentary envy that the other woman should inspire extreme passion in a man while she had been discarded so casually. Shame followed. What if the man was violent and Emmie feared for her life? There was nothing to envy about that. He could be a Steve figure, an abuser, someone far more dangerous than anything *she* had had to contend with.

Emmie regarded her with resignation. 'I wouldn't call it hiding,' she said at last, and there was pure desolation in her voice. 'I would say it's more like exile.'

'Exile?' It was a word with political connotations, one that conjured disgraced queens and fallen leaders. 'Why would you be in exile? I don't understand.'

'That's why I don't want to talk about it. *You* won't under-stand and *I* can't explain.'

'Yes, you can. You can tell me, I'll be on your side.' Tabby felt a twinge, remembering the phrase as one of her father's when she was little. And he had been, even during the Susie years, or at least he'd start off on her side and Susie would grind him down. His instinct had been for her, though, and that was better than nothing, better than anything her mother could manage.

'I doubt it,' Emmie said in a shrunken voice, almost to her-self. 'No one else was, so why would you be?'

'Because I'm different. I promise I will try to understand, whatever it is.'

Emmie breathed a long-suffering sigh. Neither of them had moved from her position on either side of the bathroom door-way, but now Emmie lowered herself on to the curved rim of the bathtub. 'If you must know, I was accused of being some-thing I wasn't.'

Tabby digested this. Accused of being, not accused of doing. It seemed an important distinction. 'What were you accused of being?'

'A bad person.'

'A bad person?' It was curiously childlike phrasing. 'Bad in what way? Did you commit some sort of crime?'

'That depends on your point of view.'

'What's *your* point of view? That's all I want to know.'

But Emmie would not say.

'Why here, then?' Tabby asked, determined not to lose the momentum of this breakthrough exchange. 'At least tell me that. This place isn't that well known in Britain, is it? Why not Paris or the south?'

'It could have been anywhere, I suppose. But I knew about Ré. I'd heard about it from a friend.' There was another pause, before she allowed, 'We were going to come here together.'

'We? This *does* involve a man, then?'

Emmie concurred, or at least implied doing so with that way she had of simultaneously dipping her chin and eyes.

'Who? Why did you break up? Where is he now?'

But Emmie held up a hand: 'Please don't ask any more. I just want to rid myself of it. I need new words, new stories.'

'But—'

'No, please!'

Tabby did not have the first idea of what to make of these declarations. What new stories? What new words? Having finally extracted the admission of heartbreak she'd been so determined to win, she was rewarded only with a feeling of anti-climax. Then she reminded herself of the practical imperative for not irritating or distressing Emmie: to protect her position as beneficiary of Emmie's good will. A good will all the more charitable now she had been given an inkling of how low Emmie must have been feeling.

'We need to get on,' Emmie said, and she resumed her scouring with an amiable air, as if they'd been passing the time in idle gossip, nothing to think any further on. 'Thank you for the water. Could you make the beds next? According to the notes, the linen cupboard is by the door to the main bathroom at the back.'

'OK, sure.'

Tabby approached the bedrooms in a tumult of remorse, not only for bullying poor Emmie into talking about events she plainly preferred to forget, but for the night of adultery that now returned to her as she entered the one room of the house she genuinely recognised. She'd thought it such a luxurious chamber and yet it was the smaller of two guest rooms, the most modest of the five bedrooms. Grégoire was a very wealthy man, clearly, and she had been a cheap and temporary acquisition.

Emmie was right, to want to free her mind. Our hearts shouldn't have such a narrow focus she thought. Men, relationships, love: they shouldn't be the only things that drive us to

103

do extraordinary things like going to a different country and starting a new life. We should be here because we're adventurers, not fugitives! There should be bigger, nobler things to motivate us.

For the moment she could not think what those big, noble things might be, but she felt utter conviction that she wanted to find them.

Chapter 8

Emily

Arthur was quite open about his womanising past, about how he had caused his wife pain not only by the infidelities themselves but also by his preference to spend the precious little time he had outside his work with someone – anyone – other than family. Had it been golf or rock-climbing or a mania for remote-control planes, it would have contributed just the same to his being a negligent husband and near-absent father. And while nothing to be proud of, his affairs were, he told me, nonetheless typical among his colleagues, some of whom lived separately from their families during the week, joining them only at weekends. Others were divorced, remarried, divorced a second time, the forgiveness of loved ones a luxury long relinquished. It was more than an occupational hazard, it was an epidemic.

'It's not the kind of marriage I set out to have,' he said. 'I didn't aim to fail. I certainly didn't aim to be the one who *made* it fail.'

'Would you act differently if you could go back to the beginning?' I asked him.

'Yes. But I'd only need to do one thing differently – say no, not yes, that very first time – and the rest would never have followed.'

Instead, he'd said yes (to a colleague, predictably), and after that the women had come and gone, an easy reward for a gruelling spell, like having a drink on the way home from work; the lovers who lasted any length of time becoming the equivalent of a favourite pub. 'I made the mistake of thinking that because it didn't mean all that much to me, it couldn't mean much to her either,' he said, of Sylvie.

'So what happened?'

'Two years ago she gave me a final warning. She'd already found a divorce lawyer and had written the email instructing him. She just hadn't sent it yet.'

'And?'

'And so I stopped.'

'Just like that?' In spite of the absurd irony of his making this claim while his naked body was hooked around mine, I listened rapt, as if to a confirmed truth.

'Yes, on the condition that *she* stopped with the constant accusations.' As I raised my eyebrows, he continued, 'I know how that sounds, I know I was the one at fault, but if I'd slept with as many women as she imagined, I would have had no time to do my job. Sometimes I was only in the pub because I was having a drink.'

'Yes, while looking out the window for who might be passing by ...'

'That's not fair.' The arch of his right foot stroked my left shin. 'Anyway, since then we've both kept our side of the bargain.'

'Oh, come on, Arthur.' The disingenuousness of his position could be ignored no longer. '*She* may have, but in case it's escaped your notice, *you*'ve started again. And I'm not sure I like being compared to a pint of lager.'

'Oh, but this is different,' he protested. 'Completely, fundamentally different.'

'Why? It's an affair like the others.'

'It's not an affair. It's the real thing, the *coup de foudre*. It's what makes me see how unnecessary the others were.'

I had not heard the phrase '*coup de foudre*' before, but I had not had a relationship with a married man before, an exceptionally overcommitted married man at that, and it had taken me by surprise how intense and fast-moving it was, an expedited version of an ordinary one. We were propelled by the imperative to make every meeting count, as if we were foreign secretaries gathering at a moment's notice to tackle the outbreak of civil war in a neighbouring territory. Critical decisions were reached in pillow talk, key announcements made as zips were refastened and belts buckled. Avowals, pronouncements, promises: they did not have to be fished for or extracted (or, in the case of Matt, forsaken), but came of their own accord and in thrilling flurries.

'I'm falling in love with you,' he told me, after only a handful of liaisons, and not even when we were in bed but afterwards, with minutes to spare, as we dressed and gathered up keys and wallets, ready to return to our respectable real lives.

'Are you?' I had halted midway back into my skirt, but quickly resumed wriggling it over my hips, telling myself he was teasing.

'Yes,' he said, very firmly, 'I am,' and when I looked across at him I saw that he was perfectly serious.

'Do you think that's wise?' In the short time of our affair I had developed a composure that represented either a persona especially for him or a sudden steep development in my actual personality. Whichever it was, Arthur embraced it wholeheartedly, telling me he had been attracted in the first place by the 'exceptional mismatch' of me, that I was someone whose humility did not tally with her appearance and he wanted to help me realise how beautiful I was.

He smiled at me, tender and indulgent. '"Wise" isn't the

word I'd use, no. Nothing about this is wise, is it? Being here isn't wise.'

Except for the first weekend, when Matt and Sylvie had been out of town, we had not been able to use the flat for our assignations and so we met in the only decent hotel in the neighbourhood, the Inn on the Hill. It was a boutique place on the high street near the station, a couple of bus stops from Earth, Paint & Fire and walking distance from Arthur's hospital department. By accident or design we were always given the same room, 'Marrakech', which had a *riad* theme: terracotta walls, patterned kilims, a big wooden bed with carved posts; in the bathroom there were cobalt-blue mosaic tiles and a polished copper basin, high-end toiletries that we never used and I longed to pocket but was too ashamed to in front of Arthur. I wondered if it was the room they always gave to couples having illicit assignations: a simulated honeymoon in Morocco. I wondered if the hotel had sprung into existence expressly to service the affairs of the hospital consultants down the road.

'I get the feeling you don't feel the same way,' Arthur said, and his face betrayed no disappointment, nor even bemusement. His was a character built to beat adversity; he did not acknowledge rejection.

'Of course I feel the same way,' I said, scooping up my shoes from under the bed without breaking eye contact. 'But I think I can still stop it happening. Rein it back before it's too late.'

His eyes widened a fraction – with interest, I thought, rather than doubt. There was never any reason with him to worry about being *too* honest. 'Why on earth would you want to rein it back?' he asked.

Because of the long human history of love triangles, I thought: all the triumphant wives, all the mistresses brought low. There was a good reason it was not the other way around. 'It's obvious, isn't it? Because I don't want to be one of those women who hangs around for years waiting for her married man to leave his wife and then he doesn't, of course, and why should he? He already knows he can have her as an extra – that's why they call it a "bit on the side", isn't it? But by the time she realises that, it's too late for her to start something with someone else, too late to have children, too late for anything. She's totally wasted her best years.' The use of the third person did not provide the safety net I'd intended and for all my bravado I experienced a direct hit of despair – a visceral recognition of how it would feel to be the woman I described, waking up at the age of forty or forty-five and seeing that only the beginning had been sensational: the rest had been no more than the aftermath of a mistake.

Evidently feeling no such neurosis himself, Arthur leaned across the bed and seized my hand to draw me to him, steadying me as I lost balance. Our faces were now close enough to kiss and I could feel my breath coming harder. 'That's what you think is going to happen? That I'll string you along, just use up your best years and then spit you out? Because that's what I do?'

'I didn't say *that*.'

'But you think it, don't you?' He was growing amused. 'Haven't you ever heard of a positive mental attitude, Miss Marr?'

'I've heard of falling in love with the wrong man, a man who openly admits he's a serial adulterer and who has no hope of changing his ways as long as he lives.'

I expected him to protest the insult, but instead he crowed, 'So you do admit that's what you're doing? Falling in love?'

This was so far removed from any discussion I'd had with a boyfriend before, it was a brand-new language. 'Yes, I admit it,' I said. 'I don't see how it helps me, though.'

'Look,' he said, and I sensed the building of deliberation that came whenever he was about to say something crucial. It wasn't in any correction to the eyes or even the tone; it was to the breathing, which became concentrated, undetectable. 'The scenario you've just described is from the Dark Ages. Divorce is as common as staying together now, especially when the kids are growing up, like mine are.'

I felt uneasy at the reference to his children. Having focused to date on the chemical rush of our sexual attraction, the sensation of flying above ordinary mortals, I had not considered his two sons at all. To me they were *among* the ordinary mortals, the ones we'd left on the ground. I knew their names, of course, Alexander and Hugo, I knew they were eighteen and almost seventeen, just one school year apart, the elder taking A-levels the coming summer and beginning a gap year soon after, the younger to repeat the sequence twelve months later. Though Arthur admitted he hadn't spent a great deal of time with them when they were young, not compared with the current hands-on breed of father, there could be no doubt that he adored them, in the primal, unconquerable way of all good parents. He never spoke negatively of them, only of his own deficiencies. And they had had Sylvie for their everyday needs, I thought: *she* had not had to earn a living as the new generation of mothers invariably did. In retrospect, it sounds callous, I know, no more than a convenient excuse, but the truth was that to me it was natural to need only one parent, to have no choice in the matter.

'You didn't want to leave last time,' I said, finally, 'when she gave you the warning.'

'Forget last time. Last time wasn't you. How I feel now only makes me realise how miserable Sylvie and I have been for a long time. But this is it. I'm clear about that.'

I could hardly believe what he was implying, that he intended to leave her to be with me, and I certainly could not allow myself to trust it. *Last time wasn't you*: I would be a fool not to consider the possibility that he'd made such intoxicating declarations to previous lovers. That the possibility existed that, however pretty my face, however individual my personal style, I was still the same as every other woman who'd fallen for him:

110

fallible, flawed, and never more so than when in love. Because I *was* in love, of course I was.

'Please, Arthur, don't try to trick me, don't tease me. I'm not stupid: I know you have far too much to lose if you split up with her, you'd be mad to do it. I'm the one who'll lose, I know that and I accept it. But please don't pretend it's going to be any other way.'

His expression did not alter. As far as I could see, he was no longer even blinking. 'I'm not pretending anything,' he said in that grave undertone of his. 'You don't know me well enough yet to know that I don't say things I don't mean. And what I'm saying is I *will* be with you. You don't need to "accept" anything less.'

'You might mean it now,' I said, moved by both his words and the loving press of his fingers, 'when you're here with me. But you'll mean it a lot less when you're back home this evening with your family around you.'

'Or maybe I'll mean it more, because the reality is the boys are never at home and Sylvie doesn't really want to be alone in a room with me, not any more.' His eyes narrowed. 'Like I say, children fly the nest, couples move on. There might be two or three spouses in someone's life. I have a colleague who's on his fourth.'

'How many do *you* plan on having?' I giggled, if only to relieve the tension, but he remained quite solemn.

'Don't make a joke of it, Emily. To answer your question: one more. You. When I leave Sylvie, it will be the first and last time I leave anyone.'

'Really?'

'Yes. It will happen. It's purely a question of timing. Tell me you believe me.'

We stared at each other with rapt devotion. 'I believe you,' I said.

And he released my hands at the exact moment my body

111

weakened with delight, causing me to fall to the side, laughing. In that moment history was forgotten and with it any woe I'd ever experienced or anticipated, the whole lot extinguished by the radiation of joy. It was the happiest I had ever felt, I was sure of it. I had reached the summit of human elation.

'But what about the boys, Arthur?' I had yet to use their names, conscious of my lack of right, strangely superstitious of the effect of such an utterance.

'I'm only leaving her,' he said, 'not them. I'll need to make sure I can see them as much as I do now. Alex will be off soon, it won't affect him so much. And Hugo, I honestly think he'll handle it fine. Sometimes I think he's more of an adult than I am. I'll talk to him properly about it, make sure every question is answered, every possible doubt cleared.'

'As you say, they're older now,' I said. 'They might have been more upset if they were younger.'

'I couldn't do it if they were younger,' he said, 'not even for you,' which put me in my place all right. But it was still a place I was very happy to be put.

By then, Matt had agreed to move out. I'd insisted on our parting even before this declaration of intent by Arthur, though the truth was overlooked later in preference of the theory that I had wilfully traded up, discarding the old only when I was sure I had the new in the bag.

In keeping with the tone of our whole relationship, we were not explicit in our break-up discussions. We made no interrogations of one another and traded no recriminations. If not able to be warm, we could not bring ourselves to be cold.

'One of us has to move out and if you don't want to, it will have to be me.' I stated this with little sense of the urgent necessity I felt, for it was important to avoid the inference that this was anything but a mutual decision. Still, this *was* my initiative and I had to be prepared to bear the greater inconvenience of it.

'You move then,' was his first response, and I agreed without argument. I then spent a fraught night considering my options, ready the following morning to begin looking for a short-term rental within easy distance of work. Away from the Grove, it would be safer for Arthur to visit, too.

But the next evening Matt announced that he had changed his mind. 'I'm not paying this rent on my own, not even for a couple of months. I'll go, all right?'

'All right.'

I gathered from this that he'd mentioned his dilemma to a friend and had had an offer of a sofa or spare room. Either that or he too was seeing someone new and she, being presumably unmarried, was happy to take him in.

During this period he asked only one question that caused me proper difficulty, partly because it could be answered in so many different ways. 'What's going on with you, Emily?' And there was confusion in his face, as if he no longer knew me, which gave rise to opposing pangs of pride and remorse in me. I knew I'd altered since becoming involved with Arthur, but I did not want to be unrecognisable to Matt. We'd been friends a long time.

'What d'you mean? Nothing's going on.'

'Is it that posh bird at work?'

'Charlotte? She's not a bird, Matt. She's a Homo sapiens.'

But his meaning was clear enough: I thought I was too good for a down-to-earth man like him; I'd developed aspirations, wanted the kind of privileges Charlotte – and most of her customers – had. I did not tell him that relations with my boss had taken a downward turn lately, ever since I'd developed a need to take time off at short notice with debilitating migraines.

'I'm exactly the same as I've always been,' I said firmly.

Matt capitulated. 'Well, you *look* the same. Better than ever, actually.'

'You're not so bad yourself.'

There was a silence then that neither of us knew how to fill, but I was glad of it, of the evidence of reflection before the separation. 'I won't be able to give you your half of the deposit until I've moved out myself,' I told him at last. 'I hope that's OK?'

'Whatever. I'll let you know the address to send it to.' And that really was that with Matt. I haven't deliberately cut his lines or diminished his significance. He simply was not a man to chase someone who did not wish to be chased. The damage he could have done had he chosen to stick around and stir trouble, or even avenge, was untold.

When I told Arthur I'd be officially free by the end of the month he was overjoyed, proclaiming our cause 'halfway there'. 'He must be insane not to fight for you,' he said, adding, only half jokingly, 'but he'd never have beaten me anyway, so it's probably easier this way.'

I suspected the same could not be said for Sylvie. A devoted wife of twenty years was a different proposition from an inattentive boyfriend of five. She would not concede so easily.

We had been involved for three months when we had our first skirmish with the real world. It was an opportunistic Saturday-afternoon tryst following a cancelled appointment at his private clinic and requiring my feigning nausea to leave work at lunchtime. ('I think it's a side effect of the headaches,' I told Charlotte, but she'd grown tired of my mystery symptoms, demanding with disdain, 'Are you sure you're not *pregnant*?' As if her livelihood did not depend on just such reproductive inconveniences.) Late afternoon, I exited the main door of the Inn on the Hill and walked directly into the path of Sarah and Marcus Laing, out shopping, judging by their armfuls of bags from the chic-er neighbourhood stores. In using a local hotel, especially at the weekend, there had always been a risk that we'd see someone – or be seen – which was why we never left together, always allowing at least ten minutes between our departures. If second and not dashing back to work, I would have a coffee in the café, extending the time to twenty minutes or longer. Today I was first.

'Hello, Emily,' Marcus said, sounding genuinely pleased to see me. 'I haven't seen you about much recently. How are you doing?'

'Really well, thank you. And you?'

As her husband chatted, Sarah eyed me with mild hostility and since I was not being the slightest bit flirtatious with him there could be no other reason than how I looked. I had not checked my reflection before leaving and hoped I didn't look too obviously like someone who had had all her make-up kissed off. If there was one thing I knew about women it was that we did not like to feel more resistible than others of our sex, especially younger others.

'Where are the kids?' I asked her, casually jovial, though I would never have assumed such a familiar air if I were not bent on concealing my own activities – and terrified of Arthur materialising too soon behind me. But the subject of children acted as both neutraliser and guaranteed digression and, sure enough, Sarah could not help supplying details.

'They're at a birthday party. Rather a nice one, actually. Horse-riding in Richmond Park and then a private viewing of that new vampire movie.'

'Wow, a bit different from parties when I was young. Aren't they lucky? I see them in the morning sometimes,' I added. 'They look so smart in their uniforms. Where do they go to school?'

I had not heard of the school she named but the pride in her voice told me it was an élite one and that I'd earned myself the credits I'd fished for. Even so, I was not home free yet. After seeing her three successive glances towards the hotel entrance – we stood practically on its doorstep – I could no longer avoid explaining my business here, though I knew very well that the offering of unnecessary details was a sure sign of a guilty conscience. I didn't want to say I'd been in the café, in case Arthur appeared and said the same. I needed a story he couldn't possibly echo. 'I've just been asking about a job,' I said, off the top of my head. 'I thought this might be an interesting place to work.'

'Aren't you at that pottery café any more?' Marcus asked. I was impressed that he remembered.

'No, I am, but I've got the afternoon off.' More unprovoked detail; they were unlikely to know I was contractually obliged to work on Saturdays. 'Anyway, they haven't got anything at the moment. The recession, you know.' A sideways glance reassured me that there were no signs in the window advertising for staff.

'The market will pick up soon,' Marcus said kindly. 'And there are always other options, aren't there?'

I'd grown adept at reading other people's thoughts, not through any special instinct but through my dealings at work with couples just like this one, and I could guess what they were thinking. Why does she do this sort of menial work? Doesn't she want a nice white-collar office job, a 'proper' career? She's reasonably well spoken and is obviously presentable. What a prospect, what an impossible thought, in a sunny street in an affluent neighbourhood, to explain to two manifestly wealthy people that I had grown up in a climate of real financial struggle, my father having left his job to nurse my mother before her death and never able to regain the security he'd begun with, hanging on by the skin of his teeth in jobs where employers were not yet enlightened enough to understand why a man would choose to raise children on his own. There had been no money for college and now there was no money for any but the most basic care for him during his own cruel illness.

I hated myself for having wanted to agree when Arthur had called me 'unlucky', but I did; sometimes, to my shame, I wallowed in self-pity. But what then did that make the poor soul who used to be my father incarcerated in a hospital unit and literally not knowing if he was coming or going (neither, in that place)? Damned, perhaps?

'I just thought it might be time for something new,' I said to the Laings, my reply girlish, anodyne. 'I've been at Earth, Paint & Fire for almost two years now and I'd like to try for a managerial position somewhere.'

'We'll let you know if we hear of anything,' Marcus said gamely, and I did not look at Sarah, preferring not to see her poorly feigned agreement.

Just as I judged it safe to sidle off, Marcus was calling out Arthur's name and raising a hand in greeting. To my relief, Arthur had not followed me through the main doors but had appeared from the alleyway that ran to one side of the hotel building, where there was a fire door. He joined our gathering with an impressively natural look of surprise.

'I don't know if you remember meeting at our party?' Marcus said to the two of us.

'Yes,' I said, cheerfully, 'I think I do. You're the eye man, aren't you?'

'That's one way of putting it,' Sarah said, and she and Marcus laughed together at my lack of due reverence. It was clear they were in awe of Arthur and thrilled by this opportunity to have him to themselves. I eyed him shyly; he did not look as if he'd just spent the afternoon having sex with me.

'I'm afraid I don't remember your name,' he said to me, apologetically, and Marcus jumped in to clarify.

'Emily. Emily Marr. Our next-door neighbour. She of the potter's wheel.'

'I don't actually make the pots,' I laughed. 'They all come factory-made and ready to paint.'

'Oh, what a disappointment,' Marcus said.

'What, you like a woman in clay-smeared overalls?' Arthur asked, amused.

'No, just clay-smeared,' Marcus said, chortling.

'Well, we all have our weaknesses.' Arthur spoke in the droll, self-confident tone I recognised from the men at the Laings' party. How I admired the ease with which he bantered with this pair – or with Marcus, at any rate, for the exchange had apparently displeased Sarah, who was struggling to suppress a scowl. Like Sylvie Woodhall's in the café, her dislike of me was instinctive. It would be ridiculous of me to protest, however, since it was fully justified, and more ridiculous still to go on wanting to be liked by them while happily making off with one of their men. I suppose I wanted it both ways and yet, standing there on the pavement with the three of them, I had never felt more out of my depth, unfit for either role, let alone both. Twenty minutes ago Arthur had told me repeatedly that he loved me, and I would have traded a hundred avowals then for a silent, secret one now. But instead he glanced at me as if he really did not know me and had no particular reason to reverse the situation.

'Well, I'll leave you to it,' I said, with a general smile. 'Enjoy the rest of the weekend, everyone.'

I left a cautious interval before texting him: *Does that alley lead anywhere besides the fire exit of the hotel?*

He replied: *It's a short-cut to the station. I told them I'd just come from Harley Street.*

Thank God. I was scared they might have guessed.

No. Don't worry.

Sarah doesn't like me, does she?

If she doesn't it will be because Marcus does. And there's nothing wrong with his vision, as far as I'm aware.

I didn't care much for this theory, but I supposed it was preferable to Sarah hating me because she suspected I was having an affair with one of her friends' husbands.

And, all things considered, I would far rather have bumped into her in that situation than into Sylvie herself – or her friend Nina Meeks.

Chapter 9

Tabby

How seamless the weeks were when you might be working on any day. They turned without pause, the island's summer season unstoppable both for the holidaymakers and those who served them. Tabby knew which she would rather be, given the choice. A regular income having lifted her from the ranks of the near-homeless, she began to feel stirrings of a desire to let her hair down. All at once it felt tightly braided, knotted to her scalp so closely she could no longer breathe for the pain.

Which was another way of saying she was bored.

Though much had happened in the intervening months, it wasn't so long since she'd devoted her own days to hedonism, to floating in the waters of the Gulf of Thailand with her arms outstretched and eyes closed, feeling the sun burnish her cheeks while alcohol or other chemicals flowed through her blood-stream. Here, she was excluded from the forces of indulgence at play around her, the daily demonstrations of high spirits in the bars and cafés of the port, and it was an exclusion that was self-imposed – and self-defeating. It began to seem absurd that she and Emmie were living in such a sedate manner, behaving more like elderly spinsters or war widows than young women in their twenties and thirties. How anonymous their lives were, how clandestine! They'd dropped out of everybody's society but one another's, a pair of oddballs with no friends among the locals and only one bicycle between them, spending their working hours preparing houses for other people's holidays, people who sat in the sunshine and drank rosé and licked ice-creams and danced and laughed and . . . everything else.

Everything else that made life a pleasure and not a punishment.

Having thought she had successfully buried the memory of her night with the Parisian Grégoire, even reached the point at which it was possible to pretend to herself it had not actually happened, she now relived with disturbing clarity her reacquaintance with his guest bedroom. As she'd stood by the bed, the deadweight of fresh linen in her arms, she'd been unable to prevent the onslaught of a series of destabilising lurches as she recalled how good it felt to have sex with a man – with Paul, ideally, who in declaring himself dissatisfied with all other aspects of their relationship had not been dissatisfied with *that*. The pitching feelings had gone on even as she tucked the sheets and hauled the quilt into its new blue-and-white gingham cover, thumped the pillows into plumpness; they startled her like hiccups that could not quite be beaten.

Which was another way of saying she was lonely.

Though her experience of that earlier feminist epiphany had been acute, she'd since continued to be painfully reminded of her aloneness, of being unequal to the task of that aloneness – not like Emmie, whose character appeared well suited to her solitude. (Or maybe she was just better at concealing her frustrations than Tabby was.)

'Why don't we have a night out?' she suggested one Saturday evening soon after the job in Les Portes. The distant music of holidaymakers' voices through their open kitchen door was always more potent with the added energy of the weekenders. 'You're not booked to work tomorrow, are you?'

'No. What did you have in mind?' Emmie asked, doubtfully,

as if there were hundreds of ways in which the two of them might risk life and limb in this law-abiding place, and she wanted nothing to do with any of them.

'Just a drink in one of the bars. All these places, and I've hardly been to any of them. You do drink, don't you?' Tabby had never seen Emmie drinking alcohol. She herself had supplied bottles of wine here and there – it was as cheap as water in the supermarkets – but Emmie had declined all offers of a glass. 'Or we could just have a coffee? Come on, you can't spend *every* night reading or staring at your computer ...' She faltered, realising too late that Emmie had not once brought the laptop downstairs but kept it at all times in her bedroom, which meant Tabby could only have known she passed evenings in this way because she'd peeked through the glazed panel of Emmie's closed door.

But Emmie didn't make the connection. 'All right, why not? Give me a few minutes to get ready.' She was unexpectedly agreeable, even pleased, which made Tabby wish she'd made the suggestion weeks ago. Why hadn't she? Money, she supposed. The bars and cafés in the port were expensive and her priority remained to save cash, not spend it. As for Emmie, while having appeared when they'd met to be in a far healthier position than Tabby, she was, it transpired, living a similar hand-to-mouth existence on the earnings she made from cleaning for Moira. Other than the bottle of expensive perfume, there'd been no evidence of any former affluence, nothing to bring to the table from her old life; even the bike had come with the house.

Upstairs, as Tabby dispensed herself enough cash from her savings for a couple of carafes of wine, the sight of the modest stash of euros caused sudden euphoria in her. Of course she should overlook her strict budget for a few hours. She'd worked hard to pull herself back from poverty, she'd hidden herself away for almost six weeks now, and it had been months since she'd made an effort with her appearance. Standing at the mirror and putting on her make-up, she felt the exhilaration grow: it felt less like the application of a mask than the removal of one, the overdue reinstating of who she really was. She was twenty-five, young! She deserved a public airing.

She hurried downstairs, wishing Paul could see her looking good again – a weak, futile desire, she knew, but at least she was now free of the belief that there was no point if he could not.

'All set?' she called up, hearing Emmie's door open and close, her footsteps on the stairs. As Emmie's lower body began to come into view, she couldn't help but stare, first at the footwear – deep-green velvet court shoes with a glamorous high heel – and then at the skirt – full and swinging, a vintage print of pink and green – which revealed itself to be a dress, cut low at the front and puffed a little at the shoulder, a garment not only at odds with Emmie's usual style but also the first time Tabby had seen her in *any* dress. Last came her face: she too was wearing make-up, rose-pink lips, kohl smudged under the eye and winged liner on the lids, bringing drama to her green eyes, and a creamy foundation that polished the contours of her cheekbones and jaw. Her hair, normally unkempt and, Tabby had come to assume, resistant to styling, was smoothed from her forehead and secured with a narrow band. It was not just a smartening-up but a complete reconfiguration.

'Wow, Emmie, you look amazing!'

'Thank you.'

'I've never seen you in make-up before. And can you walk in those shoes?'

Emmie frowned, offended. 'Of course I can. Why shouldn't I?'

'I just meant on the cobbles?'

'Oh, I see. I'll try.'

They managed the short walk without injury, Tabby slipping her hand into Emmie's elbow to help steady her on the uneven ground. This in itself was without precedent, for they had not yet developed the kind of friendship where touch was natural. They attracted glances as soon as they merged into the flow of the promenade. Tabby, in one of the sheer cotton cover-ups she'd bought in the Far East, had forgotten how revealing the fabric was, and as for Emmie's dress, well, it was very tight at the chest and hips; she must have been a smaller size when she bought it. As they took seats at the bar on the quay, she noticed the glances growing into stares.

'Well, what a beautiful evening, still so hot!' She gestured to the waiter for service. 'Let's pretend we're the ones on holiday, let other people do the work for once.'

But no sooner had they ordered their wine than Emmie was springing to her feet again. 'I'm just going to the *tabac* to get some cigarettes,' she announced.

Tabby was amazed. 'Cigarettes? I didn't know you smoked?'

'I used to, now and then.' And she was gone before Tabby could make further comment.

Alone, she became aware of two men at the table next to theirs who were looking her over with particular interest. Something about one of them reminded her uncomfortably of Steve: he had the same British complexion, the same insolence in his eyes. It struck her for the first time that it was not beyond the realms of possibility that she might meet someone she knew from England while she was here. Not Paul, of course, this was not a traveller's destination, but it was certainly a tourist's – and just a short flight from London. She was confident, however, that she would not be likely to encounter her mother and Steve. They would not be attracted here for the same reasons that they would be so out of place if they were to find themselves here: it was not flashy enough, but understated, a world of faded beach-wear and demure cotton print shifts. No wonder she and Emmie had stood out as they tottered across the cobbles, their faces vivid with make-up.

The last tables were filling, the chatter thickening around her, as the waiter returned with the wine. Tabby began without Emmie, finding she needed the drink more urgently now her thoughts were sliding in the direction she most disliked, towards the single occasion when she had voiced a complaint to her mother about Steve's attentions. For what it had been worth.

It had been about six months after he had moved in with them and only a few weeks since her mother had confided in her that she thought he was about to propose.

'I don't like the way he looks at me,' Tabby began, struggling to gain her mother's full attention. Waiting for an opportunity to get her alone meant she had to ambush her as she left for work.

'Oh, it's just his way,' Elaine said. 'He likes the ladies, but he doesn't mean any harm.' It was the pride in her voice that had disheartened Tabby most, for it was evidence that she was applying all Steve-related matters to herself, not to her daughter, prepared to turn suspicion of him into a compliment to herself. She revelled in her renewed status as a woman desired, even if it made her daughter uncomfortable. Tabby supposed all children of first marriages must encounter this when their mother began again with someone new – but they surely did not encounter the rest.

'Mum, he came into the bathroom when I was in the bath. He saw me naked!'

'He told me all about that, Tabby. He didn't realise you were in the house at all, he thought you were at school.' This, Tabby knew, was where Steve's testimony held weight, since she *had* been supposed to be at school but had skipped the class for the history A-level that she would go on to fail. 'He was as shocked as you were. Try to imagine the situation from his point of view. He was blushing like anything when he told me.'

'But he—'

'Please, Tabs, stop this.' Elaine's voice grew hard. 'It's difficult enough making a go of things second time around without having to deal with you criticising him the whole time.' And she closed the discussion before Tabby could find the nerve to give further insight into Steve's 'point of view'. Yes, she could have insisted, she could have followed her mother out to her car and spewed the full details, shouted, 'Propose? Why don't I tell you what he proposed to *me*!', but what would have been the point? She would only have been accused of attention-seeking, of trying to come between them out of loyalty to her father or jealousy of her mother, of creating disharmony where Elaine was determined harmony should reign. She could not win.

She could not forget, either, not the smallest detail of the episode. She'd been at home on her own, reading in the bath, when Steve had come home unexpectedly from work. She heard the front door open and close, his voice call Elaine's name and then, getting no response, her own.

'I'm in the bathroom,' she yelled.

She heard his footsteps on the stairs, the unhurried deliberation of them, and then, to her alarm, she saw the door handle pressing down.

His face appeared, his shoulders followed. Then he was in the room and the door was closing behind him.

'What are you doing, Steve?' she shouted. 'Get out, will you!'

'You said you were in the bathroom. Did you want me for something?' The innocent tone didn't deceive her for a second.

'No, of course I didn't! I meant I'm in here so *don't* come in!'

But he was already lowering himself on to the towel she'd left folded on the closed toilet lid, and he was looking frankly at her. He was not tall and his face – admittedly well arranged and boyish but ruined at the best of times by a compulsive moistening of the mouth – was startlingly close to hers.

She'd been in the water long enough for the bubbles to have all subsided, leaving her completely exposed. All she could do – and had done the instant his face peered in – was to cover her upper body with her arms and bring her knees closer to her chest, feet drawn tightly together. She couldn't tell what was visible to someone sitting at his angle, but it was too much whatever it was.

'Why are you *sitting*? Can you pass me that towel, please – and then get out!'

'What towel?'

'The one you're sitting on, Steve.'

He refused to meet her eye, his making a deliberate scanning of her body parts, gaze coming to rest on her forearms shielding her breasts. 'Sorry, can't reach it. You'll have to get it yourself.'

This would of course mean kneeling or half-standing, losing the protection of one arm as she tried to tear out the towel from under him, and, worst of all, having to make certain physical contact with him. She envisaged a naked tug-of-war that would be far more titillating to him than her remaining motionless in half a bath of dirty water.

Though the water was cooling, her face was searing hot, her pulse pounding. She was frightened. 'What do you want, Steve?'

'Well, that's the thing, it's what *you* want, isn't it?'

'What are you talking about? I don't want anything.'

His lips parted. 'I know you need fifty quid, I heard you asking Elaine. How about *I* give you it?' To her bewilderment, he fished notes from his back pocket and placed them on the windowsill behind his head.

'Why would *you* want to give me fifty pounds?'

But she was beginning to understand the answer.

'Don't be like that,' he said, with the temerity to look insulted. 'Seriously, you don't have to do anything. Just lie back, put your arms by your sides, or behind your head, better still, and let me have a proper look. A nice, long look. Then the money's yours. Fifty.'

'Make it fifty million and you've got a deal.' Her snarled retort belied her shame and horror; but she was determined not to cry.

'Come on, it's not much to ask, is it? Just a little favour. You must know it's driving me fucking crazy living with you.'

'You are living with my mother, not me.' The distinction was lame, her implicit departure from this house of fun too distant for anyone but her to have considered it with any seriousness; and even if she was leaving tomorrow, it could not protect her here and now from the continued prodding of his obscene gaze, as if he could use it to prise loose her arms from around her own body.

'She doesn't need to know anything about it,' he said; 'don't worry about her.'

Tabby felt nauseous with revulsion. Her hatred for him was giddying. 'I'm worrying about myself.'

Tongue and teeth appeared in another lascivious smile. 'Oh, you have *nothing* to worry about, believe me.'

As he leaned a fraction towards her, her fear began to escalate. They were alone in the house and she doubted neighbours would be in at this time to hear her scream. Was it possible that he might use physical force? Was she in actual bodily danger here, at risk of rape? He had not actually touched her and yet, if he did, in a way she'd know what to do, she'd fight back with her fists. But this staring, this invasion without touching, it was menacing, all the danger held in reserve.

'Get out!' she yelled, violently. 'Get out or I'll go to the police!'

'Take it easy. Just being friendly . . .' But at last he shifted his weight to his feet and rose reluctantly, repocketing the cash. Though still grinning, the expression in his eyes was unpleasant and she shrank from it, causing the water to move around her and his eyes to notice the additional inches of bare skin revealed. 'And don't waste your time going to Elaine because I'll tell her it was you after me.'

'She wouldn't believe that.'

'You think?'

But she might.

She'd used the lock on the bathroom door after that, even when Steve was out of town for work. She'd begun staying at friends' whenever she could, with those whose parents were away or who were kind enough not to mind, and, when they allowed it, her father and Susie.

Drinking the wine now and surveying the evening festival of Saint-Martin before her, she wondered if it had always been going to happen, her sneaking into Emmie's house that night in May. Wasn't it just the latest in an established behavioural pattern of her begging for shelter, putting the onus on someone else, forcing that person to make the choice between condemnation and pity, rejection and acceptance? When had she lost the ability to decide for herself? Had she ever possessed it in the first place? From what Paul had told her, she had not, at least not for as long as she'd been under his protection. And, in the end, he had chosen rejection.

'What's the matter?' Emmie's voice asked. She had returned to the table with her cigarettes, was looking expectantly at Tabby.

'Sorry, I was just thinking. Look, the wine's here ...' Tabby pushed Emmie's glass towards her and raised her own. 'Cheers! *Santé!*'

'*Santé.*'

It was peculiar seeing Emmie, this dressed-up, made-up Emmie, across the table from her, drinking and smoking – she held her lit cigarette self-consciously, like a schoolgirl – casting bold little looks left and right as if they'd only just arrived in Saint-Martin and were people-watching for the first time. A part of Tabby welcomed the transformation – finally they'd be having some fun – but this was countered by a stronger instinct of protestation. She might not fully understand solemn, secretive, strait-laced Emmie, but she liked her. All things considered, she'd been a very good influence on Tabby.

'So what were you thinking about?' Emmie said. 'You looked angry.' It was not like her to ask a personal question like this, a Tabby sort of question.

'Nothing. I don't know, I just wish that British guy would stop staring at me. It's making me squirm.'

Emmie frowned. 'British?'

'Yeah, I heard them ordering before, they're definitely English.'

She directed Emmie's attention to the table to her right and, still unsettled by thoughts of Steve, was careful to avoid any eye contact of her own with the men. Immediately, Emmie whipped back her head and lowered it with a dramatic flourish Tabby put down to the first effects of alcohol and nicotine.

'What is it?'

Emmie was already grinding out her cigarette. 'They're not looking at you. They're looking at me.'

'They are?' This made little sense, since Emmie had not been here to witness the scrutiny – of one man, not both – but there was nothing competitive in the way she made the claim, nothing arrogant or vain. She seemed, in fact, agitated.

'It's not a big deal, but when you were gone—' Tabby began.

'They were waiting for me to come back,' Emmie finished, voice rising.

'Well, OK. I hate it when people ogle like that. In fact I was thinking how it reminded—'

Again Emmie interrupted: 'So do I, obviously!' To emphasise this she scraped her seat to her right to put her back square to the two men. Even in the circumstances, Tabby was a little embarrassed.

'Let's just ignore them,' she said, not sure why this was starting to sound like an argument (and what had Emmie meant by that insistent 'obviously'?). She noticed the waiter arrive with their neighbours' bill. 'They're leaving now, anyway, so let's forget it.'

'I think I'm going to head back as well,' Emmie said, far from mollified.

'What? We've only just got here. You've hardly started your drink.'

'I know, but I need to leave. I have no choice.'

'No choice? *Why?*' When Emmie did not answer, Tabby softened her tone. 'Come on, at least finish the bottle with me? It's such a gorgeous evening, we can't spend it shut away in that dark house.'

'Fine.' Emmie picked up her drink again. The men left, their table claimed at once by new customers, a French couple, harmless by anyone's standards, but it was no fun any more. Emmie remained jittery, Tabby subdued, and their conversation was disjointed at best, the joviality of half an hour ago quite gone. When Emmie said again that she wanted to go home, Tabby's heart was no longer in her dissuasions. 'OK, whatever you want. I'll stay on my own for a bit. I might wander around, have a look in some of the shops.'

Emmie departed so quickly that it was only after she'd gone that it crossed Tabby's mind that she might have recognised one of the men and decided to catch up with him. How else to explain her insistence on cutting the drink so short, especially when she'd made such an effort to dress for coming out? But she could clearly track Emmie hurrying across the quay and stalking up rue de Sully towards their lane. The two men were nowhere to be seen, there'd been no connection. She'd probably imagined the harassment in the first place, mistaking a perfectly normal passing attraction for intimidation. She felt completely responsible for the abrupt termination of this first proper attempt at a social outing. So much for a well-earned night out, the first of many! Perhaps the reason for her having adopted Emmie's hermit lifestyle had been more than financial need; perhaps she wasn't ready for the wider world, still so absorbed in her thoughts of the past, not only of Paul, but of her father as well, even Steve. No wonder Emmie couldn't bear to stay; she probably sensed she was about to hear another sob story. 'Nobody loves me . . .' again and again. She bored herself.

She counted out the correct euros for their bill and left the bar. It was still light and she didn't feel like going home yet. Most of the shops were still open, tourists browsing after early dinners or before late ones, and she decided to join them, picking through the baskets of seaside bric-à-brac, the smallest piece of which equated to a week's food budget. Still, the drinks had not cost as much as she'd allowed for, perhaps she could treat herself to a trinket to cheer herself up, a souvenir of her time in this—

'Tabitha, is this really you?'

Startled, she felt a hand on the small of her back, a male voice in her ear: Grégoire. She opened her mouth to reply but was unable to say anything intelligible in greeting. Having convinced herself that she'd barely recognise him if she saw him again (and that he certainly would not know her), she now acknowledged the delusion of this. He was familiarly attractive, taller than she remembered, masculine and confident, and her thrilled physical response surely repeated the original one, the one in the bar near the Gare Montparnasse that she could not wholly remember thanks to the alcohol she'd consumed, only that they'd been drawn to one another with unambiguous speed.

'What are you doing?' she asked, unnecessarily, for he was guiding her through the open doorway of the shop and into its lantern-lit interior, by which she gathered he must have his wife nearby and required this little reunion to take place out of her sight. It was not such an extraordinary coincidence, she realised. He was a part-time local on the island, this was a Saturday evening in summer, every bar and restaurant table in the capital village taken. He must have been sitting at one of them, perhaps across the water, and seen her at hers, waited for a chance to come and confront her.

For there was no question that he was less than overjoyed to see her. Coming to a halt next to a trestle table displaying tall jars of polished shells and pebbles, he cuffed his fingers around her two wrists as if placing her under arrest.

'What?' Tabby asked him, gently extracting first one arm and then the second from his grip, if only to stop herself from liking it so much.

'You are still here?' He looked comically disconcerted, almost wounded, as if it were she who had apprehended him and hustled him into a shop.

'That would seem to be obvious,' she said, with a non-committal smile.

'But why did you stay? I thought you would go back to Paris?'

'I had no reason to go back. I hated Paris. I don't know why I was there in the first place. I've found work here and I like it. It's a special place.' She realised the truth of this only as she spoke it, and with the realisation came renewed appreciation for Emmie. Abortive night out or not, this was still the most content, the most secure she'd been since before she left England. 'But don't worry, it's not like we're in the same village. You're in Les Portes, I'm here. I won't come near you.'

She wondered what he'd say if she told him she'd cleaned his house, she'd made the same bed they'd lain in together, but it seemed a fair guess that he would be suspicious of her motives. It was the sort of thing a stalker would do, he might say. The next step would be to befriend his wife and materialise as a dinner-party guest. It struck her, as he eyed her coolly, that he was going to threaten her, to demand she leave the island, which she very strongly did not want to do, and so when he next spoke his words were a great surprise:

'Perhaps I want you to come near me.'

133

'Oh?' And predictably, pathetically, the words caused the same pleasure as a declaration of love – he wanted her and that was cause enough for her to want him back. A sudden craving for physical touch raised her body temperature like the first grip of fever. What had she been thinking, a drink with Emmie, all the strains and oddities that would entail (and, indeed, had)? *That* wasn't what Tabby had needed. 'You have a wife, Grégoire,' she said, reminding herself as well as him. 'I know it didn't bother me then, but it bothers me now.'

His flicked glance towards the door confirmed to her that his wife, perhaps his whole family, was indeed here in Saint-Martin this evening. '*Nous allons séparer*,' he murmured, inexplicably choosing this moment to switch to French. Tabby wondered if he preferred to lie in his mother tongue.

'*Vraiment?*' She raised her eyebrows to underline the sarcasm before looking away from him, reaching for a conch shell, varnished and silvery, turning it in her fingers.

Perhaps sensing a drifting of her attention, Grégoire returned to English. 'Yes. When the summer is over, when we are back in Paris, Noémie and I will be living lives on our own.'

'Right, sure. That's very likely. I believe you.' She returned the shell. To buy the whole glass jar of them would cost five hundred euros, she estimated.

'When can we be together?' he pressed. 'Next weekend? Saturday?'

'Don't be crazy,' Tabby said. It was breathtaking that he could make this approach when his wife was in the vicinity, audacious to demand she suggest a venue, as if her assent were a given and it were simply a matter of agreeing logistics. But the truth was that her protests were merely an anticipated part of the dance. Womanisers did not attempt to seduce every woman in their path, it was not a numbers game they played, it was one of calculated targets: they sensed the ones most vulnerable to their charms, they identified them by a single gesture or a look, just as schoolyard bullies selected their victims. They knew how powerful intensity could be, how successful persistence.

And so, when he said to her, as gravely, as urgently as a detective with the life of a kidnap victim at stake, a siren wailing outside, 'You have an apartment here in Saint-Martin? A room?', she was nodding, she was agreeing, yes, she *would* meet him next weekend, of course she would. But not because she was his victim, at least not only for that: she would have a use for him, too. When they went to bed together she would close her eyes and dream that she was with Paul – or she would keep them open and educate herself in the reality that she could never again be with Paul. It would only be once, but it would work the cure that their first encounter had not.

'I do have a place,' she began, but the thought of Emmie arriving home after work and finding Grégoire there brought her to her senses. 'I share a house, but it's not possible for me to have guests.'

'A hotel, then. I will find us somewhere. Give me your phone number.'

'No.' She was rallying again, battling herself in this exchange as much as him. 'Give me *your* number.'

'You must not call me.'

'I'll text. I'll text you in the week where I'll be next Saturday. I'll be working, but you might be able to come for a short time.'

Grégoire took a flyer from the pile at the counter and scribbled his number. Then he leaned forward and kissed her on her jaw by her ear, a manoeuvre that necessitated a nuzzle, an intimacy that made her feel more alive than she had at any time in the last few weeks.

'I must go now,' he said, and she remembered how he had repeated the command 'you must go' that morning in early

May. She told herself in her weakness that this change in the pronoun represented progress, a swing in her favour.

She waited a self-conscious five minutes before exiting. Outside, she saw him across the water from the bar she and Emmie had chosen, at one of the outside tables of the popular seafood restaurants. There was, of course, *la femme* Noémie, as well as two sons, the ones she'd seen in the family photographs at the house. Dishes of seafood rose from the centre of the table on a stacked stand. Grégoire could clearly be seen slicing an implement around the edges of an oyster, putting the shell to his lips.

She was far too stimulated to go home and so took a table at the bar nearest to his restaurant and ordered a glass of wine, watching for a while. Inevitably, her interest came to rest on Noémie, who was as lean-limbed and well preserved for her age as Tabby had known to expect. Her hair was silver-blond and sharply cut, her complexion smooth; there were expensive glints at her ears and wrists. She wore a linen dress the colour of biscuit. Did she have any notion that her husband liked to proposition young women under her nose? Tabby had heard of the famous French tolerance for adultery, but was it actually true? Did every middle-aged woman accept it as inevitable or was it only those married to men of a certain wealth and status? As for the man himself, how odd it must be, how complicated, to run two women in parallel.

Or not complicated at all, if Grégoire was anything to go by. He'd finished the oysters now and was poking at something on one of his sons' plates. Somehow, perversely, his utter lack of agitation, his ease with his own treachery, made him more attractive, not less. Simple as it would have been to stride over to his table and announce herself, she was going to have to borrow Emmie's phone if she intended to contact him again. Good, she thought, she'd be sober tomorrow and she might feel differently, less reckless; she might remember that she was a

136

very different girl now from the one who'd once absconded from Paris to an Atlantic island with an ageing adulterer, a man who could have murdered her.

The thought of Emmie's comments made her smile.

Returning home, she was relieved to find her housemate already in bed, her door closed, light out. As she tiptoed across the landing to the bathroom, it struck her that she was extremely drunk. Allowing herself to remember that unpleasantness with Steve had caused her to drink more than she'd intended – most of the bottle she'd begun with Emmie and more afterwards as she'd spied on Grégoire – and she was woefully out of practice. She was due at work the next morning for Sunday changeover duties on a cottage in La Flotte, one of those old village houses that was deeper than it was wide, with acres of tiles to be mopped and no fewer than five beds to be made, all of which was going to be twice as laborious with a hangover. She decided to take painkillers with a pint of water, a cure that had served her well in more decadent times. She had no painkillers, that was the problem, and knowing the pharmacy and *supérette* to have been closed since eight, she hoped Emmie had stocks somewhere.

In the bathroom there was no cabinet, only a shelf above the basin where she and Emmie kept their toothbrushes, and a lidded basket on the floor in which Emmie stored her toiletries. Opening this, she found shampoo and conditioner and deodorant, tampons and plasters and Savlon, a cream for insect bites, a supermarket sunscreen, but not a single blister pack of aspirin or paracetamol. Noticing a make-up bag, she thought again of the bold kohl Emmie had worn that evening, smudged around her eyes like charcoal, the lipstick of ripe watermelon pink, and could not resist unzipping the pouch to examine its contents. The brands were cheap English ones, the items mostly new.

Digging deeper, her fingers struck more hard plastic, this time producing an encouraging rattle, and she pulled into the light a half-full bottle of prescription medication. The label had been printed by the East London NHS Trust and was dated over a year ago. The name of the medication was Quetiapine, which Tabby had never heard of and had no idea how to pronounce but was clearly something stronger than aspirin. It occurred to her it might be medication for depression, prescribed to counteract the low feelings Emmie had been experiencing since her parents' deaths or those nameless crimes and accusations that had precipitated her 'exile'. Emmie had shared no further details since their conversation in Grégoire's bathroom and Tabby had been true to her word and not enquired again. However, she still believed entirely in the theory that it took one to know one. Their situations might not be precisely the same but each had at its heart the withdrawal of love, she was certain, and nothing could break a person like that.

I could have done with some of these myself not so long ago, she thought, rubbing her thumb across the label. It had been torn where the patient's name had been printed, but she could make out the capital 'E' of Emmie. She returned the bottle to the make-up bag, the bag to the basket, and replaced the lid.

Making her way downstairs to check the kitchen drawers, where at last she unearthed paracetamol, she experienced a sensation of intense gratitude towards her housemate. She would never forget that Emmie had thrown her a lifeline when no one else had even noticed her in the water, Grégoire included. She was, Tabby surprised herself to realise, the nearest thing she had to a friend.

Chapter 10

Emily

Soon – too soon – after the encounter with the Laings in the street, I came home from work one evening to find a note through the door from Sarah: *Emily, do you ever do babysitting? I'm really stuck for tomorrow night so if you're interested, phone me on the number below or pop round.*

'I hope you didn't mind my asking,' Sarah said on the phone, all sweetness. 'It's just I know you do parties at the café and so have experience with kids. I thought you might be interested in earning some extra cash. You said you were looking for work?'

Unsure whether a transactional relationship between us would improve or worsen matters, I followed my instinct and agreed. 'Sure, of course. If you're really stuck, I'd be happy to help.'

The hourly rate she offered was generous and we agreed I would come at seven-thirty the following evening. As it turned out, the job was a blessing, since Matt had chosen the same evening to pack up his possessions and my absence made this activity a whole lot less awkward for both of us.

There was nothing suspicious about the atmosphere at number 197 when I arrived and was led down to the basement kitchen by a confident girl of about twelve. It was exactly as you would imagine the hub of an affluent London family house on a Friday evening – full of end-of-week chaos and good-natured argument, the granite worktop piled with dinner dishes and the polished oak table now cleared for homework. In the adjoining den, I could see long, low sectional sofas in grey wool and a huge TV screen on the wall. The children – there was a boy of ten as well as the girl who'd answered the door – protested in ringing private-school accents that they didn't need sitting, and the staggering array of technology about the place suggested they could pass a year unsupervised and still be kept amused. The girl's phone, set down by her schoolbooks on the table, was a far more expensive model than my own, I noted.

'They usually stay up late on Friday nights and watch a movie,' Sarah said, 'but they're perfectly self-sufficient. You don't have to watch the film if you don't want to. And help yourself to anything in the fridge, of course.'

She was far friendlier than she'd been at our previous meetings; obviously, she was grateful for my having helped her out, but I also wondered if the change might partly be a result of her having made such an effort with her appearance (or I so little with mine). Her dress was simply cut and expensive-looking, her heels fashionable, the overall style that of a particularly chic first lady. But when I complimented her, she immediately pawed at her hair and drew my attention to the nest of grey hairs at the parting. She had not been able to get an appointment at her preferred hairdresser, she said.

'Just you wait,' she added, in a tone I couldn't quite place. 'The more you try to defy it, the faster it comes.' I didn't know if she meant the grey hairs or the passage of life generally, and thought it safest not to comment.

'Is Marcus away on business?' I asked politely.

'Yes, he's in Dubai. Back tomorrow. He was supposed to be home today but he had to stay an extra night, hence my last-minute scramble for a babysitter.'

It was awful of me, but I couldn't help imagining that

Marcus had stayed on not for work but for a female colleague. Of course it was possible *she* was the one on the illicit date that evening.

'What are you up to tonight?' I asked her. 'Something fun?'

'Oh, just a girls' night. Well, I say "girls", but obviously I mean women.'

She said this in a way that made me feel excluded from the category, as if I belonged with the children. I wondered if she realised I was thirty; or perhaps there was a point at which you could no longer judge a person's age accurately. 'Do I need to know where you'll be, in case I need to contact you?'

'Just at the bar in the Inn on the Hill, but I'll have my mobile, don't worry.'

It seemed to me that the look she gave me when she mentioned the hotel was a significant one, but I told myself I was being oversensitive.

The evening proved delightful, simply by virtue of my spending it in a big, beautiful house with people who hardly knew me instead of the tiny, scuffed flat next door where a man who knew me well enough to be willing to move out transferred unwashed cycling gear from a laundry hamper into a backpack. I watched the film with the kids and then chivvied them upstairs to clean their teeth and get ready for bed. Their rooms were at the top of the house and they had an enormous bathroom to themselves up there, too, the run of the floor. Noting the Arts and Crafts beds and designer curtains in their rooms, the rugs and framed prints I would have admired in an adult living room, I thought, What a way to grow up! The house I'd been raised in had been a fraction of the size of this and the flat I'd shared with Dad and my brother after Mum died no bigger than Sarah's master bedroom (into which I could not resist peeking: unlike the children's rooms it was stark and modern, an upholstered bed and matching ottoman virtually the only furniture). Oddly, though, I felt far less envious of Sarah's fortune this time than I had the last. Falling in love had subdued my material aspirations: I would rather have my low-grade flat with Arthur in it than this vast glittering house without him.

Of course, the reality was I had neither.

Soon after the children had settled, when I had just finished tidying the den and was drinking tea at the kitchen table, I heard footsteps on the path outside and the scratch of a key in the front door. Sarah was back earlier than I'd expected and I was disappointed to cut short such a comfortable evening: I'd been hoping to read some of her *Vogues*, too expensive for me to buy regularly for myself.

'You're down here, are you?' Sarah called, clattering into the kitchen and discarding her handbag on the nearest worktop. In her wake followed two of the 'girls': Nina Meeks and Sylvie Woodhall. I should have guessed, in retrospect I don't know how I could *not* have, but the fact was their arrival that night came as a serious shock to me. With preparation I might have done better, but to be faced with the wife of the man I was sleeping with, to suspect this might have been set up by Sarah for this purpose ... well, I was running scared. What idiots Arthur and I had been to think conclusions would *not* be jumped to that day in the street: he was, after all, by his own admission famous for his wandering eye, while I was no doubt notorious for the eye-popping dress I'd worn to the Friends' Christmas party. I imagined Sarah reporting the sighting to Sylvie and Nina: 'She claimed she was in the hotel asking for work, but I checked after she left and no one had been in to enquire all afternoon.' To this day I would put money on her having cancelled her regular babysitter in order to contrive the 'desperate' vacancy, a trap that I fell into like the fool I was.

'Hello, Emily,' Nina said. 'You seem to be everywhere these days.'

'Well, I do live next door,' I said, in no way antagonistically, and yet I immediately felt as if I had cheeked the headmistress.

'So I hear. Very cosy.'

I gave her a weak smile, already at a loss for an intelligent remark.

Thanks to Arthur, I knew more about Nina now, how her popularity both in print and online had made her one of the highest-paid women journalists in the UK. I'd seen her column several times. She'd give some cabinet minister a dressing-down or praise the stand an actress had made against her abusive estranged husband. Though her position was feminist, the subjects on whom she turned her scathing brand of common sense were often female ones. She had a gift, it was said, for sensing which public figures would get the reader's goat. She was both opinion maker and spokeswoman, and I got the feeling she was about to take both roles in this encounter with me, too.

Aware that I was both blushing and avoiding looking at Sylvie, I tried to compose myself. I began to update Sarah on the children's evening, clinging to the safe ground of PG movies and clean teeth, but she interrupted me at once. 'So long as they're still breathing and the house hasn't burned down, I don't need the full audit.' Her tone was droll, all her earlier warm gratitude now absent. 'I'll open a bottle of wine, shall I? Sparkling water for you, Sylvie?'

'Yes, please,' Sylvie said, seating herself several places from me, and her voice sounded artificially merry, almost shrill. I glanced at her for the first time. Her small face had a pixie's prettiness to it, an effect enhanced by the cap of curls from behind which her anxious eyes peeped. Unlike the others, she had not removed her coat, giving her an uncertain air, as if she thought her safe harbour here might be removed at any moment. Perhaps it was this fragility that inspired such protectiveness in her friends, such fierce loyalty, and – I gulped at the thought – the reason why Arthur had stayed with her in 'misery' when he could have left at any time.

'Have a drink with us, Emily,' Nina commanded, sensing that

I was about to get to my feet and scarper, and she and Sarah took the seats on either side of me as if to lock me down. Sarah sloshed white wine into the glasses, pushing one determinedly towards me; she was the tipsiest of the three, I saw, the most excited. Had she joined the coven? Or perhaps she'd always been in it. What had Marcus said that first time? *Not as friendly as she'd like*, that was it. Suddenly my throat was full of the fear that Sarah was delivering me to the other two as a kind of initiation sacrifice. Bring us the slut and you're in.

'Did you have a good time?' I asked mildly. 'I thought you might make more of a night of it.'

'Not at our age, dear,' Nina drawled, not quite putting me in my place, but not seeking to put me at my ease, either.

'Oh, Emily can't imagine what it's like to be an old crone like us,' Sarah said. 'She hasn't got a care in the world.'

'If you say so,' I said, using the light-hearted tone that worked well with ruder customers at Earth, Paint & Fire. Already muscular tension was causing aches in my shoulders.

I made myself look at each of them in turn; continuing to evade Sylvie's eye would have been a sure sign of guilt. As our glances intersected, I felt a brief flare of how I would respond to her if we were meeting in more innocent circumstances, and I was surprised to register pity. I wouldn't be drawn to her, not as I might be to Nina or even Sarah, were they not so overtly unwelcoming of me; she looked too needy, as if she could always find something to complain about. Even disregarding Arthur's betrayals, I found it impossible to imagine their original compatibility at all. Had he really once desired her as he now did me?

'Old crone' was ironically brutal, of course, but the fact was that Sarah had been quite right in her comment: I *couldn't* imagine being their age, I couldn't imagine how it felt to be faded or threatened or replaced, to feel the need to be snide to my youngers. And yet, didn't I know from the way twenty-year-old girls looked at me that they felt exactly the same about my age group? Perhaps for any generation the one just above its own is the most distasteful, even tragic, its company to be avoided at all costs. There is no solution to the unfairness of this, and few exceptions (my fascination with Arthur, for instance, but perhaps such instincts did not apply to the opposite sex). No, all you could do was try to experience your prime to the utmost while you were actually in it.

How you knew you were in it was not something I thought deeply enough about then. I connected it too readily with attractiveness to men, I suppose, and not enough to strength of character, to courage or grace – all of which, I know now, Sylvie possessed.

'How's the lovely Matt?' Sarah asked me.

'He's very well, thank you.' If I knew anything for sure it was that I should not reveal that we were in the midst of splitting up. 'Really been getting into his biking now the weather's better.'

'I've seen him shooting down the hill a couple of times,' Nina said, which surprised me as I did not know she had met him. Perhaps they'd been introduced the night of the Christmas party. 'You know a cyclist was knocked down last week, just outside Sylvie's house?'

'I didn't know, no. That's awful. I hope he wasn't badly injured?' I looked towards Sylvie, whose loathing, or so I imagined, had until then prevented her from speaking directly to me.

'No,' she said at last. 'A broken wrist.'

'Unfortunately Arthur wasn't at home to assist,' Nina added, 'but the medics were there in a couple of minutes.'

'They're based at the hospital, maybe,' I said stupidly, anxious to avoid further mention of Arthur's name or any reference to our little gathering outside the hotel.

'How long have you been together?' Nina asked me, and a jolt of shock made me widen my eyes and draw breath. I knew she had noticed this reaction, but it was too late to do anything about it. She had meant Matt, of course, not Arthur.

'Er, nearly five years.'

'Any wedding bells in the offing?'

I was able to laugh at this suggestion quite genuinely, and doing so relaxed me a little. 'No. Matt's not the wedding-bells kind.'

'Are you?'

I hesitated. There was no longer any way of avoiding the fact that this was an inquisition and yet there was nothing to be gained by reacting defensively. 'I don't know. I suppose I'm like every other woman, I think it would be nice to get married one day.' To avoid tumbling into the trap of discussing the 'right man' for me, I steered the discussion towards a different cliché: 'I'd like to choose the dress, plan how it all looked, that would be fun . . .' I ran out of words, suspecting that any could be dangerous in this context.

At the mention of clothing, they all looked me over, a disarming experience that made me feel like a carton of eggs getting its sell-by date examined. With their eyes dipped, their faces were momentarily free for me to check: Sarah's was disagreeable, bordering on hostile, Nina's cocked in superior amusement, Sylvie's . . . Sylvie's was, inevitably, the most unsettling. She looked defeated, a wife already in mourning.

She knows, I thought.

Nina touched the sleeve of my cardigan, a sage-green shrug with a feathery fake-fur collar. 'Yes, you obviously do the whole vintage thing, don't you? I like the Lauren Bacall hair, the retro make-up. Old Hollywood: it suits you, you've got the right figure for it. If only more girls did the same, rather than starving themselves half to death in pursuit of an ideal that will one day be considered grotesque.' But just as I hoped she'd been diverted by more political concerns, she zoomed back to me. 'Yes, you're quite a catch, aren't you, Emily Marr? I do hope Matt appreciates what he's got.'

I felt uncomfortable to hear this last comment, and stated so baldly, as a judgement rather than a compliment. There was also the clear inference that I'd been previously discussed and that the experience of me in the flesh was merely confirming an opinion formed earlier. 'I just prefer old clothes,' I said, blandly. 'I love the fabrics and the colours. And they're much cheaper than new ones.'

Nina mused, 'Vintage clothing is a very feminine nostalgia, I think. Do you find that men like it, Emily? What is it they some-times call it? Not second-hand, no one says that any more, do they? *Pre-loved*, that's it.'

I was far too stricken by the implications of her remarks to allow images of Arthur into my mind, his unreserved approval of the silk blouses and pencil skirts, the stockings and sus-penders, every detail designed for his pleasure. Even the perfume I wore when we were together was a vintage blend: he'd recently given me a beautiful old flask of it. I was glad I was not wearing it now, but saved it for him. 'Some must do, I suppose. But I'm not sure Matt's interested in anything except cycling Lycra.'

Nina laughed, seconded by Sarah. I liked to think I had scored a point for this little attempt at humour, and since it was probably the only one I *would* score, I got to my feet to leave. 'Talking of whom, I ought to get back if you don't need me any more. I've got an early start tomorrow. We've got three birthday parties in so it'll be a long day.'

'My God, that will be half the kids in the area,' Sarah said.

'Good to know our children are safe in your hands,' Nina added.

'I hope so,' I agreed, with as much dignity as I could muster. 'Thank you very much for the wine, Sarah.'

She followed me to the door and handed me the cash I'd earned. 'Thank you, Emily, I really appreciate your coming to my rescue like this.' Her glee was barely contained, her feet already pivoting from the door as she closed it, ready to dash back down to her debrief.

If I'd been offered the superpower of invisibility and been able to follow her back to the kitchen table and hear everything they said about me, I would not have taken it.

I told Arthur about the encounter when we met a few days later at the hotel. Until then, I had been in a paralysis of anxiety and couldn't begin to communicate by text what had happened.

'Hmm,' he said, listening without interruption, as was his habit. 'That *is* worrying. We need a new meeting place, somewhere less local. I'll have a think. Your flat is going to be out of the question now as well, if Sarah's on the case. That's a shame.'

'To put it mildly!' I cried, but as usual no evidence of concern disturbed the glacier of his face. It stood to reason that he would be experienced in containing a crisis, or in not letting a situation get critical in the first place, but I was not. Having turned over the episode repeatedly and even lost sleep over it, I was livid with fear and melodrama. That detail about a cyclist being run over replayed itself as a sinister threat; and the sly way Nina had said 'pre-loved', all that had been missing was a raised eyebrow in Sylvie's direction. *Good to know our children are safe in your hands . . .* Was not the unspoken second part of that clause, *if not our husbands*?

But how *could* they know? A coincidental meeting of neighbours outside a local hotel: that was all they had. Whichever, if any, enquiries Sarah might have made at reception afterwards, surely no staff member would have divulged the details of a confidential booking. Meanwhile, Arthur deleted all texts and call logs religiously and so could not have left clues that way; in any case, he had separate mobile phones for his family and work and I contacted him on the work one. There could be no calamitous mix-up of contacts. No, the answer was they couldn't possibly know. I was in the grip of paranoia and it was making my thoughts wild, reckless.

'I understand if you'd rather just dump me,' I told him bleakly. 'I'll kill myself, but I'll understand.'

He looked at me with that perfect earnestness of his. 'Tell me you don't mean that, darling?' He made an attempt at unbuttoning my top – normally we'd be undressed and in bed by now – but I captured his fingers in mine, pressing them to my sternum.

'Feel my heartbeat, Arthur, it's out of control. I feel hunted, and no wonder! It's not as if I'm not guilty, is it? Everything they suspect is true!'

'You just need to hold your nerve. They're messing with you, believe me.' Keeping his hand on my chest, he leaned forward and kissed my throat, moving once again in the direction of the exposed groove of cleavage, the first button of my top. I eased his head back up. I needed him to look at me, to acknowledge the catastrophe, to be the one I could count on to believe *me*.

He did not fail me. He stopped trying to kiss me and pulled me back to sit next to him on the covers, the pillows stacked behind our backs. He wore his gentle, willing face, the one I imagined he needed for more fearful patients, the ones who asked the same questions over and over. 'OK, let's talk about this properly. Did Sylvie say anything to you herself?'

'No. She hardly looked at me. It was all Nina. Everything she said seemed to have some other significant meaning.'

'Yes, it would. Don't forget she's a professional, she's been on the *Today* programme and *Question Time* and God knows what else. Of course she's going to get the better of you, that's her job. It's a confidence trick, a bluff. I know it's scary, but it's a trick all the same.'

I gazed at him. When he spoke like this, as an unquestioned equal to Nina and her ruling ilk, I saw how out of my league I was. Without his protection, I was the easiest of prey.

'I promise you she doesn't know anything, not for sure. If

149

Sylvie had a shred of evidence, she would have accused me by now. You mustn't worry about this, my love. This is for me to handle, and I will. Please trust me, all right?'

'All right.' And his words did reassure me. His sureness about Sylvie and the likelihood of her confronting him had to be based on experience as well as instinct. But my exposure to his wife's circle had raised other questions, ones I could not help voicing. 'So have you ever had an affair with one of them?'

'One of whom?'

'The coven. Nina and that lot.'

Arthur laughed. 'No, of course not. I'd be ritually castrated if I so much as tried. They have their code of honour, that gang. It's quite admirable, really.'

'But *you* don't?'

'What, have a code of honour?' He furrowed his brow, as if he'd never been asked such a searching personal question before. 'I've never thought of it like that.'

'But how could you not? It's obviously wrong to be unfaithful to your wife. You said she's been upset in the past, she gave you that warning? You must have thought about it then?'

This, of course, was the central contradiction of my situation, the one that presumably vexed mistresses the world over and that I'd previously avoided contemplating in any depth: how could a man be the beautiful soul his lover believed him to be when he was capable of such wilful unkindness to the mother of his children? That instinctive reaction to Sylvie I'd had, to pity some unnamed weakness in her: it was all too convenient to believe Arthur had ceased to find her attractive because of the same failing, and yet might it not be the case that the weakness had developed because of his neglect?

In which case, he was a monster and I was a fool.

Sensing that his job of placating me was not yet done, he answered me only after obvious thought. 'I did think about it, yes, which is why I ignored all temptations in the two years before I met you. But I also knew that that final warning of hers was less to do with her wanting me to be faithful for moral reasons as to do with appearances, public image.'

'You mean the socialising you have to do for work?' I imagined him moving in exalted circles, dining with Charles and Camilla or the Saudi prince he told me he'd treated years ago. I imagined black-tie charity fundraisers and lavish parties at their home, taxis and chauffeur-driven cars queuing up the Grove to deliver their distinguished cargo.

'No, we don't do that much social stuff any more, only the occasional thing we really can't refuse. Or I'll go to events alone.'

'Why?'

'Sylvie wanted to cut back on it.'

'I don't understand.' It seemed to me that Sylvie would benefit from consolidating this role. Wouldn't a wife under threat seek more ways to become indispensable?

'Emily, there's no reason why you should understand. The fact that you're not jaded and broken like we are is the reason I love you.' As usual, I never tired of hearing him say this, or of feeling the sudden listing sensation of submission that it elicited. 'You just have to take my word for it that when you've been married to someone for twenty years, you become very pragmatic. You can't stay idealistic about someone for that length of time. It's a natural adjustment.'

But pragmatism, or the fading of idealism, did not quite explain the desolation in Sylvie's eyes at Sarah's table, or the first impression I'd had in the café that time, which had left me with the idea that she had survived a traumatic ordeal and dreaded its return. It was deeper than an aversion to humiliation or loss of public face: she *did* want him to want her still, I was sure of it. I did not think Arthur was lying to me, however. I assumed that his marriage, rather like my relationship with

Matt, had not included enough frank communication, which meant that his interpretation of their respective positions was different from hers. What he imagined to be a blind eye might in fact be a sobbing one.

'Look, I can hardly deny I've been a terrible husband,' he continued. 'You know that. There've been plenty of times when I've hated myself for what I've done, for the excuses I've made to her *and* to myself. But I'm not sorry I met you. Do you want me to be sorry, is that it?'

'No,' I whispered, 'I want you to be glad.'

'Good. I *am* glad. Because I feel like I'm starting again with you, trying to do right all the things I did wrong before. I know there's a short overlapping and I wish it weren't this way, but that's all it is, a short overlapping.' He slid down the pillows a little, pulling me with him. 'Alex does his A-levels this term; I can't think about causing any drama until they're over, but once they are ...'

Even without prior experience, I knew this was the classic married man's deferral; there would always be another reason to postpone. If we waited for the younger son to finish *his* A-levels it would be another year, and by then Arthur might have decided he couldn't jeopardise their first terms at university, their finals, the early months in their chosen careers ... How easy it would be to fall into the brooding silences and secret ultimatums of the long-term mistress. What made *me* different from all the women before me who'd hoped and believed and come to wish they had not?

I didn't say any of this aloud, however. I'd already taken up half our time together today with my fears and insecurities and I didn't want to turn our liaisons into anything other than ones to be anticipated with relish. Not when desire was what linked us in the first place.

But Arthur had an intelligence that enabled him to track my emotions. He held me closer, saying, 'It will happen, I promise, *very* soon. I can't leave her right this minute, but until I can I want to support you in other ways.'

'I don't want your money,' I said, meaning it. Sylvie was not the only one with pride to protect.

'I didn't mean that.'

'What then? How can you "support" me?'

'However you need me, you tell me. Let me come with you to visit your father. I know you feel lousy afterwards, whatever you pretend. Well, let me be there for you, as proof.'

'Proof of what?'

'Proof that I love you. More than any other woman, ever.'

We rubbed our faces together. Now when his fingers unbuttoned my top, unclasped my bra, I had no power to stop them. Now when he kissed me, I responded hungrily. 'I've never wanted anyone like this,' he groaned. 'I've never loved anyone like this ... It's ... it's beyond my ability to describe ...'

'I feel the same.' And out of vanity, or for pleasure, I made him wait, made him repeat his vows. 'Did you tell any of the others you loved them more than any other woman?'

'Oh, Emily, you make it sound as if there've been whole chorus lines of them. And no, I didn't.'

'Only me?'

'Only you.'

He was true to his word and came with me to visit my father the following Sunday. Someone or something had been cancelled to facilitate this, but I did not allow myself to think about that.

Arriving at the ward, I thought how cautious I would have been of making this introduction had Dad's disease been less advanced. Back when he had been himself I would not have allowed them to meet at all, and a part of me was grateful for the convenience of his lack of comprehension. The only father in the world not likely to disapprove of his daughter's married

153

lover! How ashamed I was of that perverse gratitude – hadn't I spent years praying for a miracle? I could have wept for him, for everything he'd once known and now did not.

He'd been given a sedative to help him sleep and could not lift his head from the pillow. Arthur, seated beside me, did instinctively what Phil and I had had to be educated to do: use body language to convey warmth. He knew not to bother with words. When Dad drifted into sleep, his hand remained clutched around mine and we stayed a while. Arthur took my other hand and I felt the flooding gladness of total trust in someone, a friend to whom I could reveal the full enormity of my sorrow. He wouldn't make light of it or avoid discussion of it as Matt had. He wouldn't listen in open horror as Charlotte did, exclaiming constantly that she didn't know how she would cope if it were *her* beloved father and not mine.

In a low voice, I told him about the diagram of a pyramid Phil and I had been given by the specialist when the disease was first diagnosed.

'Maslow's hierarchy of needs,' he said at once. 'At the bottom the physiological needs, the basic ones, at the top the transcendent ones.'

'Yes. It's supposed to help us identify which bits are no longer within reach.' The upper parts of the pyramid had been shaded out long ago and we were, at best, in the middle, on the tier labelled *Belongingness and Love*. 'So long as he still knows I love him then it means he's still at that level. Do you think he knows?'

'Yes,' Arthur said, 'I do. Definitely.'

Because it was Sunday, there were no consultants on duty. I had hoped to see Dad's key worker from the care home, who had continued to keep an eye on him after the transfer and made occasional overtures regarding his return to that more comfortable facility, but she was not there either. It was strange to think of the medical staff detaching themselves from him and

154

the other patients for their weekends off, when I could hardly pass an hour without being reminded of him. Arthur did his best to gain information from the staff that I might not be able to extract myself, but it was clear to all of us there was little new to say, just new ways of saying it. He was sweet to try, though, and to tell me that if I had any questions he would ring one of the senior staff the next day for me.

In his car on the way home, we were silent at first, grateful for the congested lanes that slowed our re-entry into the city and towards the river. Normally, at some point in my solitary trek home I would phone Phil, let him know that things were much the same, give or take, hear in his voice the same horrible longing for cataclysmic change I knew must be in my own, the same claustrophobic terror that there should be any alteration at all. How consoling Arthur's silence was, just as it had been at the hospital bedside.

Presently, I turned to speak. 'You know when you see people in the street who look totally desperate?'

He glanced through his window to the street life beyond. 'Homeless, you mean?'

'Yes, or just people who are lost and distraught about something, at the end of the line. Well, I'd love to be able to say, just to one person, one time, "Come with me, stay with me until you've got yourself back on your feet." Give someone a break, totally against their expectations.'

'That's a very charitable attitude,' Arthur said, 'but it might be a bit risky to take someone in without knowing a thing about them. If they're roaming the streets and obviously desperate, they may have mental-health issues.'

'I don't mean I'm actually going to do it,' I laughed. 'Not in London. I might be murdered in my bed if I let in a complete stranger. I just meant I'd *like* to do that, one day, something that makes a proper difference to someone down on their luck.'

'A random act of kindness? I think it's natural, that sort of impulse. You feel helpless back there . . . ' – he meant the hospital – 'you worry you can't do anything to help your father. But you have to realise you *are* helping. What you said about love and belonging, honestly, he couldn't wish for a better daughter. By visiting him so much, you're helping, both you and your brother. Plenty of families cut back on the visits long before this stage. I wouldn't be surprised if some of the patients in there don't get a visitor from one week to the next.'

'That's true.' It had certainly been the case in the care home, where I knew at least one resident who had no visitors at all. 'But how do you explain the fact that I've had these feelings even before Dad got ill?'

'I don't know; perhaps you should have trained in medicine or teaching or something. A more formal way of helping people you don't have a personal connection with?' He glanced at me, placed his hand briefly on mine. 'Either that or it's plain old maternal instinct at work. Have you considered that? The lives we influence the most are those of our children – I can tell you that for a fact.'

We lapsed into silence. I didn't know if he was thinking of his sons or of any children we might have together in the future, but I had no wish to alter the atmosphere by repeating my overwrought doubts of last time, by demanding promises of fulfilment and the fulfilment of those promises. I never would again, I vowed. I would not even allow myself to consider the nearest of futures, half an hour from now, when Arthur would drop me somewhere on the outskirts of our neighbourhood because it was far too risky to take me to my door.

I'd think only of the here and now.

'When did you last go on holiday?' he said.

I had to think hard to place the answer. 'Last year – no, the one before. A whole group of us went to Spain on this cheap deal.'

'Well, as soon as this is over, I'll take you away.'

I didn't know if he meant when my father died or when he left Sylvie, but my response to the two eventualities, one so dreaded, one so desired, held an element in common: a longing for the uncertainty to end. A sense that to wait any longer might break me.

'Where will you take me?' I asked him, turning my head so my cheek brushed the headrest.

'I have the perfect place in mind. It's a little island off the west coast of France. It's very relaxed, very low-key, and the weather is great. We'll go for two weeks, hole up in a place on the beach.'

This couldn't happen this summer, I knew, for he was due to go to Sussex for ten days in August; work commitments would not permit a further two days, much less weeks. And I would never allow myself to leave Dad unvisited for so long. But at that moment, as the car moved through the City towards the river, I wanted to believe it was true.

'What's it called, this island of yours?' I asked.

'Ré. I've been there a few times, when the boys were younger.'

I felt my eyes close as he continued to describe his island hideaway. It didn't matter whether we would actually go there or not because this was a bedtime story, a fantasy, pleasurable and lulling and bespoke. The sand dunes and salt pans, the old stone cottages and terracotta roofs, the hollyhocks that grew taller than your head: they were all just for me.

Chapter 11

Tabby

Even before she'd led Grégoire up the stairs of the house on rue du Rempart, which she was looking after so reliably that Moira had confirmed the job was hers for the rest of the summer if she wanted it, Tabby knew this would become a regular arrangement too – if *he* wanted it. Worse than that, she knew it would become the highlight of her week, as if in spite of all higher ambition nothing but human intimacy was in the end worth looking forward to. (What would Steve say to that?)

Even as they were kissing, undressing, groaning, giggling, she was rendering obsolete her own justifications, creating new ones in their place. This is a link to living, she was telling herself. Without it I might disintegrate and die, and who would notice, who would care? Doing this, at least *I* care.

And Grégoire cared too, didn't he? While he was inside her, he cared; maybe for a few minutes afterwards, too.

The logistics of the thing had taxed her somewhat. She was, after all, supposed to be working and it was not the kind of work you could take home with you and catch up on later. She'd calculated that if she brought from the stocks at home a bedsheet of her own, she could still strip the beds and get the used linen in the machine at the start of her shift in the usual way; if she attacked the kitchen and bathrooms at top speed, completing them before he arrived, she could earn herself a longer-than-usual break; if she left for afterwards only the mopping of the tiles and the remaking of the beds; if she limited her time with him to an hour or so ... then she could fit it in.

The hard bit, it would turn out, was not the muscular exhaustion that followed accelerated and intensive cleaning – adrenalin and lust counteracted that well enough and she had all evening to rest, in any case – but the discipline required to limit herself to a single hour before kicking him out.

'I have no hurry,' he told her, naked and relaxed on the bed as she began to dress.

'No, but I do. I'm *working* here, Grégoire. You're my lunch break.'

'I'll watch you finish your work,' he proposed.

'I think you should go home,' she told him. 'Aren't you worried your wife will be wondering where you are?'

'She has not any consequence where I am.'

'That makes no sense.'

'Then we must speak French if you want to have sense,' he said playfully.

'I don't have *time* to speak French.'

A reluctance to leave on his part had not been scheduled for. She had expected (and would have preferred in the circumstances) an adulterer who had his clothes on and was out of the door within ten minutes of ejaculation. She did not ask what his alibi was – he would only deny he had need of one, peddle his nonsense about separating from his wife – but supposed it must have been easily enough concocted. This is surreal, she thought, hearing the washer-dryer enter its spin cycle downstairs and wondering how easy it was going to be to smuggle back home the used sheet Grégoire was sprawled upon and get it in and out of Emmie's washing machine without detection (very easy, she decided; if not at her beloved laptop, then Emmie was more often than not absorbed in a book or her own thoughts). She would have thought he'd be more aware of the risk of this situation – unless, of course, it was the risk that aroused him in the first place.

'You might be able to delude yourself, but you don't delude me,' she told him as he at last prepared to leave.

'Yes, Tabitha,' he said, sly, satisfied, happy now to joke. 'You know me so very well.'

She wished she had thought to use a false name with him, allowed herself to escape Tabby Dewhurst and be someone else completely.

At home, she dealt with the bedsheet and switched the kettle on, still on her feet but already anticipating the sweetness of the forthcoming collapse. Four hours of cleaning condensed into three, one hour of sex, thirty minutes of walking, and dinner still to cook: just as she'd told Moira, she had a lot of energy.

Judging by the sound of running water from above, Emmie was taking a bath. She had her own regular Saturday changeovers, two fishermen's cottages on the same street in La Flotte, which with a little ingenuity could just about be squeezed into the standard eleven-to-three slot. Tabby was not sure she would like to try such a feat.

There would be, of course, no drinks in the port tonight. It had come as no surprise that Emmie had not cared to discuss the incident of the previous Saturday. The following afternoon, Tabby had asked, 'Did something upset you last night?' and Emmie had replied, 'No, I'm fine' in a bright and determined tone. She'd been dressed in her usual casual clothes, all trace of the previous night's make-up removed. Later, Tabby came across the cigarettes in one of the kitchen drawers, the pack missing just the one she had watched Emmie smoke.

It was a mystery – but she was getting used to that.

All at once the lights went out and the noise of the kettle faded. She had been alarmed when this had first happened, but was used to it now. The kettle used enough power to trip the electrics, their budget tariff giving only a limited supply. 'Just wait till winter,' Emmie had told her. 'Apparently you can have hot water or the radiator, but not both at once.'

It had touched Tabby that she believed they'd still both be here, living together, months from now. She, for one, expected to be gone by autumn time. When high season ended and the work dried up, she'd be on her way. She couldn't afford to live in an expensive part of France without a regular income. As for Emmie, she gave no impression of planning a departure, presumably aiming to stay in the house until such time as its owners chose to reclaim it. Renovations were planned for the following new year, they'd told her; until then, she needed give only a week's notice.

Throwing the main switch by the front door, Tabby turned off the lights to finish boiling the kettle and then reinstated them once her tea was made. Standing idly with her mug in hand, she noticed in the centre of the kitchen table a plastic purple file that she'd never seen before and that presumably belonged to Emmie. It was the kind with loops of elastic to keep its covers closed, perhaps Emmie's equivalent of her own zipped wallet in which she stored her passport and the old travel documents and tickets that amounted to souvenirs of her trip.

Her eye was caught by the dark, shiny corner of a photograph sticking out of the top and she reached out a hand to tuck it back in. At the moment of contact, however, she changed her mind, pinched the corner and began to ease it outwards.

She disappointed herself even as she brought index finger and thumb together. This was the problem with her job, she thought: it made access to other people's possessions an everyday occurrence, it blurred the line between respect and disrespect until the two were no more than a casual step apart – one that, crucially, only you knew you had taken. What was that famous philosophical question Paul had told her about once? If a tree falls in a forest and no one is there to hear it, did it make any sound? Something like that. And in any case, if people *would* keep taping up signs saying '*Privé*' and yet not use a lock and key – well, it only made the temptation to pry greater and that was not philosophy but human nature. (She was aware only very dimly that she had a tendency to blame her transgressions on human frailty in general rather than any character flaw of her own.)

Having worked the photograph free, she held it under the light. It was a picture of a couple, a man of about thirty, eyes narrowed at the camera, cigarette between his lips, and a young blond woman whose face was averted from both him and the camera. Judging by their smart dress and the flower arrangements in the background, Tabby judged it to be a reportage-style wedding shot. She would not immediately have known the woman was Emmie had it not been for the dress being the very one she'd worn last weekend, and the similar heavy style of eye make-up. The girl in the photo was rather younger and slenderer, captured in sudden motion as she turned, tresses of hair obscuring the lower part of her face. Her hair was shoulder-length and pale blond, almost platinum-blond, and curled in the 1950s way of Grace Kelly or Lauren Bacall or one of those old movie stars. Tabby peered more closely, admiring the elegance of the dress on Emmie's leaner frame. It fitted her better here, *suited* her better.

'Hard to believe it's me, eh?'

She started at the sound of Emmie's voice at the foot of the stairs, giving a little gasp and flushing deeply. She had not heard her footsteps on the stairs, supposed the failure of power must have interrupted her bath. 'Sorry about the lights,' Tabby said helplessly. 'I hope you don't mind ...' She held out the photo for Emmie to take. 'I didn't mean to be nosy. It was sticking out of the folder and I couldn't help recognising the dress from last week ...'

It was an obvious lie, but Emmie did not challenge her, taking the picture from her but staying close to Tabby so they could both study it. She marvelled at her own image.

'You look very different,' Tabby said, unnecessarily. 'Your hair's so blond.'

'Yes. I needed a total change of style.'

Tabby wasn't sure if she meant before or after the photo was taken; certainly there'd been a drastic rethink since, for there was no doubt that the current Emmie was far drabber than this glamorous creature and had gained a fair amount of weight. Then Tabby noticed another detail: in the picture, Emmie held a cigarette at hip height – the camera had caught a curl of smoke from its end – and she recalled how Emmie had hardly been out two minutes before she'd wanted to run off and buy cigarettes. They said reformed smokers were more likely to relapse in the company of old smoking buddies; perhaps clothes could have a similar effect? Had she and Emmie not fallen into that silly argument about the men at the next table, what other old habits might she have revived? What confidences might she have been persuaded to share?

There was a pause and then Emmie said, 'I know, I know . . .' and the pleasure in her voice made Tabby turn in surprise to her. Sometimes Emmie seemed to have the ability to read her mind: she'd give an answer to a comment Tabby had only thought, and then they'd continue without needing to mention the fact. But this time Emmie had pre-empted wrongly: she wore exactly the expression of someone who'd just been paid a delightful compliment and was modestly deflecting it.

'You look fantastic when you dress up,' Tabby said belatedly. 'Really glamorous. Like I say, I'm not sure I would have recognised you if it weren't for the dress. Who took the picture? Are you at a wedding or something? Is that an old boyfriend you're with?' As an attempt to get Emmie to tell her more about her failed love affair, the 'badness' that had ended it, it was a typically unsuccessful one and Emmie merely sighed, slipping the photograph back into the folder and taking it with her towards the stairs.

'Sorry,' Tabby said to her receding figure. 'I know I said I wouldn't ask.'

When Emmie came back down later and the two ate supper together, there was something subtly different about her, a difference that became more defined as the evening wore on: self-importance, perhaps even vanity. Tabby could be wrong, of course – Lord knew she was not the best judge of character – but she thought she detected in Emmie's eyes the faint, counterintuitive sense that she was, for the first time, enjoying Tabby's curiosity.

Such was the power of this instinct that Tabby began to convince herself that Emmie had left the photograph lying around deliberately and that the reason for this was in some way connected with Tabby's liaison with Grégoire that afternoon. It was as if she needed to let Tabby know that she had once been the attractive one, the one propositioned in shops and bedded in secret assignations.

But that made no sense at all. It had to be guilt giving her strange ideas. For fear of provoking disapproval, she had not told Emmie about meeting Grégoire again and she could think of no other way of her knowing. Yes, Tabby had borrowed her phone to text him, but she had deleted the message just as soon as she'd sent it, and in any case it had contained only the address of the house on rue du Rempart and the time that he should come. Emmie was not a witch or a clairvoyant. Additionally, she had not left the photograph lying face-up; Tabby had pulled it from the folder and in doing so had invaded Emmie's closely guarded privacy, just as she had the night they'd met.

Something *had* shifted in Emmie this evening, though. However quick she had been to shut down interrogation, however able she was to compartmentalise those experiences that had led her to leave England (if nothing else, the photograph showed that at some point since she had radically altered her appearance, and everyone knew that people did that when they'd suffered some kind of trauma), that sigh of hers had been the sigh of a person accustomed to inspiring intrigue.

A person who did not wish to go on resisting other people's questions for ever.

Chapter 12

Emily

I was intensely curious about Arthur's house. It was on the uphill part of the Grove, the 'right' end (though there was hardly a wrong one), one of a row built for a better class of Georgian than the rest and now inhabited by a better class of Elizabethan. Having adjusted my route to work to pass it every day, I would steal long looks through the ground-floor windows, though there was disappointingly little to be glimpsed and nothing that ever altered. You could see a portion of book-lined wall, a standard feature on the street, a corner of a high-backed chestnut leather chair, and the pale stiff shade of a standard lamp. The curtains were of some dark, heavy fabric and possibly silk-lined – in any case, they were rarely pulled shut; the tops of a pair of blinds were also just visible. Arthur told me this room was his study, the kitchen and family room being, like the Laings', below, and the whole of the first floor – with a trio of tall polished windows and vivid flowerboxes at the front – used as a formal sitting room. The bedrooms and bathrooms were on the two floors above, while in the garden was Sylvie's studio (she made hand-decorated greetings cards, I had learned, and sold them at craft fairs and school fund-raisers).

I should say here that I never once aspired to taking possession of this house, of kicking Sylvie out of her side of the marital bed and installing myself in her place – that would have been unthinkable on every level. I may have signed that rental lease for 199 with naïve dreams of sharing the grand and romantic identity of the street, but I was an outsider here, even in my own flat. In any case, the deeper my love for Arthur grew, the less I cared about either my neighbourhood or my status within it. When I imagined us in our new life, it was in a small cottage outside the city, with stone walls, square windows, a spray of wisteria, the classic childhood home I had always dreamed of.

Of course, my enemies would argue that I thought in these terms because Arthur was a father figure to me, as if there is something evil or perverse in that. But why should there be? Why should a lover not also be caring and protective? Do young women really want what I had with Matt, the initial thrill of the chase replaced all too soon by a casual neutrality whereby he called me 'mate' and prided himself on evading any 'traps' I might set for him? Was it really such a surprise that I responded to being treasured and adored by someone older?

'*Please* can I see your house,' I'd say to Arthur. 'When she's out for the day or down in Sussex. Just a five-minute tour. It's hard to know someone properly without seeing where he lives.'

'I live at work,' he would say wryly.

I wasn't serious, in any case. I knew it was too dangerous. Having lived on the Grove for twenty years, he and Sylvie knew everyone there worth knowing. If Ed or Nina Meeks, who lived opposite, did not see me entering the Woodhalls', then someone else would and word would get back to Sylvie, if not directly then indirectly.

So it was quite a surprise when at last I got my invitation. In the middle of July, with exams over and school finished, Sylvie and the boys left to spend the summer in the house in Sussex. They would be away for six weeks, Arthur said, as had been the family's custom since they'd bought the house ten years ago. Sylvie had a sister there and liked to blow away the cobwebs on long coastal walks, while the boys swam and sailed and, these days, partied with their cousins and friends in the village. Arthur was to join them for weekends when he could, as well as for ten days at the end of August. September had been discussed as a possible time for him to break the news to her that he was leaving; after Alexander had departed on his travels.

I did not allow myself to doubt the likelihood of this, nor did I dwell on how I might endure our time apart, but instead I concentrated on enjoying how available he was to me in the present. As experiences of being 'the other woman' went, this was freedom untold: in the first week, we went out for dinner twice in the West End, and spent a night in a hotel in Covent Garden. We had never been more besotted with one another.

On the second Friday, he phoned me in the evening. 'I'm home early. Can you meet?'

'Yes.' I always said yes. I had learned early on that to contrive to be unavailable was only to cut off my nose to spite my face. And since I was already home from work, there was no need for the anxious invention of some emergency in order to hoodwink Charlotte into releasing me early. All those sudden sicknesses and last-minute days off I'd been taking were beginning to stack up.

'The thing is, the Crescent's fully booked.' This was the hotel we'd been using since the Inn on the Hill had been declared high-risk. 'We could go into town again?'

'Come here,' I suggested. 'Saves us both travelling in.' And out again – separately, in both directions. 'We could take a chance just this once: Sarah's away, I saw her leave earlier.'

Until then, my flat had remained frustratingly out of bounds. Though Matt was gone, there remained the issue of the Laings, more precisely Sarah, who worked from home around her children's hours and seemed always to be getting into or out of her huge black Range-Rover to take one of them one place or collect the other from another, even late into the evenings. Since the babysitting episode I'd had no further run-ins with her, but I rarely arrived or departed without the sensation of being observed. Having learned from her daughter that, irritatingly, the family was not going on holiday until the very day Arthur was due to join Sylvie in Sussex, I had given up on the possibility of him sneaking up to see me – until that afternoon, when I'd seen Sarah and the kids heading for the car with overnight bags. My hopes for a lucky break were confirmed when I heard the girl say she would miss Misty – their family cat – and Sarah reply, 'We'll be back tomorrow afternoon, you'll see her again then.'

Relaying this now to Arthur, I was amazed when he responded, 'You're right, we can take a risk for once. Why don't you come to me?'

'To you? Are you sure? What about—?'

'Ed and Nina left this morning for a birthday party in Italy. I don't know about the other neighbours, but carry a book or something, just in case. Then if anyone mentions seeing you to Sylvie I can say you were returning something I lent you.'

He had in fact lent me an NHS document about Alzheimer's and I held this in my arms, feeling like a student visiting her professor with an assignment to be marked. It was a bright, still evening and the street was gold and green, its beauty silent and heightened, as if special-effects had cleansed the walls and paths of any marks or sounds of human imperfection. It stirred in me the most joyful reprise of the epiphany I'd had in Arthur's car coming home from the hospital: I would not worry about the future, either in terms of my father's illness or my affair with

Arthur, but would live for the day, for the moment, and on this day at this moment I was lucky enough to be walking up one of the most beautiful streets in London towards the house of the man I loved. After all, I could be run over and killed before the night was over – would I like to think I'd spent my final hours second-guessing the travel plans of Sarah Laing or Nina Meeks, two women I hardly knew and who both loathed me? (Ironically, by basing herself in Sussex, Sylvie Woodhall was the only person making life easy for Arthur and me.)

I was in a state of exhilaration by the time I turned in to his gate, leaping up the steps and reaching for the bell with childlike glee. But the effects quickly faded when Arthur answered the door, a grudging smile on his lips, primed for any watching eyes and listening ears.

'Emily, hello. You found it, did you? Excellent. Come and have a coffee while you tell me what you think.' He acted so convincingly, I forgot that we were lovers, and though he kissed me the moment the door closed behind us, it fell well short of the welcome I received when I joined him in the hotel room – a frantic assault of lust, a proclamation that the wait had been far too long to bear. Instead he broke off almost at once, telling me he'd show me the house 'first'. As he led me from room to room, he was a diffident tour guide and my admiring comments began to be replaced by a fretting disappointment at that 'first' of his, his assumption that I was here for sex, at his service, for ever the easy conquest.

It was a lovely house, though, it really was. Whoever owns it now is to be envied, just as the Woodhalls once were. It didn't have the self-conscious dramatic touches of Sarah's, but was more casual, even dated, with clusters of sofas and arm-chairs in every space, antique rugs on the oak floors, everything cranberry and yellow and other warm hues. It was not hard to imagine the two teenage boys and their friends stretched on the huge mustard sofas in the family room, or Sylvie cooking at the double range in the kitchen, her dinner guests drinking wine at the beautiful rear window overlooking the lawn. Her garden studio, a painted wooden cabin in the New England style, was just what I dreamed of in my fantasies about starting to write.

'I like this room best,' I said of Arthur's study. There were photographs on his desk, but otherwise there was little evidence of the other three members of the family. I noticed that the blinds had been rolled down. All those times I'd passed, I'd never seen them in use, I'd been able to look in, but now I was inside I was not permitted to look out. Ridiculously, tears bubbled at my eyes at the thought that he was concealing me. I knew it was only necessary caution, but it felt like shame.

He released my hand then – it seemed to me as if to signal the end of the pretence that this site visit was anything but ill-conceived. 'Let's go upstairs,' he said, and it was the first time I'd seen him subdued and distracted like this; I knew his misgivings must be serious. Until then, I had never considered how it might be for him to see me in his home, only how I might react to being in it, but had I done I would have guessed there was a risk of his being so struck by the wrongness of it, it might shake his conviction about us. As for *my* reaction, I had scarcely prepared any better for that: would seeing the family photographs that chronicled two decades of another woman's possession of him make horribly true what had always been my suspicion, that the idea of him leaving had never been anything but fantasy, like an invalid planning the round-the-world adventure he knew, deep down, he would never take?

Following him up the stairs, I felt a certain despair that these thoughts had occurred so late, a despair that only grew when the tour came to an end at the open door of a bedroom, just as he'd assumed, a guest bedroom on the second floor. Only as we were closing the door behind us did I reach the logical conclusion that one or both of us might not relish sleeping with the

171

other this evening, one or both of us might find it so distasteful we might want to terminate the affair there and then. In fact, one of us might already have decided to do so, allowing himself one last congress for old times' sake. So convinced was I suddenly that this was the case that even as we slipped under the covers (smooth and cool with disuse), even as we made love quietly and quickly, as if the house were not empty at all but full of people suspicious of our activities and likely to spring at any moment, even then I felt like crying. My eyes kept finding our clothes, normally abandoned without care but this time piled on a single chair by the bed, the better to access in the emergency change of heart that I expected to be announced within minutes of our breaking our bodies apart and recovering our breath.

'You didn't enjoy that,' Arthur said, an acknowledgement, not a question.

'I feel funny being here.' I can't relax, I added, silently, knowing I'm about to go to the gallows. I felt a shiver at the back of my neck.

'I've got some news,' he said with ghastly timing.

'Oh yes?' As the first tear caught in my eyelashes, I did not at first understand what he said when he said it.

'I think I've found somewhere for us to go.'

'You mean a new hotel?' We were both half whispering, as if defying hidden microphones.

'No, I mean properly, somewhere to live together when I move out.'

My heart bounced so hard he must have felt the impact through our ribcages. 'When you move out?'

He pressed me to him closer still. 'Yes. It's just temporary, but a friend of mine at the clinic in town lives out in Hampshire and has a flat in Marylebone for when he's up here. He and the family are away for the whole of August and he's going to give me the keys. We'll have a month to find somewhere else, but in the meantime we'll be together. It's a nice place, in one of the mansion blocks near the High Street. If we like it, we can maybe look for a place nearby. It's as good a base as any while we decide where we want to live long-term, and while the lawyers work out what budget there is for a new place.'

I gaped, joy clenched in the tight fist of shock. 'You mean ... you mean you're going to leave her now, this summer, while she's in Sussex?'

'Yes. It's time. I'll go down tomorrow and tell her. Talk to the boys. Their exams are all done, Alex is off to South America in a couple of weeks – what difference does it make if I wait for him to get on a plane? And Hugo: we understand each other, I'm sure he'll handle it better than anyone. In many ways it's the best time for Sylvie, as well. She'll be near her family, won't have to explain to anyone what's happened until she gets back.'

'My God.' I was flabbergasted. How could my instincts have been so poor? 'Marylebone? I assumed that if it happened ... well, I thought you would just move in with me at first.'

Arthur frowned. 'Oh no, I can't stay on the Grove – and nor can you, darling. Sylvie knows every last soul here and they'll all take her side. We'd both be lynched. And don't forget Hugo will still be at school. I couldn't have him seeing us together in his own neighbourhood, it would be cruel.' Now he said it, it was obvious.

'I'll need to give notice on the flat,' I said. This I had been about to do whether Arthur left Sylvie or not; I could not afford it on my own for much longer.

He nodded. 'It'll be useful to have it for storage for a few weeks. There's not much space in the Marylebone place.'

The shock was loosening its grip, allowing euphoria to seep into the air. 'Are you sure, Arthur? Are you really ready to leave all this?'

'Yes. Actually, seeing you here has confirmed it.'

'Really?'

'Life doesn't last for ever, and I want to spend the rest of mine with you. I'm not prepared to risk you leaving me by constantly delaying. You'll lose heart, I can tell. Besides, there'll never be a perfect time to do this; people will be just as upset if it's tomorrow or ten years from now. The way I see it, now is as imperfect a time as any.'

'Gosh.'

'I know, gosh. You're pleased, aren't you?'

'Of course I am, I'm overjoyed.'

He kissed me hard. 'I can't wait to have you in my bed every night.'

'Nor can I.' I was light-headed with pleasure.

'I hope you can bear with me these next few months,' Arthur said. 'I'm going to get hell from all directions. There'll be an enormous amount to sort out with lawyers and accountants. Sylvie will get both families in her camp, God knows what they'll dream up to punish me . . .' He breathed a heavy, anticipatory sigh. 'But let's not worry about any of that tonight. We need champagne,' he added, smiling.

'Absolutely!' But I didn't really expect to celebrate the theft of another woman's husband in her own house, using her best crystal flutes.

'I'll nip out and get a bottle.'

'Oh, you don't have to go out, Arthur. Ordinary wine will do. Anything. A beer?'

'I'll still have to go. There's no alcohol in the house.'

'Isn't there?' I was astonished. I had imagined a climate-controlled cellar, its racks creaking with expertly collected bottles from the vineyards of Bordeaux; I had imagined dinner parties at the old farmhouse table for other hospital consultants and their wives, everyone knowledgeable about the various grapes and vintages.

'Sylvie used to have a bit of a problem,' Arthur said, out of bed now and buttoning his shirt. 'She's fine now, just has a glass occasionally when she's out, but it's easier for her to control if there's nothing in the house. She doesn't want the boys drinking at home, either. She worries about the example she set when they were younger and so she's very strict about it.'

'Oh, I didn't realise.' Now I understood why Sarah had given Sylvie water that night while the rest of us had wine, why she'd wanted to cut down on entertaining, what she and Nina had been joking about in the café the first time I saw her. Again, I noted how admirably discreet Arthur had been about her frailties; throughout the months of our relationship he had rarely complained about any personal faults of hers, only of his own, or of the general, natural decline of a long marriage. I wished I had been so gracious in my own assessment of her.

'Back in a few minutes,' he said. 'Stay where you are.' Naked, he meant. Ready to be ravished again the moment he returned – and this time I *would* enjoy it.

Left alone, I spent a minute or two exulting in the knowledge that this was it: we were going to be together, and far, far sooner than I had allowed myself to believe. I remembered our very first time together, Arthur's comment, '*I* pursued *you*' – and now it was he who was driving this, too. He wanted this as fervently as I did. Later, should guilt play a greater part than it did now, that would help me, I knew. I should not want to think that I had wheedled and manipulated a man into leaving his family.

I needed the loo. Defying orders and pulling on my dress over bare skin, I left the room and paused on the landing, trying to remember which the door to the bathroom was. Directly ahead was the master suite, which had not been included on my tour, but I resisted the temptation to explore for signs of marital intimacy (admittedly, I took a step inside the door, but after one glance at the large taupe and blue bed, the tan leather armchairs and deep-pile rugs, lost my nerve and retreated). Disingenuous as it may sound – and frankly unbelievable given all that happened next – my thought was that if Arthur could still treat his wife with respect, then so should I.

Returning to the guest room, I found my handbag and checked my phone, noticing I'd missed several calls from a number I did not recognise. I dialled it at once. Because of the situation with Dad, I did this routinely with any unknown number: it wasn't impossible that a member of the hospital staff was calling me from his or her own mobile phone or that Phil, who I knew was visiting that day, had forgotten his and asked to borrow one to call me.

'Hello? This is Emily Marr.' Bracing myself for cheerless news, I suppressed the brightness in my voice. I was practised now in the manual adjustments required when descending from the soaring heights of time with Arthur (and *this* time more than any!) to the lower altitudes of a distressed child at work or, as now, a concerned hospital orderly in Dad's unit. 'I think you've been trying to get hold of me?'

'Emily. Thank you for calling me back.'

I knew before she gave her name that it was her. A fraction of a second later, I had guessed that she'd got my number from Sarah. Sarah, or any one of the other neighbours Arthur had mentioned, must have been recruited to track my comings and goings while she was away and, having seen us together over the last two weeks, had duly reported to her. She was one step ahead of us, after all. I cursed myself, cursed Sarah, bloody, nosy, social-climbing Sarah.

'Sylvie Woodhall. We met at Sarah's house, if you remember?' Her tone was one of controlled determination rather than antagonism.

'Yes, of course. How can I—?' I began, hoping I did not sound as choked by cowardice as I felt, but she interrupted at once.

'You know why I'm phoning, so please don't waste your

time or mine pretending you don't. I know about you and Arthur.'

My innards twisted in fear. She knew. Of course she knew. My thoughts blundered forward: when she heard he was leaving her she would take every penny he had and leave us in penury; she would forbid him to see his sons (or if that wasn't legally possible, given their ages, then heavily influence them against him); she would ruin his life, all our lives. Or ... or she would make him change his mind and ruin only mine.

'I know you're in my house,' she said.

Instantly I was returned to the present, the crisis escalated to a catastrophe. How could she possibly know I was in her house? My chest burned and my head roared, mobbed by new terrors: what if she were no longer in Sussex but here, in London, in this street? What if she'd been watching my flat herself, or even her own house; she'd been at Sarah's window or Nina's, waiting to catch us in the act. The insanity grew: what if ... what if she were here in the house, had been all evening? What if she were hiding somewhere, in one of the bedrooms I had not seen, waiting for an opportunity to get me on my own, and was now going to come into the room and kill me? But I was not so deranged as not to see the absurdity of this last scenario. There was no one here but me.

Come back, Arthur, I pleaded silently. I imagined him held up in a queue, celebratory champagne in hand, perhaps in the very off-licence where we'd made our first treacherous plan to be together.

Composing myself was out of the question, but I did remember to breathe, which allowed me to say, 'How do you know where I am? Where are *you*?'

'I'm where I'm supposed to be – which is more than can be said for anyone else in this tawdry little affair. You may have made yourself at home on my street, but I've been there a lot longer than you have. I have a lot of friends, Emily, and I know you've been seeing him while I've been away.' So she thought our affair was brand-new, I calculated, fractionally relieved; just a dalliance while she was out of town. But this hope was extinguished seconds later when she continued: 'I know you've been sleeping with him for months, that you used to go to the Inn on the Hill. I know your boyfriend moved out. I know everything.'

I was barely able to keep track of her pronouncements, much less consider the best way to respond to them. What did an intervention *this* appalling call for? Denial, placation, full confession followed by a plea for forgiveness? Bravado, the assertion that it didn't matter what she said because she was too late? And what about Arthur, who *would* return sooner or later: should I hang up and conceal this horror from him or should I hand over the phone and let him answer for me?

'Are you still there?' she asked.

'Yes.'

'Is *he* there? In the room with you?'

'No.' So – for what it was worth – her informant knew I'd gone in but not that Arthur had gone out.

'Good. In that case, I'll get on with what I phoned to say.'

Did the previous onslaught not count, then? I lowered myself on to the bed, the first debilitating effects of her ambush subsiding a little.

'I'm only going to ask this once,' she said. 'I won't ask it again.'

'Ask what?'

'Call it off, Emily. Break up with him. Tonight.'

That took me aback. 'What?'

'I said end it. *He* won't, I know that for a fact.'

'I don't—'

'No, hear me out, please. I'm completely serious. If you have any respect for your own gender, if you have any compassion for two children who've done nothing to deserve their father's disloyalty, then call it off and let him be with his family – at least until Hugo has finished school next year. One year, Emily, and then after that it's every woman for herself.'

This bamboozled me in an entirely new and alarming way: she was speaking as if she already knew he'd decided to leave her, had heard the plan about the Marylebone flat made between these covers only twenty minutes earlier, and yet how could she? *Could* the room be bugged? Was *that* how she knew I was here? Did ordinary people do that sort of thing?

'What makes you think he's so serious about me, anyhow?' I stammered, hoping she would reveal more about her methods of surveillance.

'Oh, I know, all right. He's cheated on me before, you may be surprised to hear – I don't suppose he's advertised his faults.' Oh, he has, I thought, there's no deception between *us*. 'But this is different. I know him better than anyone and I can tell he's ready to go.' With these words she became the first person to acknowledge the strength of Arthur's love for me, the first person outside of the two of us to have had the opportunity to do so, and it was enough to draw from me the feeling she was demanding, to experience it nauseously deep in my stomach: a direct connection to her pain. She loved him as I did; my happiness existed only at the expense of hers.

'It's not up to me what he does,' I said at last, and with genuine humility. 'He has to make his own decisions, surely?'

'I disagree. Not this one. I think you and I can make it between us. One year, that's all I ask, Emily, twelve months. You're young, it's nothing to you. Hugo will be eighteen then, he'll have left school. Let him have his father for the rest of his childhood, let us wave him off to his adult life as a family. Don't you think Arthur owes his son that?'

I hesitated. There was an element of performance to this last statement, it was too word-perfect to be off the cuff, I thought. What was more, her argument had a definite strategy to it: she was deliberately confusing me by appearing to empower me

179

with the crucial choice in this, when there was only one outcome that would satisfy her. Of her own two options in this situation – that she let him go or she found a way to keep him – she had fixed upon a compromise: she kept him for a year and then she let him go. But *I* had to choose it for her. The grinding pressure of my sympathies lessened somewhat.

'He's already grown up,' I pointed out. 'What difference would it make if he's seventeen or eighteen?'

'It makes a crucial difference. While he's still living at home, he needs his father here. This period is so important – I know because I've just been through it with Alex.' Her tone was becoming more impassioned, making me wonder what events she had weathered with her elder son, and whether Arthur had weathered them with her or withdrawn to the shelter of his work, of me. If the latter, then how much practical use was he to her even if he did stay? 'His brother won't be here, that will be a huge factor, and if Arthur is thinking of going too . . .' She faltered for the first time, openly emotional, and I had no more idea how to counter this than I had her previous briskness. The ache in her voice, even disembodied like this, was hard to bear.

Then she rallied once more, her tone sharper: 'I will not watch him fall apart over exams and university applications just because his father would prefer to up sticks and start all over again with some tart. How do you think that would make him feel? Can someone like you even imagine that?'

'I don't know.' But, released perhaps by evidence of her renewed antipathy – *some tart, someone like you* – a current of delight was outpacing more complicated emotions: the implication that Arthur might want to start a family with me. What had he said, that time? 'I'm trying to do right all the things I did wrong before.'

'Twelve months,' Sylvie repeated. 'And then I will step aside. I will put it in writing if that's what you want. I'm *begging* you, Emily.'

180

Begging? And she was, she was on her knees here, a woman whose own desires had been subjugated by a primitive necessity to protect her family. Only she could judge whether her seventeen-year-old son counted as a minor or not; I could only refer to my own parenting at that age – Dad had treated me as an adult, someone to be respected and consulted – and wonder if there was not a parallel here worth considering. Phil was two years older than me, which meant he had left home when I was even younger than Hugo Woodhall, and yet I had remained with a single parent perfectly securely. The same had to be true for thousands of families. What was so special about Sylvie's? Was it because she was wealthy and grand and thought herself better than people like me? Coming to my senses, I considered what it was she was actually asking. Twelve months. No contact with Arthur until the following summer. But a year without him was a life sentence; I would not survive it.

'Look,' I said, in as reasonable a tone as I could muster, 'I know I'm the villain here, I admit that, but it doesn't stop me from feeling just as strongly about my position as you do yours. You're wrong to use the boys to make me feel bad. Half their friends must have parents who are divorced. They can handle it, plenty of people do. I didn't have a mother for half of my childhood, in case it's of any interest to you – I don't suppose it is. The point is, this is not about them, it's about you and him and me. Only Arthur can decide which of us he wants to be with and it will make no difference to how he feels about his sons. He loves them more than either of us, which is how it should be.'

I stopped myself from saying any more, conscious that I was now doing precisely what I'd just argued I could not: speaking for Arthur. My speech had felled her, though. Even before I heard her voice again, I sensed the re-emergence of the Sylvie I'd seen at Sarah's kitchen table and in the café that time: not the

181

strong, selfless negotiator that she'd set out to present at the start of this conversation but a spent force, a casualty of the changed hearts of others.

'How can you be so selfish?' she said at last. 'How can you not see what is the right thing to do in this situation?'

'How can *you* not, Sylvie? As you said yourself, it's every woman for herself, isn't it?' And I took no pleasure in saying this, none whatsoever, but only felt wretched, exhausted. I meant it, though, for Sylvie and I were, in our own ways, equally selfish, equally at Arthur's mercy.

It was only when she didn't reply that I realised she had hung up.

In the few minutes that followed, before I heard the sound of Arthur's footsteps below, I tried to wade a path through a maelstrom of thoughts. That earlier joy in his promise that he was going to be mine – even his wife had seen the imminence of the transfer of power – had been replaced by terror that he might never make good on it. Moments later, however, this had reduced to a remote, slightly shameful thrill, as if I were watching a reconstruction on television; then, by the time Arthur appeared in the bedroom doorway, bottle and glasses in hand, a plunge into near-despair.

'Thirsty?'

'Yes, very.' I didn't tell him about the phone call at once, which meant I was not going to tell him at all. He sensed, of course, that there was something wrong.

'What is it, darling?'

'Nothing, I'm just a bit overwhelmed by everything.'

'I can see that. You're shaking.' He held me, kissing me. 'You genuinely didn't think I would do it, did you?'

'You haven't done it yet,' I pointed out.

'But after tomorrow I will have. I've just left a message for Sylvie saying to expect me in the afternoon and to make sure the boys are about so I can talk to them as well.'

My heart stuttered. I feared I might vomit. 'You didn't speak to her direct?'

'She was on the line to someone else. But it will all be over by tomorrow night. I'll call you from the car when I'm on my way back home.'

'You think you'll be back tomorrow? So soon?'

'I can't see her wanting me to stay the night. If I do, if it's more drawn-out than I'm expecting, then I'll see you some time on Sunday.'

To my surprise – and his – I broke into sobs. 'Phone me as soon as you can, I'll only believe it then. Otherwise I'll think she's persuaded you ...'

As he comforted me, I tried not to think about the other woman who was, almost certainly, weeping at the same time, for the same man, and with no one to say the words he now said to me. 'Please don't be upset, my love. I shouldn't have told you my plan, I should have surprised you afterwards. I know it's hard, I know you feel guilty and scared, but when it's over I'll do everything in my power to protect you from the fallout, I promise. Sleep here tonight,' he murmured, 'I don't want you to go home.'

I shuddered. 'What if she comes back?'

'Why would she?'

'She might ... she might want to see you? When she picks up your message, she might suspect?'

'There's no reason for her to do anything but wait for me there. It's only a matter of hours now.'

'Maybe you're right,' I said. On balance (what little balance I had that night), I decided she would not be back. And even if she did come, maybe it would be better if she found me still here – she already knew I was here, after all, and at least it would put an end to the terrible suspicion that I had misjudged our confrontation, said all the wrong things; that I should have told Arthur about it the moment he appeared in the bedroom doorway. It would have placed the moral responsibility on him; he had the character to deal with it, not me.

Absurdly, it took being on this knife's edge, joy on one side of the blade, terror on the other, to make me understand that this love of ours was never going to be anything but opposed by other people, a source of condemnation and disgrace.

Even when freed to be together, our first task would be to fight the world.

She did not come. Even if he did not have the crucial new information I did, Arthur knew her far better than I and Saturday afternoon was going to be soon enough for her, after all. Her proposal last night had not been a spontaneous act and now she would need time to deliberate her next move. I imagined her on the phone, being prepared for the marital confrontation by Nina or another confidante, perhaps yesterday's trusty informant, who could this morning report to her the respective times of our departures. I wondered how it was possible to hide the crisis from her sons, to make breakfast and plan a day as if there were not every chance that it would be their last as a family. Then I remembered that teenagers, young adults, did not get up for breakfast on holiday. They lived a different shift from their parents, going to bed at three in the morning and sleeping until after lunch. When their father arrived that afternoon, they would probably just be surfacing.

Be brave, Arthur, I thought. They will still love you. I may not have been a parent, but I was still a child, and I knew that a son's love was as indestructible as a father's.

In the morning, we lingered. It was a novelty for us, lingering; it was one of the things I knew separated proper couples from illegitimate ones (there were many, many other things besides, and how I longed to get on with discovering them). I was due at work, but Arthur had a conference call scheduled with the director of his African charity and needed to take that before heading off to Sussex.

At nine, I rang Charlotte. 'I forgot to mention I have a dentist's appointment this morning,' I said.

'You always seem to be forgetting to mention appointments,' she said, in the tone of one who had held her tongue for long enough and would hold it no more. 'What's going on, Emily? It's the school holidays now, we're going to be packed today. You can't just not turn up! Are dentists even open on the weekend?'

I sighed. 'Of course they are. It's just a check-up. I'll be with you by eleven at the latest. And I'll stay late this evening to make up the time.'

'Fine.' But she was furious and I prepared to leave soon after ten, knowing I could not risk being a minute later than the time I'd given.

'This time tomorrow . . .' Arthur said, kissing me goodbye in the hallway.

'This time tomorrow. Good luck.' As I approached the front door, the bell went, startling me with its low, grinding ring and sending me scuttling back to Arthur. 'Is it her?'

'Of course not,' he said. 'She'd use her key, wouldn't she? It can't be the cleaner, it's not one of her days. It'll be a delivery or something. Stay in the study for a minute just in case . . .'

I took his seat at the desk, my heart in my mouth as I listened to him opening the door to the outside world. I noticed the light flashing on his mobile phone, charging on a shelf close to the power socket, and resisted the temptation to check if there was a text or voicemail from her.

'Hello?' Even in those two syllables Arthur's voice was different, though I couldn't immediately identify how. Afterwards, I realised that it was the first time I'd heard him express doubt.

'Good morning, sir, are you Mr Woodhall?' It was a male voice, not one I recognised. 'The husband of Sylvie Woodhall?'

'Yes, that's right. Is anything the matter?'

'I am Police Constable Matthews and this is Family Liaison Officer Louisa Wayne. Please can we come in and talk with you for a few minutes?'

'Of course, yes.'

There were the shuffling sounds of footsteps on tile, the door closing, then a female voice – presumably Officer Wayne – asking very gently, 'Are you here on your own this morning, Mr Woodhall?'

'Yes,' Arthur said, 'I mean no, I have a friend here, but ... What's going on? Is something wrong?'

I was able to get a glimpse of the visitors as they followed him past the doorway, two uniformed officers, the man about my age, the woman older, in her forties. The gait of both was informal enough, but their profiles were tight with some contained emotion, some trained attitude I could not place.

He must have taken them down to the kitchen, close enough for me to hear that conversation was taking place but too far to decipher what was being said. I heard nothing for a minute or two but indistinct voices, then a cry of 'No, oh no!', and then more cries, strange shapeless sounds that carried up the stairs towards me. I didn't recognise the anguish as Arthur's at first, but it slowly dawned on me that it could not belong to either of the officers and that by process of elimination it could only be his.

Everything about this situation pointed to the phrase 'I am sorry to inform you'.

I thought it was just Sylvie. I know 'just' isn't the right word, that it could never be 'just' anyone, and perhaps a clearer way of expressing it is to say that I thought it was Sylvie and I thought that in itself was terrible enough, certainly enough to bring an end to Arthur and me. How could it not? We were as implicated as one another, as guilty. There followed a few seconds, maybe ten, in which I succeeded in suspending reality;

though solidly seated in the chair, I felt myself hang in the air as if weightless, clinging to the last moments of us as we were, us as we'd been going to be but no longer would.

This time tomorrow.

Eventually, when love overcame fear, gravity returned and I got to my feet and left the room, with a last glance towards the two windows I'd passed twice a day since February. The blinds were still drawn; when opened again it would be on to a different world from the one they'd been closed on. I pulled the door silently behind me and walked towards the kitchen, the terrible, unavoidable questions forming on my lips.

Chapter 13

Tabby

Dear Tabby,
   I am very worried about your psychological state and am on the verge of reporting you missing – please get in touch.
   Mum

Oh, for goodness' sake, Tabby thought. Her 'psychological state'? Since when had her mother cared about *that*?

Emails from Elaine had arrived sporadically during her travels, at first chatty bulletins about family and friends, her work and, of course, her perverted husband, but in recent weeks, while Tabby had been offline, it appeared that they had contracted to urgent pleas for her to get in touch – or risk becoming a matter for Interpol.

Tabby sighed. She had enjoyed her spell without technology more than she might have expected: no communication with her mother, no Facebook with old friends whose lives appeared to have none of the troughs of hers, no glances at the British news headlines – war might have broken out and she would be completely in the dark. Then Moira had told her about a bureau in a shopping street off the market car park where you could pay to use a PC by the hour. Its opening hours were irregular, however, and she'd only managed to get online at last this evening, a Friday night in July.

She had had no illusions as to what she was hoping to find when her new email appeared on screen, the *only* thing: Paul's name. But it was not there. Of course it was not there. She was history, wasn't she? *I've tried to tell you before, but you never get the message.* And there was no new message now. Scanning her inbox a second time, even a third, did not make one magically appear.

She typed her mother the necessary reply: *Am alive. Still in France. No need for drama.*

Once or twice this last year she had considered putting it all down in writing, the distress Steve had caused her, sharing it with Elaine while she was in a position to avoid the repercussions. But each time she would decide against it: chances were, there would *be* no repercussions, except possibly to smother what little was left of the parent-daughter relationship. One day, she might wish her own children to know their grandmother (though, under no circumstances, their step-grandfather). And what was the point in any case when the bathroom incident, which had been the worst, had been dismissed out of hand as an embarrassing blunder?

For Steve had not, in the end, ever actually touched her. Who was going to believe that the effect his attentions had had on her had been so profound that by the time she left for college she hardly uttered a word at home and had developed a compulsion for privacy that bled into the rest of her life? In the sixth form, while her friends had dressed in sexually provocative ways, imitating their celebrity heroes as teenagers their age usually did, Tabby, with someone in her home all too easily provoked, dressed as unglamorously as possible and kept her hair boyishly short.

'You know Elaine's worried you might be a dyke,' Steve told her. '*I* know you're not. You could wear sackcloth and you

189

couldn't hide what you've got. Your body is unbelievable, it's a crime against red-blooded males to cover it up the way you do. Tell me what you get up to with that boyfriend of yours, tell me every detail.'

And: 'Come on, it's summer, it's way too hot for all those clothes. Put your bikini on and sunbathe in the garden. You can take your top off if you like, don't mind me.'

And: 'Getting excited, are you? Am I getting you nice and wet?'

'I'm not listening,' she would say, if she said anything at all. She would try not to show her distress, but he could sense it just the same. And even when she turned away she could still feel those horrible sliding looks that groped no differently from fingers.

They married, of course, Steve and her mother. The confusing thing was that he seemed genuinely to love Elaine, treated her perfectly well, which was part of what made it so impossible for Tabby to tell.

'You could try and look happy for me,' her mother said, the morning of the wedding. 'Please don't ruin today for me, Tabby.'

Somehow the pestered adolescent had become the killjoy, the toxic teenager every parent dreaded, the one who slunk around in glum self-absorption, plotting to ruin weddings. She heard them sometimes laughing about her. *Laughing*.

At least their marriage won her a two-week break from them, when they went to Spain for their honeymoon. Steve was scrupulous about leaving no trail, there were never texts or voicemails or emails while he was away, anything that she could take to her mother – or any other authority – as evidence. She fantasised sometimes about buying surveillance equipment, but it was clear she could not afford concealable cameras or microphones. She considered using her mobile phone to record his harassment, but it was too obvious: the moment she reached into her pocket or bag he would simply change the subject to something legitimate – 'How's the geography essay going?' – or stop speaking altogether.

No, she would never tell now. Nothing had actually happened, and actual happenings were the only things people took seriously; anything else could be considered imaginary. And it was more than likely that Steve had long ago pre-empted any complaints by reporting it all himself, his version of events, in which he'd recast Tabby as the temptress and himself as the victim, the one made to feel hunted in his own home. How easily he could have sent himself a suggestive message from Tabby's phone and stored it for use in the event of a confrontation. It was ancient history, anyhow, seven years had passed since she'd last slept under the same roof as him and her mother – what good would it do to audit her unhappiness now? She could just hear her mother saying to her friends, 'I know she's my daughter, but it's just as well she's out of the country. Even before her father died she was a handful. An overactive imagination, that's the problem.'

Having paid for an hour's internet use, she thought she might Google Grégoire, but she could not remember his surname. He was a doctor in Paris but she did not know which hospital, only that he specialised in allergies and immunology. It was too hard to understand in French.

Reminding herself of her epiphany that her life's purpose should not be so easily interchanged with the seeking of male approval, she sat for a minute or two furiously denying further thought of any of the men who routinely troubled her thoughts. Then she tapped instead the words 'Emmie Mason'.

It was a common name, it turned out, more common than she'd thought, judging by the thousands of results. The first few pages referred to an artist, a songwriter and a cross-country runner of the same name; there was also a headmistress, a florist, a dentist, an environmentalist interested in homesteading (whatever that was), not to mention the dozens more who populated the business networking sites, often known simply as 'Em' or 'Emi'. Not surprisingly, a scan of image results yielded no photograph of her Emmie, either in the current low-key incarnation or in the earlier more head-turning blond guise she'd glimpsed in the mystery photograph. She even tried 'Emmie Mason London' and 'Emmie Mason France', only to be faced with millions of possibilities where the words were combined. Her Emmie was the needle in the haystack, perhaps not even stuck in the haystack at all.

Well, it was hardly surprising, given the innate elusiveness of Emmie. She wouldn't have been surprised if it was like one of those film plots when you woke up and found your friend gone, only to discover you were the only person who thought she'd existed in the first place, everyone else insisting they'd never laid eyes on her. You then had to find a maverick detective to help you figure out if she were ever real or just a figment of your imagination, a ghost you'd created for company.

But no, that could not happen here. No matter what her mother might say, she didn't think the authorities need be alerted just yet.

She had ten minutes of her hour left. To torture herself, she reopened her email and read some of the messages Paul had sent her when they were still together and counting down to their trip. They were the memos of a mate, a fellow adventurer: *Twenty-eight days to Full Moon Party!*; *Check out this awesome surfing ashram!* (She never did find out what *that* was.) How easy it was with hindsight to read them as pleas for release. I can't be your father, he'd said, or your mother or your therapist or your friend. I just want to be freed from you.

Then she began to read the messages she'd sent in return. One stood out: *Honestly, Paul, without this trip to look forward to, I think I might go mad.* He'd had no choice but to take her with him. She had made herself his responsibility.

She re-read the last mail she'd sent him, from Paris, before her money ran out: *I still love you and am here if you want to get in touch.* It was the work of a doormat, and yet wasn't it the awful truth that she still meant every feeble-minded syllable of it?

Whatever it was she was doing with Grégoire could make no difference to that.

'Who is this man who has made you so sad?' he asked her the next day, in the master bedroom of the rue du Rempart house. The shutters were, of course, closed.

'You,' Tabby said, teasing.

'No, who?'

'No one. He doesn't matter,' she said, circumstance alone giving her words a temporary and quite credible conviction (how could he matter if she were happy to lie in bed with someone else?). 'He doesn't want me, so ...'

'If he doesn't want you, why do you want him?'

'Oh, come on,' Tabby said. 'Haven't you ever wanted someone who didn't want you? Or wanted her *because* she doesn't want you?' She was aware of sounding rather young, mouthing psychologies she'd read in magazines as opposed to having gained from experience. Luckily, such lack of authenticity was either willingly indulged by Grégoire or lost in translation.

'Never. I think this is cultural differences,' he said, and he shrugged and Tabby laughed, which made him laugh, and this was as serious as things would get between them.

It was an affair now, albeit a seasonal one. They had their routine, their honed subterfuge: early on Friday evening she would text him confirmation of their rendezvous the following day. Since she had finally bought credit for her own phone and no longer needed to borrow Emmie's, she and Grégoire even spoke sometimes, for there was no risk to it. Noémie and the boys being based for the whole summer at the house in Les Portes, he was alone in Paris during the week, joining his family on Friday evenings or – via Tabby – on Saturday afternoons. She did not ask him his cover story, assuming it was simply a matter of his telling his family a false arrival time. If he arrived instead on the Friday, he only had to fabricate some errand to run for a couple of hours the next day. Somehow, his blithe arrogance counteracted any guilt she was experiencing; nonetheless, she liked to think Noémie had her own weekly vanishing act, her own lover in a secret cottage somewhere on the island (though she rather doubted that *her* lover had been hired to clean the cottage first).

Check-in/-out procedures at the cottage also worked in their favour. Though check-out was eleven o'clock – when her own shift would officially start – the owners were Belgian and invariably their tenants were of the same nationality, leaving by nine for the eleven o'clock Brussels flight from La Rochelle. This meant Tabby could arrive early and then extend her 'break' in the middle of the day. The incoming holidaymakers were expected to occupy themselves before checking in at 3 p.m. and the entry system would be disabled until then, so they could not surprise her unannounced. Meanwhile, the owner never visited, bookings and payment taken entirely online, so there was no one for the neighbours to go to with gossip – if there *were* any neighbours who had not let their own property and entrusted its upkeep to a Tabby of their own. As for Moira, she made the occasional spot-check on her cleaners, but according to Emmie she closed shop at midday on Saturday, returning to her home on the mainland for the rest of the weekend. Since Grégoire did not arrive until after twelve, there was minimal chance of discovery.

As a matter of ritual as much as pride Tabby would check every room in turn before pulling the front door shut behind her. The interior shone, the surfaces gleamed, the light danced: the perfect Ile de Ré holiday awaited the approaching Belgians. Call it atonement, recompense, a guilty conscience – she was, if anything, doing a *better* cleaning job than she would have done otherwise.

No one would guess.

Though Moira had praised her as an outstanding worker, Emmie was a less than fastidious cleaner at home and had made no objection when Tabby offered to clean their house once a week as part of her rent.

To avoid disturbing Emmie, she tried to find a time when she was alone in the house, which she approached with the same thoroughness she did her paid jobs. The rooms were comparatively small, but the facilities more dilapidated. The bathroom in particular was in need of renovation, but she liked its worn-and-torn charm, still remembered with pleasure her first bath in it, how magical it had felt to be bathing unhurried, the polished blue sky high above the ancient glass of the skylight.

One thing she was absolutely clear about: she had not volunteered her services in order to snoop. Any search she might make for the purple folder was casual, its failure of no particular disappointment to her.

In Emmie's room she always exercised the utmost restraint as she vacuumed the rug and straightened the items in the drawers and wardrobe. Of course it was impossible not to note, alongside the utilitarian sweatpants and cotton tops, the pretty vintage dress Emmie had worn in the photograph, or the single other smart item in her wardrobe, a black boiled-wool jacket with big covered buttons and a white fur collar. It was in the same retro style as the dress, though far too heavy to be worn in summer weather here.

To do her job properly, it was important to dust the few items on the dressing table, to spray the mirror and polish the glass to a shine. To do this it was necessary to remove the postcard of the painting she had often wondered about, but she would make a point of not turning it over to read the message.

On one occasion, however, entirely by accident, the card fell from her grasp to the floor, landing with the words facing up. It was only a single line of blue ink and – well, she was only human: *For E, my* coup de foudre, *with love, A x* The painting was called *Coup de Foudre*, too, she noticed. She'd heard the term, but could not place it. There was no French–English dictionary in the house, unless you counted Emmie, whose French was fluent, but Tabby could hardly ask her for a translation: she would make the connection straight away, know Tabby had been reading private correspondence. She might not appreciate the coincidental nature of such things; she might think, First the photograph, now this.

She repositioned the postcard, telling herself that she would not give it another thought.

It was Sunday lunchtime and therefore a bit of a risk, but still she texted Grégoire: *What does 'coup de foudre' mean?*

The message came back a little later: *A lightning bolt.*

Then, a minute later, an afterthought: *The English say, love at first sight.*

And she imagined him laughing to himself at the thought of her believing this to be what *they* had, chortling as he stood in the vast kitchen scrubbing mussels with Noémie or dressing the salad, strolling with their kirs on to the sunlit terrace by the pool. No, it made little difference whether he planned to leave his wife or not after the summer (of course he didn't): the point was that if he were legitimately free he would not consider her, Tabby, for a public relationship.

She was no one's lightning bolt.

Chapter 14

Emily

Sylvie and the boys were dead. They'd come off an A-road near Horsham and crashed into a bank of trees. All three suffered fatal head and chest injuries and were pronounced dead at the scene, their bodies taken to the hospital mortuary. Such was the car's speed before the frontal impact crash that it had been described by witnesses in stationary oncoming traffic as terrifyingly over the limit. To have survived it would have been a miracle, and there had been no miracle.

The liaison officer spoke to Arthur with maternal tenderness. 'Were they on their way back to London, do you think? Was that the route she usually took?' I don't think she was pursuing any official inquiry, but was just trying to get him to speak, to say something and engage with the information. He was in shock, anyone could see that, his gaze stark and empty, his skin greyish and dehydrated-looking and his breath faint. I wanted to grip him in my arms, cover his face with my body, speak for him, breathe for him, but I knew instinctively I should not. Since I had joined them in the kitchen, he had scarcely glanced in my direction. Instead I had to rely, as the others were, on the strong, sweet tea he'd been given.

'Do you feel light-headed?' I asked.

'No,' he said in a voice that was no longer his. Like his face, it was devoid of conscious expression. 'They weren't coming back to London.' I realised he was answering the officer's question, not mine. 'They were down there for the summer. I was joining them this afternoon. There was no reason for them to come back, they must have been going out for the morning somewhere.'

The woman said the deaths had been reported to the local coroner, which was normal in the circumstances. He would probably wish to investigate, she said, which meant that registering the deaths and proceeding with the funeral would have to wait until authorisation was received.

'Investigate?' I said, when Arthur failed to query this information. 'What do you mean, the "circumstances"? You just said no other vehicles were involved?'

'Yes, but they don't know how the car came to go off the road the way it did. It might have been any number of factors. It's nothing to worry about, the coroner enquires into all unexplained violent or unnatural deaths, that's his job. An inquiry will establish the facts, the exact cause of death.'

Unexplained ... unnatural ... exact cause ... I knew what she meant, then, and it chilled the blood in my veins: whether the crash had been accidental or deliberate. Arthur, of course, had no cause yet to question the distinction.

'There must have been something wrong with the car,' I said. 'The brakes, maybe? To be driving at ninety or more when the limit was – what did you say?'

'The limit is seventy on that stretch, I believe, but we won't know the exact speed the car was travelling at until after the investigation.'

Officer Matthews added, 'I'm afraid they've had a lot of problems with speeding on that road. A motorcyclist appeared in the magistrate's court recently having been caught at a hundred and thirty miles an hour.'

'God,' I said, shocked. 'Maybe it—'

'Sylvie wouldn't have been speeding,' Arthur said at the same time; it was as if he hadn't heard me begin to speak. 'Not with the boys in the car. You can't compare this with some lunatic Hell's Angel.'

The officers were quick to agree with him, and I realised I should not have drawn the discussion in this direction.

'I need to go to them,' Arthur said. 'I need to talk to the paramedics, the police, someone from the response team at the scene.'

I'd momentarily forgotten that he was a medical professional himself and would know something of the process that awaited him. He put his tea aside as if he meant to leave that very minute. I looked to the police officers for a lead – he couldn't be allowed to travel, not in this shocked condition – but they only nodded their agreement.

'We can arrange for someone to take you,' they said.

'No, I'll drive myself.'

'I'll come with you,' I told him. I'd never learned to drive.

But he looked at me as if I were a stranger, an intruder. 'What? No. No, thank you.' I wondered if he knew my name.

'You can't drive,' I said, fighting sudden tears. 'You can't be alone, either.' I turned to the two officers, telling them my name, not sure if I was introducing or reintroducing myself, for this conversation – time itself – was creasing and stretching in peculiar ways. 'I'll make sure he gets there safely. Do you have an address for the hospital?' I could not say 'mortuary'; my brain could think the word but my voicebox could not produce it. 'We'll take the train. It goes from Victoria, I'm guessing. I'll check.' I'd phone for a taxi to take us to the station, I thought. I'd sit next to him for the whole journey, not let him out of my sight.

But I could see the police officers were uncertain of me, had picked up on Arthur's rejection of me, and neither judged it safe to supply the details. 'If you prefer to make your way separately, that's fine,' Officer Wayne told him, continuing to speak very gently, 'but Emily is right, you shouldn't drive. Is there anyone else you'd like us to contact who might take you? A family member or close friend? We'd be happy to phone them for you and wait with you until they arrive.'

'My brother,' Arthur said. 'He's in north London. He'll take me.'

'What's his name? Is his number in your phone?'

'Yes. Toby Woodhall.'

'Your phone's in the bedroom,' I said. 'I'll get it for you, shall I?' All three of them looked at me then and I regretted having been so specific, not because of the officers, who exhibited a studied lack of judgement in their appreciation of my offer, but because of Arthur, who regarded me with utter bewilderment, as if he couldn't comprehend how an uninvited guest should know the whereabouts of any of his possessions or consider it her business to roam his house. I fetched the phone, grateful to leave the room for a minute, also grateful to see that he'd missed no calls during our night together. However, returning downstairs I remembered the second phone, the one I'd seen recharging in his study. Not sure which held his brother's number, I decided to bring both. As soon as I handled the second one, the display lit up with an alert for two missed calls.

By the time I returned to the kitchen, Arthur's expression had distorted into one of near-revulsion for me. I wanted to protest, remind him that he loved me and I loved him, that we loved each other. I wanted to vow to him that he would survive this tragedy, that one way or another he would continue to live, but I could say none of those things, of course.

He noticed the missed calls at once, fingers finding the itemised log. 'There's a message from Hugo,' he said in a tone of terrible wonder, and I was relieved when the officers suggested he wait a while before listening to any voicemails. Officer Matthews then made the call to Toby, who, I gathered, promised to set off from his house directly. It was agreed that I would take interim guardianship of Arthur and, having offered final condolences, the officers departed. I was moved by how shaken they looked compared with their composure on arrival, even though they must do this every day. But then I thought, no, they don't, they can't. Not this bad. This is exceptional.

After they'd gone, I tried to hold him but his body recoiled, its resistance instinctual, and I knew, as I drew away, it was the last time we would touch. Even without his having been told about my phone call to Sylvie, I just knew. And I was not the only part of him that would be banished; he would never again be as he had been, feel as he had felt.

'I can't bear this for you,' I said. 'I know it's better if you go with Toby, but I can come to you any time if you need me. Tonight, tomorrow ... just say the word. You mustn't be on your own.'

It was an appalling choice of words and he did not reply.

Toby arrived. He was not like his brother at all, but chaotic in personal style and freely expressive of his anguish. 'This is unbelievable,' he kept saying, his voice rising and falling with the strain of an inadequate vocabulary, unpractised emotion. 'Are they sure? I mean, all three of them? Alex and Hugo? Are they absolutely sure?' I did not like to trust him with Arthur's welfare, but I knew I had to.

'I live up the road,' I told him. 'I was bringing back a document your brother lent me and was here when the police arrived.'

Having no reason to know the lie, he thanked me for my kindness and took my number before urging me to leave; he probably thought I was longing to escape and get on with my delayed day.

In my bag my phone rang and rang. It would be Charlotte, but I could not go in to work. I could not guide small children's hands as they applied paintbrush to ceramic, or lead 'Happy

201

Birthday' and call out, 'Hip, hip, hooray!' I could not explain to a mother why her child was snivelling or had lost his shoe. I could not smile hello or wave goodbye.

'Shall I phone you later?' I said to Arthur, hopeful to the last.

His eyes looked blindly towards me, as if he were able only to follow the disembodied sound of me. 'No,' he said, 'don't. Don't phone me.'

I swallowed my sorrow. 'You're right,' I said, as if in agreement. 'I'll wait for you to contact me.'

By the afternoon, the deaths had been reported online. There was nothing like the subsequent coverage of the inquest, only brief references amid warnings of severe traffic disruption and temporary road closures. A single image showed an air ambulance at rest on a ghostly carriageway, two lanes of traffic held behind a barrier and backed up as far as the eye could see. You could not see the wreckage or any other emergency vehicles.

On Monday there was a short piece on the *Telegraph* website, which named the family:

> The wife and two sons of leading Harley Street eye surgeon Arthur Woodhall have been killed in a road accident in Sussex. The coroner has opened an inquiry into the three deaths, which he has referred to the police for investigation on his behalf. Mr Woodhall is noted for his work in neuro-ophthalmology and strabismus, and lists among his patients members of the British and Saudi Royal Families. As well as running an exclusive private practice in Harley Street, he is a consultant at NHS St Barnabas' in south London and founder of the AllSight charity, which works to combat blindness in West African countries.

I must have read it fifty times.

*

I couldn't say now how many days passed before the coroner's office rang me, but it was in the immediate aftermath, I'm sure, because I was aware as I pressed the phone to my ear of my face being swollen and sore from nightly crying. The officer, Gwen, told me the investigation was under way, the police having assigned an impressively large team to it. The implication was that Arthur's VIP status warranted this commitment to maximum efficiency.

'Would it be possible for someone to come and speak to you?' she asked. Her manner melded matter-of-fact professionalism with the warm solicitude of a new friend. The former scared me, the latter made my heart clench.

'Why?'

'Because you knew one of the deceased, Sylvie Woodhall.'

'I didn't know her. I only met her twice, and even then only for a few minutes.' I felt like a criminal uttering this half-truth.

'You knew her husband, though, and you spoke to her soon before her death. You may have information that could be useful in understanding her intentions before the collision took place.'

They must have looked at her phone log, I realised. I must have been one of the last people she spoke to. Had I even been the last? It didn't bear thinking about, but I could see I was going to have to.

'Has there been a post-mortem?' I asked, speaking in painful gulps. 'I mean on Sylvie?'

It was a question that had consumed me these days – these weeks. What I was thinking, what I had by then decided to be fact, was that our phone conversation had caused her to drink and drive. Arthur had told me she did not drink alcohol, or not often, he had as good as said she was a recovering addict. Had my refusal of her 'deal' led her to relapse the night before the accident? Unused to its effects, she might not have metabolised it quickly enough and it had acted as poison, affecting her judgement at the wheel.

'A post-mortem has taken place now, yes,' Gwen said.

'What did you discover?'

'The pathologist is still preparing his report.' In other words, they weren't about to tell *me* anything. She said she would pass my number to the investigator and forward me a guide to coroners' inquiries to give me an idea of what the process would entail.

I told myself it had been inevitable that someone would name me as Arthur's lover; perhaps Arthur had already done so himself. And on a shameful, subterranean level, I couldn't stop myself from hoping that being involved in the investigation might bring me into contact with him again. Maybe it would make him remember me. Because the tragedy may have stopped him from loving me, I understood that, but it had not stopped me from loving him.

There was a succession of interviews, in the event, in which the chronology of my affair with Arthur was documented, our plans to live together resurrected, my phone conversation with Sylvie reconstructed in an official statement. I did my best to give the investigator a true and full account. Gwen kept me up to date. As I had feared, she said it had now been established that I was the last person Sylvie had spoken to on the phone, possibly the last person at all besides her sons, and I would certainly be called as a witness at the inquest. The coroner would want to understand her state of mind when she set out on the morning of the accident and my 'background information' could be crucial.

They did not say if Arthur knew this or not.

'Am I . . . am I in some sort of trouble?' I asked her.

'No, you've been very helpful and we'd like to thank you for that. The coroner's job is not to determine criminal liability in any way. He wants only to establish the facts in order to give a verdict on the cause of death.' Gwen added that the coroner had now issued the authority permitting the three bodies to be buried, and that this in itself signified that no criminal charges were likely to be brought against anyone.

I did not ask where and when the funerals were to take place. Under no circumstances could I show my face on those occasions. Sustained though I was by then entirely on the hope of seeing Arthur again, even for me the thought of watching him lay his sons to rest was unspeakable. I had a vision of Sylvie's family standing in a horseshoe around a grave, glaring at me with murderous loathing. I knew of the existence of her sister already, the recipient of the yellow dish, and of the niece who had helped Sylvie paint it, but there were probably parents still alive too, other siblings, nieces and nephews, cousins to the boys. Not to mention the relatives on Arthur's own side. The momentousness of the tragedy overwhelmed me once again and tears spilled down my face.

'Do I *have* to attend the inquest?' I said. 'What would happen if I said no?'

There was the sound of an exhalation, not quite a sigh. Gwen was too tender-hearted to let on that she was bored or irritated by the protests she must encounter day in, day out. 'I know it's upsetting, Emily, but there's nothing to be afraid of. To answer your question, you can either come voluntarily or we can issue a formal summons.'

I banished the row of faces, the branches on the family tree. There was no question that I would refuse. 'Of course I'll come, if you think I can help.'

She said there was a very good support service for witnesses and, if I wished, someone would accompany me on the day.

'I don't need that, thank you,' I said. 'When will it be?'

'We'll let you know the date as soon as it's set. It will be the new year at the earliest, depending on the complexity of the investigation.'

I felt as if I'd been struck in the chest: the new year at the earliest! The idea of reaching January of the following year, months away, was unthinkable, like being asked to swim the Atlantic. To have to swim the Atlantic before I could see Arthur again ... I admit I cried even harder after the call ended, hopelessly sorry for myself. At least it was in the morning and I was still at home, free to lie on my bed sobbing and writhing till the torment subsided. Had I taken such a call at work, I would have had to put down the phone and pretend I was not in the middle of a waking nightmare. For I had to continue working, of course. I had to or I'd very quickly be destitute.

Charlotte had accepted my excuse on the Saturday of the accident that I'd been consoling a neighbour, having become drawn into the crisis on my way to the dentist's. She'd already heard news of it and was prepared to give me the benefit of the doubt. But from the Monday, I had no choice but to behave as if as personally unaffected as she was, for I could hardly explain my true involvement and expect any sympathy. To excuse my facial swelling I told her I'd suffered an allergic reaction to a mosquito bite, which seemed to work, but when I lost control and was found in tears while washing up the chocolate fountain, I had to improvise and say my father had had a relapse. I felt the additional misery of the lie as heavily as if it were true.

'Oh, poor you,' she said. 'You know how close I am to *my* father. I can't think of anything worse to have to deal with.'

I could.

'Except that poor guy who lost his whole family,' she added. 'The surgeon. I guess *that*'s worse. You can tell something terrible's happened, can't you? I mean locally, right down the road.' Since our adult customers talked of little else but the 'triple tragedy', conspicuously shielding their children's ears from their gossip, this was stating the obvious. 'It's a relief when someone comes in from out of the area and doesn't know

206

anything about it. But even then, there's just this weird atmosphere.'

Perhaps it was me; perhaps it descended when I arrived and lifted when I left.

'I wonder if she ever came in here,' Charlotte mused. 'Sylvie Woodhall.' Her attitude of compassion was agonised, for no one embodied better than her the emotion of 'There but for the grace of God go I'. While a minute ago she had been beside herself with relief that she was not the one with a parent dying in hospital, now she counted her blessings that it was Sylvie Woodhall who'd lost control of a speeding vehicle and not her.

'I did see her in here once, actually,' I said. 'She did a plate, a yellow one, for her sister's birthday.'

'Wow,' Charlotte marvelled, 'you've got a good memory.'

My brother rang me when he discovered that for two weeks in a row his regular weekend visit to the hospital had been the only one Dad had had all week. 'They say you haven't been up for a while,' he said. 'Is anything wrong?'

'There's been something I've had to deal with here,' I said. 'It's been . . . upsetting.'

'I thought you split up with Matt ages ago?'

'Not Matt.' Oh, the innocence of an amicable break-up with a single man!

Phil paused, not one to pry.

'I will go and see Dad,' I told him. 'I hadn't realised how long I'd left it. I'll go this evening. How was he when you saw him?'

'The same.'

So *something* was the same in this upturned world, but it was hardly heart-warming news. 'It's not the same, though, is it, Phil?' I cried, and after that words came tumbling from me before I could scoop them back: '*He*'s not the same. He's unrecognisable. It's unbearable, don't you think? All those years he sacrificed everything for us and now we're older and in a position to give something back, we can't. There's nothing he wants. He doesn't *know* what he wants, he doesn't know us!'

There was a moment of cold shock, for this statement of helplessness was years out of date. Like me, Phil had grown expert in pretending, at least in conversations between the two of us. Perhaps he bared his true torment to his wife Julie, as I did – *had* – to Arthur. 'He wouldn't want you to think like that,' he said, voice determinedly steady. 'Don't crack up, Em. It's actually good that he's stable at the moment and not deteriorating.' Another pause. 'You know what we just talked about?'

'What?'

'You. When you used to have nightmares.'

'Cheery stuff.'

'Oh, come on, we were laughing about it. The third bunk, remember?'

'The third bunk?' I willed myself to get into the spirit of this, but I was out of practice. I knew what he was talking about, though. For months after Mum died, I'd had terrors in the night and become frightened of the dark, of sleeping in my room alone, and so Dad had moved me to the lower bunk in Phil's room. It was a tiny cabin of a space, every breath amplified, and all that happened now was that my crying woke him up and set him off. So Dad laid out a mattress of sleeping bags for himself next to my lower bunk, the three of us sleeping in a space not much bigger than an airing cupboard. And it worked well enough, until one morning Phil sprang down from the top bunk, forgetting about our new roommate, and landed on Dad's head. Somehow Dad managed to hide his pain from us and get us to school. Years later, he admitted he'd taken the morning off work to go to A&E to be treated for concussion.

'He didn't actually remember,' Phil confessed. 'But he enjoyed hearing about my clumsy, pubescent phase.'

At last I managed a chuckle, if only to end the call on a warmer note. Scenes from our childhood were like make-believe now, at best fables, instructive to the listener – if only for a minute or two.

Chapter 15

Emily

As I say, Arthur had to all intents and purposes dispossessed me. He'd also made it impossible for me to contact him. Having discovered that the mobile line on which I had always reached him was no longer in service, I called his secretaries at St Barnabas' and the Harley Street clinic. Both parroted the official line: he had taken compassionate leave for an indefinite period and they were not able to promise that any message would be returned. They were sure I would understand.

For the first time I turned on the old laptop Matt had left when he moved out and began checking for email from Arthur – sometimes, at weekends, obsessively, several times an hour – but there was never anything, of course. I went back to the beginning and tried the options again: mobile phone (out of service), hospital extensions (the party line), email (nothing) – an eternity ring of futility.

I had, by then, all but given up on the possibility of seeing him on the Grove or anywhere else in the neighbourhood. He had moved out of his house, at least temporarily, that was the only conclusion I could draw after I'd passed it several times a day for weeks – not only to and from the bus stop to work as of old, but also late at night, when I would find myself attracted against all reason uphill to the pavement outside

210

number 11. Every time, without exception, I found it dark and unchanged, the blinds at his study windows that had been pulled low to conceal me never again opened. Occasionally I would go to the door and ring the bell – its abrupt grind penetrated my soft tissue like a death knell – but no one came, of course, and I would scuttle away, fearful of catching the eye of a neighbour or mourner. There were numbers of the latter at any given time – often teenagers standing in pairs or clusters, the girls weeping openly – and there were bouquets of flowers in various states of decomposition. Little messages I couldn't bear to stop to read, and even drawings, had been tied to the railings with ribbon.

Somehow, partly by lingering inside my front door and listening like an animal for signs of life on the other side of the wall, I avoided running into Sarah and Marcus. I did see Nina once. We were walking towards each other in the street and I scurried to the kerb well in advance of any potential collision, my guilty eyes kept low. Of course a guiltless person would have stopped the best friend of the dead woman to offer her heartfelt condolences, but I was not guiltless; I was the offender who had repeated 'it's every woman for herself' back to the victim, no longer sure whether I had meant it in sincerity or mockery. It was a horrible coincidence that when Nina and I passed we were in easy sight of the Woodhalls' house, all those wilting flowers at the railings. She did not speak to me, but if she had, she would have said, 'This is your fault. I don't care what the coroner decides, *you* are the cause of death.'

The cause of *three* deaths. The magnitude of that defeated me: I could not absorb it. Two boys, one only eighteen, the other still at school and young enough for his mother to have begged for his father to stay to parent him to adulthood. Sons and heirs, pride and joy, apples of eyes, they must have been those things to Arthur and yet I knew so little about them, having either suppressed my interest or not considered it necessary to have any in

211

the first place. I knew from photographs I'd seen in the house that they'd taken after their mother physically, both fair-haired and blue-eyed; I knew that Alex had been the adventurer, Hugo more introspective, both equally high-achieving academically and headed for universities that would make Arthur and Sylvie proud. But what else? Were they popular? Did they have girlfriends? Had they been virgins? What were their hobbies and passions? Were they alert before they died or dozing, having been awoken against their will and herded into the car in what was supposed to be only their holiday cut short, not their lives? How many friends and classmates and teachers wept for them, for the monstrous robbery of youth and potential? Many more, I supposed, than the ones I'd seen outside the house. Their school would be in mourning, the summers of a hundred or more families darkened by the horror of this. When Hugo's class returned for the new term, it would be all anyone talked of; they'd offer the students counselling, beseech them to stop thinking, as every last one of them surely had, That could have been me. And Alexander's class, off to university or gap-year travels. What a bitter send-off they would endure, were they to continue with their plans at all.

My fault: at least some of it and maybe all of it.

Other than Gwen at the coroner's office, only one person made contact regarding the Woodhalls: Toby texted me some weeks after the event to say that the family appreciated my help on the morning of the accident and that Arthur was coping as well as could be expected. Frustrated by the stock phrases and by the absence of any coded personal message, I rang the number back, but when connected to the voicemail service I could not think how to express myself.

Tell him I love him and miss him. Tell him he's my whole life. Tell him I'm sorry for what I said to her. I wish I'd said . . .

No, better to say nothing.

*

212

Though Arthur's absolute silence during this period could be interpreted only as absolute rejection, I persisted with my phone calls to his office, and at last the available information altered: he had returned to work at St Barnabas'. I found out which day he was next seeing patients and, discovering that the hours overlapped with my lunch break, I went to the clinic myself.

It surprised me that any Tom, Dick or Harry was free to walk straight into the Ophthalmology Department without a security check, though I suppose the assumption was that no one in his right mind would want to unless they had an appointment, for it was bedlam down there in the basement unit. Every wall of the corridors leading from the stairs and lift to the reception desk was lined with plastic seats, every seat taken. The surplus patients stood or squatted, while new arrivals continued to press towards a desk staffed by a single figure acting as both receptionist and porter; with every second enquiry, he would leave his station to help or accompany an elderly, half-blind arrival to safety, having to negotiate each time for a seat already occupied. The only other authority figure I could see was an interpreter for an Asian woman, who spoke rapidly and anxiously in a language I could not identify. The clinic was plainly oversubscribed; it reminded me of bus stations in developing countries or a logjam at airport immigration lines when too many flights have touched down at once.

As I waited in the queue for reception I became aware of various medical staff emerging every so often from an adjoining corridor, calling out patient names and shepherding the chosen ones off into examination rooms. Arthur was not among those who appeared, but twice I left the queue to collar one of them, hoping to discover which room he was in and present myself unannounced. Both times I missed my chance, the patient already having begun to bombard the staff member with questions, and I was waved back to the same queue I'd left.

After twenty minutes, I reached the desk. 'I don't have an appointment,' I told the receptionist. 'I'm here to speak to Arthur Woodhall, the consultant.'

'He told you to come without an appointment? He doesn't normally do that. What's your name?'

'Emily Marr, but no, he isn't expecting me. I just need you to tell him I'm here – or if you could show me which room he's in, I could—'

He cut me off. 'I can tell you now that if you haven't got an appointment he won't be able to see you today. Yesterday's clinic had to be cancelled and we're running that alongside today's post-op – you can see how crazy it is.'

'Yes, of course.' I tried to smile. I'd forgotten by then that I used to be considered very pretty, that I'd once caught male eyes routinely and been able to extract myself from trouble on that basis alone. 'I'm a good friend of his. He'll know my name. I don't mind waiting right till the end, when everyone's been seen. Shall I just do that?'

But I no longer had the power to charm. The receptionist looked only wary and irritated by my suggestion. 'I'll have to check his schedule with his team upstairs ...'

'No, please. Could you just tell him I'm here? *Please*.'

At last he made the call, not connecting directly to Arthur, I gathered, but at least passing on my name and request to a member of his office staff. 'Yep, I'll hold.' I waited to the side of the desk, watching him check in patients one-handed, hardly able to contain myself when his phone exchange resumed: could this be it, finally? Would I be summoned to the phone and permitted to hear Arthur's voice, or directed along that overcrowded corridor to the room that held him? He could be twenty feet from me, right this minute! The yearning to be physically close to him was so strong I felt on the verge of levitation as I stood there on the tips of my toes, ready to hasten wherever I was summoned.

The receptionist replaced the phone and called me forward. 'Mr Woodhall would like you to leave,' he said. He'd tactfully lowered his voice, but the tone was quite different now, implicit of grave consequences were I to choose not to cooperate.

Though I felt as if I'd been booted in the solar plexus, I feigned mild surprise. 'He hasn't got time to see me?'

'He is only seeing registered patients today. There are already several he might not get to as it is. When he finishes his clinic he goes straight upstairs into theatre. He doesn't have a minute to spare.'

My control began to slip. 'But he must! He must have a minute, *one* minute! What about after he's finished in theatre?'

He gestured sharply, losing his patience with me. 'Look, I'm sorry, but you can see for yourself we're up to our necks here.' As those behind me agitated to check in, he reached across me to take the next appointment card and rattled the computer mouse to refresh the screen. 'This isn't the place for personal calls,' he added in a mutter.

'Then where *is* the place!' I cried, not noticing I'd raised my voice until silence fell among those waiting around me. Realising I was creating a scene, one that might later be reported to Arthur, I began sobbing into my hands.

A second member of staff now materialised, asking the first, 'Want me to call Security, Bob?'

He and Bob frowned at me in joint query.

'No,' I told them, wiping tears and mucus from my face. 'Forget it. I'm going.'

Such was my loss of a hold on reality that by the time I reached Earth, Paint & Fire I had convinced myself that my message had never reached Arthur, that his staff had refused the request without consulting him, overprotective of him in his bereavement. At the first opportunity, I phoned his St Barnabas' secretary and left a cheerful voicemail asking her to confirm that Arthur had been informed of my visit. When she did not call back that day, nor after I'd left an urgent second message early the following morning, I phoned his private clinic in Harley Street. It was nine o'clock, just before I had to leave for work, and this time I had my strategy ready. I would not claim private acquaintance but would make an appointment as a patient. But of course the first thing I was asked was if I had a referral or a health-insurance policy number, and right away I was floundering.

'Can't I just have the consultation and pay for it out of my own pocket?' I said.

'What exactly are your symptoms?' she asked.

I made something up about blurred vision and a sharp pain behind the left eye, but that only made her *too* concerned. 'It sounds as if you need to go to Accident and Emergency at Moorfields,' she said. 'They're open twenty-four hours. Can I give you the address?'

'No,' I said impatiently. 'It has to be Mr Woodhall. He's been recommended to me by a good friend.' When she asked for a name, I blurted out, 'Nina Meeks. The journalist. She knows him well.'

At last she capitulated, agreeing to check Arthur's schedule for an opening and asking for my personal details. But no sooner had I said my surname than she was changing her mind, and quite unapologetically: 'I'm afraid Mr Woodhall has no appointments available for the foreseeable future. In fact, he asks that you please do not call again.'

'What do you mean "he asks that"? You haven't had time to tell him who this is!' All at once my voice turned shrill, my breath frantic, my body struggling to process the sudden mental stress. This exceeded my distress at St Barnabas' the previous day; I was experiencing the first symptoms of a panic attack. 'Is he standing right there, listening in? If he is, can I please speak to him in person and we can get this misunderstanding sorted out!'

Ignoring my hysteria, she spoke in a low, unyielding tone: 'Mr Woodhall is not here, no. All I can tell you is that he has asked that you do not contact him again. He has been very clear about that.' The suggestion was that he had briefed all staff at the practice to turn me away – me, the one who loved him most in the whole world! The one he had kissed from head to toe, the one he had said he could not be without.

I hung up without another word and fell from the sofa to the floor, my arms protecting my head as if reacting to sudden gunfire at the window. I don't know how long I lay there, crying, but I broke off only once, in order to call into work sick. I *was* sick.

'This is your last chance,' Charlotte said, mean with exasperation (and who could blame her?). 'If you're not in tomorrow, don't come in again at all.' She was so inured now to my excuses she was able to end the call even as I wept.

I returned to work the following day, and the next and the next. As the weeks crawled by, all I could do was work, and when I wasn't working I lay on the sofa in my living room, shrunken and inert, waiting to work again. As I'd promised Phil, I resumed my visits to the hospital, only to find that the relapse I had fabricated to explain my original misery had come to pass. Dad had contracted pneumonia and been moved to a bed in the high-dependency unit. Though he was fading again, he recognised me without difficulty and for the first time in many months he struck me as substantially his own self. I couldn't explain why, but it was almost as if I believed that as long as he went on knowing me, so my own chances of survival would improve. It was the only faith I had left.

'I love you,' I told him, repeating it until the words sounded foreign and abstract, a lullaby playing even after sleep came. More than once I dozed off in the chair at his bedside and would have stayed overnight had I not been woken and sent home by the nurses.

Beyond my workplace and the hospital, I went nowhere, saw no one. I knew I needed to give notice on the flat – since Matt had gone, ninety per cent of my salary went on my rent and utility bills – but the thought of flat-hunting, of flat-*sharing*, even of packing, exhausted me. More important to me than any future debt was the fact that this was where Arthur could find me. I could not live with the thought of him resurfacing one day and needing me, ringing my bell and finding a stranger in residence.

Besides, I had nowhere to go. Phil's house in Newbury would mean too long and expensive a commute, even if he and Julie agreed to let me stay in the first place, and since I'd told no one of my affair with Arthur, there was no one to take me in and comfort me – or reproach me – now it was over. The last friendships I'd sidelined during my romance with Arthur now petered out beyond the point of no return.

Marooned both physically and emotionally, I spent Christmas alone, turning down an invitation to spend it with Phil. New Year passed unnoticed. I suppose I must have eaten and drunk enough not to expire.

Now, when I think about that time, the thoughts are confined to a dark recess. My brain has tricked itself into forgetting, just as women forget childbirth – or at least the full details of it, their memory reduced to the finer pains, the poetic part at which the peak of human endurance is reached and tips back again.

If I shone a light on it, if I granted it more space, I know I would go mad.

Chapter 16

Tabby

The purple folder had reappeared. It was on the kitchen table again, right in the centre, just as it had been before – and this time its owner was out at work. Before laying a finger on it, Tabby used coins from the nearby bowl of odds and ends to mark its exact spot on the table.

She was not sure she recognised herself any longer.

Perhaps it was living so anonymously that had somehow made her lawless – or maybe 'amoral' was the word; she was so ... so *unaccountable* here. Yes, she had given Moira and Emmie her real name, and she had shared with Emmie her true history, but she might just as easily have made both up. Perhaps it was to do with the tone she'd set right at the beginning of her time on the island: wrongful entry, first in Grégoire's wife's house, then in Emmie's, and most recently, in a fashion, at the rue du Rempart property – had she ever really improved on it? Had the eluding of consequences excited her, addicted her? Was she any different from Grégoire, for whom betrayal of trust and violation of rules were clearly aphrodisiacs?

And, perhaps the most crucial question of all: did recognising your faults diminish them in some small way, or did it make them all the harder to excuse?

Whichever the answer, a warning phone call from Moira had not been enough to bring her into line.

'Tabby, I just wanted to check that you do know it's strictly forbidden to invite friends into any of the houses when you're at work? The owner of rue du Rempart is particularly clear about that. He deserves the utmost privacy and discretion.' She was so grand sometimes, made it sound as though the owner were the Emperor of Japan, not some faceless Belgian who happened to employ a cleaner to help him rake in thousands of euros from overpaid holidaymakers.

'Of course,' Tabby said. 'I know the rules.'

'It's just that someone mentioned seeing a visitor arrive last Saturday ...'

'Oh, who?'

'That's what I'm asking *you*,' Moira said, more sternly.

'No, I mean who says he saw that?' Though she was confident she sounded as innocent and eager as ever, Tabby alarmed herself by the devious turn her thoughts were taking, even as she should be concentrating on convincing Moira of her blamelessness. Already she was wondering if her new Sunday property might accommodate her assignations with Grégoire instead. The problem was that it was British-owned and the families often drove from Calais or Saint-Malo, arriving earlier than the official check-in and knocking at the door to ask if they could just start unloading their luggage, and since they were there could the children quickly use the loo or get a drink of water? In any case, would Grégoire be able to manage a Sunday meeting? Even in this ungodly state of affairs, it was possible that Sunday remained sacred to him and his family. She had seen the locals going to Mass at the church in the village. And Sunday was a family day all over the world, wasn't it? She remembered trips she'd been taken on by her parents as a child and, later, being aware of those her father and Susie arranged for the girls.

Moira was growing impatient. 'Can you just answer the question, Tabby. Did you have a visitor at the rue du Rempart house or not?'

'No, of course not. It must have been the postman or a delivery or something.'

'What delivery?'

'I don't know. You do get the occasional neighbour knocking on the door. A kid's ball came over the wall once and the father came to get it back. Should I start keeping a log? For all the properties, or just that one?'

This was easier than she'd expected, and the original witness statement clearly not as solid as threatened, because Moira was already backing down. 'Of course you don't need to keep a log. I know I can trust you. It's a question of security as much as anything. If you were to allow a friend in for a coffee and then something went missing, it could get very complicated.'

'Nothing will go missing,' she assured Moira. 'Everything's fine.'

Nothing would go missing, that was true, but everything would be touched, including the documents the owner trusted he'd left under lock and key. It was a matter of routine now that she try any odd keys in those drawers and cupboards she found locked (the key was often in a box or jar nearby, or tucked at the side of a bookshelf). The thrill was not in the scrutiny of any plumber's estimate or insurance policy or even in the *factures* sent by Moira herself, detailing her commission and expenses, but in the fantasy of being some sort of all-seeing spirit, or at any rate something less prosaic than a snoop. It was the perversion of justice unknown to any judge, the breach of trust that would never be known by the betrayed.

And now here she was breaching the most important trust of all: Emmie's.

She snapped off the two bands and opened the folder. Somehow she had known it would not contain mundane

221

house-related documents, but she had not expected what she found, either: a pristinely ordered stack of newspaper cuttings and print-outs from internet news sites. It was some sort of research project, perhaps. The edges were so rigidly aligned, certain sections clipped in what was apparently a very particular order, she was loath to disarrange them and give herself away. She contented herself for the moment with reading the topmost page, a photocopy of a cutting from the British newspaper the *Press*. The page had a picture of two women in garden chairs, squinting into the sun, glasses of wine in hand, while in the background a group of half-naked infants circled a paddling pool. The picture was captioned *Happy days: Sylvie Woodhall and Nina Meeks in 1999, when their children were young.*

Sitting now, her back to the front door, Tabby read the article in full:

A MOTHER REMEMBERED

Nina Meeks pays tribute to the real 'other woman' in this week's media storm – the wife . . .

You will not have found any obituary of Sylvie Woodhall in the broadsheet newspapers the week she died last July. She was not famous in her life, not 'noted' or 'celebrated' for anything, not so far as the world was concerned. Only by the nature of her death has she come to our attention, and only then because of who she was married to: the eminent eye surgeon Arthur Woodhall.

It was always Arthur who was the famous one, and for good reason. There was the undisputed surgical gift, the royal and celebrity patients, the near-holy status that top-ranked surgeons like him command, inspiring as they do reverence in the rest of us, ignorant of all but the most basic medical facts.

222

But none of that impressed me. I was Sylvie's friend, not his. We met when our eldest sons started nursery school together sixteen years ago, and quickly became the closest of confidantes. I moved into a house on the same street as hers. We could wave to one another from our front doors. By happy coincidence our second children – another son for Sylvie, a daughter for me – were also in the same school year. They became friends too.

My children are now as bereft as I am.

The verdicts found by the coroner this week were, according to my legal friends, inevitable, but that does not mean we have to accept them as anything but a formality. It was Sylvie who was driving that terrible morning, yes, but the truth is she was driven to that tragic ending. She was driven to it by a woman who has come this week to represent much that is despicable in our culture today: a lack of respect for others, disregard for their emotions, for their human dignity.

A woman who thought – and I have no doubt still thinks – only of herself.

I won't use her name here, though you will know precisely who I mean. In a few short days she has become a household name, better-known than Sylvie herself. But I will not name her and sully what will likely be Sylvie's only obituary in a national newspaper. If the many of us who loved her have any hope for her to rest in peace – she is buried with her beloved Alexander and Hugo in a cemetery near her home in Sussex – we must ensure that her memory is mercifully spared any connection to the woman who, to all intents and purposes, conspired to end her life.

Farewell, Sylvie. You were a wonderful mother, a dutiful wife, a loving daughter and sister and a true friend. You never once stopped doing your best for us all and we honour your memory.

Tabby felt her eyes water, ran her thumb across the printed text as if better to understand the source of so powerful and heartfelt a tribute. To have a friend write about you like this, to lambast your enemies and protect your memory! Who was this Sylvie woman and why would Emmie want to keep her obituary?

She peered at the date. The article had been published on Sunday, 12 February 2012, almost six months ago. Emmie had said she'd come to Saint-Martin in late March. Was there some sort of link? Was Sylvie a good friend, or even a relative? An older sister, whose death had caused a grief so severe Emmie needed to leave the country? Woodhall was Sylvie's married name, but might her maiden name have been Mason? On the other hand, wouldn't a sister want constant contact with remaining family and friends so soon after the loss of a loved one? Except ... Emmie had told her both her parents were dead; she'd admitted her relationship (perhaps even marriage) was over, too. And what about that strange word she had used that Tabby had never been able to make sense of, 'exile'?

At the sound of the entry pad clicking at the door behind her, Tabby abandoned the cutting and closed the folder. She replaced it on the table and put the coins back in the bowl. The chime of metal hitting ceramic rang out as she turned in greeting.

'All right, Emmie?'

Emmie's eyes moved from the folder to Tabby, who lowered her face to conceal her embarrassment, pretending to leaf through a tourist brochure about boat trips.

'I thought you didn't finish till six?' Tabby said.

'No, five,' Emmie said.

Tabby was certain she'd said six. 'I'll make you a cup of tea. You look tired.'

She felt her face burn with shame. Had she learned nothing from Emmie's forgiveness that day in May when she'd been discovered uninvited and asleep in the back bedroom? What

224

kind of a person had she allowed herself to become? Had she really just thought that self-indulgent nonsense about being an all-seeing spirit? What she was doing was cowardly and wrong and if she couldn't stop snooping of her own accord then she needed professional help. She was becoming as self-absorbed as the terrible woman described in the article she'd just read.

She managed to compose herself while the kettle boiled, aware that Emmie was straightening the few bits and pieces on the table, including the folder. It was not like her to straighten, Tabby thought, especially not on the same day that Tabby had cleaned the house. As they drank their tea at the table, the folder placed disconcertingly, accusingly, between their mugs, she imagined herself saying bluntly, 'Who is this Sylvie Wood-hall?' or merely, 'What's in the folder, Emmie?', but even inside her head her tone sounded false and devious, her prurience plain to see. Instead, she avoided acknowledging it at all, led conversation in the direction of the beach house in La Couarde from which Emmie had come. The out-going holidaymakers had had small children and there'd been damage to the door of a kitchen cupboard and the shower curtain had been torn from its rail. It had taken her an age to vacuum up all the sand in the grouting of the floor tiles and they'd obviously taken the bath towels to the beach: they were stained with seaweed and God knew what else.

'So what have you been doing this afternoon?' Emmie asked.

'Oh, not much. I read a bit, gave this place a once-over. I was thinking I might go for a swim now if the tide's in.'

'I didn't notice.' Emmie did not swim or walk or window-shop, she did not even like to go to the supermarket, happy to accept Tabby's offer to run errands on her behalf. She did not like to do anything that brought her into contact with other people, particularly now high season was in its swing. Tabby wondered sometimes if she had a fear of crowds.

As she chattered on, Tabby became aware of a distracted air

about her friend, the sense that Emmie was unusually excited. Several times she glanced down at the folder and then up towards Tabby, almost as if daring her to ask about it, inviting her to.

Should she? The tension was excruciating, exactly the conditions that caused Tabby's imagination to make its wilder leaps and bounds. It struck her that the circumstances this evening were strikingly similar to the previous time: the folder in the centre of the table, other items cleared out of sight as if the stage had been set, Emmie off the premises or safely upstairs. It could not be mere coincidence, could it, that on both occasions Emmie had reappeared at exactly the moment Tabby was sneaking a look? And now she came to think of it, Emmie had not minded her seeing the photograph, had she? She'd enjoyed looking at it with her.

Had she, then, either consciously or subconsciously, *wanted* Tabby to open the folder? Had she told her the wrong time in order to discover her looking and engineer a conversation about its contents?

But why on earth would she need to do that?

The answer was she wouldn't, of course. There was no reason whatsoever for her to lay traps like that or to approach subjects in such an oblique way. She could simply introduce it directly into the conversation. I'll wait for her to say something, Tabby thought. Until then I'll mind my own business.

But, historically, this was not a conviction to last very long. She knew already she would go to bed that night longing to know who Sylvie Woodhall was, who she had been in Emmie's life.

Chapter 17

Emily

In the end, the period between the accident and the inquest was six and a half months: exceptionally concise, I was told, and yet an agonising stretch to a woman measuring the time since she'd last seen the man she loved not in months or days, but in hours, in minutes. In breaths drawn.

The date was to be the week beginning the 6th of February. Helpful Gwen said that while most road traffic collision inquiries could be completed in a single day, the coroner was to consider all three deaths in the same hearing and therefore this one might run into several days, even a full week. I would only need to be there for the Wednesday-afternoon session in which I was to be questioned, though of course it was a public hearing and I was welcome to attend every session if I chose. She was fairly confident that proceedings would not run ahead of schedule, though they might possibly run behind. She asked me if I had any questions.

I had just one, the only one that mattered to me: 'Will Arthur Woodhall be there?'

She said yes, he was a witness himself and she understood that he would be attending in person.

'Throughout the whole thing or just when he's being questioned?'

'I would imagine he would want to come for the full hearing. This is an opportunity for family to ask their questions.'

'You mean he's allowed to ask the police questions of his own?'

'Yes, and also the pathologist and any of the witnesses.'

Any of the witnesses? That included me. I felt nauseous.

'This is all in the guide I sent you,' Gwen said. Her resources of patience were limitless. She was the only person during this period to neither ignore nor become agitated by my wilder emotions, treating them as commonplace. 'He may not need to ask anything, of course. He may have asked for copies of witness statements in advance.'

'Can you do that? Can I get copies as well?'

'No, I'm afraid they're only for family members. And the coroner may not always agree to give them.'

She must have heard the moan of despair that escaped from me then, because she said, very firmly, 'Remember, they can't accuse you of anything, Emily. The reason the inquest is being held in the first place is because the case is not going to trial; no criminal charges have been brought against anyone. The idea is not to apportion blame to witnesses.' She'd said this several times now, which only alerted me to the fact that blame *would* be apportioned; not formally, not by the coroner, but in the room that day.

I didn't tell Charlotte the real reason for my day off. Though my attendance record had improved lately, my misery for the most part better-concealed, the warning I'd received after that disastrous phone call to Arthur's clinic and my unauthorised absence that day had not been forgotten by either of us. Pre-empting objection, I requested unpaid leave rather than holiday and told her the date could not be negotiated.

The solemnity in my voice must have caught her ear because she asked, a little irritably, 'Doing anything interesting?'

'No, just personal stuff.'

A frown crossed her face before clearing in remorse. 'Oh, Emily, your father – I keep forgetting! Is there any improvement?'

'A little. He beat the pneumonia, which is good news, though he's still in the hospital. But this is nothing to do with that.' Certain that lying on my part had ill-willed the onset of pneumonia in the first place, I no longer used Dad to excuse the effects of my Arthur-related desolation. 'I hope you don't mind but I'm not allowed to talk about it.'

I regretted this comment because she looked immediately horrified. 'Oh God, it's not jury service, is it? There's no way I can pay you *and* a replacement for weeks on end! Do everything you can not to be selected, OK? Pretend you're psychologically unstable or something.'

Pretend?

I sighed. 'Don't worry, it's not jury service.'

'Well, it's obviously *something* awful, because you look as if you're about to burst into tears.' She looked closely at me then, and her compassion was genuine, I judged. She probably now suspected a medical matter of my own, an abortion or something else better kept to oneself. Oddly, I found her sympathy harder than the previous intolerance; it gave me a bleak feeling to realise just how estranged we'd become ('I keep forgetting' – forgetting that my father was *dying*!). It had once mattered to me to impress her, to win her approval and friendship – I remembered how we'd laughed together about Matt and his friends, discussed their arrested emotional development – and yet I'd isolated myself without a second thought, my only concern to protecting my relationship with Arthur. In altered friendships like this with her, I was the one at fault; I had recast her as someone to deceive, not to confide in. I had only myself to blame.

But it was too late now. I could not bring myself to tell her about the affair, the inquest, my guilty connection to the loss of three lives. It had grown too big to explain and therefore had to remain hidden for ever.

God, I had no idea.

The building that housed the coroner's court was unprepossessing in a bland, institutional, late-twentieth-century way, the atmosphere in the lobby neutral and unpromising. Though I was not required until the 1 p.m. session, thanks to a road being blocked near the train station I arrived twenty minutes late to find the front desk unmanned. I did not have the first idea where to go for the hearing or whether I'd be admitted this late, whether I'd see Arthur for the first time in over half a year or, once again, be barred categorically from his presence. Whatever my fate, I prayed I would not create a scene.

A notice behind glass detailed the week's proceedings: THE FULL INQUEST TOUCHING THE DEATHS OF SYLVIE MARTHA WOODHALL, ALEXANDER ARTHUR WOODHALL AND HUGO BENEDICT WOODHALL. Below this was a list of witnesses, which ran to three pages and included pathologists, police officers at the scene, air ambulance staff and paramedics, three civilians listed as *Witnessed incident*, two police investigators. On the third page, amongst a group labelled *Background information*, there were three names I recognised all too well:

Nina Meeks
Emily Marr
Arthur Woodhall

Nervous emotion rose in my throat and I swallowed, making a gulping animal sound.

'Can I help you there?'

I spun on my heels to find a stout, smiling woman with a clipboard. Suddenly too overwrought to ask if she were my ally Gwen (which did not bode well for my performance in the witness box), I managed to stammer, 'Yes, I'm sorry I'm late, I'm a witness in the inquest of Sylvie Woodhall.' I couldn't bring myself to say the boys' names too. I couldn't admit to myself I had made any contribution to their ends.

'I thought everyone had already gone back in.' As she located my name on her list, I wavered between the hope that she'd say it was too late, I might as well go home again, and the exhilaration set in motion by her use of the word 'everyone', because it surely included Arthur. He was here, in this building, and I was finally going to be granted entry to the same room as him.

'Not to worry, there are still a few to go before you. I'm just taking in a message for the coroner, actually, so you can slip in with me if you like?'

'OK.'

While not having expected the Old Bailey, I was surprised that the room where the inquest was taking place was neither large nor imposing. Entering, I was met with the sight of rows and rows of backs, with only the coroner himself facing us. He was a slight, balding man of about fifty-five, seated on a raised platform, his head bent over the papers on the broad desk in front of him. Dominating the panelling behind him was the royal coat of arms. Directly in front of his desk were two rows of tables, the kind you'd see in a school or church hall, about eight places on each row, every seat taken, some by uniformed officers. I quickly identified the backs of Nina and Arthur among them, she at the front left, he on the second row to the right. Both wore dark jackets. At first I registered no reaction in myself at setting eyes on my former lover, but continued instead to piece together the elements of the room. To the lower left of the coroner sat a young woman who I took to be a clerk or stenographer, and directly in front of her was the witness box, where a male police officer now stood, a ring-bound folder open on the lectern in front of him. To the right of the tables, not far from Arthur, were seated two impassive young men with notebooks on their laps: local press, I presumed.

Behind the desks the rest of the room was filled with rows of pew-like oak seats. These were only half filled and I slipped silently into the emptiest, tucking my bag at my feet. Though a few heads had turned at the entry of the officer, who was discreetly passing a note up to the coroner, no one had noticed my arrival, and the first thing I did was take a tissue from my bag and wipe off my lipstick – the gaiety of the colour had been a bad misjudgement. Then I found a hair tie and knotted my hair into a bun at the nape of my neck. At least I was in dark clothes, I'd got that right.

I noticed in the row in front of mine a woman in her seventies: Sylvie's mother, perhaps, or Arthur's, a bereft grandparent. She was crying silently, her hand being squeezed by a companion of similar age. I wished I had someone, too, remembered Gwen's offer of a support officer and wondered why I had not accepted it.

The coroner was speaking. He had a rapid, low-toned delivery, not easy to tune into from my position at the back of the room. I gathered that the police officer was a traffic collision investigator, a witness several names ahead of mine on the list, and that his folder contained photographs and plans from the scene of the accident, a set of which the coroner also referred to as they talked.

'As I said this morning, it has been unnecessary to read aloud or discuss the more distressing material from the medical reports of pathologist Dr Michael Corrin, but you have had the opportunity to hear his evidence yesterday and to read his report in full?'

The investigator said he had.

'And the technical findings we have been discussing would, in your opinion, corroborate the conclusions drawn from the type of injuries sustained, sadly fatal in these three cases?'

'That's right, sir.'

'I would like to ask for a few clarifications, if I may. I'm interested in the deployment of the rear left-hand seatbelt: in your examination it was clear the restraint had not been used?'

'Not at the time of the collision. It may well have been used earlier in the journey.'

'There is no evidence that it had been in use but failed to function correctly on impact?'

'No, none.'

'I'm looking again at the statement of Miss Lisa Hawes, whom I had the opportunity to question on Monday, and her eye-witness evidence that the rear passenger, who we know to have been Alexander Woodhall, moved forward between the front seats and took hold of the steering wheel in an attempt to gain control of the vehicle. Did you or any of your team find any mechanical reason to disagree with her observation?'

'None, sir. Our findings corroborate her judgement of the positioning of the third passenger.'

As this dry exchange continued, my eye drifted inevitably to Arthur. His head was bowed, whether in grief or in order to look at material on the desk in front of him I could not tell, but to my great fright emotions now started to make themselves known within me, bringing cold shivers to my skin and hot tears to my eyes. Within seconds I understood something crucial: there was nothing 'former' about my love for him, I loved him the same as ever; the months of silence had had no impact whatsoever on the degree of my devotion. Even if he did not once turn his face my way this afternoon, even if I was destined never to see him again, I would love him till the end. And this was in no way a peaceful epiphany, but a horrible, turbulent one, like receiving a punitive ruling, a sentencing. I could not be happy without him; and since he wanted nothing more to do with me, I could not be happy again. Like Sylvie, I would die unhappy.

This last, self-indulgent thought jolted me from my reverie. There was an exchange about death taking place between coroner and investigator and here I was thinking about *my* unhappiness. I could hear Sylvie's voice – *How can you be so selfish?* – and was overcome with self-loathing.

I returned my focus to the proceedings.

'. . . And did you find any evidence of moisture on the surface of the road?'

'No, sir, it was a fine, dry day. There had been no rain overnight.'

'And it was light at that time of the morning?'

'Yes, visibility was very good.'

'Thank you. Now, with your fifteen years of experience as a traffic collision investigator you have gained expertise in judging speeds at which collisions occur? In examination of tyre skidmarks and crush damage and so on?'

'Yes, sir.'

'What speed have you calculated in your investigation of this matter?'

'I would judge that the car was travelling pre-impact at approximately ninety miles an hour. The extensive frontal-impact damage was consistent with a speed in that region.'

'And this would be consistent with the witness statements of both Miss Lisa Hawes and Mr Nigel Reynolds, who were able to estimate the speed from a stationary position on the opposite carriageway, and also of the paramedics of the Sussex Ambulance Service and Sussex Air Ambulance, who attended the scene, and of course the pathologists who examined the injuries and whose report we have already discussed.'

'Yes, sir.'

As I listened, I began to realise that every word that came out of the coroner's mouth was concerned with factual information: there were no right or wrong answers to his questions, no shades of personal opinion or approval, just as his staff had assured me. He gave frequent factual recaps and reminders that his job was to establish how, when and where the Woodhalls had come by their deaths.

'We touched just now on the rear left seatbelt, which you believe was functioning normally. And it was not your conclusion that there were any other mechanical faults to the vehicle?'

'No, sir.'

'No tyre defects, for instance?'

'No. The vehicle had been serviced by Camberwell Motors in south London just twenty-six days earlier. Two tyres were replaced then and so were virtually brand-new.'

'And there were no signs of sabotage to the car?'

'None whatsoever.'

'I'm looking at the photographs taken after the removal of the persons. You directed the photographs of the interior of the vehicle?'

'That's right, along with my colleague, Police Investigator Robert Timms.'

A small movement in the second row seized my attention: Arthur. As he turned to respond to the offer of drinking water by a neighbour, I saw part of his face for the first time, a glimpse of the profile so familiar and beloved it caused tremors of yearning in me; to resist them I had to hold the breath in my lungs and wrap my arms around my chest, feeling the air inside me press and press. In front, the stifled sobbing continued.

The investigator was excused and the coroner spoke at some length. 'Now, as I say, I have had the opportunity to examine the witness statements and I have shared such material as I consider necessary from three quite complex pathology reports ... I am satisfied that the identities of Sylvie Woodhall, Alexander Woodhall and Hugo Woodhall have been correctly established and that the place they met their deaths has been correctly recorded. I have been left in no doubt as to the accuracy of the recording of the times of death. I am also satisfied that I have clear knowledge as to the precise injuries that caused those deaths ...'

I exhaled. This sounded like a summing-up to me – was I off the hook, then, no longer required after all? Listening to the investigator's evidence had made me feel helpless as to what I could contribute to this inquiry; I hadn't been at the roadside that horrible morning, I was not an eye witness or a member of the emergency services. More than this, the idea of going into the witness box and standing where he had stood, only then able to see the faces – and experience the glare – of those people who detested me, made me feel faint with cowardice.

'What still remains, however, is for me to establish how the collision came to happen, not in the technical sense, which as I say I am clear on thanks to the evidence I've just heard from Police Investigator Brian Jarrett, but in the sense of being satisfied that the car came off the road accidentally, that is by pure accident and not by any deliberate act on the part of any of the persons in the vehicle. As I remarked when I opened this inquest, were such evidence to come to my attention, I would have no hesitation in adjourning this hearing in order to make further and necessary enquiries.' Throughout this speech, the coroner's manner remained perfectly avuncular – he had an understated authority that reminded me of no one so much as Arthur – but it was impossible not to be electrified by the content, with its implications of suicide and even murder. All heads in the room were raised now, all backs tensed to attention, as he spelled it out for us: 'While satisfied that there could have been no sabotage to the vehicle, I would like now to question a group of witnesses who may be able to help me in understanding if the collision could in any way have been intentional on the part of the driver, Mrs Woodhall.'

He called Josa Buxton, who identified herself as Sylvie's elder sister of Arundel, Sussex, and confirmed that she had spoken to Sylvie the day before the accident. I thought of the yellow plate, of Sylvie holding it to her chest like a trophy or a shield; I thought of a walk through a darkening park with a man who belonged to somebody else, the sense of enchantment I'd felt in his presence, the conviction that there could be no resisting what lay in store for us. What had Arthur said about our being together? It seemed inconceivable that it wouldn't happen, he'd said. He had not bargained for death, for the obliteration of his family.

'I knew there were problems in the marriage,' the sister said, in answer to a question I had missed. 'I knew that Arthur had been unfaithful to her several times over the years and she found it very upsetting.'

I caught my breath. Somehow I had not considered that other people would be questioned about the Woodhalls' marriage today; only me. Stealing a glance towards Arthur's row, I saw that his head remained facing the coroner; he did not turn to look at his sister-in-law as she laid his private life bare.

'It was not her desire to end the marriage?' the coroner asked.

'No, definitely not. She wanted to keep her family together. She felt very strongly that teenagers need their parents just as much as younger children do. She'd done a lot of reading about it.' Anticipating the direction of the coroner's enquiries, Josa declared, 'There is no way on earth she would have deliberately harmed her boys. I can't stress that strongly enough. If anything, she was sacrificing personal happiness for their well-being.'

The coroner nodded respectfully. 'You last spoke to her on the morning of Friday the twenty-second of July, when she met you for coffee at your home. You were aware of no specific problem or piece of news that had distressed her in the preceding days?'

'No. She was quite negative when I asked after Arthur, but that wasn't unusual. As I say, she had often felt let down by him. I thought he must have been unfaithful again, or she suspected he had. She'd become a bit paranoid about it and I suppose I'd stopped picking up on every little comment or criticism.'

'Paranoid in the sense that she was suspicious of events taking place that had not in fact taken place?'

'More that she didn't always know for sure whether they had or not. She didn't always have evidence. He was a master at covering his tracks and he also had his staff telling lies for him. You probably know he's quite famous, very famous in his field, and everyone treated him like a god. It's amazing Sylvie didn't ... ' She did not finish the comment, but it was clear that there was no love lost for Arthur from this quarter. Inevitably I was now thinking, Does she know about me? Do any of them? Was my testimony to be the first time they heard my name, understood my part in this tragedy? If so, I did not think I would get out of the building alive.

'To clarify: in this conversation, you were not made aware of an individual person or specific incident to which she might be having an extreme emotional reaction. Did she mention any plan to return to London the following day?'

'No,' Josa said. 'She always stayed till the August bank-holiday weekend. I'm sure she would have said if she was going back the next day, even if it was just a dentist's appointment.'

I had been the one with the dentist's appointment, I thought. Shame seemed to be manifesting itself in body temperature and, having earlier been shivering, I was now flushed and sweating.

When Josa stepped down, she took a seat next to Nina, who was called to the witness box immediately after and laid a gentle hand on the other's shoulder as she passed behind her. Again, I craved similar comfort: what had I been thinking, trying to survive this on my own?

As Nina swore her oath, it seemed to me that her confidence and authority brought a heightened significance to proceedings. She awaited questioning with an attitude quite different from that of Sylvie's sister, as if her commitment and intelligence in this matter matched the coroner's own. She was compelling, I thought, as I had when I first met her. What a friend to have, what a woman to have on your side!

How incredible it seems now that I should have had such admiration for her.

It was evident in her opening words that she had more specific insight into Sylvie's private anguish than had Josa. 'Yes, she had found out about Emily Marr about a month earlier,' she said briskly. At the first mention of my name, I coloured deeply under my make-up, lowering my eyes in anticipation of the hostile attention to come. 'She'd had her suspicions before that; she could tell Arthur was involved with another woman. But this one was different. She thought he seemed unusually happy. She said she'd seen him one day in the street when he didn't know she was driving past and he looked euphoric. That was the word she used: euphoric. She found it heartbreaking that it should be someone else who'd made him so happy and not his own family. It was about the same time that our friend Sarah had told her she'd seen him and Emily outside the Inn on the Hill hotel and she put two and two together. It wasn't rocket science.'

'What was her reaction to this deduction?'

'She was terrified he was going to leave her, she seemed convinced it was going to happen sooner rather than later, and she had to decide how to deal with that possibility. Until then, it had always been a question of her threatening to leave him and him deciding he didn't want the affair as much as he wanted to stay with his family. There'd been a pattern she could rely on. But this time was different and she didn't know what to do.'

'Her removal to Sussex for the summer was not to be considered an attempt by her to leave him?'

'No, she went there for most of July and August every year. She thought it was best to carry on as normal, especially as it was Alex's last summer before he went off travelling.' Nina paused, lingering as I did, as everyone present must have been, on those words 'Alex's last summer'. 'The boys had invited friends, there was a party planned for Alex's send-off and she didn't want to disappoint them by cancelling. Arthur always

239

went down for two weeks in August and she decided that was when she was going to confront him, when there weren't all of his work demands and, obviously, when he was away from *her*, Emily. Meanwhile she'd have time to develop some strategies to deal with the new crisis.'

'She used that term?' the coroner interjected. 'She thought her life was in crisis?'

'She thought her marriage was, yes. Not her life.'

'Did she at any time give you the idea that she was feeling defeated by the crisis?'

'No, the opposite. What Josa just said is right: Sylvie wanted to fight. She would have been returning to London to do exactly that. She probably planned to force the situation to a head.' Nina's adamant tone, her steadfast body language, made an indisputable truth of every opinion she uttered. 'She'd said in the past she found it torture to not know what lay ahead for her and the boys. For years she hadn't felt as secure as she should have done. It was almost a form of abuse, in my opinion.'

It was grotesque, worse than anything I had imagined, to hear a dead woman's fears about me announced in this way, and to what could only be a disgusted and sickened audience. I wondered if Nina knew about the phone call. She'd made no reference to it so far and yet it was laughable to imagine Gwen or her colleagues refusing a forceful character like this any requests for witness statements, blood relative or not.

'You say you did not speak to her that night, the night of Friday the twenty-second? So you did not hear directly from her what her intention was in returning to London the following morning?'

'No. As I said in my statement, she left a message for me but I was out of the country and at a location out of mobile range. I didn't pick up my messages until I got back to my hotel in the early hours of Saturday, by which time I assumed she'd be asleep. I phoned her at eight-thirty in the morning British time, but it was too late, her phone was switched off. I know now she had already set off.'

'The message you refer to is the spoken one recorded at seven-fifteen p.m. UK time on Friday the twenty-second, in which Mrs Woodhall says she has discovered her husband is with Emily Marr in the marital house in London?'

'That's right. She said one of our neighbours, another friend who was aware of the situation, had texted her to say she'd seen Emily arrive at the house at six-thirty. She begged me to call her back as soon as I could and discuss what she should do.' Nina paused then and looked down, blinking several times, the first obvious trace of emotion in her demeanour. 'When I didn't phone back, she must have decided to contact Emily. She had the number from Sarah, who lives next door to Emily.'

She did know, then, I thought. They all must. The realisation was a source of both relief and terror.

'She'd considered this course of action before and I'd advised against it, but we'd talked about what she could say if she did confront Emily directly.' The middle finger of Nina's right hand dabbed at the corner of her eye. 'Obviously, with hindsight, I wish I had stayed up all night and kept calling until she picked up. I would have told her not to go anywhere. I would have told her I'd come down myself the next day straight from the airport and we'd work out a plan.'

'The issue of the sedative would suggest she may have slept through your calls in any case,' the coroner suggested with sympathy.

'Yes,' Nina agreed.

'So, given what you've told us, and the fact that a conversation was had with Miss Marr, what is your opinion of what Mrs Woodhall would be likely to do next, faced with an evening without immediate support or guidance?'

Nina gave an audible exhalation. 'If she was really distraught, she would have had a drink.'

'You mean an alcoholic drink?'

'Yes.'

'This would be corroborated by the toxicologist's findings of high levels of alcohol in her blood and also by the CCTV evidence we have from Tesco Express near Pulborough, where Mrs Woodhall purchased two bottles of red wine.'

I felt the hairs on my arms stand on end. I'd missed the toxicologist's evidence, but clearly it was as I'd feared: my conversation with Sylvie had triggered a terrible relapse.

'One bottle would be an enormous amount for Sylvie,' Nina said. 'Half a bottle, even. She hardly drank at all any more. She never let herself get drunk. It's years since any of that. She must have felt absolutely desperate that night. And to take the sleeping pill as well: she must not have been able to bear her own thoughts.'

Nina was thanked and excused. I felt her eyes seek me out as she walked the short distance between the witness box and her desk, challenging me to answer to her monumental anger and grief. But I could not; she knew I could not.

A spry, red-headed man in his late thirties stood now and made his way to the witness box. I couldn't remember the exact order of the witness list but the first question established him as the Woodhall family GP, Dr Hanrahan of Grove Walk Surgery.

'You have said in your statement that you do not consider Mrs Woodhall to have been having any thoughts of taking her own life?'

'That's right. The last time I saw her, she was in reasonable spirits, good health generally. She had suffered from depression and had battled alcohol in recent years. I knew she still had trouble sleeping and we had discussed ways to alleviate that difficulty. In the past she had used alcohol to help her sleep but she had not done this for eighteen months or two years.'

'You had prescribed the medicine Zopiclone? This is used to treat sleeping problems?'

'Yes. I had directed Mrs Woodhall to use the lowest dose. But that had been several months earlier and she had not come to me for a renewal of the prescription. She must have had some left.'

'We have heard from the toxicologist yesterday that alcohol would have increased and perhaps prolonged the sedative effects of Zopiclone?'

'That's correct. When I prescribed the medicine, I made Mrs Woodhall aware that it should not be mixed with alcohol under any circumstances.'

'She did not, then, in your opinion, have an issue with alcohol abuse?'

'No. She had begun to rely on alcohol in the past, but I would not have classed it as chronic abuse. She did not want it to become a problem that affected her sons and she sought help early.'

'Which is consistent with Mrs Meeks' evidence that she was now living in sobriety?'

'Yes.'

'You last examined her in May of last year. In your opinion there were no signs of any deterioration in her psychological health?'

'No. She complained of stress and said she could not count on her husband for support domestically; he was extremely busy and worked long hours almost every day of their marriage, she said. She was not as close to him as she'd once been, but she had a very good relationship with her family and friends. She had a network she could rely on. She was not desperate.'

To my alarm, this was as much as the coroner wanted to know from the GP and sooner than I'd expected he was dismissing him and calling the next name – mine. Getting to my feet and putting one in front of the other was a trauma in itself: I felt as if I'd been dropped into a well and left to tread water, gasping for breath until the air ran out. It was panic, pure and simple.

I swore my oath in a tiny, childlike voice. I was aware of the row of pale profiles and dark shoulders to my right but forced myself to look only at the coroner. It was not just the prospect of Arthur's face, or Nina's, but any face, for there was no one among them who had not loved the Woodhalls – or experienced the ghastly sight of their ruptured bodies. The coroner, however, was smiling down at me, sensing my fright, and I had never been more grateful for the benefit of anyone's doubt. He was not going to accuse me, he was not going to judge me, he was not going to blame me.

'I have read your account of your conversation with Mrs Woodhall on the night of the twenty-second of July, which the police believe to be her last conversation with anyone other than her sons, save for the few words with the cashier at the supermarket. Did you make the call or did she?'

I gulped. 'I phoned her. I'd missed several calls from a number I didn't recognise and that seemed unusual. I thought it might be someone from the hospital where my father is a patient, so I called back straight away.'

'She'd made several attempts to reach you, then? How many exactly?'

'Five, I think. I saw afterwards that they were just a few minutes apart.'

'You say she did not sound drunk or under the influence of drugs during this conversation?'

'No, she sounded sober.'

'And had you had any alcoholic drinks yourself that evening?'

'No, not at that point.' Arthur had come back with champagne soon after and I'd drunk it, only minutes after hearing the despair in her voice, knowing I had consigned her to a night of abject misery.

'Did you have a sense as the conversation proceeded that Mrs Woodhall intended returning to London soon after? In order to continue the discussion between the two of you in person, perhaps?'

'No. There was no sense of that. I thought ... Well, I thought she had accepted what I said as my final word and we would not speak again.' The last of these words – *would not speak again* – resonated appallingly and I wished I could retract them.

'You're referring to your having declined her proposal that you should bow out of your relationship with Mr Woodhall for a period of one year, the length of time her younger son was to remain in the family home?'

'Yes, that's right.' A year was an eternity, I wanted to explain to him. We'd only been together six months, we wanted to be together every waking moment. Arthur was almost fifty and life didn't last for ever! Still I had not dared glance at him since I'd been in the witness box; kept my eyes fixed on the coroner, the only source of good will, of mercy. 'But I said she needed to discuss it with him, not me. I didn't think it was my place to make any kind of negotiation.'

The coroner was peering at his documents. When he removed his gaze from me I felt unprotected, unsupported, as if I might slide to the floor. 'You say you thought she accepted your decision as final: did you get the sense that this was a disappointment to her?'

'It must have been. She was ... she was begging me. To have me say no, it must have been disappointing, yes. She hung up on me.'

'I'm interested in your remark to Mrs Woodhall, "it's every woman for herself" ... '

I felt myself go pale: how horrible it sounded, how callous, even when recreated in those pleasant, fair-minded tones of his.

'Was it your intention that she should take this as a challenge to be acted on directly?'

'No,' I protested, my voice rising, 'not at all. I was only repeating a phrase she had used herself earlier in the conversation. It wasn't a challenge for her to come and find me that night, or the next morning or any time soon. As I said, I assumed she would want to talk to Arthur next. It was *their* marriage.'

He nodded as if in total accord, as if he couldn't have put it better himself, and at last I began to relax. 'Did she say *when* she would talk to him?'

'No, but Arthur had decided to go down to see her the next afternoon, so I knew it would be then.'

'She did not make reference to this?'

'She wouldn't have known yet, because Arthur left the message while she was on the phone to me. But since it was the same phone line, she would have had the voicemail waiting for her when she'd finished speaking to me.'

'You did not mention it to her yourself?'

'No.'

'And you also say you took the decision not to tell Mr Woodhall about your phone call with his wife?'

'Yes.' It was starting to sound like a farce, put like that, a comedy of disastrous errors, of missed calls and information withheld. 'As I say, I thought they'd be having their own discussion the next day.'

'Thank you,' the coroner said. 'If there's nothing else, Miss Marr?'

'No, nothing.'

And that was it, that was all he wanted of me, to hear from my own lips that Sylvie had not voiced any intention to return to London either then or the following morning. That no one knew for sure whether she understood that Arthur planned to arrive in the afternoon. That it was reasonable to deduce that I was the direct cause of her drinking, if not of her drinking and driving.

But the coroner was not dismissing me, after all; instead communication was taking place with someone in the front row: Josa, Sylvie's sister. She had a question for me, which was perfectly permissible, though the coroner wanted to remind her that it must be an enquiry with a direct bearing on the matter at hand.

246

To my discomfort, Josa rose to her feet and there was a tense moment when nobody said a word.

'Perhaps the witness might show me the courtesy of looking at me,' she said finally, with an attitude that could only be described as vicious dislike.

Shocked, I turned to face her. Her revulsion was palpable; indeed, she was trembling with it. In my peripheral vision, I was aware of Arthur's head bowed, eyes cast down. Josa spoke: 'I would like to ask you to explain further why you did not tell Mr Woodhall about such an important phone call.' The words finished there but the remainder of the message, and the accusation it contained, was as clear as if she'd stated it aloud: 'Had you told him, they would all still be alive now.' Of course Arthur would have acted on the news that his wife had phoned his mistress – or vice versa: it would have constituted a crisis point even to the world's coolest-headed adulterer. He would have got in his car and driven straight down to her and the boys. He would have reached them by ten or eleven, several crucial hours before they began their own doomed journey. He would have found Sylvie either drinking or passed out and he would have made sure she got nowhere near her car until he was satisfied she was sober. The next day, Nina would have arrived, ready to offer all the strength she needed.

Even if the worst had happened and she had tried to harm herself afterwards, the boys would not have been involved, the boys would have survived.

I took a deep breath and tried to keep my eye contact with her steady, if not confident. 'I suppose I must have been in shock. To have had this conversation with her completely out of the blue . . . She and I didn't know each other at all, I didn't recognise the true significance of it. And, as I say, the two of them were going to see each other the following day and so I honestly didn't think it would make any difference to tell him.'

But it wasn't the whole story and I could see in Josa's face that she knew this. The abhorrent truth was that I didn't want Arthur to leave that night. I wanted him to stay. I was elated and I was frightened and both emotions carried an invincible desire to be with him. I had deliberately kept him in ignorance and any thought I'd spared for the consequences of the phone call had been purely with regard to my own self. Would Sylvie come tearing back that night, I'd fretted, and, if she did, what would happen to me? Arthur and me. What was it I'd thought that night? Maybe it would be better if she found us together. Maybe it would be *better*.

Josa did not acknowledge my answer as satisfactory, but merely indicated to the coroner that she was finished. Now he said I could go.

Arthur was called next. The sight of him raising himself, moving with reluctance to the spot I had vacated, placing himself in front of us grey and diminished, it caused painful lurches in my gut. He emanated the same air of disgrace that I supposed I must have myself and, like me, he kept his head angled towards the coroner, his eyes not once straying to his enemies. Seeing the tragic line of his profile, his features downturned, untouched even by the memory of a smile, I was revisited as perhaps others in the room were by that adjective Nina had used, 'euphoric', and struck with the certainty that this was a man who could never experience that state of being again.

Or even cast a glance towards the source of that erstwhile euphoria.

'I have, as you have heard, questioned Mrs Meeks, Mrs Buxton and Dr Hanrahan,' the coroner told him, 'each of whom knew your wife well and are in agreement that she displayed no signs of considering taking her own life or those of your sons. Is that an impression you would agree with?'

'Yes,' Arthur said. 'She wasn't suicidal and never had been. I think she wasn't thinking straight, she was panicking.' Hearing his dipped, sorrowful voice brought a further assault of pain. I had never seen him cry, I realised.

'You received no word from her that she was on her way back to the family home?'

'No, but I wouldn't have heard her call, in any case. My phone was in another part of the house. After I left her a message I put it in my study to charge. I think I explained in my statement that I have a mobile line especially for family and it was this one she would have used.'

I watched the sequence of his actions in my mind's eye – leave house, make phone call, buy champagne, return home, plug in phone, pick up champagne flutes, bound up the stairs to the guest bedroom, to me – and the images were reduced, blurred, as if delivered on damaged film from a century ago. For the first time, it struck me that Arthur might have deliberately kept his phone out of earshot; he'd had his own compulsion to prolong our joyful, precious night, perhaps even his own thoughts of things being better this way.

'But you were in a position to see after the event whether she had tried to phone you?'

'Yes, and she hadn't. Only Hugo had phoned me, on the morning of the accident.' Arthur's right hand strayed to his face, touched the bridge of his nose, fell once more to his side. I saw the fingers clench.

'The voicemail you received from your son that morning, you say you did not hear this until after the accident?'

'That's right. I found I had missed two calls from him, but there was only one voicemail, the one he must have left soon before the car went off the road.'

The coroner nodded in grave agreement. 'This is the voicemail recorded at eight-twenty-six a.m., only twenty-two minutes before the time of death was given. I have had the opportunity of hearing a recording of this message myself and I do not wish to distress you by playing it during these open proceedings, but would you agree that the gist of the message is that your son wanted you to speak urgently with your wife?'

'Yes. I'm guessing he wanted me to talk her into pulling over or stopping for a break. She must have been driving erratically and it was worrying him enough to want me to intervene.'

'And could you confirm that the voice in the background is that of your wife?'

'Yes. She was shouting at Hugo not to speak to me, to get off the phone. She sounded distraught. Too distraught to be able to continue driving.'

'What is your opinion of the reason she wanted your son to end the call?'

'Maybe she didn't want him to tell me that they were on their way back to London. She wanted to catch me by surprise, not give me any warning that she was coming.'

'Even though you had let her know you would be driving down yourself later that day?'

'Yes. Perhaps she hadn't picked up that message, or maybe she didn't want to wait until the afternoon. In the past when I'd joined them, I was sometimes later than I'd estimated.' There was a pause then in which I, and perhaps others in the room, imagined untold latenesses and let-downs on Arthur's part. 'Or perhaps she thought she would catch me in the act. I know now that she knew Emily was with me in the house and it's possible she expected to find us together. I don't know what she was thinking, but I imagine, whatever it was, her judgement was obscured by the alcohol and sedatives in her system.'

'Would you say that it was typical for her to drive at the speeds we have heard discussed today?'

'Absolutely not. She never speeded, not with the boys in the car. I would agree with the investigator that she must have fallen asleep, had her foot on the accelerator. By the time the boys noticed she'd passed out, the car was going too fast for them to be able to take control. Alex tried, but he couldn't save them in time. I don't know if anyone could have succeeded in a car moving at that speed.'

'Thank you, Mr Woodhall. I know it must be very painful for you to have to return to the events of that day, and I think we can leave it there.'

No sooner had Arthur returned to his seat than the coroner announced that he was going to adjourn proceedings for the day and ask the remaining two witnesses to return in the morning. 'That will give me time to consider the evidence, including the very helpful information from Miss Marr.'

I knew there would not be a person in the room (perhaps those two local reporters) who wasn't thinking then, There's nothing helpful in what *she*'s done.

By the time I could decide whether to leave the room first or last, after him or before, most people had departed and the decision had been made for me. In the lobby I could see him some distance ahead, on his own, hastening towards the main doors, about to leave the building. I drew two conclusions from this: one, he had not waited to speak to anyone, including me, and therefore wanted no company or conversation; two, without entourage or protection, he could be easily approached. As I grappled with the dilemma, I sensed the scrutiny of someone close by, the same unmasked disgust I'd provoked in Josa. But not Josa this time: Nina, who stood with her husband Ed in a group by the front desk.

She took a sudden step towards me. I took one back, as if in a dance. Her lips parted and for a moment I thought she might be about to spit at me, or loudly insult me, but instead she spoke in a tone that was sinister in its mildness. 'If I were you, Emily, I would think seriously about disappearing.'

'What?'

'You heard me.'

'Is that some sort of threat?' I asked.

'Not at all, I wouldn't dream of threatening you. I'm just telling you what I would do if I were in your shoes.' And she looked down at mine, blood-red court shoes with bows, the kind of cute Betty Boop shoes that Arthur had once loved to see me in, the kind of shoes I should not have worn to the inquest into the death of his wife and sons.

Turning my back on her, on the mute loathing of her supporters, I hurried out of the door, my mind made up: I would speak to Arthur whether he wanted it or not. I would not go unacknowledged. Already half panicking about those seconds lost to Nina, I scanned the car park and nearby roads for him. My heart bounced. There he was, at the driver's door of his Mercedes. Rushing towards him between the rows of parked cars, I had the wild idea that I would drive with him back to London or wherever he was staying, we would talk and comfort one another. We would reconcile. We might never again experience the bliss of our beginning, but we might at least make life tolerable again.

'Arthur, Arthur, please wait!'

He turned, closed the car door with reluctance, even locking it as if he feared I'd try to climb in uninvited, and stood with his back to it, staring in my direction. Before, when he'd looked at me, it had been with an unblinking rapture I'd found spellbinding. Now it was gone, extinguished, and his eyes narrowed slightly as if to minimise the sight of me.

I hesitated. 'We haven't had the chance to speak since everything happened.' I made this sound as if we were the victims of a series of cancelled arrangements, missing each other by bad luck, not design, and in my mind an image rose of a broken woman sobbing in the corridors of St Barnabas' while staff threatened to call Security. I reached for him then, the fingers of my right hand making contact with the fabric of his left sleeve. I did not dare grip the wrist beneath. 'I need to explain ... Could we ... do you have time to get a coffee somewhere?'

He removed his arm from my touch. I could tell by the glance he shot over my shoulder towards the building that our reunion was being observed, but I could also tell that he was acting of his own accord, not for anyone else. 'I'm afraid I have to get back to London for a meeting this evening.'

'You're not staying overnight?'

Only when he looked at me with a revolted expression did I hear how my question might have sounded, like an invitation to spend the night together (in his holiday home, perhaps – was that where he lived now? Extraordinarily, the possibility had not occurred to me until then). 'I mean, I thought you would want to stay to hear the verdicts in the morning?'

He said nothing to this, had not the energy to fabricate an answer, for I knew then that there was no meeting in London. I stood, hopeless and forsaken, never in greater need of direction from him and never less likely to win it. I thought, in desperation, If I wanted to I could follow you to wherever you're going; there'd be nothing you could do to stop me. I could sit outside your door and wait, like a pet you've tried to set free but who keeps coming back.

But I was no pet, not any more.

'Please, Emily. You must see there's nothing to be gained ...' He didn't finish the sentence but if he had it would have been 'from talking' or 'from going over it'. There was nothing to be gained from *us*.

My eyes brimmed. 'I think there *is* something to be gained, Arthur. Knowing that someone loves you and wants to care for you during the worst time of your life. Not being alone in the dark night after night.'

But my appeal seemed only to pain him. I am alone, he said, without words. You do not count. 'You need to forget me,' he said simply.

'You mean that?' Though my ribcage rose and fell with every desperate breath, he remained utterly immobile. He had not lost that capacity for stillness. 'That's really what you want? For us to forget everything we ever said, everything we ever felt?'

'Yes.'

As my face convulsed in anguish, he pressed the fob in his hand and the car locks released. I watched him get into the driver's seat with the hopeless wonder of someone seeing an astronaut prepare for a shuttle launch, his destination inconceivable to an ordinary, earthbound mortal like me.

'Goodbye, Arthur,' I said to the sealed window. And the car reversed from its spot, leaving me there with my face in my hands.

I did not think again that day about Nina and what she had said. I did not think to fish from my bag the leaflet the support team had sent me, explaining the procedure in a coroner's court, the passage warning witnesses that members of the press might request a statement to include in their coverage. The afternoon I was questioned, there was not a single reporter interested in exchanging two words with me, much less requesting a statement. I simply walked to the bus stop alone; in turmoil and wretchedness, certainly, but in private turmoil, private wretchedness.

I had no idea, that day, as I waited for the train back to London, how precious my privacy was and how close it was to jeopardy.

Chapter 18

Tabby

The day after breaching the secret folder, Tabby awoke earlier than usual and in a state of nervous excitement. It was obvious to her that she had found herself in the thick of some sort of mystery and that she now had enough clues to discover once and for all the cause of Emmie's reclusive behaviour. It was also clear to her that she had not the strength of character to leave well alone. It was *not* well, she convinced herself, and that was all the justification she needed.

She could hardly contain herself as she approached the internet bureau immediately after breakfast – until she saw the handwritten card in the window: *Fermé. Ouvert 17 Août.* She could not believe her eyes: closed, in the height of the season, in the midst of her investigation! There was not the demand, she supposed, not when most tourists had their own laptops and could pick up wi-fi in one of the larger cafés or hotel bars. And all the houses she cleaned had a PC for guests to use; an internet connection was expected in the same way a high-end espresso machine was, a twenty-first-century holidaymaker's right.

She replayed the thought – all of the houses she cleaned had an internet connection – and let it lead itself naturally to the next: all of the houses had a dossier of guest information that freely gave the wi-fi code. Moira had told her that the tariff was paid by the owners monthly: the guests could use the internet and landline as frequently as they pleased free of charge. Of course it was strictly forbidden for cleaners to do so, just as it was forbidden to read confidential documents locked in a drawer or entertain lovers in bedrooms you were supposed to be airing.

Her job that day was in Le Bois-Plage and she arrived well in advance of the usual start time in order to watch the out-going holidaymakers get into their taxi for the airport (these days, she scarcely glanced at the faces of these tanned, well-rested folk; she shared no language with them, not even with the British ones). Making use of the adrenalin coursing through her, she worked furiously until the house resembled a show home. In this property, an interior-designed beach bungalow, there were numerous extra touches: towels and bedlinen to be folded and tucked just so, special local soaps for the adults and caramels for the children, a home-made lemon tart that had to be taken from the freezer at the beginning of the shift in order to defrost in good time. She forced herself to finish every detail before settling at the desk in an alcove off the kitchen and turning on the PC. She could smell the lemon in the thawing tart on the worktop nearby.

For the first time since parting from Paul she did not begin by checking her email for word from him – could *that*, at least, be considered the road to recovery? – but instead Googled 'Arthur and Sylvie Woodhall'. The screen refreshed to reveal a bombardment of references, hundreds of thousands of them. She used the News filter to select a recent item on one of the more reputable UK sites. It was dated from April, four months ago:

WOODHALL RESIGNS ST BARNABAS' POST

The surgeon at the centre of one of the biggest media sensations of recent times, Arthur Woodhall, has resigned his post

256

at St Barnabas' Hospital in south London with immediate effect. It is thought that Woodhall plans to leave the UK, though rumours that he has taken a position at the new Moorfields Eye Hospital outpost in Dubai have been denied by a spokesperson for the surgeon. It was confirmed that he will continue to treat private patients at the Marylebone Eye Clinic, Harley Street, for the foreseeable future.

Woodhall's wife Sylvie and the couple's two teenage sons were killed in a car accident in July last year. Public reaction to the subsequent inquest, which revealed damning details of Woodhall's affair with his neighbour, Emily Marr, became a media phenomenon thanks to a moral crusade led by the *Press* columnist Nina Meeks. The so-called Marr Affair has since come to be regarded as emblematic of the nation's moral decay in an age of casual, low-brow celebrity and deteriorating state education.

Tabby stared, her eyes returning to a single word in the second paragraph: 'Emily'. This was no coincidence; it did not take forensic investigation to deduce that 'Emmie' could be a corruption of 'Emily'. The only place she had seen a single letter of her name was on the pills bottle. E: she'd simply assumed it stood for Emmie. As for the surname, she had never seen her friend's passport or any other formal identification – why would she have?

She cast her mind back to the evening when she'd asked Emmie her last name. Emmie had hesitated, apparently not wanting to say, before at last admitting to Mason. Had she, in fact, made it up on the spot? Marr and Mason: the initial was the same.

Excitement making her fumble, she Googled 'Emily Marr' and selected Images. There were surprisingly few different ones, given that the subject was a figure described as a 'media sensation', and the available ones were repeated hundreds of times, often treated in some illustrative way: Andy Warhol-style or a caricature with obscenely prominent lips and exaggerated curves; a line drawing of the kind you saw in court reports.

But it was her Emmie, she was sure of it, even before she came upon the one photo she recognised: Emmie in the pink and green dress, the caption revealing both the identity of her companion and the occasion: *Marr with her former boyfriend, Matt Piper, at a Piper family wedding in Kent.* There was the cascading blond hair, the winged eyebrows and smudged kohl, exactly as Emmie had done her make-up the night they'd had drinks in the port. Some of the other images must have been taken years ago, for this woman was young, a real beauty; she did not look as if she cleaned holiday homes for a living or reacted with anything but confidence to questions about her private life.

Scrolling on to a third page, Tabby noticed two new shots, one of Emmie with an armful of newspapers, her face buried in their pages and only her blond hair visible, the second a full-length image in which Emmie had something of the morose attitude she *did* recognise. In this she was wearing a black coat and boots, black headscarf, dark glasses, no make-up: was this, then, post-'exile'? To Tabby's shock, the caption read: *Emily Marr, leaving Willbury Cemetery in Hertfordshire after the funeral of her father, March 2012.* Tabby felt her breath catch in her throat. March: so recently! When she considered how raw it felt in her own case, and six years had passed. Poor, poor Emmie, what drama and loss she had suffered, and, for reasons Tabby was now beginning to appreciate, had had to suffer in silence.

Next, she scrolled through the pages and pages of sites in the general search, scanning the avalanche of headings: IS EMILY MARR THE NEW CHRISTINE KEELER?, EMILY MARR: DIE, SLUT!, WHATEVER HAPPENED TO EMILY MARR?, MARR: PUBLIC ENEMY NUMBER ONE, I HATE EMILY, EMILY MARR JOKES, STEAL HER STYLE: EMILY MARR ... On and on it went, there had to be a year's worth of reading material here. Tabby began with the Wikipedia entry:

Emily Rachel Marr (born 13 July 1980) is a British woman who came to media prominence in February 2012 during the inquest into the deaths of Sylvie Woodhall, Alexander Woodhall and Hugo Woodhall. It was heard that Marr had been having an affair with Sylvie's husband, Arthur Woodhall, a world-renowned eye surgeon with links to the British Royal Family. Marr, who lived on the same street as the Woodhalls, the famous Walnut Grove in south London, and worked in a neighbourhood pottery café, had been the last surviving witness to speak to Sylvie before her death. Though never charged with any criminal act, Marr was widely deplored for her lack of compassion for her lover's wife, including her declaration 'It's every woman for herself,' repeated to the coroner and reported by journalist Nina Meeks in the *Press* newspaper. She was subsequently condemned by the Church of England, the Deputy Prime Minister and several feminist groups for her disregard for marital values and her absence of remorse. The scandal reached its critical mass through digital media, but its inception was credited to Meeks, winner of a National Press Award in 2007 and widely tipped to receive another for her campaigning coverage of the tragedy.

The section on early life and family lacked citation, but stated that Emily had been born in Hemel Hempstead, Hertfordshire, and gone to a comprehensive school, leaving with one A-level, in English. Her mother had died from ovarian cancer when she was nine years old and she and her older brother had been raised by their father, who had not remarried. When Emily was in her twenties, he had been diagnosed with Alzheimer's, the form of dementia that led to his death at the age of sixty-three in early March.

Tabby scanned down to the section headed *Scandal*:

It came to light through statements given by both Woodhall and Marr that they had met at a Christmas party in December 2010 and begun an affair in February 2011. So intense was the attraction between them that by July Woodhall had decided to leave his wife to live with Marr. He had been about to drive to the family's holiday home in Sussex to break the news to his wife when the police arrived at his London residence with news of the triple tragedy. Marr was present at the time, having stayed with him overnight, a detail that distressed Mrs Woodhall's relatives and was considered deeply distasteful by Marr's critics.

Subsequent life

Little has been heard of Emily Marr since she left her flat on <u>Walnut Grove</u> in late February 2012.

Complaints were made to the Hertfordshire Constabulary following the funeral service of her father early the following month, which was disrupted by photographers attempting to access the burial site, and again following an incident in <u>Newbury</u>, Berkshire, where Marr is believed to have been in hiding at the home of her brother Philip. It is thought she may since have settled overseas to escape the widespread hate campaigns she was suffering in Britain. Internet reports have placed her variously in <u>Morocco</u>, <u>Australia</u> and the <u>Netherlands</u>. In spite of her infamy, she has not once spoken to the press or made a statement in any media, remaining, as the *Sunday Times* labelled her in a feature in June 2012, one of the 'Top Ten Great British Disappearing Acts', alongside <u>Agatha Christie</u> and <u>Lord Lucan</u>. Latterly, public opinion has shifted to include admiration for Marr in her eschewing of the celebrity and commercial opportunities that have undoubtedly been available to her.

Riveted, Tabby continued to read about her friend's infamous alter ego, article after article of mostly damning criticism, some of it expressed in obscenities and even death threats, until at last she was interrupted by the ringing of her phone. Predictably, tiresomely, it was Moira, checking that the job was done. She'd been making calls like this ever since her reminder of the rules regarding visitors.

'I'm just leaving now,' Tabby told her, rising to her feet and surveying the kitchen. The phone clenched between ear and shoulder, she sieved icing sugar on to the softened lemon tart. It looked perfect.

'So late? You should have finished an hour ago. The family will be on their way from the airport by now.'

'I know, I wanted to do a great job. The place looks fantastic. I'll be gone in two minutes.'

She could tell Moira was frustrated to be having to micro-manage and that Tabby apparently continued to warrant it. 'You know you'll be paid only for the official hours of the job?'

'Of course. That's fine.'

She turned off the PC and tucked in the desk chair, washed, dried and put away the sieve, and then headed for the front door. For once, she hardly cared if she would be paid at all.

She charged home on Emmie's bike through the vineyards, scarcely registering the swarms of tourists in her path. She could wait no longer, would pussyfoot around Emmie and her strate-gically placed folders no more. No one could be expected to contain knowledge of this magnitude (suspicion, she corrected herself. It wasn't knowledge yet), and if confrontation led to her being asked to leave the house that night, then so be it.

Inside the house it was quiet and cool, the shutters closed, as usual, on windows that could be overlooked only by a contortionist. But at least she now knew why. Emmie had been dozing on the sofa, but was roused at the sound of Tabby's arrival, the bike clattering over the threshold, the door swinging shut with a thump that made the lights flicker. Tabby propped the bike against the nearest wall and came to a halt herself by the fireplace, catching her breath, preparing her lines. You'd never guess, she thought, looking at the yawning woman in front of her, the wan complexion and dank hair, the softening jawline and fleshy build. Even the distinctive eyebrow shape had grown out. You'd never guess it was the same person.

'You gave me a shock,' Emmie murmured, sitting upright. 'What's wrong?'

Tabby waited for their eyes to meet before saying, 'I know, Emmie.'

'You know what?'

There was an odd moment between them, a sense that there was still a chance for Tabby to hold fire or for Emmie to dodge the bullet, but it did not last.

'I know you're not who you say you are. You're not Emmie Mason.'

Emmie forked nervous fingers through her hair, brow creasing. 'What are you talking about?'

'You're Emily Marr, aren't you? The woman in the Woodhall case? Please don't deny it, Emmie, it won't help. I've just read it all online. I saw the picture of you in the same dress, the one you wore when we went out. It's got to be you.'

There was a silence. Emmie let her hands fall to her lap and fixed her eyes on them.

'I knew you knew,' she said presently, and Tabby crossed the rug to sit down beside her, both relieved that the surrender had come so swiftly and excited by the thought of the revelations to follow. 'Have you known all along?'

'I haven't, actually. Not until today. I was in Asia when it was in the news, I must have missed the whole thing.' It felt wrong to call it a 'thing' when it was someone's life, someone's life altered beyond recognition.

All Emmie said was, 'Oh.'

Tabby leaned towards her, keen to resume eye contact. 'Will you tell me about it, Emmie? I know it must be hard to talk about, but I'd like to understand. Tell me from start to finish what happened, every detail. How you met Arthur, how it could possibly come about that you could be so well known and so ...' she remembered the word that had cropped up in the coverage she'd read, 'so *hated*. It's hard for me to make sense of it.' When Emmie remained silent, she added, 'Only if you want to, of course. I just thought, maybe you've been wanting to confide, you know, subconsciously, leaving the folder out yesterday, after I'd seen the photo that time.' She reminded herself that Emmie did not know she had read the obituary yesterday, though the distinction was hardly of relevance now she had made the leap she just had.

Emmie appeared to reach a decision. She got to her feet and rolled back her shoulders, looked down at Tabby with a startling new expression: where once her eyes had only repelled Tabby's curiosity, reflected it directly back at her, now they sucked powerfully at it, promising a limitless capacity to satisfy it. The sudden change in demeanour confused Tabby, for there was an air of grandeur to it also, almost as if Emmie were a Hollywood star who had been living undercover to research the role of an ordinary person and could finally unveil herself, instantly more comfortable once her rightful station was restored.

Without saying a word, she headed for the stairs.

'Emmie?' Tabby called after her. 'Are you all right? I didn't mean to upset you ...' Now she was the one at a loss. What had she stumbled into here, and had it been wise to confront Emmie like that? Had she sounded too accusatory, as if she

263

meant to condemn Emmie in the same way the rest of the world evidently had? Shouldn't she have instead reassured her, as she had once before, that she was on her side, no matter what? Did she genuinely care about Emmie's feelings or had she only been satisfying her own appetite for personal information, the unattractive part of her that had bloomed during her time here, fast coming to define her?

This unpleasant chain of thoughts was broken by Emmie's heavy-footed return. She stood before Tabby once more, this time with her laptop in her arms. That odd sense of pride was gone now, as was the voracious gaze; instead she looked fretful, grief very close to the surface of her features. Tabby knew then that the woman in front of her could not be the one described as heartless and scandalous and deplorable, and far, far worse. Even before she had mastered the basic elements of the story, she was starting to grapple with the full scale of the injustice that might have been done to her friend.

She reached up and touched Emmie's arm. 'Listen, I should have said before I started that I'm not going to make any kind of judgement. Whatever you've been involved in, I'm just a shoulder to cry on, that's all. A friend.'

Emmie did not respond to this in words, but placed the laptop gently on Tabby's lap, the greatest gift she could bestow. 'It's all in here,' she said.

'What do you mean?'

'Everything you want to ask me, all the details you want to know, it's all explained here. It's easier if you just read it.'

'You kept a diary?'

'Not exactly, not day by day, but my side of the story. Everyone was so sure they knew what happened, what kind of a person I was, but this is *my* version of events. This is the truth.'

Tabby steadied the laptop on her knees, her fingers fiddling with the catch and lifting the screen. 'That's what you've been doing all these nights? Writing?'

Emmie did not answer but stood staring at the laptop, as if already regretting allowing it out of her possession. It was heart-breaking to see her face. She looked older than her thirty-two years, a broken and tortured version of the exquisite young woman Tabby had seen online an hour ago.

'You're sure you want me to read it?'

'Yes. But please be careful with it. It's all I have.'

Tabby needed no second invitation. She turned the power on. It took a few moments for the desktop to display, it was an old thing. 'What's the password?'

'Woodhall.'

'As in . . . ?' But it was a stupid question. 'OK. What's the file called?'

'It's on the desktop. It's called "Emily Marr".'

It was a sizeable file and clicking it open Tabby saw that it was in fact over a hundred pages long. She already knew she wanted to read it in solitude; it would be impossible to concentrate if Emmie were standing over her like this, agitated and expectant, ready to repossess the computer at any moment. 'Is it OK if I take it upstairs to my room to read?'

Emmie nodded.

Tabby stood up, moved past her towards the stairs. A thought struck her then, not an urgent one, just something to bridge Emmie's rather tragic relinquishment of the material with her own indecent desire to devour it. 'You didn't tell me it was your birthday,' she said, her voice bright, only a little strained.

'What?'

'It was a couple of weeks ago, wasn't it? The thirteenth of July? I had no idea or I would have given you a present.'

As Emmie's face darkened, Tabby feared she'd said precisely the worst thing she could have done, but a moment later Emmie's expression had cleared again. 'Birthdays are the last thing on my mind,' she said.

Chapter 19

Emily

In all the research I've done since, I have never seen a coroner's inquest into the death of an ordinary citizen get the coverage this one did. By 'ordinary' I mean someone who was not in her life a famous personality or a celebrity, for there had been nothing ordinary about Sylvie's world, of course, with her three-million-pound Walnut Grove house, her celebrated husband and her privately educated children. Her 'coven' of high-status friends.

Nina Meeks, for instance, her closest friend of all, a newspaper columnist of impressive power and reach. If I had not appreciated before the full extent of that power and reach, I soon would. Normally she commented on stories already in circulation, scandals under way, but this time she decided to create one. She made the distinction herself in the article that began it all – 'it' being not so much my fall, since I was already on bloodied knees, but my public disgrace, my character assassination.

Whatever you want to call it.

But that was not until Friday morning. When the coroner announced his verdict on the Thursday morning, it was not immediately reported online. Very little came up when I Googled 'Woodhall inquest' on the PC at work that afternoon, only the original brief reports of the accident from the previous summer, and so I waited till Charlotte was out of range and phoned the coroner's office. A verdict of accidental death had been recorded, I was told, and just in time, because it was almost four o'clock by then and the office was about to close for the day.

Still stupefied by the pain of my encounter with Arthur, I felt nothing distinctive on hearing the news. It was what had been expected, wasn't it? A formal ratification that Sylvie could never have meant to kill herself or the boys; if she had wanted anyone dead that morning it was me. It was only when I got home from work that I found I had been given only half the news – or a third. Searching the internet once more, I saw that a local paper in Sussex had posted a report, including the full wording of the coroner's conclusions:

On the balance of probability, Mrs Woodhall's death was not the result of any deliberate act. I do not believe she intended to harm herself and for that reason I have recorded a verdict of accidental death. In the matter of her two sons, however, I believe that a sober person would have understood that the boys were at risk of involuntary manslaughter.

It has been established that the rear passenger, Alexander Woodhall, was not wearing a seatbelt at the point of impact and that this would have given him a significantly lower chance of survival than if he had remained in his seat with the legally required restraint. It has been reasonably demonstrated that he unbuckled his seatbelt in a bid to take control of the vehicle following Mrs Woodhall's loss of control. I have to conclude that it was an avoidable end for him, just as it was for his brother, Hugo Woodhall, seated in the front passenger seat, and my verdict in the deaths of Alexander Woodhall and Hugo Woodhall is therefore unlawful killing.

I cried for Arthur then. How could it not devastate him to hear that his wife was responsible for his children's deaths, if not her own, declared a criminal in all but name? When I fell asleep that night, it was with his face held tightly in my thoughts. How I longed to be able to cradle his head in my hands on the pillow next to mine, put my lips on his skin, console him, protect him with my love on this night of all nights.

To be fair to Nina, when she published her column the following morning, she probably did not dream it would have the impact it did. Possibly, in her own mind, she meant it for my eyes only. That was certainly my assumption when at 8 a.m. my doorbell rang and, hurrying downstairs, I found the doorstep unoccupied and a copy of the *Press* sticking through the letterbox. Pulling it free, I dislodged a yellow Post-it on the front page with the scribbled clue *See page 13*.

It was her regular Friday slot, a full right-hand page. I would soon be aware that her column was more than simply a popular read; it was a national institution, and many people bought the paper expressly for it. Even in the digital age, what Nina said on a Friday was often what the nation discussed at dinner parties that weekend.

The headline today was REMEMBER MY NAME and the picture was not of a movie star or a politician or of anyone widely recognisable, but of me. *Me*. Even before I could form my first intelligible thought my nervous system had skipped ahead, quickening my lungs and heating my skin. Standing there, barefoot and in pyjamas in the draughty hallway of 199, I tried to focus on the picture, make some sense of it, and soon identified by my dress and hairstyle that it must be one of the reportage-style shots taken at the wedding of Matt's cousin Gemma two years earlier. Matt had been cropped out, his hand just visible on my right elbow, and devoid of context I looked light-headed, remote, as if I didn't have a care in the world. I had not seen the shot for ages and supposed it must have come from Gemma's or another guest's Facebook page or blog.

The article began:

> It's not often I write about so-called 'civilians', those who are not famous and do not wish to be. As a columnist, my stock-in-trade is public figures, people we all know and feel a common urge to discuss. But there are times when I cannot escape the paradox of modern journalism: we must make a sensation of events that should barely pass as notable in the lives of household names, while overlooking the truly sensational among those we've never heard of.
>
> Well, maybe sometimes we *should* have heard of them.
>
> Personally, I think you should know the name Emily Marr. Say it out loud. Remember it. Emily Marr. I know it already, of course, for it belongs to the most despised woman in my neighbourhood.
>
> It strikes me that she also deserves to be the most despised woman in Britain. I'm pretty sure a certain coroner in Sussex agrees with me.

My breath coming now in painful gulps, I read on in horror as Nina summarised the events of July 2011 before offering choice cuts from my testimony earlier in the week, including, inevitably, 'it's every woman for herself!' – on which she bestowed an exclamation mark – and other damning admissions from my witness statement (of course she had got her hands on a copy, by fair means or foul, she was a *journalist*). I did not understood then that, although the verdicts were included in it, the main part of the piece had most likely been written before the inquest, timed to launch a campaign about British morals, a campaign that would later gain her editor a mention in the New Year's Honours list. Nina had had months to hone her hatred, to set me up.

Every woman for herself: that was the challenge Marr threw down that terrible July evening, and, just as any good wife and mother would, Sylvie got in her car and set off to claim the husband she had loved and honoured for over two decades.

She made no mention of the fact that Sylvie had drunk the best part of two bottles of wine and taken a sedative before doing what any good wife and mother would do. I read on:

Don't get me wrong, Miss Marr's was not a crime that will be remembered for centuries, she is no Lizzie Borden. Hers was a smaller, more familiar one, one that she hoped would remain secret – until it suited her to reveal it. She had an affair with a married man, a father; she ignored the pleas of his wife made on behalf of his children. In doing so she caused, indirectly, the deaths of three people. She is no serial killer, no, but in my opinion she has taken children's lives and I call now for a public reckoning. On the day this newspaper launches a new campaign for old morals, I ask you again:

Remember her name.

Emily Marr is a young woman who symbolises all that has decayed in our society. She has no respect for anyone else and an inflated regard for herself. She wants what she wants without earning it, and without caring that it might already belong to someone else.

Well, I hope she's satisfied now.

As I say, naïve as it now sounds, my first theory was that Nina had had this article mocked up especially for me, to scare me, punish me; I could not see that it could possibly be her actual column that day. I needed to double-check, though, for peace of mind, which meant I could pick up a copy from the newsagent on the way to work or I could look now to see if her column was available yet online – I'd often read it in that form before.

Upstairs in the flat, I dialled up and found the site for the *Press*. That was when the full horror surfaced: this was no private psychological torture but a public denouncement, because there it was, in full, exactly the same copy as the printed version I held in my hand. Nina Meeks had told the whole country, her millions of readers, about *me*.

Scrolling down, I saw that there were already dozens of comments, at 8.30 in the morning:

Sounds like a complete whore to me . . .

Selfish, heartless bitch. Meeks is right to bring real cases like this to public attention. I blame our culture of reality TV. People want something for nothing, even if it means stealing it from someone who's worked for it.

What a c∗∗t. Terrible dress sense as well.

Even the one less vitriolic comment I managed to find was unpleasant: 'I'm not being funny, but look at her, she's a babe! The wife must have been knocking on the door of fifty, who would you rather do?!! Bet the doc tampered with the brakes himself!!'

Another user had responded to this: 'Read the article, you insensitive tw∗t. The poor man lost his KIDS in that crash!'

Shaking, I closed the page. After a pause, I searched for the name 'Lizzie Borden', quickly finding a notorious killer from the nineteenth century. I was not to be compared with her, no, but our names were printed in the same sentence in a national newspaper along with the declaration that 'in my opinion she has taken children's lives' – and so what else were people expected to do?

271

I disconnected. Absurdly, I still intended to go to work, was dressed and about to leave the flat, when Matt rang. I had not heard from him since the evening he had moved out and so his call was a confirmed sign that I was in a critical situation.

'What the fuck is going on, Em? I've just got into work and there's some kind of viral thing about you on the internet.'

'What do you mean?'

'I don't know what it is, but you're everywhere. It's like a hate campaign. There's a photograph of me doing the rounds as well, it's mental!'

My pulse began to trip once more. 'It must be to do with what Nina's written about me in the *Press* ...'

'Who's Nina?'

'Our neighbour – I mean my neighbour. The journalist, dark bob, high heels, friend of Sarah Laing, do you remember?'

'Not really. What's her second name? I'll look her up on Twitter.'

I spelled it for him, hearing the fear in my own voice.

'Here's the link to her article, hang on ...'

I waited while he read, my breathing strained and shallow.

'You were seeing the bloke whose family died last year? You had to go to an inquest?'

'Yes.'

Matt wouldn't need to delve too deeply to see the overlap between the last months of our relationship and the start of the affair with Arthur, but that was the least of my worries – and his, evidently.

'Seriously, you might want to close down some of your accounts, email and Facebook and stuff. You're going to get hate mail. This woman has over half a million followers. Fuck, she was tweeting about you just now, this is surreal. Listen to this, she's just said, "I agree, she deserves nothing less. And I say that as someone who has sympathy for Ruth Ellis's memory." Who's Ruth Ellis anyway?' he asked.

'Wasn't she the last woman to be hanged in Britain?'

'Oh, yeah, that makes sense, here's the thread: she's responding to some loony who tweeted her, "Bring back the death penalty!" She means for *you*. Jesus, this is bad . . .'

'Don't tell me any more,' I begged. My hand was trembling, the phone bumping against my ear.

'Isn't this libel or something? I think you need to get a lawyer.' I could hear the new edge of outrage to his voice.

'I don't have money for a lawyer,' I said.

The call ended, I sat on the sofa, head in hands, eyes tight shut. I couldn't comprehend the hair-trigger brutality of this. I felt as if I were witnessing an explosion, still too blinded by the light to see how the particles had been blown apart. Only yesterday morning, the coroner had closed his inquest to a half-empty room. Was he aware yet of Meeks' article? Could he do anything to get the *Press* to retract it? What had she said, *I'm pretty sure a certain coroner in Sussex agrees with me . . .* Was that true? Were you allowed to print comments like that? Underneath that scrupulous fairness, that egalitarian compassion, *would* he agree with every word she'd written?

He might.

Matt was right about the hate mail. I closed my Facebook account just as activity on it began to go haywire. My email inbox was swelling second by second in the same way it had when the computer had once had a virus; I logged straight out.

I saw that I couldn't possibly go to work. I phoned Charlotte, grateful to get her voicemail and not have to speak directly to her. I said there was a legal emergency to do with my day off on the Wednesday, but I would be in, as usual, the next day, Saturday, always our busiest of the week thanks to the standard back-to-back birthday parties. I could only pray she did not discover what the emergency was, if she had not done so already.

That done, and Matt's voice already fading from memory, I

sensed the beginnings of what would become the defining emotion of this period: besieged, hunted – and it was still a full day before any photographers would arrive at my gate. I tried to do normal things, treat this as a spontaneous day off: I took a shower, but the water felt like an assault, the nerve endings in my skin ten times more sensitive than usual; I watched television (I was not on air myself – not yet) and did some laundry, anything that allowed me to pretend for two minutes that I'd never seen Nina's article and she had not set in motion something truly diabolical. I successfully ignored my ringing phone, declining call after call, including one from Phil, but I could not keep myself from the laptop. By the early afternoon, a search of my name yielded thousands of listings – *thousands*, from a standing start six hours ago! – and the numbers were increasing with every minute. I was fixated on those comments below Nina's column, which now numbered many hundreds. There were breathtakingly bold statements of opinion regarding my appearance and sexual desirability, shockingly easy expressions of agreement that I was a hateful witch who deserved to die or a slut who would not be kicked out of bed. Thankfully the killer angle had not been so readily embraced, but other notorious women of history were freely referenced, mostly famous prostitutes and mistresses. Some became queens, others remained the grubby cast-offs of sportsmen, but not one, from Mata Hari to Monica Lewinsky, was a woman to whom I had ever wanted – or thought – to liken myself.

It was less a sick joke now than a waking nightmare. Scanning my text messages, I read one from Matt: *I hope you're managing to lie low. My supervisor just told me to go home early. First time ever!*

He was my unlikely sole supporter that first day; there was an unconditional loyalty in our communications that reminded me of the happier days of our relationship. There were times that terrible Friday when I wished he were back in the flat with me, that we'd never parted, never moved here, never met the Laings or the Meekses or the Woodhalls.

That evening, as guides began to appear to the background of this contagious new scandal (GET UP TO SPEED ON THE EMILY MARR CRASH!), I took the opportunity to read the evidence of those questioned before and after me at the inquest. Alexander's girlfriend, a gentle, dark-haired beauty who had a place at Oxford in the autumn and whose photograph was placed next to mine for good/evil contrast, explained that she'd received a text from her boyfriend when he was *en route* that final morning, established as the penultimate communication from any of the three (the very last being Hugo's voicemail to his father): '*Mum insisting we come back to London. In a state but won't let me drive. Call you when back.*'

Exact findings were given of the toxicology tests, heard by the coroner on the first day: Sylvie had had a blood alcohol level of 260mg per 100ml of blood, the legal limit being 80mg per 100ml. Paramedics had described how she and Hugo had had to be cut free from the overturned wreckage; Alexander had been thrown through the windscreen and been 'close to decapitation'.

The pathologist had been present to answer questions and Arthur had asked him if any of the three might have been conscious between impact and death. The pathologist replied that death would have occurred instantly. I wondered if that was any comfort, given the statements of some of the witnesses. One, a woman called Lisa Hawes, had said of Hugo as he flashed by at ninety miles an hour or more, 'He had a look of total terror on his face. I've never seen anything so awful in my whole life. It was like someone on a rollercoaster who's just seen that he's come off the track and is plummeting to the ground.'

I tried to go to bed early and escape these terrible details through sleep, but I couldn't steady my thoughts enough to lose consciousness. I'd spent so long at the computer my brain continued to sift and search, as if the thousands of pages I had not yet seen were backed up, opening one after the other, never quite fast enough to outpace the incessant arrival of new ones.

The following morning, Saturday, almost every national newspaper reported on the inquest, less for the value of the story itself (it was a tragedy to be sure, but whatever Nina liked to believe Sylvie Woodhall was not Princess Diana) as for unprecedented social media activity that had followed the original column, which was described as 'campaigning', 'incendiary', 'electrifying'.

In the *Press*, there was a new piece by her entitled WHY I BLAME EMILY MARR FOR THE LOSS OF ALL OUR LIVES, in which she linked me with drug dealers and fraudsters. 'At best, she is a poster girl for brainless Britain,' she wrote; 'at worst, the most casual and amoral of killers-by-proxy'. Elsewhere in the national press, a rival tabloid had a feature called WHY 30 IS THE MOST DANGEROUS AGE, based chiefly on the fact that I had begun my affair with Arthur at this age. The same picture from the wedding was shown, with the caption: *Emily Marr: A Danger to Society?* A second photograph from the same event was captioned *Beautiful on the Outside, Ugly on the Inside*.

I was in no fit state to work, concerned though I was that this would be my third day off that week. As I dithered, Charlotte phoned and made the decision for me. She was in a state of high agitation. 'Why didn't you tell me you were mixed up in all that business?'

By then it seemed remarkable that there should be any living soul only just being made aware of my infamy. 'I told you I was there the morning of the accident,' I reminded her quietly.

'But you said you hardly knew the guy?' She didn't pause for an answer, exclaiming, 'This is a disaster, Emily, he's some sort of world-famous doctor!' as if I had not noticed of my own wit. 'Ash said people have been taking photos of the shop on their phones, and we've had two reporters on the line already, on a Saturday!'

But I was rapidly learning that there was no such thing as a weekend on the internet, no closing hours, or even minutes. 'Will you be able to cope without me?' I asked her.

'Well, we'll have to. You can't possibly come in, it's all anyone's talking about. We'll be mobbed for all the wrong reasons.'

'I'm sure it will have died down by the end of the day,' I said, hearing the pathetic plea in my voice. 'Shall I aim to come in as usual on Monday?'

'Let's leave it for a while, speak again on Monday or Tuesday,' Charlotte said. 'See if it *has* died down.' But I knew – and understood – that, whether the frenzy had abated or not, she meant we would talk only about formalising my departure. My poor attendance record was one thing, but she couldn't risk her business being associated any more closely than it already was with a woman fast becoming known as the country's most hated home-wrecker. *Ugly on the inside.*

Having been indoors now for thirty-six hours, I decided to brave an expedition to the shop for bread and milk. For fear of being recognised, I tucked my hair inside my collar and, for the first time in years in public, wore no make-up at all. Managing the errand without being accosted, I walked back the long way, past number 11. The flowers and notes were back on the railings, though none of the reports I'd read stated with any certainty that Arthur had returned to live there. My instinct told me he had not.

Returning to 199 with my bag of provisions and a stack of newspapers in my arms, I noticed a cluster of men at the gate, young, casually dressed, apparently familiar to one another: photographers, four of them. Spotting me, they began to issue a stream of low-key questions and comments, as if we were good friends delighted to meet accidentally: 'Here she is'; 'All right,

Emily?'; 'What do you think about Nina Meeks having a go at you like that?'; 'How do you feel about being an internet sensation?' It was chummy, almost festive, the way they bantered as they followed me up the path to get their shots (there was none of the shutter-clicking you associated with paparazzi, only the silent surveillance of digital equipment). It would later be considered a 'PR strategy' but when I hid my face in my newspapers it was in fact because I was too shocked to look up from my feet; the result was that none of the photos would identify me clearly.

They stayed until early evening and then returned the next morning, pioneers of what by Monday would become a pack befitting the winner of a television talent show or a homecoming Olympic medallist. It was a surreal development to a situation already impossible for me to absorb or comprehend, and, inevitably, my value system began to lose its solidity. I unearthed the 'emergency' cigarettes I'd hidden in a kitchen drawer when Matt and I moved in and smoked my first one in almost eighteen months – then a second and a third. I was promptly sick.

I received more voicemails and texts that day than I had in the previous year. I made only one myself, to the hospital ward. 'I don't think I'm going to be able to visit this weekend,' I told the sister on duty, trying to sound unflustered.

'That's probably for the best,' she said matter-of-factly, which told me that the news had reached even secure hospital units. I begged her to try to keep any offending newspapers from my father. Though he had lost the ability to follow anything longer than a sentence or two, he might see a picture of me he recognised, something dredged up from my childhood, and become confused or distressed. He certainly didn't need to know his only daughter had been elected a national hate figure.

Again, with no excuse but cowardice, I avoided calls from my brother.

That evening, I had the discombobulating experience of

seeing myself discussed on television. On one of the twenty-four-hour news channels, two journalists and a retired coroner debated whether or not the media storm begun by Nina heralded a brave new age of journalism, the death of celebrity culture and wannabe reality TV in favour of real stories about ordinary people.

'What has captured everyone's imagination is that this is real-life drama, as opposed to "reality" drama, in which no one actually behaves as they would in real life because their aim is to become a celebrity.'

'But aren't we just making a celebrity of Emily Marr? Isn't this just a different way of getting to the same result?'

'It's not the same at all. There's nothing whatsoever to suggest this woman has courted our attention.'

My breath caught at this note of support: did it mark the end of this nightmare, the return of reason?

'You're saying this is a private tragedy and it should have remained private?' asked the presenter.

'I'm saying this is a personal agenda on the part of Nina Meeks, not a story of national importance. Inquests into road traffic accidents take place every day of the week up and down the country. There's nothing about this one that merits more than a report in the local paper, or maybe a summary of the more lurid elements in the *Daily Mail*.'

'But the fact that there *is* so much interest suggests Meeks' instincts were right, people *are* finding meaning in this one in particular. Don't you think it's possible that every so often we get a young woman in the public eye who is representative of her generation, and Emily Marr is ours? She's a Christine Keeler figure, a Monica Lewinsky, an important symbol?'

'Our first poster girl for immorality this century?' the presenter asked, clarifying.

'Well, I could name plenty of others who might take that honour.'

There was knowing laughter and then the supporter spoke up once more: 'But there's nothing new about having an affair with a married man and not thinking about the consequences, is there? All this "old morals" stuff the *Press* is peddling is hogwash. We all know there's been sexual infidelity since time immemorial; there's always been this sort of scandal in communities. And the man Marr had an affair with is hardly Jack Profumo, is he? Or Bill Clinton? He's not a major political name—'

'He's one of our leading surgeons,' the presenter interjected, 'with an international reputation.'

'Yes, but he's not a public figure in their league, is he? He's not a household name.'

'He is now!'

The one I thought of as my defender grew exasperated. 'Look, if you want my opinion, this is a witch-hunt, pure and simple, and we should be very careful about taking part in it, because normal citizens are not equipped to deal with sudden persecution of this intensity. This young woman has had no preparation, no media training. She could be sitting at home watching this, completely terrified by the situation she finds herself in.'

'I doubt that! She may not be working the press right now, but who's to say she won't pop up later this year in the jungle or the *Big Brother* house? Publishers would pay a fortune for her story, if she acts quickly enough.'

The retired coroner, asked his opinion at last, said, 'I'm pleased to see the public being educated in the nature of coroners' inquiries, the work these unsung heroes do. Inquests like this answer important questions for loved ones, they explain what would otherwise have remained unexplained, and that can be a great consolation to surviving relatives.'

On this gentler note, the presenter brought the discussion to a close. I told myself the story would get no further than this cable channel, which couldn't have huge viewing figures, especially on a Saturday night, when most people were out meeting friends, letting their hair down, starting love affairs that were nobody's business but their own.

The next day, I read Nina's belated obituary of Sylvie, published that morning in the sister Sunday of the *Press*. People reported on Twitter and other sites that they'd been reduced to tears by it. There were, when I looked, 812 comments posted under the online version. If anything, activity seemed to increase at the weekend. Was this all anyone did? Read about how sexually depraved a woman they'd never met was and post a comment saying the country had gone to the dogs?

Did Arthur read the obituary too? And if he did, had he, as I had, lingered on one sentence in particular: '*It was Sylvie who was driving that terrible morning, yes, but the truth is she was driven to that tragic ending*'?

What were his feelings about the monstrous circus that now surrounded the deaths of his wife and sons? Did reporters hound him as they did me, and if they'd run him to ground, where was that ground? The cottage in Sussex, where Sylvie and the boys had spent their last night? The Inn on the Hill? His office in Harley Street? *Where was he?* Was anyone comforting him as he needed to be comforted?

Even then, I longed with all my heart for it to be me.

On Monday morning, with reporters and photographers multiplying in the street outside, my doorbell rang incessantly and the thumping on the door could be felt in vibrations on the first floor, in rattling window frames and shuddering floorboards. Voices called up to me from below, sometimes rough, as if waking me in an emergency, other times more musical – 'Em-i-lee, Em-i-lee' – in the hope of enchanting me to an open window, preferably half naked and camera-ready. They did not seem to consider that mine was only one of three flats in the building and that others might be disturbed by this harassment. By chance, the couple in the lower flat were on holiday; the occupants of the flat upstairs, three medical students from St Barnabas', kept irregular hours and so I could never quite be sure when they were in or out. A point of particular drama and distress came when one of the students, a Malaysian called Ashraf, let himself in downstairs and reporters forced the door as he tried to close it behind him. His footsteps, the soft, familiar ones of a neighbour who often came home at dawn, were followed by a stampede of others, coming to a halt, inevitably, at my door. I don't know how long the hammering and shouting went on but I wedged a heavy armchair against the frame and earplugs in my ears to try to wait it out. I had no doubt that poor Ashraf's image would appear online, with the suggestion that he was yet another lover of the murdering slag on the first floor.

In the evening, watching from a painful angle by the living-room window, I saw Marcus Laing come down the road on his way home from work and, reaching his gate, turn to face the assembled media next door. His demeanour was relaxed, his expression open-minded. A minute later, my bell rang in the short, abrupt way of a genuine caller, as opposed to the lengthy din caused by a thumb pressed down for minutes at a time.

I did not answer, of course.

'See? You're wasting your time, guys,' I heard him say as he returned to the pack. 'She's gone away. We haven't seen her since last week. Why don't you try her work?'

I didn't hear the response, but guessed he was being told I had failed to turn up for work again. Perhaps Charlotte had even announced my dismissal.

'There you go, she must have left town.' I didn't know whether he was trying to protect me or just voicing wishful thinking. 'I don't blame her, either,' he added, 'with you lot on her case!'

'Know her well, do you?' one of them called out. 'A friendly kind of neighbour, is she? Got a thing about married men, apparently,' which caused the rest to shout with laughter and rain further questions down on poor Marcus. His gait visibly tenser, he paced back up the path, head down as he turned in to his own gate, so I couldn't see his face.

Switching on the TV later that evening, hoping to be distracted by a film or documentary, I caught the opening minutes of BBC's *Newsnight*:

'Tonight we'll be reporting on the first big internet story of 2012: the overnight sensation of Emily Marr. Just who is Marr and why has she become one of the top trending subjects on Twitter? Joining us in the studio will be the woman who set the story alight in the first place, the *Press* columnist Nina Meeks, who is fairly certain *she* knows the answer. I should say that, in the interests of fair play, we have invited Emily Marr to come and defend herself, but as yet have had no reply from the woman at the centre of this story, the woman who, remarkably, has yet to speak to a single journalist or post any message online.'

And nor would she.

Chapter 20

Emily

Nina's wish was granted and I became, for a time, Britain's most hated woman. In fairness, the press were only the prosecutors: they brought the recommendation that I be hated, but people still had to hate me of their own accord.

I gave up noting the names of my detractors early on, even in passing. I had – and still have, presumably – tens of thousands of them, hundreds of thousands possibly. Visualising the reach of the internet was giddying, overwhelming; the feeling it gave me reminded me of the aftermath of my mother's death, when Dad had never been able to explain where it was she had gone. He spoke of heaven and angels and eternal rest, leaving me to make sense of the abyss on my own.

This was a new kind of abyss.

The haters pursued me from the morning of Nina's first article, mostly by email, since I had closed my Facebook account, and then, when my mobile phone number was widely published, by voicemail and text message. Later, perhaps most disturbingly, vitriol arrived by post and I would amass bagfuls of it in the small flat, not daring to throw it in the communal bins for fear that members of the resident media might steal and publish it. My 'crime' elicited the full gamut of hysterical responses, from threats of death and rape to declarations of admiration and love; I even had three marriage proposals, one from a man already married ('but that doesn't bother *you*, Emily, does it?').

I soon found myself in a catch-22: I couldn't ignore the letters and leave them unopened, or shut down my email account or change my phone number, in case Arthur wanted to contact me by one of these methods, and yet the messages I had to endure in (vain) search of one from him only reminded me, one by one, hour by hour, of how worthless I was, how unlikely ever to be communicated with again by a decent and civilised person. How implausible the notion that a man like him could ever have loved me.

Funny, but over time it was the supporters rather than the critics who made me most anxious. While the opponents got their hatred off their chests and retreated – they wanted no actual relationship with me, only a temporary target for their righteousness – the 'fans' persisted. Since my address was apparently publicly available (a photograph of Walnut Grove was more often than not preferred, to illustrate the gracious and élite social circle I had infiltrated and made toxic), it was only a matter of time before they began to turn up in person. Some were awed, speechless figures at the gate, their phones held aloft in readiness for a silhouette at the window, others were more forceful, coming to the door with the photographers to buzz insistently and, in their case, post passionate handwritten notes through the letterbox. A handful in particular would not take no for an answer. One woman came night after night, until I sobbed into the intercom, 'Please leave me alone. I *have* to sleep.' We both fell silent then, I at my flat door and she on the front step, stunned perhaps to have heard my voice, and then I heard the letterbox rattle once more: she'd posted a message. *You are not alone*, it read. *I know exactly what you are feeling. Your pain is my pain.*

And so on.

I soon discovered that such people were also acting on my behalf, disturbing a certain other Grove resident in their attempts to clear my name. Early one morning during the week after the verdict, my buzzer rang and, knowing it to be too early for the photographers and sensing unusual command in its application, I picked up the intercom.

'Yes?'

'Nina Meeks. Is that you, Emily? Can I have a word?'

I let her in, realising after a full minute of waiting that she did not intend coming up to the flat but that I was to join her in the hallway downstairs. Even then – more than ever, perhaps – this was for her a question of power, every move a strategic one. My heart thudded at the sight of her, the sound of her, the woman who had ruined my life. *If I were you, Emily, I'd think seriously about disappearing*, she'd said, and, long before that, *He wouldn't dare* ... That's what she'd said to Sylvie that first day in the café: why had I not recognised it as the warning it had been?

She did not spare me the courtesy of a greeting. 'Call your little friends off,' she said curtly, as I drew up in front of her. 'I've had them on the phone all hours of the night and at my door leaving hate mail.'

'What?' I assumed she must be talking about the doorsteppers and was unable to understand how she could have been affected at the far end of the Grove, Arthur's end. 'I would have thought you could do more about the reporters than I can.'

'Don't be ridiculous, not the media. I mean the imbecilic members of the public trying to harass me in my own home. Ed caught one of them posting *dog shit* through the door.'

Circumstances forbade me from finding this funny. Not quite meeting her hate-filled glare, I began to defend myself: 'How do you know they're anything to do with me? They could be objecting to something else you've written? You've claimed plenty of scalps.' The phrase came from the depths of memory –

the party perhaps, which now felt like a hundred years ago, thousands, before my own scalp became worth claiming.

She smirked, unimpressed. 'Oh, do me a favour, Emily. It's fairly obvious who they've been inspired by.'

Mystified by this, I could only gape like an idiot, at a loss as to how to respond. Of course, later I saw online a picture of a group of people wearing T-shirts printed with the slogan: EMILY MARR, GET OFF HER BACK! They did not have their own website, at least not one that I could find, but the caption referred to them as a protest group, one that had heckled *Press* staff as they came and went at their offices in Farringdon and, presumably, Nina at home.

I took a long, shaky breath, wanting to tell her how miserable she had made me, how unnecessarily cruel I thought her act of revenge. It could neither bring back the Woodhalls nor make any difference to Arthur and me, since he had finished with me long before she'd made a public enemy of me. No amount of misery heaped on me by her and her colleagues could make me feel worse than I had in the car park that day at the coroner's court, when I'd been rejected by him once and for all. But no words came. That early morning in February, standing in the hall under a lightless bulb, it was my first – and only – opportunity to confront her, to ask her to explain *herself*, but I was too cowardly to take it. Watching me cower and choke, she tossed me a last scornful look before leaving. 'Just call them off, all right, or I'll have no choice but to get the police involved.'

But I couldn't help her even if I wanted to. I could hardly stop people from harassing her when I could not stop them from harassing me. The siege came to a head that same afternoon when another 'admirer', a middle-aged man, rang and rang the bell, at first calling up, 'I love you, Emily!' but, when I failed to appear, turning aggressive and shouting horrible insults, calling me a fucking whore and threatening to break down the door. Sarah Laing stormed out of her house then and, unable to beat the madman, decided to join him, screaming up at my window, 'Can you *please* do something about this, Emily! I've got kids next door who don't need to hear this filth!' – as if I didn't know she had children and hadn't once been entrusted with their care. 'And while we're on the subject, if you don't get rid of that disgusting graffiti, I'll do it myself! I'll do it right this minute!'

I didn't have a clue what she meant by this and in the time I'd searched online and found a photograph of my garden wall daubed with the words DIE, SLUT, she was already standing in the street with tin of emulsion and paintbrush, a look of right-eous fervour on her face. Conscious that the whole scene would be reported by my personal press corps, I called the police before she could.

Presently, two male officers arrived and persuaded the admirer/abuser to leave. They then spoke in pacifying tones to Sarah, whose voluble complaints had drawn other neighbours to the gate, all of whom evidently had gripes of their own to share, before at last ringing my bell and asking to come up.

I was interested to see if either of the officers might be the one who'd been sent to break the news to Arthur that morning – I even remembered his name, PC Matthews – but of course nei-ther was. I don't know what I thought I would have gained by that: solace in the tiniest of remaining affinities, perhaps; the brief company of someone who had seen us in the same room at the same time and could vouch for our having once been together.

'This is reaching the point where you need to think about your own safety,' the older of the two policemen told me. He was about Arthur's age, I thought. He had probably never planned to leave *his* wife for trouble like me.

'Oh, there aren't as many photographers now,' I said. 'If any-thing, I'd say it's getting better.'

'It's not because of the photographers that you phoned us,' he reminded me. 'In situations like this, members of the public can be more threatening than the press. They're interested for personal reasons, not professional ones. They feel a connection that isn't there on your side. You have to be very careful. Are you living here alone?'

'Yes.'

'Is there anyone you can go and stay with for a while? Anyone we can phone for you?' The words, if not the tone, recalled those I'd heard in Arthur's kitchen that morning long ago.

'This is where I live,' I said, but not as defiantly as I might have in previous days. 'I won't be hounded out. I can sit it out.'

I could sit it out, but I still couldn't sleep. Only when, late in the second week, I began slipping out early in the morning to travel across the city to Hertfordshire to see my father, making the journey home again after dark, only then did the nervous energy involved in evading detection exhaust me enough to guarantee proper sleep.

Though I dressed unobtrusively for those public forays, I did not want to alter my appearance too radically for fear of confusing Dad. Since my hair was the chief giveaway, I wore a knitted hat to cover it up, tucking the strands inside it like a swimming cap and keeping it on even on the stuffy Underground. Passing a charity shop, I picked up a pair of glasses with uncorrected lenses, hoping I looked merely unstylish rather than hopelessly badly disguised. In the hospital toilet, I ditched the hat and frames, combed out my hair and added a little of the make-up Dad was used to seeing me in. I would then reverse the process before departure. In the context of my new, fugitive existence, it was not nearly as absurd as it sounds.

Once on the ward, I was able to recover a sense of perspective (there couldn't have been many other places in the land that made being the object of mass hatred look like a marginal concern). Dad was fading again and no one was pretending it was ground that might be recovered. This, too soon and yet at last, was the final stage of the disease. There was so little of him left, hardly anything recognisable: no voice, no spirit, no humour. In having been robbed of the last vestiges of personal identity – his sense of place and his position in time had gone long ago – he had also been robbed of his last physical likeness to himself.

'Dad,' I would say to his motionless, emaciated figure, and sometimes 'Daddy', an infant again. 'I love you very much, and I need you. Please get stronger.' Please make everything better again, like you used to.

But he hardly responded to me now, either as a daughter he knew or a desperate stranger he did not. I could see my words had no meaning whatsoever and it would have broken my heart, had not my heart been already pulverised.

During one visit, one of the last I would make, his consultant took pity on me and arranged for me to see one of the hospital psychiatrists, who wrote me a prescription to collect from the pharmacy on site. (Going to the GP was impossible during this period, as was any situation in which I was required to say my name aloud or have it called out in public.)

The medication came only just in time, for by then I was breaking, pieces of me coming loose and floating out of reach. Even when I wasn't being harassed I imagined that I was. Once, when I was leaving the hospital and walking to the station, I had a very strong sense I was being followed; by the time I reached the platform I had convinced myself someone was going to dash forward and push me under the approaching train. At home, I started to believe there was someone hiding in my bathroom or behind the sofa. I thought I could hear someone breathing on the other side of the flat door, would suspend my own breath for a minute at a time to try to catch the sound. I had reached the point where I didn't know what was real and what was imagined.

It began to feel only right and natural that Dad no longer recognised me, for I did not recognise myself by then, either in the media's depiction of me or in the altered woman in the mirror before me. I felt as if I was dissolving, disappearing. It was as if Emily Marr no longer existed.

Only Arthur could bring me back to life.

The day my father died, I travelled across London in absolute, if not blissful, ignorance, believing only that I was headed for a routine visit with him. For once, Phil and I would be there at the same time and I might have to face some awkward questions from him, but that was my only source of apprehension, most of my energy having been diverted in any case to the now customary imperative of not being identified by strangers. There were delays on the Northern Line, but I had a Sunday paper with me to while away the minutes. Indeed, I had time to read every word of a five-page profile of myself in its magazine.

It was the third weekend since the 'story' had broken and I was pleased to see that I was already being written about in the past tense. The article was headed WHATEVER HAPPENED TO EMILY MARR?. This, I learned, was a clever dual reference, first to my current status of having gone 'into hiding' and second to my childhood, for the journalist had taken the line that I'd begun life an innocent girl and been made degenerate and dishonest by family circumstances. 'A series of events pushed a carefree, fun-loving girl into premature adulthood ... From an early age Marr was familiar with domestic upheaval ... The loss of her mother caused a wrenching insecurity that would soon manifest itself in the search for an older protector ... ' And so it went on.

They'd *sort* of got it right, I suppose. It was a bit like one of those early drawings of exotic animals done by someone who has never actually seen his subject. The features were there, there were the right number of limbs, but the scale was off, the markings misjudged. The tail was in the wrong place.

No stone had been left unturned in this 'under-the-skin' portrait, but there was some satisfaction that not all yielded dirt. Phil 'could not be reached', for which I was grateful, while Matt, now with a new, 'less capricious' girlfriend, played down our relationship. 'I didn't see her very much before we split up. I had no idea any of this was going on.' Charlotte, sadly, believed she did: 'She used to be very conscientious, but after she met Arthur she got flaky. She started walking out without completing her duties, she constantly called in sick, and she had more dental appointments in six months than I've had in ten years. The weird thing was that in the days after those poor people were killed, she was no different from usual. When I think about it now, she must have had ice in her veins.'

There was truth in this from her perspective, I supposed, and it hurt to know it.

An employer from five years ago, whose face I struggled to recollect, offered this: 'I always got the feeling she didn't know what it was she wanted. She always seemed a bit lost to me. To be honest, because she was so pretty I think she'd got used to relying on her looks to get her through life.'

I didn't know which was more peculiar: learning the opinion of an unremarkable colleague from years ago or knowing that a nation of readers would that very day be sharing it.

Nina, of course, had been interviewed and was both more interesting and more articulate than anyone else:

Sylvie knew she was dangerous the first time she met her. I think we both did, not only because Arthur had a history of infidelity and liked her physical type, but also because she's one of those women who you instinctively know will use her sexuality to her advantage. Women like her exist for men, not for women. She'd perfected that sexy-but-vulnerable Marilyn Monroe thing, the child-woman. And she didn't seem to have anything else in her life, either, not a career or a strong social circle, no moral structure. I'm not saying she's a sociopath, but I think events prove that she found it all too easy to disregard other people's feelings when it suited her. The problem is that when enough people behave individualistically like this, society breaks down. Eventually, lives are lost, precious lives that should never have been sacrificed.

There was a sense that Nina had stepped back from the feeding frenzy that was my character assassination, as if she had not been the one to start it in the first place. Now, her interest was intellectual, her focus widening to the bigger picture, to the moral welfare of British society as a whole. The feature included a photograph of her standing with the Prime Minister and his wife at a drinks party.

Whatever her own complaints of harassment, it seemed to me she was doing very well out of this story.

The journalist commented next on my status as a Luddite:

One of the oddities of Emily Marr is that she rarely used the myriad social networking sites that characterise her generation. Her last contribution to her Facebook account was almost a year ago. For this reason we have relatively few images of the woman whose dangerousness lay in her physical allure.

'She was really into vintage clothes, and that ran into other things,' says a friend. 'She was a bit of a throwback. She only had the most basic mobile phone and hardly used that. She didn't have a clue what Twitter was.'

Almost all those quoted spoke of me as if I were deceased, though the writer kept his options open in his closing remarks (I thought of journalists as amateur barristers: always they put the case for the prosecution):

It is a central irony of this affair that Miss Marr's one official public appearance, at the inquest into the deaths of Sylvie, Alexander and Hugo Woodhall, became of interest only after it had taken place, and therefore we do not have a single photograph of her entering or leaving the coroner's court (by law, photography is not permitted inside). Miraculously, she continues to evade journalists and photographers, who have since spared her none of the doorstepping treatment afforded other attractive young women in the media spotlight. One of the few recent images we do have, in which her face is partially concealed by a hat, was taken outside the Hertfordshire hospital where her father is a long-term patient in the dementia unit. There is no evidence of the trademark blond mane and sex siren styling, the bewitching beauty that we must take others' word for. The Emily Marr who wrought havoc, the overnight sensation, seems to have vanished as suddenly as she appeared.

This was borne out when I phoned the hospital and was told that visits to her father's bedside had fallen away notably in the last month. 'I haven't seen Emily in quite a while,' the ward sister admitted. Have intrusions into her private life caused her to curtail contact with her ill father? This is certainly the view of Matt Piper. 'I think everyone should just give her a break and let her get on with her life,' he comments. 'She hasn't actually done anything illegal, as far as I can see.'

But others, Nina Meeks and the bereaved Woodhall family among them, are quick to suggest that a more likely reason for Miss Marr losing interest in her father's care is that another man has entered her life.

If so, we can only hope that her new romance is an altogether quieter one than the last.

At the very time I was reading this strange work of half-truth, half-fiction, Dad had passed away. Phil was already at the hospital, had been with him at the end, and I was very grateful for that. Having previously deferred to me in all arrangements for Dad's care, he now took one look at me and reversed our roles.

'Come with me, Em.' He slipped a hand under my elbow and held it firmly. 'I've just been told we can see him.'

I'd heard that to see a dead man was like seeing him sleeping, but it was not; it was like seeing him dead. Absence of life compressed the room with its cold magnetism, our two intruding figures obscenely thermal, glowing hyper-real. Hard as I tried, I could not keep thoughts of the three Woodhall deaths at bay, even this personal tragedy of my own was contaminated by theirs: my own father versus a woman I'd met twice for two minutes and two boys I'd never met at all. Of course, I felt guilty for weighing them up like that, but guilt consumed so much of my existence at that time, it was a feeling that had lost all shape and size. Every thought I had felt wrong then; I could not trust my sanity.

After we'd said goodbye and begun arrangements to get the death certificate issued, we thanked for the last time the staff we'd got to know over the last year. Phil suggested I go home with him to Newbury and I agreed.

As we drove, we were too splintered with shock for coherent conversation. Whenever he spoke and I glanced up in response, he radiated even in his devastation the pure, unmingled relief of being allowed to live and perhaps I did the same.

Only once, when we were close to arriving at his house, did we address the fact that his sister had become a media hate figure.

'I'm sorry I haven't phoned you,' I said. 'It's been difficult.' I did not add that paranoia had caused me to suspect – against any physical evidence – that my phone and email had been hacked.

'What the hell's all that stuff in the papers been about?' The way he said it, I knew it was not just from the perspective of fresh bereavement, but of a general lack of comprehension that what I'd done should ever have become of wider interest. 'I thought it was just someone with the same name as you at first, and then I saw the pictures. Are you with this surgeon guy or what?'

'Not any more,' I said, and I began abruptly to cry, the sobs breaking in horrible tumultuous convulsions that sounded hardly human. I surrendered freely to it, not knowing who I was crying for: my father, Arthur, myself, all of us.

Phil said nothing for some time. Eventually, when he did speak, he was choking back his own emotions: 'Oh, Emily,' he said. 'This is not a good day, is it?'

'No.'

And I truly did not think there would ever be one again.

Chapter 21

Emily

It was ironic that I was forced out of my home just as the press ceased to plague me in it. Inevitably, the other tenants and neighbours had complained to my landlord about the ongoing drama and he had written to give me notice, mentioning that the Friends' Association had been particularly insistent on my removal. It was senseless protesting against the order, as senseless as continuing to imagine that Arthur was going to materialise at my door one day and declare the whole seven-month estrangement water under the bridge, beg me to pick up where we had left off.

Instead I was the one begging: my brother, to let me stay for a while. He said yes before consulting his wife, for which I was tearfully grateful. If the request had been deliberated properly and then refused, I would not have blamed either of them for a moment.

I left Walnut Grove two days before the funeral. Packing up was unutterably sad. I still recalled that joyful interlude – the half an hour or so between Arthur's announcement that he had found a love nest for us and Sylvie phoning to tell me she knew – when I'd imagined a lovely, lazy period of notice in which I would visit the emptying flat and marvel at how my life had changed since I'd moved into it the previous winter. In that version, when I locked the door for the last time I'd be walking away towards a new life, if not out of reach of those I'd hurt then certainly protected from them. Protected by Arthur.

Instead, I'd stayed and the flat had been refuge and cage in one. I hated being in it as much as I longed to stay there for ever. And I loved it, if only for the first trysts with Arthur it had contained. *I can't stop touching you, Emily . . .*

Now I was the untouchable.

I had little furniture of my own and what I had I donated to a local charity, which sent a van to collect it. Many of my clothes I sold back to the vintage shop I'd bought them from, across the road from my old place of work. Charlotte had paid me a month's severance, as well as the previous month's work in arrears: I was not penniless. I also had half of the deposit from the flat, paid far more promptly than any I'd applied for in the past. Everyone wanted a clean break from me, the sooner the better.

The collection of hate/fan mail I tore into shreds and mixed in the bin with food remains. I had few personal bits and pieces: a folder of financial documents, some family photos, a postcard Arthur had given me soon after we confessed our love for each other. In a pile of old papers Matt had left behind, I made a fitting discovery: a print of the photograph the *Press* had used in Nina's first piece about me, the one from Matt's cousin's wedding that had since been used over and over. Matt had been cropped in that first publication, but he was here now, exuding that sardonic detachment I'd once found so attractive. Next to him I looked insubstantial, unearthly, a ghost in a pink and green dress come back from troubled times to haunt him. There was a card attached: *Dear Matt and Emily, Thank you for your beautiful gift and for sharing our special day with us. We hope the enclosed photo will help you remember in years to come! Love Gemma & Nick x*

It certainly would, I thought, and I decided to keep the picture, as much in tribute to Matt's recent kindness as anything else.

I put everything left in my backpack and got the tube to Paddington, where the train left for Newbury. It was unseasonably warm, too hot for the hat, and so I debuted my new haircut, which I'd 'styled' myself a few days earlier at the bathroom mirror (out of necessity, not madness – I couldn't risk being recognised in a salon). Cropped short, the blond mostly grown out, it was not the look to attract a second glance. The early-March sunshine warranted dark glasses, which helped conceal my newly gaunt face. I'd lost so much weight I looked ill, the victim of some unspecified wasting disease. The old Hollywood curves were no more.

On the train, even as the miles stretched and stretched between the city and me, I thought I could hear the mutters from Nina and Sarah and the other residents of Walnut Grove: 'Good riddance, Emily Marr.'

I see now that it was too much to expect that we'd be allowed privacy at my father's funeral, but at the time I wasn't thinking clearly. I was anaesthetised with grief, little thought spared for my media persecution, and I had not warned the police or even the funeral director of the possibility of intrusion. But the internet had gone restlessly on and I supposed details must have leaked on to the various Emily Marr forums; astonishingly, there were still people who were interested.

We noticed them as soon as we arrived at the burial site, even before the hearse had pulled in.

'It's not just photographers,' Phil said, bewildered, 'there's a whole load of gawkers as well.'

'Ghouls,' said Julie, quicker to understand the situation and rightly disgusted. 'What kind of a person hangs out at the funeral of someone they don't know?'

'I'm so sorry,' I said. Gawkers and ghouls, that was what I inflicted on my poor father as he was laid to rest.

'What's happening, Dad?' the younger of Phil's kids asked. 'Was Grandad famous?'

'No,' Phil told him. 'Nobody's famous. They've got the wrong man.'

'Emily!' Having spied me, the gatecrashers began calling out my name in a horrible gleeful chorus. 'Emily Marr! There she is, wearing that dark headscarf!'

'Oh, for fuck's sake,' Phil muttered under his breath.

It was easier for me to ignore them – I was used to it, after all – but I felt terrible guilt for the distress it caused the other mourners. I was glad I'd got Julie to search out the headscarf for me. If photos were taken, even with a long lens, they'd get no satisfaction from me.

'Pretend they're not here,' I told the children, advice meant for their parents' ears as much as for theirs. 'Pretend it's just us.'

We tried. But being 'just us' was what was so devastating about the occasion in the first place.

That was nearly two weeks ago. It will be April before long: springtime, new hope, new life. I probably won't write much more now; I'm getting towards the end of the story, I think. I couldn't cope with anything else happening, I couldn't live with any more loss. In the event, I've lost Dad *and* Arthur, I've lost my job and my home. I've lost myself.

I'm still living with Phil, Julie and the boys. 'How are you feeling?' Julie asks me every morning. It's taken me a while to realise she's talking about my sorrow over Dad's death, not the fact that I've been hounded from my home into a state of suspension from which I might never break free. I think that is what I'll find hardest to forgive in the future, that my own grief has been stolen from me, and that of my family has been tainted.

'I'm fine,' I lie. 'The same.'

At last the story has faded, as it was always going to, and the few journalists who tailed me here have gone, having failed to interview me just as the nationals, the BBC, even a writer for a magazine in New York, failed before them. Someone else is now Britain's Most Loathed and I wish him or her the briefest and least disruptive of tenures.

Phil and Julie both work full-time and the boys are at school all day so I spend long hours alone in the house. Of course, writing this has occupied me, perhaps even obsessed me. I don't know if it has fulfilled my original hopes, but I've gained something from putting it all down in the right order. Reconstructing it in full before casting it aside once and for all.

When feelings of captivity feel like leeches on my skin, I put on my trainers and go for a run. I pull that black woollen hat low over my ears and eyebrows, and I run to the park a few streets away. I run as if someone is chasing me. When I've completed a circuit, maybe two, I ignore my protesting lungs and run back. Once or twice I sit on a bench and look about me, trying to make sense of my changed world – how I came to be separated from all other groups in it, dispossessed, orphaned. After weeks under surveillance, I now can't shake the sensation of being watched. Perhaps I never will.

I've been weaning myself off the medication Dad's hospital gave me, and a few days ago, when I woke up, I thought I noticed a difference in my outlook. Suddenly I could identify easily what it is that I need: a job, an income, a purpose, however basic, however temporary. Surely no one will recognise me now? If I don't trust my reflection in the mirror, I need only see the faces of my nephews every time I walk into the room: the matching expressions of incomprehension in their eyes, before they remember I'm blond and smiling Auntie Emily, just no longer blond, no longer smiling.

The problem, as Phil points out, is going to be less my appearance, which is sufficiently altered, as my name. It is a household one now, whether I like it or not. Even if I were to overcome the liability of it to secure a position, at the very least I'd suffer constant curiosity, more likely abuse, from my colleagues. Phil knows about the anonymous threats I've received: if just one of the many thousands were to be put into action, I could be hospitalised.

'I could use a false name?' I suggested. 'I could be Emmie Mason or something, keep the same initials.'

'Is Emmie actually a name?' he asked.

'I don't know, but it could be short for Emmeline, or Emilia. I prefer Emmeline, like the Suffragette.' I smiled, trying, and not quite succeeding, to be playful. Opportunities for humour were scarce these days.

But Phil struggled to get into the spirit of it. 'It won't work. If you go through a company's books, you'll have to show ID, give bank account details.'

'OK, then maybe I'll get lucky and find someone who's never heard of me? Who's been out of the country the last couple of months?'

He looked doubtful. 'You could try. But I bet human resources Google applicants these days. You're bound to come up against someone who knows all about it. Unless you work for cash and don't have to fill in any forms or sign anything?' he added, his face clearing.

'What work can I do for cash?' Cleaning, perhaps childcare, babysitting, all of which would require references. I have old references, but they all give my real name.

There was a silence as we both ran out of ideas. I looked out of the window at the suburban cul-de-sac beyond, neither pleased nor displeased with the safe dreariness of it, so different from the Georgian glamour of the Grove. 'When will I be able to live again?' I asked, though I hadn't meant to say this aloud and did not expect Phil to know the answer.

'Have you thought about leaving for a while? Travelling?'

'Travelling?' I didn't tell him that I am dreaming more and more of the island Arthur told me about, the one on the Atlantic coast of France. I'm dreaming of a remote cottage, a *real* hideaway, of salt in the air and sand in my shoes.

'Don't think I'm trying to push you into anything, but it might be the solution. Go and have a long break somewhere, then when you come back maybe people will be more likely to have forgotten your name.'

'But—' I began, but he interrupted me, guessing the fundamental impediment.

'I can help you out with a bit of money.' I knew then that he had discussed the idea with Julie. It was what they thought best, the only reasonable option left. 'I would visit the grave for you,' he continued, anticipating my second objection too.

'Maybe,' I said. 'Let me think about it for a week or two.' Again, I tried to raise a smile between us. 'There is one other possibility: I could pay someone to marry me. Or change my surname by Deed Poll? See, I *do* have options.'

'Yes, Emily.'

'Not Emily, *Emmie*. I told you. Emmie Mason.'

We exchanged small, rueful smiles.

You read all the time how people want to be famous. 'I just want everyone to know my name,' they say. 'To walk into a room and for everyone to know who I am.' They don't care what it is that gets them attention, they just want the attention. '*I'll do anything*,' they say.

And then they find it's a different feeling from the one they expected. They never think it through, you see, they never consider that 'who I am' might be open to interpretation and that the number of people ready to accept the worst portrayal of you will far exceed the number willing to believe the best. The moral, the message, is always the same: be careful what you wish for.

But I never wished for this and that's the truth.

I never asked for this.

Chapter 22

Tabby

Though hours must have passed while she read, Tabby found Emmie exactly where she had left her, on the sofa, the room saved from darkness only by the dusk light entering through the glazed panel of the kitchen door. She switched on a lamp and approached uncertainly. As her gaze came to rest once more on Emmie's face, she knew she could never think of her in the same way again.

At last the cat was out of the bag – but she could never have imagined such a creature as had emerged.

She lowered herself on to the seat beside Emmie, the laptop in her arms, document still open on the screen. 'Oh, Emmie, this is such a sad story. I can't believe you've been through this terrible situation. I think you've done incredibly well to survive it.'

'I've tried,' Emmie said, in a voice so small it was hardly audible.

'I'm really sorry about your father. It's so recent, you must still feel very raw.' It seemed important to say this first. Somehow, in Emmie's recent history, her bereavement had been classified as a secondary tragedy, but Tabby knew very well the complicated sadness the loss of a father caused in a daughter. At this stage – even now it was for Emmie only six months after the event – Tabby had still been crying herself to sleep at night. Had she had any idea that Emmie's loss had been so fresh, she would have … She allowed the thought to sink before she could consider it properly. The truth was, she did not like to imagine what she would have done differently, whether she would have been capable of meeting the challenge of selfless compassion.

She glanced through the door pane to the wall of the neighbour's courtyard. If chatter filled the lanes outside she could not hear it; if there was ocean beyond she could not smell it. The house had never felt so sealed into itself as it did in that moment, and yet to Emmie it must have represented safety and freedom. 'So this was why you came here,' she said. 'Like you say, you had no choice but to leave the country, so you used the name you joked about with your brother and you chose the part of France that he said he was going to take you.' She was cautious about using Arthur's name, not wishing to presume ownership of a figure so critical to Emmie's past. 'It must have felt unreal,' she added, 'to go from being the centre of attention like that to living underground like this.' She'd laughed about Emmie behaving as if fleeing the Mafia; in fact, it had been the media, the flight quite real. 'I see why you took the work you did: it's so you never have to meet anyone. If you'd worked in a bar or a shop or something, you might have been recognised by English people on holiday.' A connection struck her. 'Those guys at the port that night, they must have realised who you were, mustn't they? Especially dressed as you were, in the dress from the photo?' How reckless that public display seemed now, entirely out of character for Emmie; she'd been lucky not to blow her own cover more disastrously. 'Why *did* you dress like your old self, Emmie? Was it because you missed being you? Do you still miss it?'

'Sometimes,' Emmie murmured. Though she looked Tabby's way, her eyes were not focused. She had listened to Tabby's deductions as if under hypnosis.

'But the press haven't tracked you down here, have they? The journalists who staked out your flat and the ones who followed you to your brother's place?' The clues continued to fall into place for Tabby as she spoke, leading her back through the months to the beginning: 'Is that who you thought *I* was when I came? A reporter or some mad Emily Marr hater who'd broken into your house?' Of all the houses on the island she could have chosen to break into, she had found the one in which someone was already hiding. 'Had you thought you'd been discovered before? I can't imagine what it's felt like all this time; you must have felt like you could never lower your guard?'

To all of these questions Emmie only nodded, her body growing limp before Tabby's eyes. When the nodding stopped, she closed her eyes and rested her head on the back of the sofa as if unable to support it with her own neck. It was not quite what Tabby had expected of the debriefing, especially in light of episodes such as the one the previous day – how ancient an occasion that seemed now – when they'd sat at the table with the folder before them, the atmosphere sparking with the tension between what was known and what was withheld. Perhaps, by releasing the whole story, Emmie had also surrendered the last of her energies. For Tabby, the opposite was the case: knowing the truth, being delivered from intrigue, it invigorated her, freed resources previously employed in darker contemplation.

'Is that why you don't have an internet connection? To stop yourself from reading all the hate stuff on the web? What about your phone, can't they reach you on that?' But Tabby remembered that, of course, Emmie's phone was a French one. She must have given up her English one when she came here, eliminating any last ways in which she might be traced.

'I just wanted to shut myself away from it all,' Emmie said, her voice dreamy.

306

'Of course you did.' Had their positions been reversed, Tabby knew she would have spent every waking moment reading what people were saying about her, she would have become obsessed, maddened. What strength it must have taken for Emmie to turn from it, resist its pull. 'What I don't understand is how it caught on the way it did. It's not like he was the Prime Minister or a movie star or someone really famous.' But then she remembered the pictures she'd seen online, the handful in circulation: in each one Emmie had possessed an ethereal glamour that seized your eye and held it on her. It wasn't easy to believe now, but the enervated woman slumped next to her had once been beautiful, and maybe in a slow summer for news that beauty, along with Arthur's minor fame, were enough – that and the fact that it had led, however indirectly, to death. 'It must have been one of those viral things that takes on a life of its own, d'you think? You know, a phenomenon, like those clips on YouTube that get ten million hits and then they report it on the news and the next day it's up to fifty million.'

'I only want Arthur to forgive me,' Emmie said. 'That's all I ever wanted. Only he can bring me back.' It was odd for Tabby to hear the phrases she'd just read on the computer file repeated aloud in this way, like a mantra. Losing him still feels brand-new to her, she realised. It still *is*. And with this came the first inkling of doubt that exposing the truth might not have been the best course of action.

'What if he's been trying to get in touch with you, Emmie? Do you at least have the same email account?'

Emmie did not blink. 'There's been nothing.'

'But have you actually checked? How?' She had not been aware of Emmie using the internet bureau as she did, but perhaps she had done so secretly, better apprised of its opening hours.

'Sometimes, in clients' houses, I look up the password and use their computers.'

'That's a good idea,' Tabby said, almost as disarmed by the notion of Emmie as a breaker of Moira's rules as she was by the extraordinary recent history just unveiled. 'And you've heard nothing from him?'

'I have to accept that he doesn't want me. It's an absolute rejection.'

'Oh, Emmie,' Tabby said again, 'I can sympathise with that.' But what had once been a whole-hearted belief in their common ground had now been exposed once and for all as false. What she had had with Paul was not like the relationship Emmie had described in her story. She and Arthur had had some kind of rare passion, one of those one-in-a-million forms of human alchemy that had made him willing to risk his whole world for her. Married men were not supposed to be like that, they were supposed to be like Grégoire, happy to take what was offered, willing to walk away again when it was withdrawn. No hard feelings – or at least none to cause lasting damage. What had torn Arthur and Emily apart was probably the only thing in the world that could have: the death of his children. Maybe that was what Nina and her colleagues had responded to, not glamour or beauty, but something you couldn't see, a kind of fatal charisma, something that had made Arthur chase her down the street, something that compelled those who didn't have it to destroy it, before it diminished their own lives, their own loves. And yet it was doomed already, doomed in itself.

'To have everyone reading about you like that – and some of it not even true! It must have been so frustrating to not be able to correct all the lies.'

'It didn't really feel like me,' Emmie said, and Tabby remembered her description of the drawing of a wild animal made by someone who had never actually seen one.

'Even the basic things they got wrong, didn't they? They said you didn't get good qualifications at school, as if you're some sort of dunce, but look how well you write! And your French is perfect. It's amazing you've become fluent so quickly, especially when you don't have much chance to practise, keeping yourself to yourself the way you do. Maybe that's what you should do next, Emmie, when you go back? Go to college and study languages. You must be some kind of natural linguist.'

But Emmie was not engaged by Tabby's enthusiasm, every visible part of her depleted, wasted. Noticing the time – close to ten-thirty – Tabby admitted defeat. 'Let's talk more tomorrow, shall we? We should both get some sleep.'

'Yes.' Emmie closed the laptop and rose to her feet. Having her talisman back in her possession seemed to power the movements required to get her upstairs to bed. Tabby followed, weary in body if not brain.

Only as she undressed for bed herself did it strike her that Emmie had stated in her story that she had written it while staying at her brother's house in Newbury, before she came to France. She'd poured it from her in a matter of two or three weeks. What, then, had she been doing during the hours she'd spent on it here? Refining the text, night after night, adding little details, or simply re-reading what she had written months ago? Tabby was not sure how helpful, how healthy, either of those activities could be for a woman whose declared aim was to forget.

I only want Arthur to forgive me ... But he had not and it tormented Emmie, haunted her. Would it always?

Tabby struggled to fall asleep that night and, when she finally did, there was precious little rest in it.

The next day was Saturday, her rue du Rempart day. Usually, she put on music as soon as she arrived at the house, to bring energy to reluctant muscles and help the hours pass, but this time she began her work in silence, Emmie's story filling her mind to the exclusion of all else. To think what the poor woman had lived through! Not only the media persecution that drove her from her home, but also the anguish of knowing that the man she loved had suffered – was still suffering – the very worst pain that life could subject him to, and that she could do nothing to alleviate it. And for her father to have passed away so soon afterwards, it was the height of cruelty. Tabby could not bear it for Emmie, and as she worked she surrendered to a violent fit of tears.

Clear though she was that Emmie's losses far exceeded her own, it was impossible not to identify closely with certain elements of the story. She was, after all, sleeping with Grégoire, an older, married man, if not a father figure to her then certainly a father, and to two boys, just like Arthur. And just as Emmie had, she had chosen to take a self-regarding, short-term position and ignore the existence of those sons. 'Are you disappointed you didn't have to work harder to get me?' Emmie had asked Arthur, while she herself had been no more than a foregone conclusion, as hard to get as half a dozen oysters at the quayside. She'd even deluded herself that she was not to be deluded: it was pathetic.

Only now was the true criminality of her behaviour clear to her. Her adulterous affair was far less forgivable than Emmie's for its very casualness. She did not love Grégoire, but was using him to distract her from the pain another man had caused her and to assuage her loneliness. How often she had thought to herself that they were all consenting adults, that she deserved a little pleasure as much as the next woman, and yet there was nothing 'consenting' about Noémie's position, was there?

Nina Meeks should take a look at *my* set-up, she thought. She was combining three clichés in one: a rebounding broken heart, a holiday romance and an affair with a married man. She was far closer than her poor, hunted friend to the poster girl for feckless immorality Emmie had been cracked up to be.

Such were her thoughts when Grégoire rang at the door that she wished she'd thought to cancel him. Belated feelings of guilt aside, her connection with him seemed cheap and dirty now that she had shared Emmie's descriptions of how love could feel. If she hadn't had the willpower to resist starting up with him again, then she should at least have had the decency to end it before now. In he came, heading straight for the bedroom. She was conscious of rushing through the sex to get it finished, out of the way so they could have a few more minutes' conversation. But it was far too late to hope to build a meeting of minds. Lying on the mattress, she explained to him the basics of the scandal, careful not to make any link to Emmie, and asked if the sensation had ever reached France.

'I have not heard about this news,' he said, examining his fingernails. Any minute, he would persuade Tabby to have a cigarette with him, even though its pleasures would not be worth the feat of room-airing required after he'd gone. His ironic detachment was the very opposite of what Emmie had described of *her* lover: Arthur's earnest intensity, the rapt way he had looked at her, listened to her, desired her. 'This is very English to me,' he added. 'The way the newspapers are there.'

'What,' Tabby demanded, 'hounding a woman from her home, from her country, maybe, when she's done nothing wrong? Organising a witch-hunt?'

'Believing that sex is such a bad thing,' he corrected. 'When it is always good.' He began to tell Tabby about the French privacy laws, the understanding that what a man did in his personal life was his own affair. Tabby found she was growing tired of hearing how sophisticated the French were, how much more pragmatic than the English in their sexual politics. How, even if someone were not indulging in extramarital adventure, he or she would accept the need for it in a spouse and, in making that acceptance known, waive any rights to express pain.

Well, she did not believe a word of it. Not when there were stories like Emmie's in the world. And just because you played

311

the game of concealing pain it did not mean you did not feel it. For the first time since their liaisons had begun she found herself getting angry with Grégoire, found herself itching to get back to her cleaning.

It took her by surprise, the knowledge that being in possession of the truth about Emmie was going to be enough, an end in itself. Her burning curiosity had been slaked, the discovery had been made, and that was that: she had no interest in exposing Emmie's hiding place or making reference to her history to anyone in the outside world. And even in their private one she was soon satisfied: after one of two more discussions, neither of which yielded any more than she already knew from the compelling written account, she had used up all her questions. She had only a renewed admiration for Emmie, a determination to support her.

Any light this cautionary tale might have shed on her own relationship history was a fringe benefit worth taking. I'm thinking about Paul much less, she decided. I'm thinking that one day I might see how events between us occurred as they did. I'm thinking there may have been issues I laid at his door that I should have taken elsewhere. Personal growth, indeed! She was free now to get on with the remains of the summer and with making plans for the rest of her life.

The problem was that she had not considered how the urging of a confession would affect Emmie.

At first she put the change of atmosphere in the house down to the one outside. It was by now early August, the height of the season, torrid and oppressive, the village overpopulated to the extent that moving among pedestrian traffic on the shopping lanes was a grievous experience. In their narrow alley, the air swarmed with tiny insects, the dust rising and falling in slow motion, the hollyhocks drying on their feet. The sun had at last warmed the terracotta tiles of the roof, the heat they'd till now been able to escape by stepping between cold thick stone walls suddenly following the women indoors, slowing them as they moved. In her sleep, Tabby dreamed of a house on stilts, right out on the water with the gulls where there was still a breeze to be caught.

When she slept at all, that was. Waking on Sunday night in the early hours, she heard sobbing from the main bedroom. It happened the next night, too, and then the one after that, until it was established as habit, the sound she expected to hear first every day even before the church bells. That flicker of unease she had felt when confronting Emmie now returned, growing constant and impossible to ignore.

On Wednesday and Thursday mornings, Emmie was late for work and Moira had to phone to chivvy her along. On the Friday, unknown to Moira, she finished over an hour early, presumably compromising her trademark thoroughness in order to do so. The all-important Saturday shift at her two cottages in La Flotte was missed completely after she called in sick and stayed in bed. She'd gone from being reliable to unreliable virtually overnight. When more absences followed, Tabby phoned Moira herself with the fabrication of a virus, offering to cover Emmie's missed shifts herself where her schedule allowed. Emmie, however, would have preferred them both to stay at home, for it was clear that where once she had rebuffed overtures on her house-mate's part, she wanted now to talk ceaselessly of herself and of the events of her past. Her persecution by Nina Meeks was her most frequent lament, and it was evident that, as Tabby had feared, the scenarios were entirely current to her, right at the surface of her memory.

'Without her, I think we could have stayed together. The article, the hate campaign, she made it impossible for him to have anything to do with me. She thought she was just crucifying me but she was actually crucifying both of us. I know I could never have made it better, but if I could have been with him, it would have been something. He must have been feeling so deserted, so alone.'

'You must try to forget,' Tabby told her, after several days of this. 'Like you said in your journal, you've written it down to get it out of your system, not to keep going over—'

'I'll never get it out of my system! It's not fair, I didn't ask for this. What did I do to deserve it? I don't understand!'

Tabby was helpless in the face of such a maelstrom of despair – and ever more convinced of her own guilt in its creation. The fact was that, left to her own devices, Emmie had found her own way of coming to terms with the injustices she'd endured; it was Tabby who had induced this disastrous relapse. There had been nothing cathartic for Emmie about the enforced confession: it had only reopened the wound, and now she was as vulnerable, as volatile, as broken as she'd described herself to be at the worst of her collapse.

'Emmie, what happened was you fell in love and it didn't work out. Relationships fail all the time because of far less. Yours didn't stand a chance, no relationship could survive what happened to you two. The media scandal – well, of course I don't think you deserved that at all, but you have to put it behind you and concentrate on this new life you've made for yourself. Let yourself grieve for your father without cluttering your mind with Nina Meeks – *she*'s not important. Come on, you were doing so well. Should I get in touch with your brother? You were obviously close before you left; talking to him might help?'

'I just want Arthur,' Emmie wailed. It was a phrase Tabby would hear over and over again during this time.

And she had only herself to blame. She was Pandora, and the consequences of her actions could not be undone. Since the box had been opened, she had not touched a single cupboard in her clients' houses marked '*Privé*'.

*

314

The situation deteriorated. As the air temperature settled and slowly, teasingly dipped, the atmosphere in the house grew only more febrile.

'Emmie,' she said, coming home from a job on the second Friday to find her friend still in her pyjamas, the journey from bed to sofa evidently the extent of her day's exertions, 'it's none of my business, but how about we see a doctor and get you something to help with this?' She was thinking of the pills she'd found, medication she now knew to have been prescribed by Emmie's father's doctors to subdue just this emotional torment.

'There's nothing wrong with me,' Emmie said, her voice distorted by the swelling of her nose and throat from weeping. 'I'm completely fine.'

'But a doctor might be able to help you feel even more fine.'

'I said I don't need a doctor!' This was uttered with vehemence, its effect strengthened unsettlingly by the reddened whites of her glaring eyes.

'OK, but if you change your mind … I know how it feels to—'

'You *don't* know,' Emmie broke in, impatient of the repetition of any ideas but her own. 'How can you?'

And Tabby had to admit she could not, not any more, and if she was to be of any use to Emmie it would not be by claiming affinity but by offering condolence after condolence.

The following day, Saturday, she became officially out of her depth. At the rue du Rempart house, her phone rang over and over in her bag downstairs while she lounged with Grégoire in the bedroom above. Fearing interference by Moira, she went to fetch it, only to find eight missed calls from Emmie. Having phoned in sick a second time for changeover day, Emmie was now screaming for her to come home.

'I have to leave,' Tabby told Grégoire. 'I'm worried she's going to harm herself. She's completely hysterical.'

'What is she crying about?' he asked, and Tabby noted the

dryness of tone. She could not confide in him about this crisis, knowing instinctively that Emmie and Grégoire would not mix to anyone's advantage, but even so, it disappointed her that he did not offer to help. He wanted only to help himself to her and head off home. Turning him out, not bothering with the usual safe interval between their respective departures, she vowed that this would be the last time they would be together. She would not text him the following week or the one after. She would entertain him no more, not in any sense of the word. And if he turned up at the usual time she would not answer the door. She did not say this to him, of course. Theirs was not an arrangement that called for formality and in any case she didn't have the time to waste arguing. She left him at the door, dashing to the end of the street without looking back.

In the house, Emmie was sitting on the floor of the living room, delirious with woe and apparently unable to get herself up. The contents of the purple folder were fanned out on the rug, a spew of vile headlines vying with one another for attention: MARR IS TOXIC, SAYS DEPUTY PM; IS EMILY MARR MURDERER OR MINX?; SURGEON'S GIRL NO BETTER THAN WHORE. Tabby sat down next to her, but knew better than to confiscate the cuttings. What had been the point of Emmie removing herself from the media's reach if she was only going to gorge herself on this catalogue of its worst abuses?

Having placated her a little, Tabby opened one set of windows and pushed back the shutters to let in some light and fresh air – she was convinced that before all else Emmie needed release from this entombment. She made tea, but Emmie misjudged the simple motion involved in taking the mug from her and it crashed to the floor, making a horrendous mess. Seeing some of her papers stained with the tea, Emmie began gathering them up with a hectic energy, wailing in the eerie, grief-stricken way Tabby was becoming so used to hearing, her eyes burning with some primitive, animal life force.

'Please, Emmie, you *must* calm down. I think you need to get out of the house, get some air; you're going stir-crazy here. And stop reading all this stuff! Maybe we should throw it away, and the laptop as well. Or at least let me put them where you can't find them ...'

'No!' Emmie screeched. 'You can't, they're mine!'

'Fine, well, let me put it all back together, at least. There's paper all over the place. Why don't you have a bath and relax? I'll go and run it for you, shall I?' To her knowledge, Emmie had not washed for two or three days.

'I just need to rest,' Emmie said, but less defiant now, and she levered herself on to the sofa with her arms, like someone who had lost the use of her legs. She did not remark on the contraband sunlight now slanting through the window and spotlighting the lamp table next to her, but just stared out at the wall as if transfixed by the sight of bare brick. How Tabby longed to smash down that wall and steal sight of their neighbour's courtyard.

She brought more tea, studying Emmie with wariness as she judged whether it was safe to leave. 'I have to get back to work. Will you be OK for another hour?'

'I'm fine,' Emmie said, half in surprise, half in resignation. The feral intensity had gone from her eyes.

There was an unwelcome element of farce to all of this when Moira phoned to harangue her. 'For goodness' sake, where are you, Tabby? The guests have arrived early at rue du Rempart. They're in the house now.'

'I'm so sorry, Moira, I had to go home in a hurry – there was an emergency. I've just got the bedrooms to do, I'm on my way back right now.'

'There's no need,' Moira said crossly. 'I've sent Sophy to finish the job. Luckily she was in Saint-Martin already and agreed to cover for you.'

'Oh, that's good, thank you. I promise it won't happen—'

317

'I don't want to discuss this now,' Moira cut in. 'I see there's nothing in the diary for you tomorrow, which is just as well. Can you come to the office on Monday morning?'

'Yes, of course,' Tabby said, though it had hardly been a question of choice. In any case, Moira had hung up without waiting for an answer.

Freed now to deal with Emmie, she persuaded her to put on some shoes and leave the house for a walk by the sea. They took the coastal path towards Loix, to anyone else a route of the most restorative beauty but to Tabby merely a method of surviving another hour or two in a hostage crisis she could not begin to fathom, much less resolve. She kept walking long after she would normally have turned back, for she needed to exhaust Emmie as she'd once seen her father and Susie exhaust the two young girls. She was thinking that perhaps Emmie's breakdown had been exacerbated by her having been denied the physical exercise she normally got from work.

'Moira's not happy,' she said presently, and when Emmie made no comment, she found she had nothing to add herself. Moira, like Grégoire, was a transitory connection, a relationship conducted on the black. Priorities had shifted and it was no longer important enough for her to want to fight for it. She had worked her heart out this summer; she owed Moira nothing.

Emmie, however, was different. She owed her everything.

The next day, Sunday, to her great relief Emmie had calmed. She did not eat or bathe, it was true, but she at least submitted to another walk, another sustained avoidance of conversation on the subject of her downfall. Tabby tried not to worry that she was simply continuing her rant in her head. She'd decided that any more fits of mania like the one yesterday and she'd need to get a doctor involved, whether Emmie cooperated or not. She was no health professional, but the anger and helplessness between which Emmie veered daily were surely both symptoms of grief, delayed or suppressed during the course of the past few months and only now finding expression. Searching in Emmie's toiletries basket for the pills she'd seen and finding the bottle gone, she hoped Emmie had begun taking them of her own accord, cheered herself with this likely evidence of self-help.

On Monday, she suggested Emmie walk with her to La Flotte for her meeting with Moira, intending to harbour her safely in a café while she pleaded her case to their boss. Her amateur practitioner's insistence on exercise therapy appeared to be succeeding, for Emmie was fast returning to her usual self, or rather the self she had constructed to conceal the original one. Tabby was grateful for the regeneration of it; she could cope with it far better than the shattered reality.

In La Flotte, to her surprise – and faint trepidation – Emmie insisted on coming up with her to Moira's office for the conference.

'I'm not quite sure why *you're* here,' Moira said. 'I thought you were still unwell?' Her displeasure with both of them was plain. She did not offer them coffee or waste time on pleasantries, wordlessly gesturing to the two chairs at her desk before seating herself opposite.

'She *is* unwell,' Tabby replied when Emmie did not. It was only in seeing her friend in the artificial light of Moira's office that she could appreciate how pallid she'd become; she'd lost weight in recent weeks, too, and the bones of her face were startlingly angular. Moira would be able to see this too, which was no bad thing, she decided. She resisted reminding their boss that Emmie was not being paid during her absence; the cash-in-hand arrangement had benefits for both parties.

Moira turned to address Tabby. 'We need to discuss what happened on Saturday at your rue du Rempart job.'

'Yes, I—'

'Let's begin with my telling you what *I* know. I had a call at two-thirty from the new arrivals, saying the house was not fit for occupation. They shouldn't have been able to use the entry system until the property was ready, but you obviously forgot to disable it when you left.'

'I'm sorry,' Tabby said. 'I was in a rush, there was a situation at home. I thought I'd be able to get back and finish up before they arrived.'

Moira did not acknowledge this interruption. 'When they got into the house, they found signs that one of the bedrooms had been in use.'

'It was in a bit of a mess upstairs, yes. As I said, I hadn't finished.'

'The mother was extremely upset: the children found a condom wrapper on the mattress. There were also cigarette butts, a used sheet, and an item of underwear.'

Tabby had no choice but to bluff her way through this sordid inventory. 'I suppose they must have been from the previous occupants. As I say—'

'Hardly,' Moira interrupted. 'The outgoing tenants were an elderly couple on holiday with their grandson. They were unlikely to have been using those items.'

'The grandson maybe?'

'He is eleven.' Moira glared unpleasantly at her. 'Tabby, please stop lying. The family saw you leave with a man just as they pulled up further down the street.'

'Oh.'

'And it's not the the first report of this kind, is it? You need to tell me truthfully, have you been using the house to meet a boyfriend? Have you been smoking there? Have you been using the premises for sex?'

Tabby gazed dismally at Moira, hoping she might appear to her employer more apologetic than she felt. She was in deep trouble – might there even be an accusation here of prostitution? – and yet the situation felt tangential, a distraction from the imperative of keeping Emmie on an even keel. The procedural details of Moira's investigation were laid out with a cold fury that would once have scared her but now seemed unimportant, possibly even bordering on comical. She found she had neither the energy nor the desire to defend herself.

At her side, Emmie was clearing her throat, preparing to say something, causing Moira to glance in her direction. 'Do *you* know anything about this situation, Emmie?'

'Yes, I do,' Emmie said, all of a sudden as animated as Tabby had seen her in twenty-four hours. 'You've got it wrong. It was me, not Tabby.'

'Don't be crazy,' Tabby told her, sighing.

'No, it was,' Emmie insisted. 'Tabby wasn't feeling well in the morning and so I went to her job instead. I invited someone I've been seeing to visit me while I was there.'

Moira gave a huff of exasperation. 'I thought it was *you* who called in sick on Saturday?'

'I did, but I was lying. I cancelled because I'd arranged to meet this person. But when Tabby said she genuinely felt ill, I offered to cover for her and I invited my friend to visit me there instead of at home. It was me who had to go home for an emergency. We had a leak from the washing machine.'

This surely sounded as implausible to Moira as it did to Tabby, and while noble of Emmie to try to save her skin, Tabby knew she had no hope of success.

'Who is this person you were meeting?' Moira demanded. 'I'd like to phone him if I may.'

Emmie was silent for an ominous moment, before replying, 'Arthur. His name is Arthur.'

'Oh, Emmie, stop it,' Tabby said. 'You know that's not true.'

Moira looked from one to the other with disbelief. If anything, she was growing more furious as she awaited the explanation that would never come, and couldn't have satisfied her even if it had. 'I don't know what's going on between you two, but I can tell you both equally that it is unacceptable to meet a boyfriend or any friend when you are supposed to be working. Has this been a regular stunt you've been pulling? Treating your place of work as some sort of short-stay hotel? I wouldn't expect this of *students*, let alone adult women. I think you need to tell me exactly what's been going on this summer.'

'Don't listen to Emmie,' Tabby told Moira. 'She had nothing to do with this. It was me. Ask the people in the house for a description of the girl they saw leaving and you'll find it was me.'

'I shall do no such thing. They've been troubled quite enough for one holiday and, I might add, are paying my client two and a half thousand euros to rent the house this week. They have no intention of getting involved in the seedy ins and outs of your dalliances.' Moira was becoming pompous now, stirring in Tabby a horrible urge to laugh. 'Yes, they arrived early, but they should not have been able to get in using the code until three o'clock. And even if your emergency were a genuine one, I have my doubts that you would have had enough time to get back and finish by three, anyhow, which would have made it unprofessional in a different way. I can only hope that these poor people don't contact the owner direct about this, because if they do, he will want to find a new agent to manage his rental, and I won't blame him if he does. You have completely abused the trust the client and I have placed in you and you have potentially damaged my business reputation. Do you understand that?'

The heat generated by this diatribe seemed to linger in the air after she'd finished speaking, repelling apology and denial equally. The compulsion to giggle had left her, but Tabby still wasn't sure she could bear much more of this meeting – this day – and yet, according to Moira's wall clock, it was not yet eleven. She glanced across at Emmie, whose thoughts were now elsewhere, her mood apparently unperturbed. 'I'm sorry,' she said to Moira, finally. 'I don't know what else I can say.'

It came as no surprise when Moira announced her decision: they were both sacked.

The following days were the strangest of Tabby's life. If ever she had valued the structure imposed by work, any kind of work, it was now. Without any formal obligation to leave it, the house became a jail and Emmie her jailor – though the reality was the other way around. *She* was responsible for Emmie now.

Emmie had spoken little since her spirited moment in Moira's office, either of her own drama or of the one that had caused them to lose their jobs. Not once did she ask Tabby if Moira's allegation were true or who the man was who'd been visiting. She had no interest in it, just as she had none in eating or looking after herself – both she managed only with Tabby's near-forcible encouragement. The same went for their walks, which continued only in short and painful form, rarely drawing them beyond the fortifications of Saint-Martin. Emmie was drinking now, a couple of glasses of wine before bedtime, and in camaraderie or defeat – she was not sure which – Tabby joined her. Any thoughts of a parallel with poor Sylvie Woodhall were best left unvoiced. Sleeping hours began to exceed waking ones for both of them.

By Thursday, the normality of working for Moira was so far out of reach as to feel like a job she'd done long ago, or perhaps only read about someone doing in a novel. For the first time, Tabby wished she could leave Ré. Without an income, the island was an untenable base, besides which she had enough cash now either to move on or travel back to England. But she couldn't leave Emmie in this condition, not when she had caused the collapse. Without her meddling, Emmie would not have had to relive her traumatic recent past, she would not have lost the job that was anchoring her to the present.

Somehow, it had all gone catastrophically wrong again.

The next morning she found the number of a doctor and phoned to ask for advice. Thankfully, his English was better than her French, good enough for her to understand that he could do nothing without examining Emmie in person. House calls were not available, so she would need to bring Emmie to his surgery. This, Tabby knew, was impossible: even if she could somehow trick Emmie into it, she would turn on her heel the moment she realised she was in the presence of a doctor. If only things had not ended so badly with Moira, she could have appealed to her for help. Tabby thought again of Phil, the brother in Newbury who obviously loved and cared for his sister, and the next time she had access to Emmie's phone she searched it for his number. To her disappointment, there were only three names listed: Moira, Emmie's landlord M. Robert, and Tabby herself. There were no UK numbers at all: she had cut herself off well and truly.

As Emmie slept, Tabby took the laptop and read again parts of her story, hungry for clues as to what she might try next to improve her friend's spirits. Finding none, she did however note one passage that she must have missed the first time, or read too quickly to absorb its significance: 'I'd love to be able to say, just to one person, one time, "Come with me, stay with me until you've got yourself back on your feet." Give someone a break, totally against their expectations.' Here, after all this time, was the explanation to the one remaining element of Emmie's behaviour she had not been able to fathom: why she had allowed Tabby to stay on the night of the break-in, why she had invited her to move in. Tabby was the recipient of her random act of kindness, her attempt to do a stranger a good turn. It broke her heart to know how the sweet, open-hearted girl in the story – flawed, yes, but as she said herself no more flawed than any other woman in love – had been reduced to the lost and broken creature in the bedroom upstairs.

At last, the following weekend, she woke up knowing just what she had to do. She made the phone calls as she shopped for food.

'I need to leave the island for a few days,' she told Emmie that evening. 'I'll be gone when you wake up. Will you be OK?'

'Of course,' Emmie said. 'There's nothing wrong with me.'

This was plainly incorrect, for she had scarcely left her bedroom since Wednesday, but other conditions encouraged Tabby to proceed with her plan. One, Emmie had not touched the laptop since Tabby had slipped it downstairs (nor had she asked where it was); two, she had had a bath and washed her hair; three, she had eaten the scrambled eggs and bread Tabby had taken her that lunchtime.

Having stocked the fridge with the healthy foods of recuperation – as if this were the simple matter of feeding a cold! – she left a couple of paperbacks by Emmie's bed. She reminded her friend that she would be gone in the early hours and promised she would be back in a few days' time and that everything would go back to normal. Whatever *that* was.

It was a little like leaving a young child to fend for herself, but Tabby reminded herself that Emmie had coped perfectly well before she arrived. Being on her own again might be just what she needed.

Meanwhile, Tabby would go back to England and find Arthur Woodhall.

Chapter 23

Tabby

It was the last weekend in August, a bank-holiday Monday in the UK, she discovered, and there were no available flights to London from either La Rochelle or Nantes that would not swallow her entire cache of euros. The Eurostar from Paris was fully booked. She would need to travel cheaply and slowly by train and ferry.

She began in the darkness of early morning, taking the bus to La Rochelle Station and marvelling at the length of the famous bridge she had first crossed with Grégoire. She still had no whole memory of her arrival in Ré that night in May. Such was the strangeness of the last few weeks, she thought that if she were to return and find the bridge gone, the island vanished, she would not be entirely surprised.

The train to Saint-Malo involved a change in Rennes, and then the ferry to Portsmouth took most of the day. It didn't feel like a homecoming and she was grateful for that. She did not need the distraction of a sentimental journey. Arriving in England close to 7 p.m., she decided to take a cheap hotel room near the station for the night rather than risk arriving in London without a reservation and having to use every last penny on an expensive room there.

It was the right decision: in the morning she was well rested and optimistic, certain that by the time her head returned to the pillow that night she would have made progress, perhaps be on her way back to Emmie with news to lift her from her despair, even propel her to happier times.

She did not know London well, was not certain she had ever set foot in Emmie's old neighbourhood, and so on arrival at Waterloo was pleased to find herself on the right side of town and just a bus ride away. Of course, she was not so naïve as to assume Arthur Woodhall would simply answer the door and welcome her with open arms, willingly returning to France with her that same day. For one thing, he probably didn't live there any more – Emily had not once seen the lights on in his house during the period between the tragedy and her departure from the neighbourhood – and for another he would surely be at work, though not at St Barnabas'. Having remembered the news report of his resignation, Tabby had phoned the hospital for confirmation that he no longer held a post there. She could only pray that he had not, like Emmie, changed his name, making it impossible to follow his trail.

She'd forgotten how beautiful England could be in late summer. The sun was high when she reached the turn into Walnut Grove and saw at her feet the steep slope of shimmering green so familiar from Emmie's descriptions. It was a narrower street than she'd expected, the trees on either pavement meeting at their tops to create a canopy, under which she began to walk as if through an enchanted forest. It was easy to see why Emmie had fallen in love with the place, how she'd been charmed into believing that being in possession of a set of keys was the same as belonging. Walking down – she'd begun at Arthur's end, the 'good' end on the hill – she was struck by the height of the houses, so tall and imposing after the low roofs of Saint-Martin. Number 11 was dauntingly grand, what Tabby would consider a mansion, the white stucco exterior immaculate and the win-dowboxes on the first floor bright with summer flowers. The watered blooms and the gleam of light through the fanlight were promising signs: the house was open, lived in once more. But by Arthur? Would a man so catastrophically bereft live in a house so large, would he be able to use its rooms without seeing the ghosts of his own children?

She rang the bell. A Nigerian woman appeared: a cleaner, Tabby assumed, like her. She automatically relaxed.

'I'm looking for Arthur Woodhall. Does he still live here?'

The woman shook her head, readily enough for Tabby to see this was a misunderstanding she'd had to correct before. 'He moved out. Another family live here now.'

'Oh, I see. When did he leave?'

'I don't know.'

'Do you know where he went? Is he still in London?' But the poor thing clearly knew nothing and was anxious to get on with her work. The closed door caused a prickle behind Tabby's eyelids and she berated herself. It was scarcely likely to be the only one today: she needed to toughen up if she was to accomplish what she'd set out to do.

She turned and surveyed the row of houses across the street. These ones were narrower, with brickwork painted black, but were nonetheless large and smart, rising to four floors. Two houses might be said to be directly opposite number 11 and she approached the one on the right first, fixing her smile as she knocked. The woman who answered was too young, in her thirties, hair loose and feet in flip-flops. She could not be the famous Nina Meeks. The cries of young children from within supported this, for Nina had older children, the same age as the Woodhalls'. The thought made Tabby swallow hard. This was where it had all begun: this street, these houses.

'Oh.' Seeing her, the woman wore the crestfallen look of someone who'd been expecting a delivery of cakes and been handed instead a council tax summons. (Don't think of Susie, Tabby told herself.) 'Can I help you?'

'I'm looking for Nina Meeks. I was told her house is near here, is that right?'

The woman frowned. 'Who's asking?'

Of course, Nina was famous. What neighbour of a celebrity would just give the information to a stranger, especially when the whole street had so recently been crawling with press? Then Tabby remembered that Nina *was* press, the sort that trampled over people's lives without any thought for the harm they were causing; how many other Emmies had she ritually tortured? Tabby need make no special allowances for her.

'My name's Tabby Dewhurst. I've come all the way from France in the hope of talking to Nina about something very important, to do with her work. Please, I'm sure she won't mind meeting me.'

'Shouldn't you try her office first?'

'I could, I suppose, but I'm in the area now and I don't have much time before I have to get back.'

The woman considered the factors: Tabby's innocuous appearance, the name redolent of sleeping cats, the distance travelled. 'She's two up, number sixteen. But she probably won't be in, so don't get your hopes up.'

'Thank you.'

At number 16, there was an agonising wait before a young man came to the door, which startled Tabby into temporary silence as she thought again of the boys she'd read about in Emily's story. This must be the good friend of Alexander; nineteen or so now, college age. There were no obvious signs of bereavement, but it was over a year since the accident. Life went on, as it had for all involved, even for Emmie for a period.

'I'm looking for Nina. Is she your mum?'

'She's in town, at the paper, I think.'

'The *Press*?' This was more promising. It would be easy enough to find the address of a national newspaper.

'But she'll be back later,' he added.

329

'Do you know what time? I've come quite a long way to see her.'

Tabby was lucky that the boy had either been raised to be helpful or kept unaware of any harassment Nina had been subjected to during the scandal, because he answered quite guilelessly, 'She said about five o'clock, maybe earlier.'

'OK, I'll come back then if that's all right?'

'Sure.'

It was frustrating to have to wait almost three hours, but she did not wish to risk going into central London only to find that Nina had passed her on a train heading home. On the other hand, it was heartening to have positively located one of the people she'd come to see and to have won the boy's casual permission to return. She took her time walking down the Grove towards the high street, at last reaching the other two houses mentioned by Emmie: 199 and 197. One-nine-seven was the Laings', hosts of the party at which Arthur and Emmie had met, but otherwise undesirable components of her story. There was Sarah Laing's black and gleaming four-by-four parked outside. Tabby was glad not to be looking for a meeting with her. The woman had been jealous of Emmie, spitefully so. With all she had – this house, her family, wealth, security – she'd still found the space and energy to envy someone with so much less. In her own way, she had been as responsible for Emmie's ostracism as Nina.

Next door stood one of the most down-at-heel houses on the whole street. The door was shabby and dented, the paintwork on the window ledges dark with dirt, a mismatched array of cheap roller blinds at the windows, hanging at various careless angles. She tried to picture Emmie behind the window of the first floor – was the living room on the left or the right? – somehow finding a viewpoint at which to watch the reporters below while not being seen herself. It seemed incredible that an ordinary woman should find herself the object of such interest, such intrusion. No wonder she had said it hadn't felt as if it were really happening to her.

All at once, the door to number 197 jerked open and a short woman in jeans and wedged heels clopped down the path towards the Range-Rover. Sarah. As she climbed into the driver's seat she cast Tabby a look that was neither friendly nor unfriendly, a kind of acknowledgement that she was not worth registering.

She thinks I'm one of her neighbours' cleaners, Tabby thought. She wasn't sure she liked Walnut Grove. It felt like the kind of street where the residents made it clear if you offended their superior sensibilities, adulterous affair with a neighbour or not.

Just before five, she arrived at the gate of number 16 at exactly the same time as Nina Meeks was parking her Prius in a bay opposite – she recognised her cap of raven hair from the news coverage. It was not ideal to have to accost her kerbside, but it at least allowed her to catch her prey off guard.

'Ms Meeks? My name's Tabitha Dewhurst. Your son said it might be OK to come and have a quick chat with you.'

Busy juggling an armful of bags and papers, Nina hardly glanced her way. She looked much older than Tabby had pictured, the strains of her profession pinching the skin between her eyebrows and drawing down the corners of her mouth. 'You're a friend of his?' she asked.

'No.'

'Then what do you want to talk about, exactly?' She spoke rapidly and in a sharp tone, hovering rather than pausing, in anticipation of a succinct response. Her eyes were an arresting blue, with flecks of yellow-gold, and to experience their focus was to feel your defences fall as fast as your nerves rose.

'It's about Arthur Woodhall,' Tabby said. She'd planned every last word of her approach, judging that his name might open doors wider than Emmie's.

331

'I can't think of anything you might have to say about *him* that would interest me,' Nina said. She was on the move again, but not objecting when Tabby followed her up the path. Nor did she close the door in her face, instead standing looking at her uninvited guest from just inside, her head slightly cocked. She had the unmistakable energy of the innately inquisitive, the same kind that had got Tabby involved in this affair in the first place.

'Would it be OK to come in, just for a couple of minutes?' Tabby persisted and Nina sighed, 'If you must,' and then Tabby was in, closing the door behind her.

She lingered in the hallway, noting the framed caricatures of political figures, the table and radiator cover stacked haphazardly with post and newspapers, while at the foot of the stairs Nina called up to her son that she was home. Not receiving an answer, she turned to Tabby to say, 'Come down to the kitchen, we might as well have a cup of tea.' While you prove that you have nothing meaningful to say to me, was the implication.

Tabby readily accepted the offer; though she'd had two coffees in the café while she'd waited, she thought it might buy her a longer interview if she did. No one threw you out when your mug was still full. Taking a seat at the table, an old scrubbed thing bearing the ancient marks of children's felt-tips and fresher red-wine rings, she couldn't help thinking of the scene Emmie had described of her own kitchen interrogation, the one held in Sarah's basement. She was determined not to let Nina intimidate her. They had no personal connection, they would never see each other again after this.

Nina delivered the mugs of tea and sat directly opposite her, blue eyes meeting her visitor's with a certain pitiless indifference. 'So how can I help? You said it was about Arthur?'

'Actually, it's more about Emmie.'

'Who's Emmie?'

Tabby was taken aback, before she remembered that the

name was a fabrication and not a commonly used nickname. 'I mean Emily, sorry. Emily Marr.'

'Oh.' Instantly, Nina's lips thinned and her vivid eyes seemed to darken. 'What about her?'

'Well, I've got to know her quite well recently and, the thing is, she's very upset.' The words sounded absurdly understated – she'd be ejected before she started at this rate – and so she began again, this time more boldly: 'More than that, she's having some sort of nervous breakdown. I'm really worried she might self-harm or do something really terrible.'

'Makes a change from harming other people, I suppose. And unless you've been living on the moon, you'll know she's already done something really terrible.' Not blinking, Nina raised an eyebrow and took a sip from her tea. In the face of such aloofness Tabby began describing some of Emmie's symptoms, struggling with feelings of betrayal as she did. 'She won't stop crying, she hardly eats, she can't work any more. I found her on the floor, completely hysterical. She feels the whole world hates her and she'll never be forgiven.'

'I find that very hard to believe,' Nina said, unmoved. 'She's probably just acting, trying to get your sympathy. She's extremely manipulative, you know. She can persuade people to do whatever she tells them.'

'I've never met anyone less manipulative!' Tabby said, her voice shrill with outrage, but Nina merely looked down at her tea as if she might fathom in its depths what on earth it was she was doing here, sitting with this ridiculous person when there were so many more pressing errands to turn her mind to. Tabby composed herself. 'I know it's your job to write about people in ... in strong terms, and I'm sure some of them have got it coming to them, but not Emily. She's not a politician or someone used to that sort of attack, she's an innocent member of the public. She didn't deserve it.'

'Innocent?' Over the top of the mug, Nina's eyes narrowed

with displeasure. 'That's the last word I'd use to describe that woman.'

'I mean innocent of any actual crime. You have to admit that, surely? She had an affair, that was all, but you wrote up the inquest as if she was in the dock. She was never on trial for anything, was she?'

'I'm impressed with your grasp of the basic premise of a coroner's court,' Nina said, regarding her with a new expression, somewhere between indulgence and disdain, which made Tabby feel very small.

'But she didn't *make* Sylvie Woodhall do what she did, did she?'

At her friend's name Nina roused herself, sensing perhaps that her visitor would simply go on in this vein until forcibly halted. 'Yes, she did. That's the point that you seem to have missed. Emily directly caused Sylvie to drink far more than she was used to and to take a sleeping pill because she was so over-wrought she couldn't get any rest without it. These acts would not have taken place without Emily having said the things she said that evening: that is a fact.'

'But how can—?' Tabby began, but Nina was in her flow now and not to be interrupted.

'Emily filled her with such fear about the future of her family that she thought she had no choice but to tear off back to London the second she woke up. She lost consciousness at the wheel, did you know that?' At the sight of Tabby's uncertain response, Nina made a rough, exasperated noise. 'I can't believe I'm even discussing this with you. You obviously don't know the first thing about it.'

'That was only a theory, wasn't it, that she passed out at the wheel?'

'Only a theory? The coroner accepted it as the most probable cause of death!' Nina's face darkened with a terrible anger. 'How dare you come here and spout about that disgusting woman's innocence? I'll tell you who was *innocent* in this: the three people who died.'

Tabby nodded, lowered her eyes in humility. This was not going well. 'What I mean is, she didn't *have* to drive, did she? Knowing she might be over the limit, she could have waited, or got the train.'

'The train? Is this some sort of joke? She didn't sit there pondering her travel options like she was going to the beach for a picnic! She needed to get to her husband as fast as was humanly possible and save her marriage!'

'But she didn't *have* to take the boys with her. They were adults, old enough to stay on their own.'

'Which shows how little *you* know about parenting teenage boys,' Nina sneered.

Tabby was puzzled. 'One was already eighteen, wasn't he? Couldn't he have been left in charge? And even if the younger one was seventeen, I remember going on holiday with friends on our own when I was that age.' It had been a highlight, as she recalled, providing as it did a week's respite from Steve.

But Nina neither knew nor cared about Tabby's adolescent troubles. She glared at her, a full-beam bearing-down that made her previous surveillance seem benign, and it was all Tabby could do not to crumple under the savage heat of it. 'I'm not sure it's relevant what your parents chose to do with you – it's certainly of no interest – but I imagine Sylvie wanted her family all in one place. She may not have been as clear-thinking as she should have been, but her instinct on that point must have been very strong. She didn't want to separate from them at the very time she was fighting to hold them together. And leaving them behind still wouldn't have saved *her* life, would it? *She* would still have gone off the road. Or do you not consider her life as significant in any way? Just some middle-aged woman with her best years behind her? So long as the kids lived, who cares? Well, I've got news for you, "Emmie's" friend: *none of them lived*.'

Frightened now, Tabby battled to conceal her powerlessness. 'No, that's not what I'm saying at all. I'm sure all their lives were equally precious. I'm just saying Emmie can't be held responsible for the loss of them. In the end, it *was* an accident.'

Nina chuckled with a cold pity for her dim-witted visitor. 'She's obviously worked her charms on you, hasn't she? How did you meet her? I'm interested to know.'

'Just by chance. Our paths crossed.'

'That's what happened to poor Sylvie. Are *you* married?' Her tone was brittle, utterly unforgiving. Tabby knew she could achieve nothing here and yet she felt magnetised by Nina, unable to remove her gaze, much less her whole self.

'No, I'm single.' What this woman would say if she knew Tabby had casually acquired a married man for a holiday fling didn't bear thinking about. Who was Noémie's Nina? Might she too have a plan for her friend's betrayer? Were her own problems actually just beginning?

'Probably just as well, I'd say. Where's she working now?'

Regretful of her previous outpouring of personal information about Emmie, Tabby checked herself. 'For obvious reasons, she doesn't want anyone to know that.'

Nina pushed her seat back from the table and Tabby took a few gulps of her own full mug in the hope of gaining an extension. It worked: Nina poured herself a second mugful from the teapot and returned. 'Look, I'm not sure I really understand the purpose of this visit. I've met Emily's supporters before, you know, and they always try to convince me she's wonderful. This is slightly barmier than usual, but it's nothing new.'

Tabby thought hard. It was clear now that if she wanted to make her request she would need to make it soon. 'I just wanted ... I just thought it was time someone stood up for her. Everything you wrote, and all the other reporters, as well, it wasn't balanced. It didn't take into account her side of the story. It incited unnecessary bad feeling.'

'"Incited unnecessary bad feeling"? What is this, a one-woman press inquiry? I'm sorry we didn't meet your exacting editorial standards, but I'm afraid you're just going to have to live with the injustice. There's always the Press Complaints Commission if you're really offended – I can give you their email address?' Nina sniggered unpleasantly. 'It's months ago now, anyway. That's a very long time in news, I can tell you, and practically a century in internet terms.'

'Not for her, for her it's still current! The thing is, it ruined her life. She feels as if she can never come back.'

'Don't make me laugh,' Nina said, and, indeed, was no longer doing so. 'She got off lightly compared to Sylvie and the boys. And why would she want to "come back"? You mean to the Grove? She'd be insane to show her face around here, even now.' There was a sudden catch in Nina's voice. 'Listen, as I say, this story has gone cold. The only people who still care are Sylvie's family and friends, and we can do without some goody-two-shoes going around running a PR campaign for Emily Marr. I can save you a lot of bother by telling you it's going to fall on deaf ears and you might as well cut your losses and give up.'

She was right. Tabby's dreams of persuading her to write a more positive story about Emily were too childish to voice. Which left her to her original mission: appealing to Arthur. And the likelihood of Nina being willing to disclose his new where-abouts was virtually nil.

'So Arthur doesn't live on the Grove any more, either?'

'No. He sold up after the inquest. I don't blame him.' But there was no warmth in Nina's tone, no compassion, and Tabby understood she meant life would have been a misery for him if he'd remained among Sylvie's friends, Sylvie's mourners. And yet he was both, too, wasn't he, whatever Nina chose to think? His life was a misery wherever he lived it. Tabby recalled Emmie's torment at not being able to comfort him.

'It must be awful for him,' she said. 'Whatever he did, he still lost his wife and sons. That doesn't happen to every man who has an affair. It's a terrible, terrible punishment.'

Nina sighed in grudging accord. 'I agree with you on that point, yes. But he'll be all right, in time, take my word for it. As you must be well aware from your new pal, there's always someone willing to console men like him.'

That meant he had a new girlfriend, Tabby realised; perhaps she was even implying he would have a new family, a second chance. She thought of poor Emmie in the house in France. She'd thought she was his second chance, but now her desolation was such that she couldn't be in the same country as him.

'Where is he now?' she asked Nina. 'Is he still in London?'

'*You* tell me. Why would I have any idea what their address is?' Nina looked as if she'd just been struck: pain suffused her face, her eyes became wet and shiny. 'Their', she'd said, and Tabby guessed she'd been thinking of the Woodhall family as it used to be, a set of plurals, a couple and their children. How long did it take for such instincts to adjust? Did they ever?

Next time she looked, Nina had recovered herself. 'Why did you do it?' Tabby blurted, sensing that the meeting might soon be terminated. 'Why did you write those articles, make her into some sort of public enemy? You could have done it privately. You'd still have got rid of her.'

Nina regarded her with new interest. At last, here was a question that challenged her. 'I see how this is,' she said slowly. 'You think I should be sorry for doing it. You want to punish *me*, get me to punish myself by printing some sort of apology.'

This had been Tabby's hope exactly, but now the idea had been explicitly stated she saw how inadequate it would be, even in the miraculous event of Nina agreeing to it. What good were a few words buried somewhere in a newspaper where no one would notice them? She thought of Emmie and the sheaves of cuttings spread out around her, the vitriolic headlines about her.

What she needed was retraction on the same scale, and that could never be achieved. The clock could not be turned back.

'Do you really not see,' Nina said, 'that I've had my punishment? All of us who knew and loved Sylvie and the boys, we've been punished for every single one of our bad deeds, ten times over. We've lost far more than Emily has. No loved one of hers died in the crash.'

No, but Arthur might as well have, Tabby thought, because Emmie mourned him like a death.

Nina stood, signalling that Tabby's audience with her was at an end. 'Look, if you want to know where Arthur is, all you have to do is ask her.'

'You mean Emmie? She's the last person who'd know,' Tabby said.

Nina made a sharp barking sound that Tabby realised was laughter – the sound of mocking amusement. 'Oh, Tabitha, what on earth are you doing getting involved in this? You're clearly out of your depth and don't know Emily half as well as you seem to think. Now, I'm sorry, but I really must catch up with my family and then get on with some work. I have a deadline in the morning.'

Tabby stood and followed her to the front door. 'Thank you for your help. I know you're very busy.'

'Glad to be of service,' Nina said mechanically, and even before Tabby had cleared the first step, she could hear the journalist's heels stalking back down the hallway, no split-second hesitation, no trace of self-doubt.

There was nothing left but to try Arthur's private practice in Harley Street. His biography remained on the Marylebone Eye Clinic website, though the last entry in the Staff News section was months ago and it was possible his departure was among the updates yet to be made. Or perhaps he remained a business party without seeing any patients? She decided she would learn by Emmie's mistakes and bypass the phone in favour of an investigation in person.

It was almost six o'clock, however, and the clinic line offered only recorded information about consulting hours and the suggestion she contact the hospital by email. She realised she would have to wait till morning, no bad thing given how she felt after the encounter with Nina: not so much demoralised as war-torn. It was a surprise, when she next looked at her reflection, not to see blood. Searching online for a local hotel, her eye was caught at once by a name she recognised: the Inn on the Hill near the train station. Walking there, it was hard not to think of Emmie in her glamorous earlier guise, the erotic wiggle in her step as she made her way to those longed-for assignations with Arthur, dressed in the vintage skirts and blouses he liked so much, the high heels and candy-pink lipstick. What was it Emmie described herself as? A confection, that was it: sweet, mouth-watering, edible.

It was a Tuesday, the place was near-empty, and so she was able to negotiate a cheap rate. Checking in, she wondered if it was the same member of staff who had checked Emmie and Arthur in and out, trained to treat their separate arrivals and exits as nothing untoward. On the wall was a framed feature from one of the glossy magazines: 'Boltholes for Bad Girls', a guide to the best hotels for dirty weekends. The Inn on the Hill had made it on to the map thanks to Emmie, of course: 'No longer as clandestine a choice as it once was, having been revealed as the favoured hideaway of Emily Marr and her married lover Arthur Woodhall. Best room: a little bird tells us Marr and Woodhall favoured "Marrakech", with its huge wrought-iron bed and copper *en suite* fittings.' For once, a piece of reporting that was accurate, thought Tabby.

She was becoming aware of an underlying thrill in the retracing of her famous friend's steps, in verifying the knowledge that the low-key, defensive woman who barely allowed herself to make eye contact with other people had so recently been a notorious *femme fatale*, albeit just for a few weeks. She was gaining a sense of what it might be like to be one of Emmie's 'fans', the ones whose admiration she grew to fear as much as she did the loathing of her detractors. Perhaps it was less problematic to consider herself, instead, a pilgrim.

Either way, it was a relief to be handed the key not for Marrakech but for Stockholm, a compact, pale single at the back of the building.

She was in Harley Street for 9 a.m. It was a smaller clinic than she'd expected, with no open-door access to reception, but she benefited from the fact that a member of staff was just arriving and held the door for her. The receptionist was on the phone, evidently consoling a caller over some misunderstanding to do with eye drops, and Tabby kept a discreet distance from the desk. She took the opportunity to look about her. It was a beautiful property, its original architectural features stylishly restored, the floors polished and glossy. The few waiting patients Tabby could see sipped mineral water and read *Tatler* or *The Economist*. How different from the overcrowded scene at St Barnabas' that Emmie had described. Tabby wondered what kind of a man it took to move between the two environments without being distracted by the injustice of it. (And then there was the West African charity: presumably, conditions there must make St Barnabas' look like Harley Street.) Standing there, she had a sudden and acute sense of identification with Emmie; how could girls like the two of them have a chance at success in this world? Just because you had nothing, it didn't mean you were worth nothing, deserved nothing. Perhaps the truth was that you deserved more?

The receptionist had finished her call and turned her attention to Tabby. 'Sorry to keep you waiting, Miss ... ?'

'Dewhurst.' Tabby could see at once past the pleasant, capable exterior: this woman was used to handling VIP arrivals, she'd be vigilant to a fault, immune to persuasion – and was therefore best approached with honesty. 'I don't have an appointment, but I've just arrived from France and I'm trying to get hold of Arthur Woodhall. I thought he might still be at St Barnabas', but apparently he left some time ago. I'm hoping he might still be working here?'

'Are you a former patient of his?'

'No. I'm a friend of a friend. I know that sounds a bit vague, but I do have a good reason to see him. I'm only in the UK for a few days and it's quite important.'

The receptionist gave Tabby a look that said, 'If your reason were good enough, you'd already know where to find him,' but she continued to give every other impression of cooperation. 'He is still working here, yes, but only a few days a month and today is not one of his days. He won't be back down until next Monday now.'

'Back down': he'd left London, then. It was her first clue, scarcely useful in itself. 'Are you his secretary?'

'No, that's Mrs Herne. Though she works mostly for Mr Ali now.'

'Could I have a quick word with her?'

'I'm afraid she's on leave for two weeks. We have a temp in but to be honest she'll probably know less than I do.'

'Do you know where he's living now?'

'I'm afraid I'm not authorised to give you the home address of any member of staff. I'm sure you understand that.'

Tabby felt the day's first vibrations of dejection. It was becoming clear that she was not suited to private detective work. 'Could you at least tell me if he's working anywhere else? You said he comes down just a few days a month, so has he moved to a hospital up north? Or does he not have an NHS post at all now?'

Faint surprise crossed the other woman's brow. 'Well, it's

public knowledge that Mr Woodhall divides his time between here and the Mapleton Eye Clinic in Leeds. I can give you the phone number if you'd like it?'

'Thank you.' Tabby was so pleased with the break that she took her leave at once, as if delaying would give the woman the opportunity to repossess the information from her brain. It may have been public knowledge that Arthur had taken a job in Leeds, but it had not appeared on the first four or five pages of search results for him she had worked her way through the previous afternoon.

In the street she rang the number, discovering that it was a new, private offshoot of the General Infirmary located to the north of the city and that Arthur would be seeing pre-op patients there that afternoon. At King's Cross, she bought the cheapest train ticket on sale and began the two-hour-plus next part of her journey. She tried not to worry about money, the fact that the three hundred euros she'd brought with her was disappearing fast. There was more cash in her room in Saint-Martin. Leaving the house two mornings ago, she had not wholly trusted herself to return and had left the fund there as a kind of insurance, a secret promise to Emmie that she would come back.

Lord only knew what she would bring with her – and what she would find – when she did.

Chapter 24

Tabby

On arrival in Leeds, and with little hope of tailing a man by public transport, she plundered her shrinking fund to hire a car and drive to the quiet suburb in which the eye clinic was located. She took her time to circle the car park and vehicle access roads before parking in the near corner of the visitor car park, as close to the exit as she could get and facing the main doors. She turned off the engine. Again, she had learned from Emily's past mistakes and did not plan to attempt to bluff her way into Woodhall's consulting rooms in the guise of patient or friend. She would simply wait until he had finished for the day.

The question was, how long? It might look suspicious to walk in and ask the receptionist outright. Might they tell her over the phone? Watching a taxi pick up a patient and his companion from the main door, she had a better idea, and headed to the doors herself.

'Car service for Arthur Woodhall,' she announced to the receptionist, hanging back slightly, as cab drivers did.

The receptionist looked up the extension on her database and made the call. 'Car for Mr Woodhall.' There followed the mildly perplexed attitude that Tabby had been expecting. 'No, that's what I thought. Thanks.' She turned back to Tabby, who kept her body language easy, her expression guileless. 'Are you sure you've got the right name? That particular surgeon is in theatre until seven o'clock.'

Tabby frowned. 'Must be some sort of mix-up. Not to worry. I'll check with my controller.'

'Which cab firm are you from?' she was asked, but she pretended to be out of earshot, on her way out of the door. Outside, she toured the staff parking bays and noted a Mercedes among the vehicles. Of course, Arthur might have changed his car since Emmie had known him, but there was a good chance he had not needed to. Given the excitable emphasis on Emmie in the press coverage, Tabby suspected that his relocation owed less than his former lover's to harassment – after all, the name of his new place of employment had been freely given by London staff – and more to overwhelming grief. Possibly he had not registered the public furore, not in a real sense; surely it would have been meaningless in the face of the losses he had suffered? He probably didn't give a damn what he drove or where he worked.

Seven o'clock. It was only three now. She bought something to eat and drink from the nearest shop and settled in the car. She had an excellent view of the doors and of the staff parking bays, and was able to position the book she was reading against the steering wheel in such a way as to keep peripheral note of them as she read.

She knew what Arthur looked like from the internet images. Yes, there might be several senior staff of similar age and appearance, but she would have to trust to memory and, if necessary, instinct. She couldn't miss this opportunity, for the simple reason that she would not be able to afford another; by her calculation she had enough money left for only one more night in a budget hotel, preferably with breakfast included, so she could fill up and not waste funds on expensive snacking. But so far, so good, she told herself. She'd had some lucky breaks today. The clinic was on the outskirts of the city, with free parking and, so far, no CCTV surveillance that had brought any security staff scurrying her way. It was a fine, dry day and the light would be good till late; she would easily be able to see which car was his and start her own in time to follow him in suburban traffic, a manoeuvre that would be almost impossible in London or in Leeds city centre.

She watched, she read, she watched. She closed her eyelids and then forced them open before she could lose muscular control of them. She watched some more.

It was close to seven-thirty when the man she identified as Emmie's lost love came out of the building, not by the main doors but by a rear one situated closer to the silver VW he now approached. He wore a dark suit and white shirt, and moved with a lithe dynamism that caught her eye even before she'd matched the short, ash-grey hair and rather solemn features to those in the images she'd committed to memory. By the time she'd started her engine and pulled out, a third car and a shuttle bus had put themselves between him and her, which made it difficult to see if he, at the head of the queue at the first lights, was indicating left or right. But she was lucky: the vehicles in between turned the opposite way and soon she was directly behind him, keeping sufficient distance so as not to strike him as too eager a constant in his rear-view mirror.

After a short while he turned on to an A-road and travelled at careful speed past a large golf course and into countryside, exiting and following a quieter road for a few minutes before pulling up at the gates of a detached brick new-build. They were electronic gates, Tabby saw, and without wasting a moment she parked at the kerb opposite, dashed across the road and slid inside the gates before they had fully closed behind the VW. It was a short driveway and absurd to imagine Woodhall had not seen her in his mirrors. Sure enough, a moment later he was out of his car and looking straight at her. 'Who are you?' he called. If he felt at all threatened, he didn't show it.

346

She took a single step forward. 'My name's Tabby.'

'Tabby who? Do you have a surname?' He spoke in fine-grained, patrician tones, but there was no mistaking the cold intolerance of his manner.

'Tabby Dewhurst.' Surveying the car park that afternoon, she had considered little else than how she would introduce herself, how best to gain his confidence, but now the time had come she found she had forgotten her lines, was intimidated by him.

'Right,' he said, 'listen to me, please. I know you've just followed me from the hospital. I assume you are also the woman who pretended to be from a taxi service earlier. You may be surprised to hear that that trick has been used before. I suggest you just tell me right now what it is you want, otherwise I'm going to go phone the police. Don't run off: you won't be able to scale the gates and in any case I've made a note of your registration, so you'll be easily tracked down and questioned.' He had his phone in his hand, ready to carry out his threat. He was not like Nina, displeased to be ambushed but by nature intrigued; he was unambiguously enraged. She'd been wrong to think him impervious to unwanted attention. He'd gone to some lengths to separate himself from his old life – other than the form of work, none of the original elements remained – and now here she was, determined to reassemble them.

He'd also been performing surgery for hours and was plainly exhausted. She should have waited, she realised, come in the morning when he had more energy and patience.

'I'm waiting,' he said.

'I'm here on behalf of Emily,' she said, finding her voice at last.

This did not perturb him as much as Tabby might have expected. But then, as Nina had pointed out so scathingly, she was not the first to try to plead Emily's case and, as he had just told her, she was also not the only one to try to trick her way into his company.

'You're a reporter?' He regarded her with a new attitude of distaste. He had, she saw, extreme self-possession and in that respect he was not so different from Nina. He was accustomed to having his commands obeyed, used to setting the agenda; he was going to be just as resistant to her cause as Nina had been and, very likely, much briefer about it.

But she couldn't allow herself to think of lost causes, not yet. 'No, nothing like that,' she said. 'I've come from France – from near La Rochelle, actually.'

'La Rochelle?' He looked surprised; this, then, was a new line for him.

'I know it's late, I know this is your private home and I'm trespassing, but I really need to talk to you about Emily.'

'Look, Miss Dewhurst, there is very little you can tell me about her that I won't already know, and even less that I'm prepared to tell you.' There was gentleness in the way he spoke Tabby's name – gentlemanliness, perhaps – and a reserve to the statement itself that gave her sudden hope. He didn't spit at the thought of Emily, or sneer at the idea that she should be worthy of discussion.

'It's very important. Couldn't you just give me five minutes?'

'I said no.'

'Please. *Please*. Five minutes and I'll never bother you again, I promise on my father's grave.'

As he turned from her, she regretted instantly the invocation of graves of any sort, following him to his front door in hope rather than expectation. He let himself in and left the door half open, the invitation to enter quite wordless, as Nina's had been, a shared acknowledgement that no matter how they tried, they could not close this business of Emily; she was owed a last hearing. Inside, he ushered her into the first room on the left, a small lounge, blandly furnished, curtains already drawn. Tabby could not help noting the difference between this modest place and the huge period residence on Walnut Grove she'd peered into the previous day.

'Wait here, please,' he said. He closed the door after him and she heard him go upstairs. When he returned a few minutes later he had removed his jacket and was drinking from a bottle of mineral water. He offered her nothing and was still openly suspicious of her. Seeing him at closer quarters, she registered a disappointment in him that may have been connected with the ordinariness of the interior, even the withholding of the offer of water. Though she'd known what he looked like, she realised she'd been expecting an obvious handsomeness, a magnetism of the type Grégoire had. But *this* inveterate womaniser gave the impression of not caring if he never set eyes on another female again. In that respect, he was changed fundamentally from the man Emmie had described, and it occurred to her that if Emmie were to understand this, she might be able to start to let go.

He sat at the end of the sofa nearest her armchair and regarded her in a way that said, without words, 'You've got a nerve,' before commenting aloud: 'Right. Five minutes.'

Tabby didn't intend to waste a second. 'I've been talking to Emily about everything that's happened and—'

Almost at once he was interrupting. 'Hang on, you *are* a journalist?' He placed the water bottle on the coffee table, ready to spring up and show her the door.

'No,' Tabby told him, very firmly. 'I said I wasn't. I've never met a reporter in my life.'

'Well, if you're a therapist you know as well as I do you shouldn't be sharing confidential material.'

'I'm not a therapist either.' Tabby wished he would just let her speak, otherwise her five minutes would be over before she had begun. 'I'm a friend of hers, a good friend.'

Looking as if he'd need some convincing on this definition, he nevertheless resettled and gestured for her to continue.

'I've been talking to her and reading her journal and I've

come to ask if there's any chance you might be able to forgive her. I don't mean you have to see her in person, though it would be wonderful if you could, but just let me know you don't hate her, so I can go back to her and tell her she doesn't have to go on punishing herself the way she has been. I mean, she knows it's all over between you, but she can't move on while she thinks you still blame her. She's in a terrible, terrible state and I'm scared she might do something serious, something self-destructive. I wouldn't have come all this way if I weren't extremely worried, I promise you. No one knows I'm here, not even her. This is a completely secret appeal.'

As she came to a halt, having run out of breath rather than words, Arthur gazed at her, perplexity having given way to a kind of enthralment. The growing silence was no less disarming than his initial quickness to jump to conclusions and interrupt.

'Where is this journal?' he asked finally, and his tone was suddenly so pleasantly mild as to be almost sinister. Emmie had written that his intensity was in his stillness, and she was starting now to sense that power. He had something, certainly, but whatever it was he was going to use it to defeat, not to seduce.

Trembling slightly, she removed the laptop from her bag. Having known it would be necessary to prove her claim and not having access to a printer, she had taken it from Emmie's house, her justification to herself being that it contained nothing that Arthur didn't already know and much that might remind him of things he'd once known but had come, in the darkness of grief, to forget. The strength of Emmie's devotion, for instance, the purity of it. To have banished her from his life so categorically, to have given her no chance to defend herself, not even the five minutes he was permitting Tabby now, to have cut her dead at the inquest, he had to have suffered some kind of post-traumatic stress, a stress that might by now have begun to subside. She did not allow herself to think how Emmie would react if she knew her former lover was at that moment being offered the contents of her heart and soul; nor had she allowed herself to imagine what Emmie's behaviour would be if she discovered the laptop missing.

'It's not a diary, exactly,' she told him, noticing him eye the laptop with circumspection. 'She wrote it after the inquest. But it's *like* a diary. It's everything that happened from her point of view. It's Emily's story.' She clicked open the file and slid the laptop across the coffee table towards him. He did not touch it and nor did he ask further questions. He seemed not to know what to say, not to know whether to accept her offering or dash it to the floor in indignation. 'It's quite long,' she added. 'It took me a couple of hours to read. I could leave it with you overnight if you prefer, and then we could talk again in the morning?' She would sleep in the car, she decided. She could not expect him to let her watch him read, but would have to trust him not to delete or remove it.

'Excuse me,' said a low, quiet voice, and when Tabby looked up she saw that Arthur had not closed the door to the hallway when he had returned and that there was a female figure standing just outside, partly in the shadows. 'Where did you get that?'

'You called the police?' Tabby said to Arthur, stricken. But of course he had, he must have phoned when he'd gone upstairs, perhaps even from the car. How naïve she'd been, tailing him like some sort of idiotic Nancy Drew, spotted even before she'd pulled out of the hospital and joined the traffic behind him; and what a fool to think he had remained unaffected by becoming a media pariah – had she not seen for herself the electronic gates, the fact that the detached house was not overlooked on any side, details of far greater importance to Arthur than stylish furniture? This was a man who, like Emmie, had been driven from his home and his job. But unlike poor Emmie, he had status and wealth, the means to establish a supportive relationship with the

351

local police and proper security at his new place of work. He was not a fugitive of no professional standing, like Emmie, but a man whose skills remained highly prized by society no matter what mistakes he'd made in his personal life. He was a victim *worth* protecting. Of course he could, and would, call for professional back-up the moment a stranger popped up talking of the Marr Affair. This police officer and her colleagues probably had their own keys, permission to enter the moment Arthur raised the alarm. No matter how hapless Tabby had looked, no matter how apparently well-meaning, he would still have needed to suspect that she could be dangerous. He would know to trust no one.

She'd judged it all wrong, as usual.

'I got it from Emily herself,' she said, speaking towards the door. 'She lent it to me. It's not stolen,' she added. The last thing she needed was a charge of theft on top of harassment.

'Oh, I think you know it is,' Arthur said, at her side.

Indignant, Tabby spun back to him. 'I know it is *not*. She gave it to me a week or two ago.' She had lost all sense of time and could not spare precious seconds to puzzle over precise dates. 'That's when I read it myself for the first time. She wanted me to read it – and I'm glad I did. It helped me to understand her position, and that's all I'm asking you to do. Is it *so* terrible a request? After everything you went through together?'

'This is insane,' Arthur said, speaking so softly it might even have been to himself. 'Completely insane.'

The word irritated Tabby, who felt now, in the presence of the police, that she had nothing left to lose: the worst was already upon her and it was now a question of keeping her self-respect – and respect for Emmie, too. 'What's insane is the way she's been treated, like someone on a murder charge. No,' she corrected herself, heated now, 'like someone already convicted of murder! She may not have behaved very honourably, but I don't think what she did was unforgivable. And a member of *her* family died as well, you know. I think it's awful how everyone turned their back on her, obsessed with blaming her, turning her into a scapegoat, when what she needed was love and sympathy.'

'Everyone,' Arthur repeated with a strange, sorrowful wonderment, and Tabby saw she'd gone too far, after all, she'd caused new offence.

'I don't mean you, of course, and that's not what she thinks either. I mean, you have obviously had a worse time even than her. I'm so sorry for your loss, Mr Woodhall, I should have said that first. I really am sorry. I didn't know anything about the accident, or this whole tragedy, until very recently. I'd been out of the country.' She was tying herself in knots now, all the while being regarded by Arthur as if she were the bearer of fantastical, bizarre tidings.

'What is it?' she asked. 'You don't believe me?'

The door opened fully then and the policewoman took a few steps into the room. She was dressed very casually, was clearly some sort of plain-clothes officer, her neutral, reticent body language no doubt the product of special training. I'm going to have to give up, Tabby thought; if I can somehow get out of this situation with only a warning or a caution ... She thought with sudden longing of the ferry crossing to Brittany, of the quiet lounge of reclining seats where you could drop off to sleep to the motion of the Channel. On the way, it had been an exasperatingly sedate mode of transport, but now she could think of nothing more tantalising.

Then she noticed something peculiar: the policewoman was not wearing shoes. Her feet were bare, her toenails the vivid white of the inside of oyster shells. She stood with a natural grace, drawing Tabby's eye up the length of her languid, curvaceous figure. Though dressed, she must have just showered, because her wet hair was combed off her face, her skin scrubbed pink. She was extremely pretty. With a sudden flush for her own

353

stupidity, Tabby recognised the truth. The woman must live here; she was not a police officer at all, but the new girlfriend Nina had hinted at, the inevitable source of consolation of which Meeks had disapproved. It was not considered seemly, perhaps, for Arthur to form a new relationship so soon after the death of his wife.

The woman gazed at the laptop with an expression of simple fascination, attracted, perhaps, by the promise of secrets about Arthur's infamous former lover. Did he talk about Emily to this woman? Tabby thought. Did he think of her ever? She felt the downward pull in her stomach of final defeat and thought, once again, Poor Emmie ... She would have to go back to her with some false story, a succession of little white lies of the kind Emmie herself had once told her distressed father. The need to tell her what it would benefit her to hear exceeded any old-fashioned attachment Tabby might have to the truth.

'Tabby,' said Arthur, with the supreme weariness of one who had spent the afternoon in the operating theatre and had no energy for further physical investigation, 'that was what you said your name was, wasn't it?'

'Yes, that's right.' Should she have given him a false one? she wondered. The strange, staring woman in front of her wasn't a police officer, fine, but Tabby sensed that she was not out of the woods yet.

'Well, Tabby,' said Arthur, standing now with a certain polite formality. 'I would like to introduce you to Emily Marr.'

Chapter 25

Tabby

Tabby stared at Arthur with the bafflement of an infant who had not yet learned sufficient vocabulary to follow adult conversation and must therefore rely on visual clues for clarity. She could tell something interesting had been said, something critical, but she could not make sense of the words. Meanwhile, Arthur and the barefoot woman had forgotten all about her, it seemed, and were gazing at each other instead, too many emotions crossing their faces – indignation, pleasure, bemusement, suspicion – to help her to reorientate.

Then the woman came to sit beside Arthur. She was interested in the laptop, Tabby saw, rather than in its keeper. 'I thought I'd lost it,' she said, and her voice, breathy and low-pitched, had a quality of humility to it. 'I never printed it out. It was just a file on my hard drive.'

'I don't understand,' Tabby said, appealing to Arthur, the authority figure here, but he was still concerned with the woman with pearl-white toenails, the woman he said was Emily Marr but who could not be. She obviously could not be because Emmie was Emily, she was quite clear on that.

The odd thing was that this woman looked a little like Emmie. Not like the Emmie in the old photos but the current incognito one. They had the same head of carelessly cropped dark hair, similarly wide-set eyes; an unselfconscious, unadorned personal style in common. This woman had finer features, however, and that soft-voiced sexiness. She was elegant and gently sorrowful; maybe 'melancholy' was the word, Tabby thought. Whatever it was, it made Arthur close his arm around her waist, cup her and protect her. He loved her, it was plain.

'You're not Emily,' Tabby told her, and she sought Arthur's eye for reassurance. 'Is she?' He, of all people, would know. But he wanted to let the woman speak for herself.

She drew a deep breath and sighed. 'There are still times when I wish I wasn't, but I am. It's obvious you don't believe me – I suppose I could show you my passport, if you like?'

'You have no need to explain yourself to this person, darling,' Arthur said, and Tabby stared at him in bewilderment. He agreed, then, that she was who she said she was.

'I don't understand,' she said, once more. 'This laptop belongs to my friend Emmie. She's had it since I've known her and we met in May, nearly four months ago.'

'It was stolen from me in March, from my brother's house in Newbury,' the woman said, as if in agreement. 'Just before I left for Paris.'

Paris? Newbury? The earth had shifted and time was stretching. Perhaps that was why Tabby was being so slow to understand. 'Your brother's house?' she repeated. 'In Newbury?' Fear of police arrest had now been replaced by some other, unnamed apprehension.

'Yes. It was reported stolen to the police, but they said straight up they didn't think I'd ever get it back.'

Tabby just breathed in and out, in and out, her vanquished brain straining to make the connections required for a first stab at an interpretation of this mystery. 'So you think Emmie got it from whoever stole it from you? But if that's the case, how did she get into it? How would she know the original password, if it wasn't her own?'

The couple exchanged a glance.

'"Woodhall",' Tabby remembered. 'That was *your* password?'

'I don't suppose it was a hard code to crack,' the woman admitted.

'It's an old thing,' Arthur commented, reaching across her to stab at the keyboard. 'I'm surprised it still works.'

'Technically, it's Matt's. But he left it for me when he moved out. I didn't use it much at first.'

Tabby being Tabby, she had investigated the other files and found documents to do with Matt Piper, the man in the wedding photograph, the one who had spoken up for Emily in the newspaper profile. 'Matt, as in Emily's ex-boyfriend?' she asked.

'Yes.' The woman looked frankly at her then – she had very dark indigo eyes, not like Emmie's in colour or shape – and grimaced in embarrassment. 'God, you must know everything about me if you've read this. I mean, the *real* everything. I have to tell you it feels a lot weirder than when people read the lies. What a bizarre situation.' She was preoccupied once more, scrolling through the file, her eyes rolling up and down, up and down. 'I wrote more after this, you know. There was another chapter. I wrote it after I left England. Just by hand, in a notebook; I couldn't afford a new computer.' She closed the lid, a tremor visible in her shoulders. 'It didn't finish here.'

'Clearly not,' Arthur said. 'Otherwise we wouldn't have this confusion now.' He turned to Tabby. 'I think you'd better tell us about this friend of yours you seem to think is Emily. You say she's using her name?'

'Well, Emmie. She's called Emmie Mason.' It was the name in the document, of course, Emily's own idea for her new identity.

'And she's in La Rochelle, is she?'

'Near there.' Tabby was reluctant for the time being to be more specific, not knowing what trouble poor Emmie might soon find herself in.

'And I suppose she looks a bit like me?' the new Emily asked. 'I mean, like I used to look?'

Tabby frowned as she nodded. Still mystified, she sensed that the other woman was closer to comprehension than she was. 'That's the strange thing. She looks more like you do right now. Short hair, no make-up, she dresses really low-key. It makes no sense.'

'Oh, it does, believe me.' Emily rose to her feet. 'I think I have an idea what's going on here. Do you have time to stay a little while, Tabby?'

'Of course.'

'Then let me get the last chapter for you. You'd better read it before we talk any more.'

'Emily,' Arthur protested, reaching for her hand and taking it in both of his. 'Are you sure you want to rake over it like this? I'm sure Tabby won't mind if we just ask her to leave. There's obviously been a misunderstanding. This other woman is nothing to do with us.'

He had a kind of unassailable calm, Tabby thought, a quality of being in the right; and so he was, for she wouldn't mind being ordered to leave – at least she wouldn't beg to stay. Though still unclear as to its precise nature or cause, she had entered into a state of humiliation, on Emmie's behalf as well as her own. She did not know what had happened, only that she had somehow been deceived. A part of her longed to do as Arthur suggested and just go, not another word uttered, and yet ... if this woman thought she had material that might cast light on Emmie's situation, then she wanted to read it. Always, for as long as she could remember, when given the choice between knowing and not knowing, she wanted to know.

'She needs to read it,' the woman was telling Arthur, gently extracting her hand from his. Something in the way he reluctantly let it go, letting her fingers slide from his grip fraction by

358

fraction, made Tabby's heart contract with acute pain. Paul had *never* released her like this. In the end, he had wanted to push her away, send her flying. 'I promise you it's the only thing that will make sense.'

'Fine,' Arthur said, rising too. 'You get what you need and I'll pour us all a glass of wine. Stay here,' he added to Tabby.

For a second time, Tabby was left alone. She could hear the distant chime of wineglasses knocking against each other, a bottle being opened, while overhead footsteps scurried into a bedroom and then back again, towards the stairs. The door had been left open and she had a side view of the staircase. So indecipherable was the situation, so unfamiliar the atmosphere, she would not have been surprised if the woman returned dressed as Emily Marr, just as Emmie had that strange Saturday night when they'd walked together, arm in arm, down to the port. The shoes would come into sight first, then the flared skirt of the dress, then the bare shoulders, the pink loveheart lips and winged eye make-up of a Fifties siren.

But when the new Emily returned she was dressed just the same. She moved very gracefully, light-footed and silent, like a dancer or a model; it was hard not to be transfixed, to want to keep your eyes on her all the time.

'Here.' She'd brought two items: a notebook the size of a paperback novel and a passport. This she showed Tabby first, drawing her eye to the name, Emily Rachel Marr, and the date of birth, which was the same as the one Tabby had seen on Wikipedia and other sites. In the photo she had platinum-blond hair, the trademark style of make-up: this was plainly the face that matched the one in the pictures online and in the print Emmie kept in her folder. Then the new Emily gave her the notebook. 'Ignore the French,' she said. 'I didn't get very far.' Tabby saw that the pages at the front contained lists of French vocabulary, household objects and flowers and animal names, the basic foods: beginner's French, well below Emmie's impressive level. But Tabby supposed that this discrepancy was the least of what she was about to discover.

'It's at the back,' Emily said, 'the bit you need to read.'

Arthur arrived to deliver a glass of wine and then the two of them murmured something about food and left her alone to read.

Chapter 26

Emily

I'm not at Phil's house any longer. I'm renting a tiny studio at the top of a house in Ivry in south-eastern Paris. My view across the rooftops is not of Sacré Coeur or the Eiffel Tower but of a warehouse for Chinese foods. It's a proper hideaway, or maybe a safe house is closer to the truth. I've finally managed the disappearing act Nina Meeks advised me to do.

I still fantasise sometimes about going back and getting my revenge – something Machiavellian and intricately plotted – but the truth is I don't know how to avenge myself on a woman like her and I don't think I ever will. If I did, I don't suppose I would have been her victim in the first place, because bullies don't choose victims of equal strength to their own. She's a bully, I realise that now, a bully dressed up as a moral crusader, and no one will ever persuade me otherwise.

Actually, since I've been here, I've thought of myself less as a victim and more as a survivor, which is progress of sorts.

I have enough money to stay for five or six months without working, provided I buy only the bare essentials. If I can find a job, something that requires only minimal French, then I'll stay longer. If not, I'll return to England and take my chances. There must be *someone* there who either doesn't know what I did or no longer cares. I can't live in solitary confinement for the rest of my life. Maybe I'll take a new name after all, reinvent myself the correct, legal way, like those juvenile killers who get given a new identity for their adult return to society.

I can't remember exactly where I ended my story last time or when my last entry was made, but it must have been only a day or so afterwards that Phil's house was burgled and my laptop taken. I knew my days – perhaps hours – were numbered just as soon as the break-in was discovered. There was no evidence that the intruder had taken anything belonging to Phil, Julie or the kids, but just knowing a stranger had walked through their house and climbed their stairs to the bedrooms was violation enough. I'm sure I would have felt exactly the same in their position.

It was no surprise that everything taken was mine, and none of it of any monetary value: the bottle of bluebell perfume Arthur had given me, a lipstick, a dress, a pair of shoes; a post-card from Arthur that came with a gift he'd sent to me soon after we had fallen in love (I don't need to record the message he wrote on it: it will never be forgotten, whether I have the card in my possession or not); and the photograph of Matt and me I'd kept, the one from his cousin's wedding that the *Press* used first and was so widely published afterwards. I'd looked at it now and then since leaving Walnut Grove; it had become an unexpected source of comfort. The signs in Matt's face of his love of easy times and paths of least resistance: I'd thought how fond I was of him. That, at least, had come of the tragedy.

Though I cried for my stolen belongings, especially the postcard, it was only the loss of the laptop that caused real trepidation, more specifically the one document stored on it that I had authored. It seemed impossible that I could rewrite my story, remember the painful and joyful details, survive a retelling when the telling had been so difficult. But over time I've begun to realise that it doesn't matter that it has gone because I've achieved my original aim: in writing it I've purged myself of the worst of it and been able to take heart in the best. I don't need to see it again. As I said at the beginning, it was never meant for posterity.

No, my fear, of course, was that my words should find their way on to the internet or into a newspaper. Were they reproduced in full, it wouldn't be so bad (it's the plain truth, after all), but I of all people know how sentences are sliced up, phrases taken out of context and used to damn the author herself.

Though I can make a reasonable assumption that the document will be kept private, I tell myself that even if it does surface and the media appetite for the story is rekindled, I'm away from home, I'm out of range. I'm in old-fashioned exile in Paris, just like Wallis Simpson, whom not so long ago I had the pleasure of appearing alongside in one tabloid's 'fun' countdown of women who'd caused their man's downfall. I was the only twenty-first-century representative in the list; perhaps there are none in recent years thought likely to stand the test of time.

I won't either. Someone so easy to fictionalise will be just as easy to forget.

I reported the theft to the police in Newbury, but they were powerless. Of course, I had a fair idea who the thief was, and so must they, given my previous complaints. For in the days prior to the theft I'd come to realise that the sensation I had of being followed every time I left the house was not lingering paranoia but well-honed instinct. There *was* someone shadowing me, a woman. I couldn't be sure, but I thought I recognised her from the regulars at the gate of my Grove flat. Not one of the haters, but one of the sympathisers.

The police were reluctant to use the word 'stalker', though Phil and I did – out of earshot of Julie.

I'd noticed her for the first time just as I'd begun to believe I was anonymous again. It was mid-morning, mid-week, and I'd just left the house for a run when I collided with someone in the street, about four houses up from Phil's. Apologising, I moved off without making eye contact (head low, eyes on my feet: this was habitual now, hence the risk of collision), but not before noticing the person's shoes. They were green velvet, like the pair I'd included in the bags I donated to the charity shop on the high street near the Grove.

I tried to dismiss it as a coincidence but, reaching the end of my laps and panting towards the gate, I saw the velvet-shod feet again. They belonged to a woman sitting alone on a bench in the drizzle. When I'd crashed into her, she'd been walking in the opposite direction from me, which meant she must have intentionally turned and followed me to the park. Now, quite openly, she rose to tail me again.

Sprinting home, I quickly lost her, not giving her the satisfaction of knowing I was aware of her, but I might as well have invited her to stroll by my side since she already knew where I lived and could find me again whenever she chose. It struck me she must have been watching me for some time, keeping her distance so I'd only sensed the surveillance rather than noticing the observer.

That now altered. Suddenly I saw her every time I set foot outside, if not in Phil's street then wherever it was I'd walked to. There was no eye contact between us, for I made a point of not looking directly at her. It was surprisingly easy to marginalise her, or, if my mood was particularly upbeat, to see her in a good light, as a guardian angel or a protector – only possible, I imagine, because it was a woman and not a man. But the reality was I did not go out often, rarely more than once a day, and she must have been prepared to wait in all weathers for my sporadic appearances. That meant she could not be holding down a job; was she even sleeping at night, and if so, where? She was devoting herself to me, to staking me out. Male or female, it was unsettling behaviour.

We came face to face just twice and they were two of the strangest experiences of my life.

The first was a Monday. I'd been to the corner shop for chocolate – how modest my adventures! – and was letting myself back into the house when I turned to find her right behind me, just a couple of feet away. She'd followed me up the drive quite silently and I let out a squeal of surprise before composing myself. I pulled off my hat and jangled my keys to signal to her that her presence had not bothered me and I would be putting myself indoors and out of reach within seconds. Phil happened to be working from home that day, so I knew I need only call out to him if I was in trouble. I was quite safe.

Key in the lock, something made me turn back and for the first time look square at her. 'Can I help you?' I asked.

Two things startled me. First, the way her face collapsed in front of my eyes. I assumed it was a reaction to the sound of my voice, it had disappointed her in some way, but I was soon put right on this score. 'What did you do to your hair?' she asked, the distress audible in her voice. 'It was so beautiful.'

'My *hair*?'

But she continued to stare at the top of my head, her eyes quite horrified, as if someone had tipped something unpleasant over me. It was the most peculiar response.

'I cut it off,' I told her impatiently. 'A while ago.'

'But why?'

'Oh come on, I would have thought that was fairly obvious. I don't want to be recognised – and I thought I'd succeeded.'

Her mood seemed to cheer in an instant, facial muscles springing up again, mouth smiling brightly. 'We have succeeded,' she said eagerly. 'No one knows.'

'What are you talking about?' I asked, but received no answer, only that continuing vivid beam of a smile. I concentrated then on the second reason I'd been startled by her, the cause of the cold feeling now crawling across my skin: the fact that she looked so very like me. I don't mean we were doppelgangers – it wasn't that close in terms of our bone structure –

but we were the same height and build, no more than a year or two apart in age, similar enough to be mistaken for sisters or half-sisters. It wasn't that, though, that chilled me; it was how she was dressed, the way she had done her hair and make-up, and obviously with painstaking care. All of it was a clear tribute to me, or rather to Emily Marr, to the woman in the images that had circulated after the scandal. Standing there, looking at the beige boiled-wool swing coat just like the vintage mustard one I'd once worn, the shoes, which I saw with relief were not my own but a rounder-toed copy, I had a moment of sudden understanding: I'd lost myself, I'd lost myself the first day I stepped from my besieged little flat with my head covered. I'd been in disguise ever since. I'd thought it was the day Sylvie died and Arthur gave me up, but it had come later. Even at the inquest, when I'd wiped off my lipstick and regretted my footwear, I'd still been myself. Now, six weeks later, all that was left of me was imitators like this.

'Who *are* you?' I demanded. 'Why are you dressed like this?'

'Because we're the same,' she said happily.

'No, we're not. We don't know each other.'

To my relief, the front door opened and Phil appeared in the porch behind me. 'Who's this, Em?'

'I don't know, but she's been following me. I'm trying to find out why.' I had half a notion to invite the girl in, satisfy her curiosity once and for all, fail her with so much evidence of my new ordinariness that she would lose interest of her own accord. But Phil had other ideas. He threatened her with the police, rudely telling her to get lost.

'You have to go,' I agreed, but more civilly. In spite of the invasion, I couldn't help wanting to treat her respectfully; she must have been damaged in some way to have let her fascination with me take such a grip of her. She was like a teenager at the stage door waiting for the star, except she was a grown woman and I was no star. I remembered now the 'protest' group who had doorstepped Nina Meeks; they'd had special T-shirts made. And there had been fan blogs, too, one of which, I seemed to remember, had brought news of a new girl group called The Emilys.

This fan was not as singular as she supposed and, watching her scamper off down the drive, I felt a little sorry for her.

Inside, Phil begged to differ. 'Who the hell is that freak show? She looks more like you than you do.'

'Than I *did*, yes. I think she might be one of the ones who hung around in London. I don't think she means any harm.'

'That's not how Julie will see it.' It was true that my sister-in-law would be anxious about the children's safety if she heard someone had been watching the house. 'It's not how you should either,' Phil added. 'Anyone who's mad enough to come from London and turn up at a stranger's house dressed exactly the same as them is potentially dangerous.'

'Well when you put it like that . . .' I tried to joke.

'We need to report this headcase to the police.'

He duly phoned to report the incident but, without a name or any threat of ill-intent, we could not expect any intervention. I had not had police protection in London when I lived under permanent siege, so I was unlikely to get it now.

I didn't see her the next day, but the one after that she was back, ringing the doorbell, a bold new step for her. I was in the house on my own and did not answer the door, but she returned after dark when the whole family was at home and Phil made me stay indoors while he handled it.

'We've filed a complaint against you,' I heard him tell her. 'If you keep coming back here, we'll apply for a restraining order. What's your name? Come on, don't be a coward, spit it out. Don't you want your hero to know who you are?'

Only when she was goaded to repeat her answer did I catch it. 'Emily.'

'Yes, I know you know *her* name. I'm asking you what *yours* is.'

I understood before he did that she was saying her name was Emily as well. I didn't believe that, of course: she had simply appropriated my name just as she had appropriated my style of dress. Peering over Phil's shoulder, I saw with horror that this time she was wearing something that really had once been mine, a black wool jacket with oversized buttons and fake-fur collar that I'd sold back to the vintage shop near work where I'd bought it. Had she followed me that day I'd lugged bin liners down the Grove to the bus stop? Had the shop assistant recognised me and made a virtue of the items' provenance? *As worn by the famous slut Emily Marr!* Had she, and others like her, taken possession of my entire wardrobe? Were there pieces of me for sale now on eBay?

I called out, 'I'll be leaving the country any day now. You won't find me where I'm going. So whoever you are, just forget this, forget me and go back to your life.'

I felt the words catch in my throat, because it applied to what I was supposed to be doing about Arthur: forgetting him, forgetting us, going back to my life.

Perhaps this woman's 'real' life was as elusive and frightening to her as mine was to me, in which case we were more alike than I had thought.

After she'd agreed to go, Phil, bless him, tried to joke. 'She puts the fanatic back into fan, eh? If she goes around looking like you, maybe she'll get a stalker of her own. Now *that* would be news.' With Julie hovering, I quickly gathered that the levity was for her benefit, and I joined in with a show of laughter.

Julie's eyebrows were pinched anxiously together. She cared about me very much – I couldn't have asked for a kinder, more thoughtful sister-in-law – but there was not a single word she uttered or breath she took that did not prioritise concern for her young sons. 'I bet she's not the only one out there, Emily. People in these news scandals always get this sort of thing.'

Still aiming to keep the mood light, I told her that at the peak of the media interest I had read that women were saying to their hairdressers they wanted a haircut like mine.

She nodded, face still tense. 'It's the blonde thing. Seriously, I bet even Myra Hindley spawned a few sick lookalikes in her day.'

'She means someone with a distinctive look,' Phil said hastily. 'She doesn't mean you have anything in common with one of the most infamous child killers of the twentieth century.'

This time I could not share the joke. Recalling Nina Meeks' reference to Lizzie Borden and the other writers' constant comparisons of me with criminals and low-lifes, I felt tears rise at the idea that my own family could make the same casual references. Mortified, Julie began apologising. I accepted her words but, even so, I was upset.

'The best thing you did was chop off your hair,' Phil told me. 'You don't need the hat any more. No one will recognise you now.'

'Well, this woman has,' Julie pointed out.

'She's the only one, though, isn't she? She must have heard you had a brother, looked up the address, struck lucky to find you here.'

I knew what Julie was thinking: if one louse had come out of the woodwork, any number of them might follow.

No matter. The point was, there was a finality to these conversations that all three of us recognised. Phil had as good as asked me to hide abroad – offered me the money to do it, no less – and I had as good as agreed. I'd delayed and delayed, but now I had to leave them in peace; my refuge here was no longer tenable.

And then, the very next time the house was left empty, came the break-in. As burglaries went it was an orderly, almost sensitive one. She'd broken glass in the kitchen door, but collected up the pieces and placed them on a sheet of newspaper on the kitchen worktop. She disarranged no contents of drawers or wardrobes, upturned nothing. She'd merely picked out the items she needed to complete her Emily Marr wardrobe and while she was at it gained access to my innermost thoughts. She couldn't have expected *that* bonus material. Soon she would know me almost as well as I knew myself. In the immediate aftermath, I felt sick with helplessness, but later, as I say, I've found it was actually the catalyst I needed.

The following evening, after another fruitless report to the local police, I prepared to leave. Without the laptop and other stolen items I had even fewer possessions to take with me than I'd arrived with, and it took less than an hour to pack. I told Phil and Julie where I was going only in the morning, before they left for work. I knew they were filled with pity for me, but also relieved to have me go of my own volition, and I could hardly blame them for that.

Phil promised to transfer some money to my account to top up the little I had. 'Keep in touch,' he said. 'Don't disappear so well that we can't find you.'

'I won't,' I promised.

As I went through passport checks at St Pancras I thought I saw the official narrow her eyes slightly at the sight of my name – and my photo, too, which was from my better-known blonde incarnation. She made no comment, however, just handed the passport back to me and let me pass. There was no final humiliation. In Paris, three hours later, there was not a flicker of recognition at Immigration, and as I walked through the Gare du Nord without attracting a single sideways glance, I knew I'd done the right thing.

As Phil says, the best I can hope for is that when I come back – if I ever do – people will have forgotten I was ever anyone they'd heard of in the first place.

*

The last thing to say is that I have contacted Arthur a final time. I did it the old-fashioned way, by letter, addressed to his Harley Street clinic and marked *Private & Confidential*. I slightly disguised my writing on the envelope and hoped the Paris postmark might pique him into opening it. But of course he must have been receiving unwanted mail just as I have, plenty of it innocently marked *Private* (I imagined it still falling in handfuls through the letterbox of 199, for of course I'd left no forwarding address). As the days pass and no reply comes, I've come to suspect that his two secretaries, the ones who denied me any contact by phone, must continue to shield him from any but the essential correspondence. 'I'm sure you understand,' they would say.

I don't suppose I'll ever know.

All I know for sure is that I had to write it in the spirit of believing it would be read, otherwise there would have been no point in writing it at all. I told him that I understood why he has been unable to see me or even speak to me since his wife's and sons' deaths. I told him I was sick with remorse for contributing to those deaths and that I would give my own life to bring theirs back. I told him that I adored him and always would. I asked him if he remembered my telling him my belief that falling in love could be averted or willed, it was not simply a question of magic. Loving him, then, was my choice. I said that even if we were never again in the same city, much less living as neighbours, that I believed the love still mattered, even if it was only mine now and neither welcomed nor returned. I reminded him of what he said to me the first time we met, and how I still know it is true:

Everybody counts.

Even Emmie Mason.

Chapter 27

Tabby

She found Arthur and Emily in the kitchen, half-eaten servings of chicken salad on dinner plates in front of them. 'It's got to be her,' she said, halting in the doorway. 'There's no other explanation. She's not Emily. She's not you.'

'No,' Emily agreed. 'Oh dear, you've had a shock, I think.' She got up from her seat and guided Tabby to a place at the table, fetching from the fridge a plate of food for her. She brought salt and pepper, salad dressing, a glass of iced water. Even as she continued to grapple with the larger situation, Tabby registered how very kind Emily was, even further from the woman portrayed by the media than Emmie was – whoever Emmie was.

'She doesn't even look like you,' Tabby told her. 'I mean, a little bit, but not properly, not now I can compare you one after the other. It must have been so obvious she wasn't who she said she was, but I was so stupid I wasn't the slightest bit doubtful. I was totally fooled.' But the word 'fooled' felt wrong. Talking like this felt wrong, like she was betraying Emmie.

'You weren't stupid. I think we're similar enough, and with the hair and make-up, the same clothing, you could easily be deceived if you only had photos for reference. It was quite a distinctive look and she copied it well – that was what unnerved me when I met her. But as it was, there would have been no

372

reason for you to be looking for differences. She told you it was her and why would you disbelieve it? Why would someone make it up?'

'Why indeed,' Arthur said. He, Tabby saw, was pallid with exhaustion.

'For attention?' Emily wondered.

'No, definitely not that,' Tabby said. 'Until she met me she was living secretly, she wasn't going around telling people she was famous. In fact, I practically had to force the truth out of her – well, not the truth, but you know what I mean, *her* truth. And there's no monetary gain, either. She's not selling her story – *your* story – or dining out on it in any way. She's working as a cleaner and isn't paid much at all, but her fear of being recognised means there are only certain jobs she can take.' Though seated, still Tabby reeled from the shock of it, of her own gullibility as much as the fraud itself.

She noticed Arthur glance at the wall clock. It was half-past ten; not the evening he had expected or wanted. Tabby wondered if she would ever know the end of his and Emily's story, how they had come to be reunited, when it had seemed so hopeless at the end of Emily's last written instalment. 'Whatever this impersonator's motives, we have to make a decision about what to do about her,' he said, and he drank deeply from his wine glass.

'The more I think about it, the more I think she's not an impersonator,' Tabby said. 'I think it's weirder than that. I'm fairly sure she genuinely thinks she *is* Emily.'

'I had a feeling you were going to say that,' Emily said.

'But what does it mean? How could that be?'

'It means she must be extremely unwell,' Arthur said. 'Whatever's going on, it's obsessive and potentially harmful and I think we need to tell the police about her.'

'But she hasn't come near me in five months,' Emily said. 'Who's she going to harm?'

'Herself, for one,' Tabby said. 'The reason I came here to

look for you was I was very worried about her. She's having some sort of breakdown. I feel more concerned than ever now. I'm not sure I should have left her on her own.'

'Exactly my point,' Arthur said. 'She needs treatment, psychiatric attention. I wouldn't be at all surprised if we find she already has a therapist here, a history of irrational behaviour of this sort. You were right to come back to England, Tabby: this is where you'll find your answers.'

Tabby agreed. 'Before I can do anything, I need to find out who she really is. She calls herself Emmie, but that can't be her name, can it? She must have got that from the journal.'

'You didn't ever see her passport or any other identification?' he asked.

'No. I would have questioned the discrepancy if I had. I wouldn't be here.'

'Thank God she didn't steal *my* passport,' Emily said. 'Otherwise it could have got very complicated.'

'It's complicated enough as it is,' Arthur said. 'Do you know where she lived in the UK?' he asked Tabby. 'If she was one of the ones who used to come to Emily's flat, might she have been based in London?'

'Well, she *said* she'd lived in London. Once she knew I knew, she talked about the Grove all the time, how it was a bus ride from her work and close to St Barnabas'. But of course she read all that in your document. She never mentioned Newbury or anywhere else. Did your brother ever see her again after you left for Paris?'

Emily shook her head. 'Not that he ever mentioned. But then it would fit with what you say if she went to La Rochelle at about the same time.'

'Actually, she's across the bridge from La Rochelle,' Tabby said, 'on the Ile de Ré.'

'The Ile de Ré?' Arthur and Emily looked at each other, perturbed, dismayed.

374

'You mention it in your account, do you remember? I think that must be where she thought you'd be going.'

'She's delusional,' Arthur said, 'and I mean clinically. As I say, I'd be amazed if she weren't known to a hospital somewhere over here.'

An image rose to the surface of Tabby's mind then, causing her to exclaim, 'Hang on, there is something! The pills. She had medication.'

'What kind of medication?'

'I don't remember exactly, but it had been prescribed by a hospital in London. And her name begins with E, that's right. I saw the label on the bottle, it was torn ... Oh, unless she stole it from you?'

She looked at Emily, who shook her head.

'No, it's not mine. She didn't take anything like that from me. And the only medication prescribed to me was by the NHS Trust in Hertfordshire, not a London hospital.'

'Hers was definitely London. I can't remember where. East London, possibly.'

Arthur looked up. 'The East London Trust? That's a specialist mental-health trust. I can ring them in the morning and see what I can find out, though the letter E isn't much to be going on with, I have to say. Do we know a date of birth?'

'Only Emily's,' Tabby said. 'She looks older, though, I would say.'

'What about other clues?' Emily said. 'Family? Has she ever mentioned them?'

'All she ever told me is what she must have found out from your journal.' She'd been struck by the phrases Emmie repeated from the manuscript, phrases she hadn't written herself but must have absorbed and borrowed. Had *anything* been Emmie's own? 'She said her parents were dead and she has a brother and two young nephews.'

'Maybe that's the true bit? The coincidence that triggered the original interest?' Arthur suggested. 'Not a name, but a family parallel, an emotional connection. This could be some sort of grief-related behaviour?'

It was a staggering thought, that grief could cause a person to withdraw from her own life and begin living in a state of complete self-deception. But both Arthur and Emily, and presumably thousands of others up and down the land, were also recently bereaved and they had not hijacked other people's identities.

'OK, let's think this through,' Emily said. 'Assuming it's not a chance family parallel, then her parents or other family may well still be alive, and if they haven't heard from her in all this time they'll be worried sick.'

'She's had no contact with them since she's been in France,' Tabby said. 'I'm certain of that.'

'So they might have reported her missing?'

Emily and Tabby looked at each other, neither blinking.

'Well, there's your first place to look,' Arthur said. 'It sounds obvious, but you could do worse than to start with Missing Persons.'

In the end it was as simple as that. There were fifty white females in Emmie's age range registered as missing in London and she was one of them. She was neither an Emily nor a Marr, of course, and not an Emmie or a Mason, either. She was called Eve Barron, born in the same month as Emily but three years earlier. It was all there on the website:

Eve Barron
Date of birth: 2 July 1977
Eve has been missing from London since 18 March 2012.
There is concern for Eve's safety and she is urged to call our confidential Freefone service for advice and support.
Eve is 5 feet 5 inches tall and of medium build. At the time of

her disappearance she had shoulder-length bleached blond hair, worn with a black ribbon.

The photograph was of a woman whose style inspiration was plain: the hair was the same length and blondness as Emily's original cut, the eye make-up a faithful replica, the short-sleeved baby-blue cardigan just the kind of garment vintage-loving Emily would have worn. The occasion was not obvious, but there was a cottage window with leaded glass in the background, china ornaments on the sill: it didn't look like a London flat or an office. A relative's house, perhaps? Her parents' home? Eve smiled with a pride that might once have seemed a perfectly ordinary response to the camera, but that now seemed to Tabby to be perverse, volatile, tragic.

Arthur left the room and Emily cleared up quietly while Tabby made the call to the twenty-four-hour helpline. 'I think I know the whereabouts of one of the people on your website. I think she has mental-health issues and I'm guessing her family will probably know that.'

She gave the reference number from the website before being asked a series of questions about timings, location, whether she had noticed CCTV equipment in the village. When the woman began to ask about Eve's clothing, Tabby wondered if she'd made herself quite clear. 'This wasn't a one-off sighting,' she said. 'I've been living and working with her. She wears lots of different clothes. I can tell you what she was wearing three days ago, but she'll have changed by now. And she doesn't really leave the house at the moment, anyway.'

'Where are you both now?'

'She's still there, at the address I've given you. I'm back in England.'

'Where does she think you are? Does she know you're making this call?'

'She thinks I'm visiting my family.' It occurred to Tabby that she was not so different from Emmie/Eve. While not listed with any missing-persons organisation, she had broken off contact with her family and hardly allowed herself to think of her mother, was generally behaving as if in denial of being anyone's daughter. She supposed she ought to phone Elaine and let her know she was alive.

'The next step is for us to get in touch with the police with this information. We'll do that first thing in the morning.' The helpline worker told her the service was confidential and there was no way her phone number could be traced; however, the police would probably want to speak to her directly if she was willing.

'That's fine,' Tabby said. 'You can give them my number, and her family as well. I'm going back to France myself, so I can show them where she is if they like. The house is quite hard to find if you don't know it.'

After the call had ended, Tabby sat in surprise. She'd said she was going back, but was that true? Shouldn't she keep her distance now she'd discovered that Emmie was an unstable and troubled individual? But hadn't she suspected that anyhow? Hadn't she noted her peculiarities time and again and yet still decided she liked her, still longed to repay her friend's original act of mercy?

'Well done,' Emily said. 'That's not an easy thing to have to do.' She stood with her back to the whirring dishwasher. 'Arthur's gone up. He's shattered.'

'I should leave you in peace,' Tabby said, pushing back her chair. 'Head back into town for the train. You've both been amazingly understanding about this situation, when I'm sure it's the last thing you need to get involved with this person.'

'Don't be silly,' Emily said. 'How can we not be involved? And it's far too late to be thinking about getting a train. I think you should stay here, in the spare room, get a good night's rest.'

'Oh.' Tabby knew the offer was more than she deserved –

and a huge leap of faith on Emily's part. Somehow, just as Emmie had, she had chosen to trust her. 'Thank you, if you're sure. That's really kind.'

'Let's have another drink. It's been a very strange evening for both of us.' Emily poured them each another glass of wine. 'One for the road,' she said, slipping into her seat, 'though I must admit I'd hoped we'd got to the end of it by now.'

She really was unusually beautiful, Tabby thought, watching the way she rested her chin on her knuckles, elbow poised elegantly on the table. Her skin was flawless and glowing, those dark blue eyes slightly upturned at the outer corners and extravagantly long-lashed, her mouth broad and curved. She had not needed the painted mask she'd worn. Tabby imagined the men she knew being faced with such a creature: Paul would be in awe of someone so exquisite; Steve wouldn't dare utter a word of insult or lasciviousness; perhaps even Grégoire might hesitate.

'I have a favour to ask you,' Emily said.

'Of course?' Tabby said. 'Anything.'

'The file you've read, and the extra chapter I showed you tonight: could you keep what you know confidential? I don't suppose anyone's interested now, but just in case ... ?'

Tabby's eyes widened in surprise. 'Of course! I won't tell a soul. I'll try to forget, in fact. It will be hard, though. It's an extraordinary story.'

Emily bowed her head, unable to deny this.

'I know it's none of my business,' Tabby heard herself say, the words as fitting as any others for her gravestone, 'but I'd love to know one final thing.'

Emily smiled. 'One final thing you'll try to forget?'

'Yes.' She conceded the absurdity of it, but still longed to ask.

'I'm sure I can guess what it is, anyway,' Emily said. 'How Arthur and I came to get back together.'

'He read your letter, I suppose? The one you sent from Paris?'

'Yes. He read it and he came to find me.' Emily's eyes glimmered with sudden tears. 'He just appeared one day out of the blue. It was ... it was like a miracle. I'd been trawling the local bars one afternoon, looking for work, but my French was just not up to it, I was getting nowhere, and when I got back to the house he was on the doorstep, sitting there, reading his English newspaper. At first – for ages, actually – all he said was, "Sorry. I'm sorry." I thought he'd forgotten how to say anything else.' She paused, and Tabby knew she would not be invited to share the part that followed; she would have to imagine the reconciliation for herself, in all its bitter-sweetness. 'When he went back the next day, I went with him.'

'After all that time, he changed his mind? You'd given up on him, hadn't you?'

'I thought too long had passed for him to be able to remember us. But now I think there's no such thing as too long. It was only eight months. I would have waited eight years.'

'Wow.' Tabby felt envy so acute it caused internal pain. Had envy also been at the heart of Emmie's imitation, or whatever it was, not imitation but identification, immersion? The intuitive certainty that this person was special, or at least her connection with Woodhall was. 'How long have you been up here, in Leeds?'

'Arthur's been here since soon after the inquest. He'd already arranged the move, but brought it forward when the *Press* story erupted. I came in May. It hasn't been easy, as you can imagine. We've had to start again, pretty much without friends. We know we can't ever see anyone from before.'

'Not even your family? What about Phil?'

'He's been all right about it, yes. He's visited us here with the boys a few times. And Arthur's brother has been OK too, though not his wife or their sister. And none of Sylvie's family, none of the nieces or nephews on her side.' She bit her lower lip, obviously upset. 'We're hoping that when they're older they might decide to get in touch with him again themselves. We'll have to see.'

'Are you here long-term, d'you think?'

'I don't know; it depends on Arthur's work. Neither of us wants to go back to London. There are new eye clinics opening overseas, we might go to one of those.'

'And you're still writing?'

Emily blinked softly. 'No, I've written all I'm going to write. I'm training to become a counsellor, so I could work anywhere English-speaking, I suppose.'

'Somewhere people would be less likely to recognise you.'

'Yes, though it's been fine here so far. The staff at the summer school where I'm doing my course have been great. They agreed I could register under a different name and so far no one has questioned that. And the few times I've been recognised, it hasn't been as bad as I expected. Often they just know they know me but can't think where from. Someone thought I'd been on a reality show, one of those singing ones. If only!'

Tabby wanted to ask what Emily's assumed name was (just out of interest), but Emily had talked enough and said she was going to bed. She showed Tabby the room in which she was to stay and again Tabby acknowledged the significance of a person required to be so vigilant about privacy deciding to lower her guard in this way. It made her feel proud.

Too stirred up to sleep, she asked Emily if she could use the computer downstairs for a little longer.

'Of course,' Emily said. 'Just turn out the lights when you come back up.'

Seconds later, the door to the main bedroom was closed behind her. Tabby could not quite comprehend that in the space beyond was the couple who had so recently incited national damnation, whose reunion was a miracle even in their own eyes. Arthur Woodhall and Emily Marr, together after all. From what Emily had said, they had very little left *but* each other. They'd been prepared to make sacrifices for each other right from the beginning; in the end, the sacrifices were larger, unspeakably graver. Everybody counted, as Emily had insisted, but nobody won.

Downstairs, Tabby returned to the Missing Persons site. She read that the majority of missing adults had chosen to disappear, a significant percentage having mental-health problems, which ranged from mild depression to severe psychosis. In some cases the missing were patients who had absconded from hospital mental wards. One other statistic caught her eye: seventy per cent of those who'd made contact with the helpline said that being missing had positive aspects to it.

Certainly Emmie had been content with her existence: comfortable in Tabby's company, absorbed by her work for Moira, happy with her little house by the port where you could run either the water heater or the washing machine but not both at once. Life, unsupervised, unmedicated, it *had* had positive aspects to it. She'd only become unhappy when Tabby had insisted on exposing her history. Her 'history', she corrected herself. So much concerning Emmie had now to be thought of in inverted commas, including her name.

She found the site for the East London Trust, which, as Arthur said, was a major mental-health facility. Idly browsing this and others linked to it, she came across an alphabetical list of medicine and studied it carefully. She thought she recognised one name near the bottom: Quetiapine. Could that be right? None of the others looked familiar in the same way. She clicked on the link and read:

Quetiapine is a type of medicine known as an atypical antipsychotic. It works in the brain, where it affects various neurotransmitters, in particular serotonin (5HT) and dopamine. Neurotransmitters are chemicals that are stored in nerve cells and are involved in transmitting messages between the nerve cells.

Dopamine and serotonin are known to be involved in regulating mood and behaviour, amongst other things. Psychotic illness is considered to be caused by disturbances in the activity of neurotransmitters (mainly dopamine) in the brain. Schizophrenia is known to be associated with an overactivity of dopamine in the brain, and this may be associated with the delusions and hallucinations that are a feature of this disease.

Quetiapine works by blocking the receptors in the brain that dopamine acts on. This prevents the excessive activity of dopamine and helps to control schizophrenia. It is also used by specialists to treat episodes of mania and depression in people with the psychiatric illness bipolar affective disorder (manic depression).

Tabby frowned, her pulse beginning to pound. Schizophrenia? Bipolar disorder? She didn't even know what the terms meant, associating them with Jekyll and Hyde split personalities. Beginning to read a second time, she halted almost at once at the term 'antipsychotic' and searched for a simple definition: *'Psychosis' is the word used for conditions in which the patient loses touch with reality.*

Becoming dislocated, separated, isolated. Becoming, perhaps, a different person entirely . . .

She turned off Emily's PC, put out the lights and tiptoed upstairs.

The spare room was at the back of the house, the clean bedding cold from lack of use. She remembered the first evening in the house off rue de Sully, Emmie saying, 'So what's your name? I assume it's not Goldilocks?', and at the sound of her friend's voice, the amusement in it that had been all the sweeter for being so undeserved, she began to cry into her pillow.

When she came downstairs in the morning, Tabby found that Arthur had already left for work and Emily was packing a satchel for her college class. She declined the offer of breakfast: she'd imposed on the two of them for long enough, long enough to be leaving with a second riddle to unravel, a disturbing new set of mysteries to solve. As she prepared to leave, her phone rang. It was a staff member from the missing-persons charity, asking if she would take a call from Eve's parents, who wanted to meet her at the airport and fly to France that afternoon.

She agreed at once.

'They're so pleased you've come forward,' the girl said. She made it sound as if Tabby had witnessed a crime, but there had been no crime, not in her opinion.

'You're meeting them today?' Emily asked her as they were about to part.

'Yes, later on, at Stansted Airport. They want to come back with me straight away.'

'I hope she's going to be all right, their daughter.'

'So do I.' Tabby hesitated; then, knowing she might never meet this woman again, she threw the last of her caution to the wind and asked, '*You're* all right, aren't you, Emily?'

Emily looked moved by the simple enquiry, and out of practice in answering it, making Tabby remember what she'd said last night about starting again without friends. 'Yes,' she said, after a pause, 'I'm more all right than I thought I could be. Thank you.'

'And Arthur? He's not ... Well, he's not like you described in your story, when you first met. I mean, it's obvious why, I just ...' Tabby could not find the words.

Emily drew her hands together, squeezing the ends of her fingers as if suddenly cold. 'He's very low, to tell you the truth, lower than you or I can understand. I don't think you can ever recover from what he's lost. But in the end you have a choice: you give up or you go on. He has enough reasons to go on. I hope that every year there'll be more reasons.'

'Yes.' Tabby swung her bag on to her shoulder. She travelled

384

ighter than ever today, having left the laptop with its rightful owner. She dreaded having to explain to Emmie where it was, very much hoping she would be relieved of the responsibility by someone better qualified to take it. 'Goodbye,' she said.

'Goodbye,' Emily said. 'I won't come to the front door with you if you don't mind. It's an old habit – you never know who might be lurking.'

Chapter 28

Tabby

She had arranged to meet Ray and Kerry Barron at Stansted
Airport by the airline desk; even without seeing the red carry-on
luggage she'd been instructed to look for, she would have
known them, for they radiated a distinctive nervous energy. An
uneasy combination of prayer and resignation, it filled Tabby,
already anxious, with a strange fatalism.

Greetings barely out of the way, Ray was buying her a seat
on the late-afternoon flight to La Rochelle that he and Kerry
were already booked on and suggesting the three of them go
through to Departures before they talked.

In the queue for Security, Tabby watched them when they
weren't aware she was looking, fascinated to see shades of
Emmie in Ray's face – the same eye colour, the same slightly
flattened planes of brow and nose – and in Kerry the perfect
original of that hushed, sober bearing Emmie had and that
Tabby still associated her with, in spite of recent volatilities.
When the Barrons caught one another's eye, it was with wariness, she saw, a sense of shared qualms that she could not help
relating to herself. They'd been in purgatory and were now
being led from it by a saviour they did not know and could not
yet trust. Was the pain about to end or would it in fact grow

worse? The responsibility made Tabby so nauseous she felt close to retching.

Only when they'd cleared the departure controls and found a table in a café did anyone mention Eve by name.

'We've brought some photos to show you,' Kerry said, 'just to double-check it's her.' Close up and in unforgiving lighting, the emotions in her eyes were startlingly raw: impotence; vulnerability; a livid, half-mad hope. Tabby looked quickly away, relieved to focus on the photographs.

Two separate incarnations of Eve had been captured: first, the most recent, Emily-inspired one – there were several snaps from the same occasion as the image posted on the missing-persons website – then an earlier one, in which her long hair was dark, her eyebrows thick and shapeless and her lips sore-looking and unsmiling. In this, rather than in the more recent one, she looked like the deeply damaged woman Tabby now knew her to be.

'So you obviously knew she had changed her appearance to look like Emily Marr?' Tabby said. She had spoken to Kerry at length on the phone that morning on the train from Leeds, telling her what she knew about Eve's contact with Emily in Newbury, the appropriation of the laptop and other personal items, Emily's suspicion that she had been among those who'd harassed her while she still lived on the Grove. 'She must have done it quite soon before she went missing, because Emily was only in the media from mid-February.'

'Yes, it was a complete change of image since we'd last seen her,' Ray said. 'We had a family party for her grandmother's birthday at our house – that's when these photos were taken – and when Eve arrived everyone remarked on the new look. The blondness was a big transformation in itself, she'd always had her natural dark hair before that. Of course, we'd all read about the Marr scandal in the papers and a couple of people remarked on the influence. There'd been a feature about her that morning in the *Mail*, how she'd left London and gone into hiding.'

'We easily might not have known, though,' Kerry added, 'because she almost didn't come to the party. She said she couldn't leave London because of work. We hadn't seen her for a few weeks, which was unusual for us. We were worried she was obsessing about her job, but we found out after she went missing that she hadn't been working for over a month.'

She'd been busy staking out Emily's flat, Tabby thought, and then Phil Marr's house in Newbury. Handing back the prints, she said, 'It's definitely her, but she looks different from both of these now. Her hair is short – to be honest, it looks like she cut it herself. She doesn't wear any make-up. She's quite scruffy, very understated.'

'Is she healthy?' Kerry asked. 'Physically?'

'She *was*. But just before I came back here, after she lost her job, she wasn't in such good shape. She wouldn't eat very much. She wasn't looking after herself the way she had been. That's why I came to get help.' Hearing her own insinuation that it was the job loss that had set the emotional collapse in motion, Tabby felt that ever-present undertow of guilt tug hard at her intestines. Whatever was the matter with Emmie, or Eve as she must now think of her, she *had* until recently been physically well. She *had* been looking after herself. It was Tabby who was responsible for the deterioration, both in her forcing of Emmie's confession of her 'real' identity and in causing her to be fired from the job that had anchored her.

'I think we ought to tell you a bit about her medical history,' Ray said, as if sensing her self-blame and hastening to set the record straight. 'You need to know that this is a natural continuation of an existing problem, a problem she's had for half her life, years before she met you.'

Tabby nodded, grateful to let him lead both this discussion and any necessary action to follow, to deflect all that hopeful anticipation from her.

As the story unfolded, it seemed to her that Eve had had the childhood Emily Marr had not: healthy, wealthy parents, a stable family environment, a peaceful and secure Home Counties lifestyle. There were two brothers, both younger, their decent, caring characters brought vividly to life in a matter of minutes and making Eve's denial of her family even more unfathomable to Tabby than it already was. To have identified so intensely with a complete stranger while the people closest to her in the world wept for her, longing every day for a word of contact: it beggared belief. To have grieved for someone else's loss of a father when her own lived and breathed and made huge sacrifices for her (both Ray and Kerry had reduced their working hours in order to support Eve in her illness, Tabby learned, and latterly to coordinate the nationwide search for her): it seemed obscene, almost blasphemous.

But the Barrons knew differently. Clearly, the two of them had educated themselves in mental health and were keen to convince Tabby that Eve could not be held responsible for her actions. They explained the history of depression in the family, the elder brother of Ray who had committed suicide in his late twenties. 'Eve suffered from her teenage years, but it grew worse in adulthood,' he said. 'She saw a series of professionals and was eventually diagnosed with a delusional disorder. At that stage, it was what they call "persecutory". In layman's terms, she thought everyone was against her.'

'We would say paranoid,' Kerry added, 'but that's not what it means, in fact.'

'There was a series of worrying incidents, the last one being with a man at work. It was what we call stalking; the experts call it "erotomania". The more he rejected her and the firmer he tried to be about it, the more she lost touch with the reality of what he was saying to her. She made contact with his wife, who felt threatened enough to call the police. Eve lost her job, of course.'

'What sort of job did she have?' Tabby asked.

'She was a teacher.'

'A teacher?' It was impossible to imagine Emmie in front of a class, confident and animated, sharing her knowledge rather than guarding it.

'Of course she hasn't always been able to manage work. Her employment has been sporadic. Before this last position, she hadn't worked for two years. She's lived with us on and off and then there've been spells of independence. It's been unpredictable.'

The Barrons told her that in the time it had taken Tabby to travel to Stansted, they had been able to confer with Eve's latest – indeed, current – psychiatrist. 'He says she may have developed what they call a "grandiose delusion". That's when someone exaggerates his sense of self-importance and is convinced he has special powers or abilities. It's quite rare, of course, but it does happen occasionally that someone actually believes he's a famous person, like a member of the Royal Family or a religious leader.'

Or the object of passing media fixation, perhaps, an object with whom physical similarities exist and are mistaken for something more profound than coincidence – in this case, likenesses in age, facial features and height, ones that Emily herself had noticed. From what Emily had written and Tabby had read online, the whole nation had become fascinated by her, if only for a week or so, but it had somehow tipped in Eve to fanaticism, and then to something more extreme still.

'He says that what could have happened is that Eve's interest in this woman – her empathy with her – began to exceed natural limits and convince her of some sort of kinship, a kinship that became total identification. She began to behave as Emily would, or how she thought Emily would, and because of the nature of Emily's circumstances, that meant living as if in hiding.'

'But she never gave me the slightest clue,' Tabby said. 'She never once slipped up.'

'But that's just it, Tabby, it's not a question of slipping up, it's not a conscious pretence, like acting. She simply hasn't been aware of her real identity.'

Tabby remembered the description she'd studied of the antipsychotic medication Eve had been prescribed. 'So it's a split personality? Schizophrenia?'

'No, not that, not if she's had no access to her own self, only the delusional one. That's one of the differences between this and a schizoid disorder, a dual or multiple personality: with that, there'd be incongruities, inconsistencies. The behaviour would not match the claim, whereas from what you've told us Eve's behaviour is completely in keeping with that of the person she thinks she is: a fugitive, concealing her identity, living under the radar.'

Tabby struggled to absorb medical concepts she'd never been faced with before. However convincing Emmie's 'portrayal', it was impossible not to continue to find fault with her own gullibility. 'I feel so stupid not to have realised. I honestly thought she was getting over a broken heart or something.'

'Well, she was, in a way,' Ray said. 'It just wasn't her own heart, it was someone else's. As I say, there'd be no inconsistencies for you to pick up on, no clues, and in any case, how would you be able to recognise one anyway? You didn't know her *or* Emily before. You didn't stand a chance.'

This was a more medically informed variation of what Emily had said the night before, and it gave Tabby a comfort of sorts to know that they at least did not hold her accountable for Eve's dangerous slide. 'It still doesn't make sense to me, though. OK, so she's cut off contact with you and shut herself away, thinking she's Emily, but I've been living with her for months and I can tell you she does everything a normal person does. She cooks dinner, she works, she manages her budget. We've been out for walks, for drinks.'

During which she had believed people were recognising her – recognising her as Emily.

Ray and Kerry both murmured in agreement. It was clear that there was no argument they had not already raised themselves. 'According to the psychiatrist she would be highly functional and persuasive,' Ray said. 'To the casual observer, she would appear to be managing perfectly well.'

'Really? But for so long? It's incredible!'

'Delusions can last for weeks or months, even years.'

'Given how extreme this is, we have to be grateful she didn't continue to pursue Emily Marr after she stole from her,' Kerry added, 'or Arthur Woodhall, who from what you say would have been easy enough for her to locate. It's actually very good news that she went to France, out of their sphere.'

This raised another baffling detail. 'But she speaks fluent French,' Tabby said. 'The real Emily doesn't, she's beginner level. So Eve isn't being *that* much like her. Anyone who knew anything about the real Emily would have guessed straight away.'

'I'm sure that's true,' Ray agreed, 'but sadly she was not among people who did, or better still, people in a position to recognise her as Eve. In terms of the French, she would have had access to her previous skills, just not to the knowledge of how she attained them. Eve has a degree in French, she taught it at GCSE and A-level. She would be able to go on being able to speak it even in her delusional state. And she chose to make her way to France, didn't she? There must have been some underlying reason for that.'

This, at least, Tabby could explain. 'She knew about the island because Emily mentioned it in her journal. Arthur was going to take her there for a holiday.'

Ray was pleased with the detail. 'So it was the natural place for her to go. Well, as Kerry says, we have to be grateful for that, because from what you say she's been relatively safe there. She's kept herself to herself.'

The three sat for a moment in silence, sipping their drinks, their intense little conference in bold contrast to the lighter spirits of the other travellers in the airport café. Emily's written account was at the centre of the crisis, Tabby thought. Perhaps reading it had been what triggered Eve's slipping from obsessive interest to the more severe state that Ray called grandiose delusional psychosis. 'It's awful,' she whispered. 'If what you say is true, then it's like she's been trapped, sealed away from her real self.'

Ray nodded. 'She can be unsealed, though, if we can get her the right treatment, which we need to do urgently. What you described to us on the phone, how she's been the last two weeks, sinking into helplessness and not looking after herself, her psychiatrist says it could be an acute depressive episode. She's had those before. She needs medication, but more importantly she needs psychotherapy.'

And I gave her sea air and a glass of wine to help her sleep, Tabby thought. Had she done *anything* right? 'I tried to persuade her to see a doctor, but she refused point blank. She insisted she was feeling fine.'

'That's one of the hardest things for the professionals, and for family, in situations like this: often the sufferer doesn't accept that he or she is suffering. They feel perfectly all right and can get very defensive if you suggest otherwise. Of course, if they realised they were ill, they wouldn't abscond to other countries and live like hermits, would they? They would try to stop the behaviour and get help.'

'It must have been terrible for you,' Tabby said. 'Knowing she was out there somewhere, really ill but not realising or accepting it. I wish I could have known and put your minds at ease sooner.'

'It's been a living nightmare,' Kerry said. 'When your child goes missing, there's nothing worse.'

Except if they die, Tabby thought. But then she wondered if that were true. Arthur had his sons' graves to visit and, in time, if not yet, that might be a source of comfort. Was what the

Barrons were experiencing actually any easier? To not know: was it worse than knowing the worst?

'It just seems so selfish that she didn't let you know she was alive. Or she could have asked me to let you know, just to stop you from worrying so much.'

'That's not how this works,' Ray said. 'She's not selfish. If she thinks she *is* this other woman, then we no longer exist for her.'

'You think she'd see "Mum and Dad" listed on her phone,' Tabby said, before remembering and adding aloud that Emmie had had a new phone with no contacts on it except the few to do with her life in Saint-Martin. 'But if she checked her email or Facebook or whatever, wouldn't she see messages from you?'

'She wouldn't though, would she? She wouldn't check anything to do with Eve Barron, she wouldn't see messages from us or from anyone trying to contact her. Perhaps she opened a new account in the name of Emily Marr. Did she say she was using email?'

'Yes – at least not in so many words. All she said was that she hadn't heard from Arthur.'

Ray and Kerry looked hard at each other, some unspoken interim acknowledgement of the severe challenge they faced. Then Kerry peered up at the departures screen. 'The flight's boarding,' she said. 'Shall we go to the gate?'

As they walked, Ray leading the way, she fell back alongside Tabby. 'Thank you for doing this, Tabby. Without you, she could have been lost for much longer, maybe for ever.'

The word 'lost' squeezed at Tabby's heart; it was as if Emmie were a defenceless infant, abducted or disastrously strayed. She thought again, briefly, of her own mother, and understood in that moment that she had to tell her story. Years had passed, yes, but the past had not changed because of it. Paul was gone for good. She had no other family.

How her mother reacted to her story would be out of her control.

With the hour's time difference, it was almost seven o'clock by the time they landed. They took a taxi to Ré, rain splashing violently against the windows as they crossed the bridge. Even allowing for the poor weather, you could see as they drove through Rivedoux and towards La Flotte that the island had emptied this week. The French holidays were over.

'This is La Flotte,' Tabby told her companions, thinking without pleasure of Moira, who was now about as significant as the wicked witch in a fairy tale. 'We're the next village along on this side. Only a few minutes now.'

Ray and Kerry peered through the glass at the watery green scenery as if it might hold important clues for them. 'Should we have warned her?' Kerry said, half to herself. They had already debated twice whether Tabby should phone or text Eve with word of her return, but in the end had agreed it might work against them and they would be better to arrive unannounced.

'We don't want to scare her off,' Ray said, as he had during the original discussion. Tabby was learning that when it came to their daughter, conversation between the two of them was characterised by the painful repetition of doubt, a matter of amateurs guessing what professionals might think best. It was astonishing that their marriage had survived the strain of it.

'Will she recognise you?' Tabby asked him.

'I don't know. If she does, it may not be helpful in terms of getting her home. There've been times in the past when she's convinced herself that we're her enemies. It may be like that this time, as well.'

'Then how would we get her back?'

'We can't force her. To do that, we'd need to get her sectioned, and I don't know how we'd go about that in another country even if we wanted to. The consultant says we should handle it very gently, work on persuading her gradually to return with us, not pressure or coerce her.'

'Yes, hopefully she'll want to come. There's nothing to stay here for now.' But as they neared the walls of Saint-Martin, a wild, irrational suspicion assailed Tabby, quite different from the guilty emotions she'd been suffering until then. Perhaps it was the dissection of Eve's mental health, but what she was thinking was, what if she had imagined all of this? What if she'd never met Emmie, but was leading this poor couple on a wild goose chase? What if they got to the house and it wasn't there, there was no alley leading off rue de Sully. What if *she* was the deluded one?

It seemed to her that the line between trust in reality and a loss of that trust was terrifyingly easy to cross.

The taxi dropped them at the centre of the village, by the church, and they trudged down the wet cobbles, Ray supporting Kerry, who wore leather soles and feared tumbling. Water dripped as they fought past the overgrown bush that stood at the entrance to the lane. The lane was there. The door was there. It was all real. Tabby drew a deep breath and keyed in the code. The lock released.

'This is it,' she said, sounding, if not feeling, quite dauntless. She led the others through the stone passageway to the hidden room beyond, crying, 'Emmie!' She called the name several times, but there was no answer. The house was silent but for the low whirr of the fridge.

She opened the windows and shutters to let in some air. The rain fell softly into their narrow hollow of outside space.

'So this is where she's been all this time,' Kerry said. 'I'm glad it's nice.' Tabby could tell she was despondent to find the place unoccupied, but given all that she herself had discovered between her departure on Monday and her return now, there was almighty relief on her own part in finding it looking as it did, much as she'd left it. The folder of cuttings was intact, still at the back of the kitchen drawer where she'd placed it, and there were no signs of any frantic search for it or the laptop.

In the fridge, the stocks she'd supplied were untouched.

'Let's look upstairs,' she said. 'Perhaps she's sleeping.'

The Barrons did not remark that it was far too early for someone to be in bed; clearly, they knew better than she did what to expect of a – what had they called it? – an acute depressive episode.

Upstairs there was a pronounced stale smell, and Tabby went to flush the loo and open the skylight in the bathroom. Emmie's toiletries were spilled on the floor, in too much disarray for Tabby to be able to tell if anything was missing.

'This is her bedroom.' She pushed open the door, unsure of what to expect and careful to enter first, just in case ... But she'd lost any sense of what the 'case' might be. Certainly, what she saw was no worst-case scenario: it looked messier than usual, yes, with clothing on the floor and bedclothes twisted as though wrung dry, but it was not anything squalid. As the Barrons absorbed the dimensions that had formed their daughter's temporary sanctuary, Tabby noted those details that concerned her the most: the postcard from Arthur was gone from the mirror, the perfume bottle no longer stood on the chest of drawers. In the wardrobe, the pink-and-green dress was missing, as was the large bag she'd seen Emmie with the first time they'd met.

Emmie, she felt sure, was now gone.

'I'll check my room,' she said. 'There might be some clue in there.' But it was precisely as she'd left it: her backpack at the foot of the bed, the collection of folded clothes in the drawers, the secret stash of banknotes. Emmie had not set foot in it.

'Maybe she's popped out somewhere?' she said, rejoining the Barrons. She didn't have the heart to share her conclusions so soon. 'To go for a walk or get something to eat? She might have been feeling more herself?'

No one remarked on the phrasing being decidedly inappro-priate – or appropriate – for the situation.

'Should we look around the village?' Ray asked Kerry. 'Check all the bars and restaurants?'

'I think one of us should stay here.'

'I'll stay,' Tabby said. 'It will be less of a shock for her if she comes back. But if you think you've seen her and need my help, phone me and I'll come.'

She gave them a map of the village, directing them to the port and the main streets off it, but she was fairly sure there would be no sighting. While they were out she packed her possessions in her backpack and began making supper with the usable items in the fridge. Only when she'd run out of chores did she fetch her phone and compose the message to her mother she had been avoiding writing for so long: *I will be back in England soon. Can we meet? I need to talk to you on your own.*

She pressed Send.

There was no immediate reply.

Ray and Kerry returned after an hour or so, puzzled and dis-consolate. Over the meal, Tabby confided her discovery of the missing Emily paraphernalia, and it was reluctantly agreed that Eve must have taken the items and left. Timings were clarified: Tabby had left for the UK in the early hours of Monday and it was now Thursday night; Eve could have left at any time in between. Even so, Kerry turned sharply at the slightest noise from the lane, still hopeful that her daughter had been out on an errand or some other innocent excursion.

'I don't like this,' she said to Ray. 'Why would she leave? Something's wrong.'

'Well, we knew that,' he said. 'She disappeared once, she could do it again.'

'But why now, when she knew her friend was returning?'

'I don't know. She must have cast it from her mind.'

'She might have suspected I would bring someone with me,'

398

Tabby said, and she coloured as she remembered her original foolish dream of delivering Arthur Woodhall to the house, of facilitating a rapprochement, if not a full-blown romantic reconciliation.

Kerry made no comment, but she was assiduous in clearing the table, washing up, replacing the plates and cutlery in their correct places, putting the house in order for when her daughter returned.

'Is it too late to find a hotel, do you think?' Ray asked. But Kerry wanted to stay in the house in case Eve returned overnight.

'We can't sleep in her room. Imagine if she did come back? She'd get the fright of her life.'

'You take my room,' Tabby suggested. 'I'll sleep down here on the sofa, then if Eve comes back her room will be there for her, just as she left it. She might get a surprise if she sees me again, but I'll handle it.' And it filled her mind once more, with a pleasurable warmth close to nostalgia, that memory of Emmie discovering her asleep and demanding, 'Who are you, tell me? How did you find me?'

The Barrons agreed to her suggestion with some relief, both visibly bone-weary. Ray said, 'In the morning, if she's not back, we'll go to the police.'

And it seemed to Tabby that not even Kerry now believed this could be avoided.

Chapter 29

Tabby

She was awake for much of the night, alert to the creak of the front door, to the rush of cold night air that never came, but at last slid sideways into sleep. Awakening to the whispers of strangers in the room, she took a moment to focus and recognise her new comrades the Barrons, both dressed and shod, conferring over a newspaper under lamplight. She remembered she had slept downstairs on the sofa. It had been her fourth bed in as many nights.

'Did you sleep well?' she asked them, sitting upright. 'You don't have to read in the dark, put the main light on.'

Kerry looked up, her brow knitted in fresh patterns of anxiety.

'What is it?'

'Come and have a look at this, Tabby. There's been a development.'

It transpired that Ray had been up early, scouring the village for his daughter in the dawn light, and on his way back to the house had bought a copy of the British *Press* from the newsagent on the waterfront to read while he waited for the two women to surface. In it, he'd found a disturbing news item about Emily Marr.

'Remember this is not today's paper,' he said, passing it to

Tabby. 'They sell the British papers a day in arrears, so it's from yesterday, Thursday.'

Tabby looked at the feature in horror, not least because it included a picture of the front of the very house in which they now stood. In it, the door was ajar, the figure of Emmie caught in the shadow of the passageway within. It was captioned *Emily Marr at the house in western France where she has been in hiding since April.*

'What *is* this?' she asked Ray and Kerry, but they gestured for her to read for herself.

The article was headed MARR FOUND IN FRENCH HIDEAWAY and began:

One of the media's most tantalising mysteries of recent times was apparently solved this week when this newspaper received a tip-off as to the whereabouts of Emily Marr. For those with short memories, Marr was the young woman at the centre of the storm that erupted after the *Press* revealed the sordid and adulterous circumstances surrounding the deaths of the wife and children of famous eye surgeon Arthur Woodhall. Marr's sudden disappearance soon after led to the sort of conspiracy theories we haven't seen since the flight of Lord Lucan, but unlike the murderous aristocrat this fugitive has now been located, if not officially identified.

Though rumours have centred of late on the north of England, where Woodhall is thought to have relocated with a new, younger partner, this whisper came from the Atlantic coast of France. I flew to the chi-chi Ile de Ré, where Marr has reportedly been living incognito in the picturesque fortified village of Saint-Martin-de-Ré.

The woman I encountered was a far cry from the glamorous siren of the original scandal. Dishevelled, lank-haired, barefoot, she was a very sorry sight indeed. It was impossible to believe this was the same woman whose sexy style once won words of admiration from the likes of Karl Lagerfeld, no less. Agitated and evasive, she refused to answer my questions. 'You are Emily Marr, aren't you?' I asked her. She made the expected denial before admitting she goes by the name of Emmie Mason these days.

'Where is Arthur?' she asked repeatedly, before becoming incoherent and closing the door in my face.

This is the latest sad instalment in a dark and doomed affair, and an indictment, perhaps, of the press intrusion that caused Marr to flee her homeland in the first place. Above all, the discovery of this troubled wreck is a cruel reminder that while some young women hunger for celebrity, others do not have the stomach for it.

Tabby looked up, aghast. '"Press intrusion"? What does he think *he*'s doing, with articles like this?' Her indignation was reflected in the two faces looking back at her. 'Oh, I wish I'd been here. When he came I could have got rid of him before Emmie saw him. This must be why she's gone.'

'I'm calling the *Press* offices,' Ray said. He checked the time. 'It's eight o'clock in the UK; will anyone answer the phone this early?'

'Someone will eventually. I'll put coffee on,' Tabby said. As the machine gurgled, a thought struck and she turned to Ray and Kerry. 'You know the tip-off didn't come from me, right?'

'Of course not,' Kerry said. '*You* know she's not Emily.'

'But I didn't until two days ago, did I? For this to be in the paper yesterday, the journalist must have written it on Wednesday or even earlier.' Who, then? Not Emily or Arthur, surely, for the information must also have come before they knew that the Newbury stalker had been living in France as Emily – not that Tabby would have suspected them of colluding with the press in any case. Nor did she imagine they had been aware of the feature themselves, for it was likely they did not read the papers any longer, particularly not the *Press*. Still, if it was true that rumours had circulated about Arthur having relocated in the north of England, it would be no bad thing for Emily and him for any remaining fans or foes to be sent so decisively off the scent.

'It could have been anyone,' Ray said. 'That night you told us about, when she went out in the clothes she stole from Emily, someone might have seen her then and thought it was Marr.'

Tabby's mind was turning, updating timelines, bringing events into focus. 'But what about Emmie – I mean Eve? *She* must have thought it was me. No one else knew her "true" identity. It would fit: she confesses to me, I disappear off without much of an explanation, and then a couple of days later a reporter turns up. No wonder she left.'

Ray raised his palm. 'Hang on, I'm through ...' Having managed to connect to someone in the editorial department of the *Press*, he did not take long to discover that the journalist in question was a freelance. With the promise of additional information, he extracted the phone number, which he dialled at once. 'Voicemail,' he said, disconnecting. 'It's too early. I'll try again in half an hour.'

'Where is she, Ray?' Kerry said, in a forlorn voice that broke Tabby's heart. 'Where's Eve gone?'

'I don't know, love. But horrible though this article is, it might help us get closer to finding her.'

They drank their coffee, Ray keyed up and restless, Kerry close to tears, Tabby absorbed once more by regrets of her own miscalculations, but all three surely picturing the same image: Eve alone and in distress, resting by the roadside, wandering a town (shoeless, perhaps?), hitching on the *autoroute*, lost in a place where no one knew her or could help. Then Ray tried the number again and this time the reporter picked up, ending their interlude of tense helplessness. After introducing himself, Ray put his mobile on speakerphone so Kerry and Tabby could hear the conversation.

'I'm calling because I saw your report in yesterday's *Press*. I believe the woman you met is not Emily Marr but my daughter, who's been missing since March.'

'This was Marr, all right,' the reporter replied. 'Pretty unrecognisable, but definitely her. As I said in my piece, she's Emmie Mason now.'

'Emmie Mason is our daughter,' Ray said.

'She's called Emmie Mason as well?'

'No, neither of them is called Emmie Mason.'

'You've lost me, mate.' The reporter sounded bored, irreverent. Had he been in the room, Tabby would have slapped him.

'Let's start this again,' Ray said, with admirable forbearance. 'Please listen carefully to me. My name is Ray Barron and I am working with the police and a missing-persons organisation to locate my mentally ill daughter. The police will undoubtedly be getting in touch with you separately since you are possibly the last person to have spoken to the missing woman, but in the interests of urgency, please forget all about who she may or may not be and tell me whatever else you can remember about her.'

There was a startled pause, before the journalist spoke again, his tone altered. 'What do you need to know?'

'How bad a way was she in? You say she was incoherent?'

'She was in a terrible state, to be frank. She was rambling, asking for Arthur over and over. That's how I knew it was really her, because she looked so different from before.'

'Was she dressed? It's hard to tell from your photo.'

'I think so, she was in black sweatpants, a T-shirt, maybe. It could have been dark pyjamas, I suppose. No shoes. At first I thought I must have woken her up, but then I saw how unhealthy she looked, like she hadn't left the place in weeks. She didn't smell great, either. Then when she spoke I realised she was . . . not all there. And she turned extremely hostile – it wasn't much fun.'

Tabby wanted to call out, 'What did you expect? People like you and Nina Meeks destroyed her life!' But then, as with every thought now, she had to remind herself that the woman she had befriended was not Emily. Eve's life had not been destroyed by journalists.

'You didn't think to help her?' Ray was asking. 'If you thought she was in such a worrying state?'

'I asked her if she had someone with her and she said yes. Then she slammed the door in my face and refused to open up again. She was shouting obscenities at me from the other side.'

'You didn't go back later?'

'I had another try the next morning before I left town, but there was no answer. Then I got a call to go to Paris on another story. I'm back in London now.' Tabby imagined him sitting in an inquest, another lost life he was able to reduce to a few sentences, another stranger he was happy to condemn. She knew that was unfair, he was simply doing his job, but she couldn't help it.

'You didn't see her leave the house after that?' Ray asked. 'Or the island?'

'No. I would have approached her if I'd seen her again.'

'Can you tell us which day it was that you spoke to her?'

'I saw her on Tuesday evening. So it was Wednesday when I went back and she wasn't there.'

Ray and Kerry exchanged looks: if she'd left on Wednesday, or even late on Tuesday, perhaps rattled by the visit, then she'd had at least two days' advantage – she could be halfway across the continent by now.

Tabby could contain herself no longer. 'Who tipped you off?' she asked the journalist. 'How did you know the house?'

'I'm not able to tell you that.'

'But this person just called the paper out of the blue, saying they knew where Emily Marr was?'

405

'Something like that, sure. It happens a lot. Not just her – other public figures, faces in the news.'

'But you're a freelance, how did you get the story? Are you based in France?'

'I've got relatives there. I do a lot of stuff in Paris and the south.'

'Did your source want money for the information?'

But he would not say, of course, and as Ray ended the conversation with admirable courtesy, Tabby rechecked the by-line in the newspaper. John Spreadbury. The name wasn't familiar, but she had an idea it might illicit a flicker of recognition when she used it.

'Can you handle meeting the police without me?' she asked the Barrons. 'There's someone I need to talk to.'

She used Emily's bike to cycle to La Flotte, flying down the rougher coastal path that she'd always preferred to the congested roadside lanes. It was mid-morning and there was no one in the office above the *immobilier* she'd first visited when saved by Emmie from homelessness. Knowing the Barrons might be some time with the police, she decided to wait, and was rewarded thirty minutes later by the sight of Moira parking her car in a bay down the way.

'Tabby,' she said as she approached, her voice flat with lack of delight.

'Moira. Can I have a quick word?'

'I'm rather busy, actually. Can it wait?'

'No, it can't. Two minutes, that's all.'

'If we must.' Upstairs, Moira didn't invite her to sit, but stood in front of her in the small entrance hall, as if barring further access, her expression resistant. 'What can I do for you?' Her tone made it clear she thought the possibilities severely limited.

'Emmie has disappeared,' Tabby said baldly.

406

'Oh?' To Moira's credit, she did look faintly alarmed. 'What do you mean? She's gone back to Britain without telling you?'

'We don't know where she's gone. She could be anywhere. She could be in danger.'

Obviously Moira sensed the note of accusation because her next reply was defensive. 'Well, *I* have no idea where she is. I haven't seen her since the morning you two came here together.' The unspoken suffix was that she had rather hoped she'd seen the back of them on that occasion. 'So I'm not quite sure how I can help you.'

'You can't,' Tabby said, staring her in the eye. 'We're in touch with the police about it. I'm here because I wanted to ask you why.'

Moira blinked. 'Why? Why I had to fire her? I think I made that quite clear in our meeting.'

'No, I mean why you decided to tell a British newspaper she was here? And not just any paper but the same one that made her life a misery before?' There was no point in putting Moira right on the matter of 'Emmie's' identity; she did not deserve the truth, and since she would only divulge it to others, Tabby considered her best left in the dark.

Moira flushed, which undermined her reply somewhat. 'I don't know what you're talking about.'

'Or perhaps you know the journalist, John Spreadbury? He's a friend of a friend, is he? Maybe a relative? I know he's got family here in France. Come on, Moira, it's obvious it was you, there *is* no one else. Emmie didn't know a soul here except for you and me.'

Moira shook her head. 'What about the new boyfriend she talked about?'

'He didn't exist. She was just covering for me.'

'You'll have to forgive me if I'm still a little unclear on that score.'

'Rubbish. You heard her call him Arthur as clearly as I did. You know who Arthur is, don't you?'

Moira sighed, in concession if not capitulation. 'Yes, I know who he is. But the fact is anyone could have recognised her and phoned the tabloids. You, for instance, Tabby, *you* need the money, don't you? You told me yourself you were penniless when you came here.'

Tabby glared at her. 'So it was for money, then? They paid you for the address?'

'Look, I took a big hit when the rue du Rempart clients ended their contract. I was lucky not to be sued.'

'Oh, for God's sake,' Tabby cried. 'The house was left in a bit of a mess, that's all. It's not as if there was a dead body in there.'

'It's all relative,' Moira said sourly.

'OK, then how does not finishing a cleaning job on time weigh up against not paying proper taxes?'

'*What?*'

'You paid Emmie and me in cash all summer, didn't you? I'm guessing that's more of a crime in the eyes of the French authorities than anything *we* did.'

Moira did not reply. Remembering the invoices she'd seen, the lucrative commission rate her former employer had charged, Tabby returned to the point: 'Whatever payment the paper promised you couldn't possibly have made up the difference in lost earnings.'

'You're right there.'

So it had been bitterness then; petty revenge.

'How did you know who she was?' Tabby asked.

'Because I'm not an idiot, that's how. I suspected from the moment I met her. An English woman appears out of the blue, nothing like the people who usually come here, behaving almost comically as if she's on the run. She wouldn't even tell me her *name.*'

'But the scandal wasn't in the French media.'

'I'd followed it online. It was all over the English news sites. She'd changed her appearance, obviously, but I made an educated guess.'

'Did you ever ask her about it?'

'Of course not. I respected her privacy.'

'You've got a strange way of showing it.' Tabby felt suddenly extremely weary, not sure now what it was she'd hoped to achieve by this confrontation. Without the skills of a Nina Meeks, she had always been destined to leave empty-handed. 'Anyway, it's too late now. I have to get back. Her parents are waiting for me in Saint-Martin.'

'Her parents?' said Moira. 'I thought they were dead?' This incensed Tabby afresh, for if Moira remembered enough of the Marr case to know this, then she must also know Emily's father had passed away recently – and yet still she had sought to sabotage her attempts to escape the spotlight. No matter that none of this actually applied to the woman under discussion; it was the principle of it that offended Tabby.

'You know nothing,' she told Moira rudely. 'And since that's the case, it would be better if you said nothing as well.'

'Oh, go away,' Moira said, turning from her in anger. 'And don't come here again, either of you. You're as bad as each other.'

'That's where you're wrong,' Tabby said. 'Neither of us is bad.'

Moira looked back at her with an expression of raw contempt. 'I'm afraid I disagree. You've been nothing but trouble, both of you, and I'll be damned if it's my job to aid and abet a pair of low-life sluts.'

Startled, Tabby could not stop the gasp rising to her lips. It was a taste of what Emily had had to deal with, she thought as she left, recognising for the first time the role played in this affair by spite – plain and simple and, invariably, female: Moira's, Nina Meeks', Sarah Laing's, perhaps Sylvie Woodhall's too.

She was not sorry to close the door behind her in the knowledge that she would never lay eyes on the woman again.

At the house, she said nothing about her unedifying errand, letting the Barrons update her on their meetings with the *gendarmerie* and the police. Eve had been reported missing and the authorities would soon be conducting a search on the ground across the whole island, as well as alerting colleagues on the mainland. Airports and ferry ports were to be contacted and a photograph circulated. It was nothing, Ray and Kerry admitted, that they had not been through before in the UK.

'They want to talk to you and the reporter,' Ray said, 'but I get the impression they think she's gone back to England. This is a tourist destination: everyone goes home eventually.' The police had taken his contact details and promised they would phone in the event of any positive identification.

What Ray did not say, but judging by his face was certainly now thinking, was that they were looking for Eve dead or alive. Accident, suicide: anything was possible, given her illness. Tabby felt a surge of fighting spirit at the thought of Emmie sitting in this same spot less than a week earlier, eating with her, talking with her, *living*. 'She must be somewhere,' she said with new resolution. 'Let's search the island ourselves as well. Let's hire a car this morning and get out there, every village, every street. Then, if we don't find her here, we'll go back to the area in London where Emily and Arthur lived. We'll follow the trail as Eve might have thought to follow it. There's a hotel near Walnut Grove we should phone, in case she's checked in there. And there's Arthur himself. If I found him, she will.'

'I think we should also get back in touch with the police in London,' Kerry said. 'Cover every possible eventuality.'

'Fine,' Ray agreed. 'The police are contacting the owners of this place, but I imagine it will be acceptable for us to stay one more night. We'll scour the island, then we'll pack up Eve's things and bring them home, continue the search there.'

The three of them left the house together and walked in single file down the cobbled alleyway, past the linen shop and other chic boutiques, on to the waterfront and through the café tables towards the *boulangerie*, then across the eastern quayside in the direction of the tourist information office. There they would be able to enquire about car rental and catch any necessary bus or a taxi.

'We'll find her,' Tabby told Kerry, with a conviction she felt deep inside her. 'She may not be right here under our noses, but we'll find her, I promise.'

Kerry smiled gratefully at her. 'Thank you for staying to help us, Tabby. It makes such a big difference. You know this place, you know *her*.'

'You know her best,' Tabby corrected her. 'You and Ray.'

'Not at the moment, we don't. If we don't know Emily, we don't know Eve. But you know Emily, that's the crucial thing.'

Tabby did not reply. It was a glorious morning and she allowed herself to be distracted by the way the sun bounced off the freshly hosed cobbles, light exploding in the air around them, and by the way the water in the harbour had become a wobbling looking-glass at their feet. Already holidaymakers filled the terrace tables, ordering their coffees and fishing sunglasses from pockets. In every direction people were exulting in their morning, breathing the salty Atlantic air, planning their day's pleasures, guilty or innocent. She did not think Ray or Kerry had been able to pay any attention to their surroundings, much less take any joy in them.

'You could have just walked away,' Kerry added at her side. 'No one would have blamed you if you had.'

Tabby linked her arm through Eve's mother's, surprising both of them with the sudden intimacy of the gesture.

'No, I couldn't,' she said.

Reading Group Questions

1. How significant are the two settings in the book: Walnut Grove, a leafy Georgian road in south London, and the Ile de Ré, an island off the Atlantic coast of France?

2. The connection between Arthur Woodhall and Emily Marr is instant – *a coup de foudre*. How do you feel about their affair and were you surprised by how it developed?

3. What were your early impressions of the character of Emmie? What does she mean when she refers to her circumstances as 'exile'?

4. What is your reaction to the media witch-hunt of Emily Marr and the orchestration of it by tabloid columnist Nina Meeks?

5. Are there any similarities between the two adulterous relationships in the book?

6. Arthur and Emily are said to have been 'punished' by the tragedy that befalls the Woodhall family. Does the punishment fit the crime?

7. How did you react to Tabby's discovery of Eve's history?

8. One of the themes of the book is isolation. Can you relate to any of the feelings of alienation felt by Emily Marr or other characters?

9. How surprising is the psychiatric condition suffered by one of the characters?

10. In what way does Emily Marr 'disappear'? Do any other characters lose a sense of their own identity during the course of the book?

The author on
The Disappearance of Emily Marr

What inspired the story?

The story is told in two strands and one of those strands contains my original idea: the sudden and entirely unwanted propelling to notoriety of an ordinary person. This was inspired directly by the book *The Lost Honour of Katharina Blum* (*Die Verlorene Ehre der Katharina Blum*), a superb and disturbing novel by Heinrich Böll published in 1974, which I first read in German class in school and have re-read several times over the years. Katharina Blum is a young woman discovered to be romantically involved with a man wanted by the police and she is hounded to the point of breakdown by the tabloid press.

Her ordeal occurs in more innocent times, in the respect that it is well before the digital age and she has 'only' the more sensationalist print newspapers to contend with. The character assassination of Emily Marr takes place in the present day, in which virtually all media is sensationalist and, thanks to the internet, ceaseless. Her notoriety happens overnight: one day she has the normal privacy of an ordinary citizen, the next everyone knows her name, her address, her mobile phone number, email address, and the rest.

I'm very ambivalent about social networking and the news sites that spawn vitriolic member comments; I don't think they draw from us the finest of human impulses, and so this plotline was partly an exploration of that.

The other strand, which follows the journey of Tabby on the Ile de Ré, came out of an interest in certain psychiatric disorders. I took some time in thinking how the two plotlines might be blended and when I hit on it, it seemed so natural and obvious.

Emily's story is told in the first person and Tabby's in the third person. Was it hard to alternate and was one voice easier or more enjoyable to write than the other?

Having more than one voice is often more interesting for the author and creates natural changes in pace for the reader. In this case there is also the difference in context: Emily writes her account with the benefit of hindsight, which automatically makes hers a very knowing voice, and poignant too, all her broken dreams and regrets right there in the telling, while Tabby's story is told as it happens, which makes her naïve, direct, in the moment. She is young as well, naturally optimistic. I preferred writing Emily's strand because her character is more like mine and so I found she came more fluently. I felt great love and sympathy for her and spent a lot of time working out if I could possibly give her a happy ending because I felt she really deserved one.

As heroes go, Arthur Woodhall, who is not good-looking and is pushing fifty, is not typical, is he?

My books aren't romances and Arthur is certainly not a classic romantic lead. He is a proper flawed grown-up and an extremely jaded individual – he's been unhappily married for twenty years, has two teenage children and has been a workaholic for three decades. My aim was to convince readers of the chemistry between Emily and him in light of her family history and sense of isolation, rather than to share her attraction for him. Having said that, I must admit he is the kind of person *I* would find attractive, because what he has is intensity and I like that – and I think most women do. The character of Grégoire was intended partly as a counterpoint: he is much more the heedless and arrogant adulterer we can all disapprove of. In disliking him, readers will, I hope, let Arthur off the hook a bit.

Tabby's story takes place on the Ile de Ré in France, a setting you have used before. Why?

I know the Ile de Ré very well and personally think it is heaven-sent as a backdrop for suspenseful plotlines. I'm amazed there hasn't been a detective series filmed in Saint-Martin-de-Re, a seventeenth-century village inside immense Vauban fortifications. It's hugely atmospheric, the old houses connecting haphazardly, the grey Atlantic pressing against the walls.

Yes, it features to a lesser extent in *The Second Husband* (2008) as well, and in both cases is a remote hideaway for characters experiencing a form of exile. In fact, in summer the village is very, very busy, but Emmie and Tabby live in a house hidden from the throng, and they keep their shutters closed at all times.

I love the contrast between a carefree holiday atmosphere, with people wandering around in the sunshine, their only concern which beach to picnic at, and a hidden, much darker situation just a street away. Ten metres from the beautiful people there's a house you can't see into, and inside it a mysterious and potentially tragic situation is unfolding.

Given the book's ending, do you plan a sequel?

No, though I have decided for myself what becomes of each of the characters, as I usually do. But I always wanted the story to end with a vanishing. Readers are very welcome to contact me individually and I'll share my thoughts on the poor soul we've now lost track of.

What kind of people are your readers?

The ones who come back for more are people who enjoy an intriguing emotional dilemma and an unpredictable outcome. My characters don't always get what's coming to them. Nobody is perfect and everybody is imperfect. Also, the books are emotionally quite honest; I try to write candidly and not to pull any punches. And I like to write about sudden passion because it's a form of madness and it makes people behave urgently and irrationally.

The feedback I get the most often is 'I never guessed that would happen', which always reminds me that however absorbed I get in the writing, the phrasemaking and the polishing, what people want is a story they haven't read before, which is exactly what I want from a book, too.

Discover Louise Candlish

I'LL BE THERE FOR YOU

Hannah and Juliet Goodwin have been best friends since childhood, but when Juliet's boyfriend Luke is killed just as Hannah marries the affluent Michael, the divide between the two is suddenly too painful to bear. While Hannah prepares for the birth of her first child, Juliet begins to neglect her job, her health, and all those who love her the most. Hannah is the last person she'd appeal to for help.

But then she finds herself drawn into a secret betrayal that threatens to destroy Hannah's happiness before she even has a chance to enjoy it . . .

SINCE I DON'T HAVE YOU

At the birth of their daughters best friends Rachel, Mariel and Jenny make a promise: to love and care for each other's girls exactly as they would their own.

Six years later and a tragedy has torn them apart.
Within weeks, Rachel has packed up and gone. Settling on the beautiful, windswept Greek island of Santorini, she can't forget the pledge she once made. She hires a private investigator, the enigmatic Johnny Palmer, and arranges for him to send regular updates on the girls she has left behind. Over the years, with Palmer's help, she is able to secretly soothe their growing pains. But in Rachel's new island life far from home, who will be there to guide her?

THE SECOND HUSBAND

When Davis Calder moves in next door to Kate Easton and her two children, no one has any idea of the devastation about to be unleashed. With Kate struggling to accept her teenage daughter Roxy's independence and with tensions between Kate and her ex-husband Alistair still very much alive, there's enough family drama to go around already.

Before they know it, glamorous, charismatic Davis is the only one who seems able to keep the peace. Soon Kate has fallen in love and agreed to be his wife. At last she can come to terms with the betrayals of her first marriage. At last she dares hope she has the happy ending she deserves . . .

BEFORE WE SAY GOODBYE

The day Maggie Lane dies, she sends her daughter Olivia a letter containing dangerous information: the address of Olivia's first love, Richie Briscoe. Olivia has not seen Richie for over twenty years.

Convinced that the note represents an admission of guilt, Olivia sets off for the idyllic seaside village where Richie now lives with his young daughter Wren. Soon she has fallen for him all over again – and found in little Wren the daughter she never had.

But there is a problem. For Olivia already has a husband and two sons. And where does this second chance at happiness leave them?

OTHER PEOPLE'S SECRETS

Ginny and Adam Trustlove arrive on holiday in Italy torn apart
by personal tragedy. Two weeks in a boathouse on the edge of
peaceful Lake Orta is exactly what they need to restore
their faith in life – and each other.

Twenty-four hours later, the silence is broken. The Sale family have
arrived at the main villa: wealthy, high-flying Marty, his beautiful wife
Bea, and their privileged, confident offspring. It doesn't take long for
Ginny and Adam to be drawn in, and there is something about Zach
that has everyone instantly beguiled, something that loosens
old secrets – and creates shocking new ones.

THE DAY YOU SAVED
MY LIFE

A child falls into the river.
A stranger jumps in to rescue him.
And four lives are changed for ever . . .

On a perfect summer's day in Paris, tourists on the river
watch in shock as a small boy falls into the Seine and disappears
below the surface. As his mother stands frozen,
a stranger takes a breath and leaps . . .

A spellbinding story of passion, heartbreak and destiny – an
unforgettable novel about mothers and daughters, husbands and
wives, and the extraordinary ways that life and love intersect.